Real Digital, A Hands-on Approach to Digital Design

Clint Cole

XIDIAN UNIVERSITY PRESS

2009

Content Introduction

This book first gives an introduction to electronic circuits: various electronic components, basic FET construction and operation. Then discusses structure of combinational logic circuits and logic minimization, introduces several combinational circuits that are frequently used by digital designers, including a data selector, a binary decoder, an encoder, and a shifter, also discusses several combinational circuits that perform arithmetic operations on binary numbers, including adders, multipliers, and comparators. Finally, introduces the concept of electronic memory and the founding concepts used in the design of sequential circuits.

图书在版编目（CIP）数据

数字设计进阶. 入门篇=Real Digital，A Hands-on Approach to Digital Design: 英文/(美)克林特 (Clint, C.)著. 一西安：西安电子科技大学出版社，2009.5

ISBN 978-7-5606-2166-1

Ⅰ. 数…　Ⅱ. 克…　Ⅲ. 数字电路—电路设计—英文　Ⅳ. TN79

中国版本图书馆 CIP 数据核字(2008)第 193853 号

策　　划　戚文艳
责任编辑　张　玮　戚文艳
出版发行　西安电子科技大学出版社(西安市太白南路 2 号)
电　　话　(029)88242885　88201467　　邮　编　710071
网　　址　www.xduph.com　　　　电子邮箱　xdupfxb001@163.com
经　　销　新华书店
印刷单位　西安文化彩印厂
版　　次　2009 年 5 月第 1 版　　2009 年 5 月第 1 次印刷
开　　本　787 毫米×960 毫米　1/16　印　张　16.5
字　　数　333 千字
印　　数　1～1000 册
定　　价　35.00 元

ISBN 978-7-5606-2166-1/TN • 0476

XDUP 2458001-1

如有印装问题可调换

Chapter 1: Introduction to Electronic Circuits

1. Overview

This chapter presents a brief, non-rigorous introduction to electronic circuits and systems. Only the most essential concepts are presented, with emphasis on topics used in later chapters. As with all chapters in this class, a companion "Exercise1" document must be completed and submitted for credit.

Before beginning this chapter, you should…

- Find a quiet place to sit and read.

After completing this chapter, you should…

- Understand the definition of voltage, electric current, and resistance, and be able to apply Ohm's law to basic circuits;
- Be familiar with various electronic components;
- Understand basic FET construction and operation, and their use in logic circuits;
- Understand logic gate function;
- Be able to sketch a logic circuit based on a logic equation, and write a logic equation based on a logic schematic.

This chapter requires:

- The ability to read, and the desire to learn.

2. Background

All matter is made up of atoms that contain both positively and negatively charged particles (protons and electrons). Surrounding every charged particle is an electric field that can exert force on other charged particles. A positive field surrounds a proton, and a negative field surrounds an electron. Field strength is the same for every electron and proton, with a magnitude of one "fundamental unit" of 1.602×10^{-19} Coulombs. A coulomb is a measure of charge derived (in a somewhat circular fashion) from a measurement of electric current – one coulomb of charge is transferred by one ampere of current in one second (to get a matter of scale, one coulomb of charge flows through a 120W light bulb in one second). If one coulomb of protons could be isolated and held one meter apart from one coulomb of electrons, an attractive force (given by Coulombs law) of 8.988×10^9 Newtons, equivalent to almost one million tons at the earth's surface, would exist between them (likewise, two one-coulomb groups of protons or electrons would exhibit an equally large repelling force). It is this large intra-particle force that is harnessed to do work in electric circuits.

A positive electric field surrounding a group of one or more protons will exert a repelling force on other groups of protons, and an attracting force on groups of electrons. Since an electric field can cause charged particles to move, it can do some amount of work, and so it is said to have potential energy. The amount of energy an electric field can impart to unit charge is measured in joules per coulomb, more commonly known as voltage. For our purposes, voltage may be thought of as the "electro-motive force" that can cause charged particles to move. A power supply is a local, contained imbalance of electrons, with material one side (the negative side) containing an abundance of electrons, and material on the other (positive) side containing a relative absence of electrons. The electrical potential energy available in the power supply, measured in volts, is determined by the number of electrons it can store, the separation distance between negative and positive materials, the properties of the barrier between the materials, and other factors. Some power supplies (like small batteries) output less than a volt, while others (like power generation stations) can output tens of thousands of volts. In general, power supplies of up to 9V–12V are considered "safe" for humans to interact with (at least when skin layers are intact), but some people can have adverse (and potentially fatal) interactions with even low-voltage supplies. In our work, we will not encounter any supplies above 5V.

Electrons carry the smallest possible amount of negative charge, and billions of them are present in even the tiniest piece of matter. In most materials, electrons are held firmly in place by heavier, positively charged protons. In such materials, called insulators, electrons cannot move freely between atoms. By contrast, in other materials (like metals) electrons can move more easily from atom to atom, and these materials are called conductors. The movement of electrons in a conductor is called electric current, measured in amperes (or amps). If a power supply is used to impress a voltage across a conductor, electrons will move from the negative side of the supply through the conductor towards the positive side. All materials, even conductors, exhibit some amount of resistance to the flow of electric current. The amount of resistance determines how much current can flow—the higher the resistance, the less current can flow. By definition, a conductor has very low resistance, so a conductor by itself would never be placed across a power supply because far too much current would flow, damaging either the supply or the conductor itself. Rather an electronic component called a resistor would be used in series with the conductor to limit current flow (more on resistors later).

Around 1825, Georg Ohm demonstrated through a series of experiments that voltage, current, and resistance are related through a fundamental relationship: Voltage (V) is equal to Current (I) times resistance (R), or V = I·R. This most basic equation in electronics shows that when any two of the three quantities voltage, current, and resistance are known, the third can be derived.

Resistance is measured in ohms, with the symbol Ω. According to Ohm's law, one volt impressed across 1 ohm of resistance will cause 1 amp of current to flow (and one coulomb of charge will pass through the resistor in one second). Similarly, 3.3V impressed across 3.3Ω will cause 1A of current to flow. In the schematic figure to the right, the lines leaving the positive and 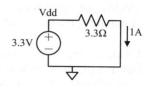 negative sides of the power supply represent conductors with an insignificant amount of resistance. Thus, the voltage delivered by the power supply is present at both sides of the resistor—3.3V at the left side of the resistor, and GND and the right side of the resistor. As current flows through the resistor, collisions occur between the electrons flowing from the power supply and the materials in the resistor. These collisions cause electrons to give up their potential energy, and that energy is dissipated as heat. As with any physical system, we define the time derivative of energy as power; in electric circuits, power, measured in Watts, is defined as (voltage x current), or P = V·I. The power transferred to the resistor at any given time results in resistor heating. The more power transferred to the resistor, the hotter it gets. For a given voltage, a smaller-valued resistor would allow more current to flow (see Ohm's law), and therefore more energy would be dissipated as heat (and the resistor would get hotter). The total energy consumed in an electric circuit is simply the time integral of power, measured in Watts per second, or Joules. Thus, in the circuit above, the electric power delivered to the resistor is P = 3.3V × 1A, or 3.3Watts, and in one second, 3.3W × 1second or 3.3J of energy is dissipated.

Electric and Electronic Circuits

A collection of electronic components that have been assembled and interconnected to perform a given function is commonly referred to as a circuit. The word circuit derives from the fact that electric power must flow from the positive terminal of a power source through one or more electronic devices and back to the negative terminal of a power source, thereby forming a circuit. If the connections between an electronic device and either the positive or negative terminals of a power supply are interrupted, the circuit will be broken and the device will not function.

Many different types of components and devices can be found in modern circuits, including resistors, capacitors, and inductors, semiconductor devices like diodes, transistors, and integrated circuits, transducers like microphones, light sensors and motions sensors, actuators like motors and solenoids, and various other devices like heating and lighting elements. Devices in a circuit are connected to one another by means of electrical conductors, or wires. These wires can move electric currents between various points in a circuit. Once a wire connects two or more devices, the wire and all attached device connectors are said to form a single circuit node or net. Any electrical activity on a given net is communicated to all devices attached to the net. Certain nets provide electric power to devices, and other nets carry information between devices. Nets that carry information are called signals, and signals transport information encoded as voltage levels around a circuit. Signal nets typically use smaller conductors, and transport very small currents. Nets that carry power are called supply rails (or just supplies) and supply rails transport electric power around a circuit. Power nets typically use much larger conductors that signal nets, because they must transport larger currents.

Electric circuits use electric power to perform some function, like energize a heating or lighting element, turn a motor, or create an electromagnetic filed. Electronic circuits differ from electric circuits in that they use devices that can themselves be controlled by other electric signals. Restated, electronic circuits are built from devices that use electricity to control electricity. Most electronic circuits use signals that are within 5 to 10 volts of ground; most circuits built within the past several years use signals that are within 3 to 5 volts from ground. Some electronic circuits represent information encoded as continuous voltage levels that can wander between the high and low voltage supply rails—these are called analog circuits. As an example, a sound pressure level transducer (i.e. a microphone) might drive a signal between 0V and 3.3V in direct proportion to the detected sound pressure level. In this case, the voltage signal output from the microphone is said to be an analog if the sound pressure wave itself. Other circuits use only two distinct voltage levels to represent information. Most often, these two voltage levels use the same voltages supplied by the power rails. In these circuits, called digital circuits, all information must be represented as binary numbers, with a signal at 0V (or ground) representing one kind of information, and a signal at 3.3V (or whatever the upper voltage supply rail provides) representing the other kind of information. In this series of chapters, we will confine our discussions to digital circuits.

Physical Circuits vs. Model Circuits

Physical circuits are constructed of real, physical devices. They can be inspected, tested, and modified. They consume electric power when energized, and they can function properly and do some meaningful work, or they can malfunction and create serious hazards to health and property. Even small circuits that are quickly and easily constructed still take time and money to build, and they can take a very long time to perfect.

Engineers learned long ago that prior to building even the simplest circuit a document showing all pertinent construction details is indispensable. Serving much the same purpose as blueprints for a building, a circuit schematic shows all devices in the circuit, and all signal and power connections between the devices. A schematic can be sketched, analyzed, debated, re-sketched, and iterated as many times as needed before the more cost and time intensive task of building a real circuit begins. Once computers became available, it didn't take engineers long to realize that if a circuit schematic could be "captured" in a computer program, it could be simulated to any degree of accuracy before it was constructed. And indeed, it could well be argued that circuit simulators represent the most useful and powerful application of computers that has ever been found.

Capacitors

A capacitor is a two-terminal device that can store electric energy in the form of charged particles. You can think of a capacitor as a reservoir of charge that takes time to fill or empty. The voltage across a capacitor is proportional to the amount of charge it is storing — the more charge added to a capacitor of a given size, the larger the voltage across the capacitor. It is not possible to instantaneously move charge to or from a capacitor, so it is not possible to instantaneously change the voltage across a capacitor. It is this property that makes capacitors useful on Digilent boards and in many other applications.

Capacitance is measured in Farads. A one Farad capacitor can store one Coulomb of charge at one volt. For engineering on a small scale (i.e., hand-held or desk-top devices), a one Farad capacitor stores far too much charge to be of general use (it would be like a car having a 1000 gallon gas tank). More useful capacitors are measured in micro-farads (μF) or pico-farads (pF). The terms "milli-farad" and "nano-farad" are rarely used. Large capacitors often have their value printed plainly on them, such as "10 μF" (for 10 micro-farads). Smaller capacitors, appearing as small blocks, disks or wafers, often have their values printed on them in an encoded manner (similar to the resistor packs discussed above). For these capacitors, a three-digit number typically indicates the capacitor value in pico-farads. The first two digits provide the "base" number, and the third digit provides an exponent of 10 (so, for example, "104" printed on a capacitor indicates a capacitance value of 10×10^4 or 100000 pF). Occasionally, a capacitor will only show a two-digit number, in which case that number is simply the capacitor value in pF. (To be complete, if a capacitor shows a three-digit number and the third digit is 8 or 9, then the first two digits are multiplied by 0.01 and 0.1 respectively). Often, a single letter is appended to the capacitance value — this letter indicates the quality of the capacitor.

Capacitors are used on Digilent boards to keep the voltage supplies and some signals stable regardless of circuit activity, and to store charge when inputs are activated in order to slow their assertion times. The majority of the capacitors on the Digilab boards are used to "decouple" integrated circuits from the power supply. These "bypass" capacitors are placed on the board very close to the Vdd pins of all chips, where they can supply the short-term electrical current needs of the chips. Without such bypass capacitors, individual chips could cause the Vdd supply across the entire Digilent board to dip below 5V during times of heavy current demand. Nearly every chip in every digital system uses bypass capacitors. Bypass capacitor value can be determined if the worst-case current requirements are known, but more typically, capacitors in the range 0.001 μF to 0.047 μF are used without regard to the actual current requirements. Digilent boards also use bulk bypass capacitors near the power supplies and around the board to provide extra charge storage for the entire circuit board. These larger capacitors (typically 10 μF to100 μF) can supply the smaller individual bypass capacitors during times of exceptional need.

Capacitor
schematic symbol

Depending on the size of the capacitor, the PCB silk screen will show either a circle or rectangle to indicate capacitor placement (usually, smallish capacitors are shown as rectangles, and larger capacitors as circles). Some capacitors are polarized, meaning they must be placed into the circuit board in a particular orientation (so that one terminal is never at a lower voltage than the other). Polarized capacitors either have a dark stripe near the pin that must be kept at a higher voltage, or a "−" near the pin that must be kept at a lower voltage. Silk-screen patterns for polarized capacitors will also often have a "+" sign nearest the through-hole that must be kept at a relatively higher voltage. In circuit schematics and parts lists, capacitors typically use a "C__" reference designator.

Input Devices (Buttons and Switches)

Circuits often require inputs that come directly from users (as opposed to inputs that come from other devices). User-input devices can take many forms, among them keyboards (as on a PC), buttons (as on a calculator or telephone), rotary dials, switches and levers, etc. Digilent boards include several input devices, typically including push buttons and slide-switches. Since digital circuits operate with two voltage levels (LHV or Vdd, and LLV or GND), input devices like buttons and switches should be able to produce both of these voltages based on some user action.

The slide switches are also known as "single throw-double pole" (STDP) switches, because only one switch (or throw) exists, but two positions (or poles) are available (a pole is an electrical contact to which the switch can make contact). These switches can be set to output either Vdd (when the actuator is closest to the board's edge) or GND. The push button switches are also known as "momentary" contact buttons, because they only make contact while they are actively being pressed—they output a GND at rest, and a Vdd only when they are being pressed. The figure below shows typically pushbutton and slide switch circuits used on Digilent boards.

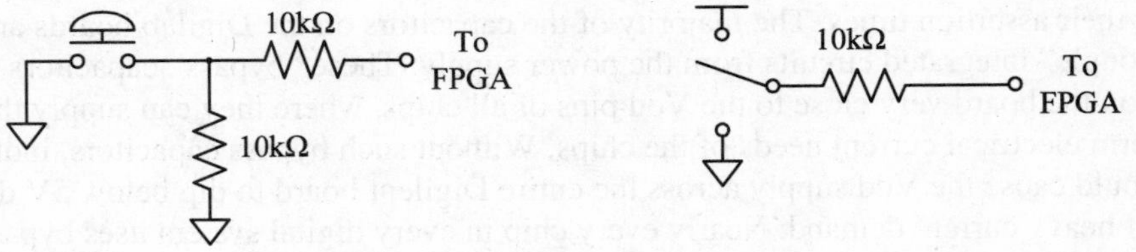

Output Devices (LEDs)

Circuits often require output devices to communicate their state to an user. Examples of electronic output devices include computer monitors, LCD alphanumeric panels (as on a calculator), small lamps or light-emitting diodes (LED's), etc. Digilent boards include different output devices, but all of them include some number of individual LED's, and seven-segment LED displays that can display the digits 0−9 in each digit position (each segment in the seven-segment display contains a single LED). LED's are two-terminal semiconductor devices that conduct current in only one direction (from the anode to the cathode). The small LED chips are secured inside a plastic housing, and they emit light at a given frequency (RED, YELLOW, etc.) when a small electric current (typically 10–25mA) flows through them.

Individual LED's are denoted with an "LD__" reference designator on Digilent boards, and seven-segment displays are denoted with a "DSP" reference designator. Individual LED's are typically driven directly from a Xilinx chip on Digilent boards, but LED displays may require the use of an external transistor to supply higher currents to the digits. Typical LED circuits on Digilent boards are shown in the figure.

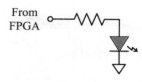

LEDs will not turn on unless their anodes are some minimal voltage above their cathodes — typically about two volts. If less than the minimum threshold voltage is applied to an LED, it will remain dark. In the example shown, the LED requires a 2V drop to turn on, leaving 1.3V to drop across the resistor. Thus, a 130Ω resistor is required to cause 10mA of current to flow in the circuit (3.3V−2V = 1.3V, and 1.3V / 130Ω= 10mA).

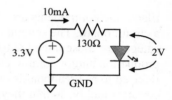

Connectors

The Digilent boards use several connectors for various purposes, but in general, they all communicate electronic information between the board and outside devices. By convention, connectors are given the reference designator "J__". Since connectors come in so many different sizes and shapes, they are usually shown on the PCB silk screen and on circuit schematics as just rectangular boxes. The following connectors are used on various Digilent boards (but not all connectors appear on all boards):

- The PS/2 connector allows connection to a mouse or keyboard;
- The DB25 connector allows a parallel cable to be attached for programming or data transfers;
- The DB9 port is used for RS-232 serial communications;
- The DB15 connector can be used to drive a VGA monitor;
- Various DIP sockets can be used to load accessory chips and to access various signals;
- The power jack can accept any compatible DC power supply;
- The audio jack can be used to drive speakers or receive microphone inputs;
- The BNC connector allows for easy connection of test and measurement equipment.

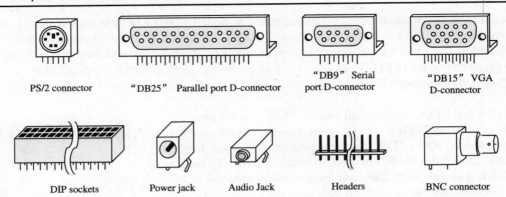

PS/2 connector   "DB25"   Parallel port D-connector   "DB9"   Serial port D-connector   "DB15"   VGA D-connector

DIP sockets   Power jack   Audio Jack   Headers   BNC connector

Printed Circuit Board (PCB)

Electronic components are often assembled and interconnected on a flat surface known as a circuit board. The several types of existing circuit boards may be divided into two broad categories: those intended for prototype or experimental circuits; and those intended for production and/or commercial sale. Circuit boards used for experimental work are often referred to as breadboards or protoboards. Breadboards allow engineers to construct circuits quickly, so that they can be studied and modified until an optimal design is discovered. In a typical breadboard use, components and wires are added to a circuit in an ad hoc manner as the design proceeds, with new data and new understanding dictating the course of the design. Since breadboard circuits exist only in the laboratory, no special consideration need be given to creating reliable or simple-to-manufacture circuits—the designer can focus exclusively on the circuit's behavior. In contrast, circuit boards intended for production or commercial sale must have highly reliable wires and interconnects, permanent bonds to all components, and topographies amenable to mass production and thorough testing. And further, they must be made of a material that is reliable, low-cost, and easy to manufacture. A fiberglass substrate with copper wires (etched from laminated copper sheets) has been the PCB material of choice for the past several decades. The Digilent board is a simple example of such a board. Note that most often, production circuit board designs are finalized only after extensive breadboard phases. Components are permanently affixed to production boards using the soldering process.

Production circuit boards typically start out as thin sheets of fiberglass (about 1mm thick) that are completely covered on both sides with very thin sheets of metal (typically copper). A "standard" circuit board might use a 1 ounce copper process, which means that one ounce of copper is evenly spread across 1 square foot of circuit board. During the manufacturing process, wire patterns are "printed" onto the copper surfaces using a compound that resists etching (hence the name Printed Circuit Board or PCB). The boards are subjected to a chemical etching process that removes all exposed copper. The remaining, un-etched copper forms wires that will interconnect the circuit board components, and small pads that define the regions where component leads will be attached.

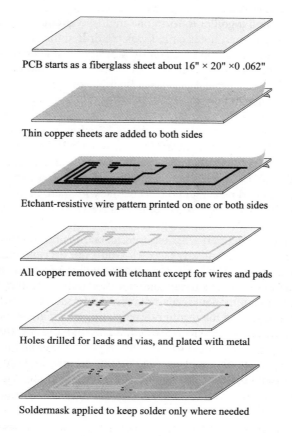

PCB starts as a fiberglass sheet about 16" × 20" ×0 .062"

Thin copper sheets are added to both sides

Etchant-resistive wire pattern printed on one or both sides

All copper removed with etchant except for wires and pads

Holes drilled for leads and vias, and plated with metal

Soldermask applied to keep solder only where needed

In a PCB that uses through-hole technology, holes are drilled through the pads so that component leads can be inserted and then fastened (soldered) in place. In a PCB that uses surface-mount technology, component leads are soldered directly to the pads on the surface. Each set of pads (or holes) in the PCB is intended to receive a particular component. To identify which component must be loaded where, reference designators are printed on the circuit board immediately adjacent to the pads using a silk-screen process. A parts list links a designated set of pads to a physical component by describing the component and assigning it a particular reference designator. The reference designators guide assemblers and testers when they are working with the PCB. Many components must be placed into the PCB in a particular orientation. By convention, components that require a particular orientation have one lead designated as pin 1. On the PCB, a square pad or silk-screen indicator typically denotes pin 1.

On all but the simplest PCBs, wires must be printed on more than one surface of fiberglass to allow for all the required component interconnections. Each surface containing printed wires is called a layer. In a relatively simple PCB that requires only two layers, only one piece of fiberglass is required since wires can be printed on both sides. In a more complex PCB where several layers are required, individual circuit boards are manufactured separately and then laminated together to form one multi-layer circuit board. To connect wires on two or more layers, small holes called vias are drilled through the wires and fiberglass board at the point where the wires on the different layers cross. The interior surface of these holes is coated with metal so that electric current can flow through the vias. Most Digilent boards are simple 4 or 6 layer boards; some more complex computer circuit boards have more than 20 layers.

The unloaded PCB appears green because thin sheets of green plastic have been applied to both sides (otherwise the PCB would appear pale yellow). Called solder masks, these sheets cover all exposed metal other than the component pads and holes so that errant solder can't inadvertently short (or electrically connect) the printed wires. All metal surfaces other than the exposed pads and holes (i.e., the wires) are underneath the solder mask. Not infrequently, blue or even red solder masks are used.

Circuit components are manufactured with exposed metal pins (or leads) that are used to fasten them to the PCB both mechanically (so they won't fall off) and electrically (so current can pass between them). The soldering process, which provides a strong mechanical bond and a very good electrical connection, is used to fasten components to the PCB. During soldering, component leads are inserted through the holes in the PCB, and then the component leads and the through-hole plating metal are heated to above the melting point of the solder (about 500 to 700 degrees F). Solder (a metallic compound) is then melted and allowed to flow in and around the component lead and pad. The solder quickly cools to form a strong bond between the component and the PCB. The process of associating components with reference designators, loading them into their respective holes, and then soldering them in place comprises the PCB assembly process.

Examine the Digilent board, and note the printed wires on either side. Wires on one side go largely "north and south" while wires on the other side go largely "east and west". The perpendicular or Manhattan arrangement of wires on alternate layers is very common on multi-layer PCBs. Locate some vias, and note that they connect wires on opposite sides. Locate various components, their hole patterns, and associated reference designators. Identify pad 1 for the various components. Note that the through-holes are somewhat larger than the vias, and that component leads can easily be inserted into their through-holes, but not into vias.

Integrated Circuits (or Chips)

The terms "chip" and "integrated circuit" refer to semiconductor circuits that use collections microscopic transistors that are all co-located on the same small piece of silicon. Chips have been designed to do all sorts of functions, from very simple and basic logical switching functions to highly complex processing functions. Some chips contain just a handful of transistors, while others contain several hundred million transistors. Some of the longest-surviving chips perform the most basic functions. These chips, denoted with the standard part numbers "74XXX", are simple small-scale integration devices that house small collections of logic circuits. For example, a chip known as a 7400 contains four individual NAND gates, with each input and output available at an external pin.

As shown in the figures below, the chips themselves are much smaller than their packages. During manufacturing, the small, fragile chips are glued (using epoxy) onto the bottom half of the package, bond-wires are attached to the chip and to the externally available pins, and then the top half of the chip package is permanently affixed. Smaller chips may only have a few pins, but larger chips can have more than 500 pins. Since the chips themselves are on the order of a centimeter on each side, very precise and delicate machines are required to mount them in their packages.

Smaller chips might be packaged in a "DIP" package (DIP is an acronym for Dual In-line Package) as shown below. Typically on the order of $1" \times 1/4"$, DIP packages are most often made from black plastic, and they can have anywhere from 8 to 48 pins protruding in equal numbers from either side. DIPs are used exclusively in through-hole processes. Larger chips use many different packages—one common package, the "PLCC" (for Plastic Leaded Chip Carrier) is shown below. Since these larger packages can have up to several hundred pins, it is often not practical to use the relatively large leads required by through-hole packages. Thus, large chips usually use surface mount packages, where the external pins can be smaller and more densely packed.

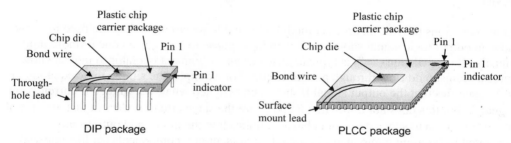

DIP package   PLCC package

On schematics and on the circuit board, chips are often shown as square boxes denoted with a "U__" or "IC__" reference designator. Some chips are loaded into sockets so that they can be easily removed or replaced. Chips, even in their plastic packages, are quite fragile are subject to damage from a variety of sources, including electrostatic discharge or ESD. Care should always be taken not to touch the leads on chips, as it is likely this will cause permanent damage.

5. Logic Circuits

As discussed earlier, a digital circuit represents and manipulates information encoded as electric signals that can assume one of two voltages—logic-high voltage (or Vdd) and logic-low voltage (or GND). A digital circuit requires a power supply that can produce these two voltages, and these same supply voltages are also used to encode information in the form of two-state, or binary signals. Thus, if a given circuit node is at Vdd, then that signal is said to carry a logic "1"; if the node is at GND, then the node carries a logic "0". The components in digital circuits are simple on/off switches that can pass logic "1" and logic "0" signals from one circuit node to another. Most typically, these switches are arranged to combine input signals to produce an output signal according to basic logic relationships. For example, one well-known logic circuit is an AND gate that combines two input signals to produce an output that is the logic AND of the inputs (i.e., if both input 1 and input 2 are a "1", then the output is a "1").

The three primary logic relationships, AND, OR, and NOT (or inversion) can be used to express any logical relationship between any number of variables. These simple logic functions form the basis for all digital electronic devices—from a simple microwave oven controller to a desktop PC. We can write a collection of logic equations of the form "F = A AND B" that use these three relationships to specify the behavior of any given digital system. Pause a moment and think about this: *any digital system*, up to and including a highly complex computer system, can be built entirely of devices that do no more than implement these three simple functions.

As engineers, we must address two primary concerns: how to express a given requirement or problem statement in terms of these simple logic relationships; and how to build electronic devices (or circuits) that can be used to implement these relationships in real devices.

Logic equations provide an abstract model of actual logic circuits. They are used to show how an output logic signal should be driven in response to changes on one or more input signals. The equal sign ("=") is typically used as an assignment operator to indicate how information should flow through a logic circuit. For example, the simple logic equation "F = A" specifies that the output signal F should be assigned whatever voltage is currently on signal A, but this does not imply that F and A are the same circuit node—in fact, the use of a logic equation to specify circuit behavior implies that the inputs and outputs are separated by a circuit component. In digital circuits, circuit components act like one-way gates. Thus, the logic equation "F = A" dictates that a change on the signal A will result in a change on the signal F, but a change on F will not result in a change on A. Because of this directionality, assignment operators that indicate direction, such as "F <= A", are often used.

Most logic equations specify an output signal that is some function of input signals. For example, the logic equation "F <= A and B" specifies a logic circuit whose output will be driven to a "1" only when both inputs are driven to a "1". Below are six common logical functions written as conventional logic equations. The AND relationship, F = A·B, can be written without an operator between the A and B (but more properly, a dot (·) should be placed between the variables to make the relationship clear). The OR relationship uses the plus sign, and the NOT or inversion relationship is shown by placing a bar over the

voltages must be reversed. Refer to one of the many available texts for a more proper and detailed presentation of FET operation.

As the figure below shows, both the source and drain diffusion areas of an nFET are implanted with negatively charged particles. When an nFET is used in a logic circuit, its source lead is connected to GND, so that the nFET source, like the GND node, has an abundance of negatively charged particles. If the gate voltage of an nFET is at the same voltage as the source lead (i.e., GND), then the presence of the negatively charged particles on the gate repels negatively charged particles from the channel region immediately under the gate (note that in semiconductors such as silicon, positive and negative charges are mobile and can move about the semiconductor lattice under the influence of charged-particle induced electric fields). A net positive charge accumulates under the gate, and two back-to-back positive-negative junctions of charge (called pn junctions) are formed. These pn-junctions prevent current flow in either direction. If the voltage on the gate is raised above the source voltage by an amount exceeding the threshold voltage (or Vth, which equals about 0.5V), positive charges begin to accumulate on the gate and positive charges in the channel region immediately under the gate are repelled. A net negative charge accumulates under the gate, forming a channel of continuous conductive region in the area under the gate and between the source and drain diffusion areas. When the gate voltage reaches Vdd, a large conductive channel forms and the nFET is "strongly" on.

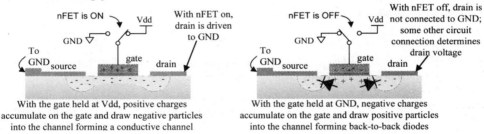

With the gate held at Vdd, positive charges accumulate on the gate and draw negative particles into the channel forming a conductive channel

With the gate held at GND, negative charges accumulate on the gate and draw positive particles into the channel forming back-to-back diodes

As the following figure shows, nFETs used in logic circuits have their source leads attached to GND and Vdd on their gate turns them on, while pFETs have their source leads attached to Vdd and GND on their gate turns them on.

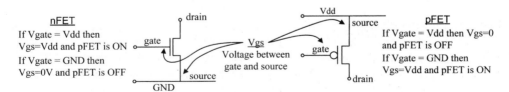

For reasons that will become clear later, an nFET with its source attached to Vdd will not turn on very strongly, so nFET sources are rarely connected to Vdd. Similarly, a pFET with its source attached to GND will not turn on very well either, so pFETs are rarely connected to GND.

Logic Circuits Built from FETs

Armed only with this basic description of FET operation, it is possible to construct the basic logic circuits that form the backbone of all digital and computer circuits. These logic circuits will combine one or more input signals to produce an output signal according to the logic function requirements. The following discussion is restricted to circuits for basic logic functions (like AND, OR, and INV), but FET circuits can readily be built for more complex logic circuits as well.

When building FET circuits to implement logic relationships, four basic rules must be followed:

- pFET sources must be connected to Vdd and nFET sources must be connected to GND;
- the circuit output must always be connected to Vdd via an on pFET or to GND via an on nFET (i.e., the circuit output must never be left floating);
- the logic circuit output must never be connected to both Vdd and GND at the same time (i.e., the circuit output must not be "shorted");
- the circuit must use the fewest possible number of FETs.

Following these rules, a circuit that can form the AND relationship between two input signals is developed. But first, note that in the circuit on the right, the output (labeled Y) is connected to GND only if the two inputs A *and* B are at Vdd. The two nFETs labeled Q1 and Q2

Series configuration:
Y = LLV if A *and* B are LHV

Parallel configuration:
Y = LLV if A *or* B are LHV

are said to be in series; in general, a series connection of FETs is required for an AND function. In the circuit on the right below, the output Y is connected to GND if A *or* B are at Vdd. The two nFETs labeled Q3 and Q4 are said to be in parallel; in general, a parallel connection of FETs is required for an OR function.

Keeping in mind the rules for FET logic circuits, an AND structure is created from Q1 and Q2 below. Using just these two FETs, Y is driven to GND whenever A *and* B are at Vdd. But we must also ensure the output Y is at Vdd when A and B are *not* both at Vdd; restated, we must ensure the output Y is at Vdd whenever A *or* B are at GND. This can be accomplished with an OR'ing structure of pFETs (Q3 and Q4 below). The AND'ing structure and OR'ing structure are assembled in the circuit on the right below. The adjacent operation table shows the input and output voltages for all four possible combinations of inputs. Note that this circuit obeys all the rules above—pFETs are connected only to Vdd, nFETs are connected only to ground, the output is always driven to Vdd or to GND but never to both simultaneously, and the fewest possible number of FETs are used.

22

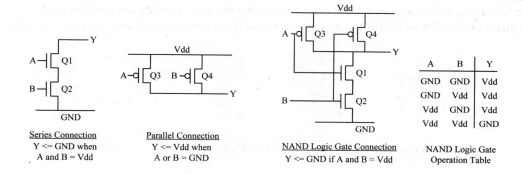

Series Connection	Parallel Connection	NAND Logic Gate Connection	NAND Logic Gate
Y <= GND when A and B = Vdd	Y <= Vdd when A or B = GND	Y <= GND if A and B = Vdd	Operation Table

A	B	Y
GND	GND	Vdd
GND	Vdd	Vdd
Vdd	GND	Vdd
Vdd	Vdd	GND

This AND'ing circuit has the interesting property of producing an output signal at *GND* when both inputs A and B are at *Vdd*. In order to have this circuit's performance match the AND logical truth table above, we must associate an input signal at Vdd with a logic "1" (and therefore, an input signal at GND must be associated with a logic "0"); and we must associate an output signal at GND with a logic "1". This creates a potentially confusing situation—considering the "1" symbol to represent a signal at Vdd on the input of a gate, and then considering that same "1" symbol to represent a signal at GND on the output of a gate. Note that if the outputs in the Y column of the truth table were inverted (that is, if Vdd were changed to GND and GND were changed to Vdd), then a "1" symbol could represent Vdd for both the inputs and outputs, resulting in the AND truth table presented earlier. Because of this, the circuit shown above is called a NOT AND gate (were NOT means inversion), which is shortened to "NAND" gate. To create an AND circuit in which both the input signals and output signals can associate a Vdd signal with a logic "1", an inverter circuit must be added to the output of the NAND gate (as the name implies, an inverter produces a Vdd output for a GND input, and vice-versa).Shown below are the five basic logic circuits: NAND, NOR (for "NOT OR"), AND, OR and INV (for inverter). The reader should verify that all truth tables show the correct circuit operation. These basic logic circuits are frequently referred to as logic gates.

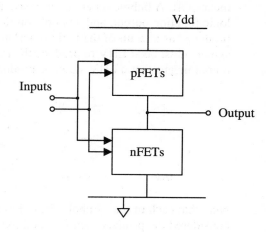

In each of these logic gates, a minimum number of FETs has been used to produce the required logic function. Each circuit has nFETs "on the bottom" and pFETs "on the top" performing complementary operations; that is, when an OR relationship is present in the nFETs, an AND relationship is present in the pFETs. FET circuits that exhibit this complementary nature are called Complementary Metal Oxide Semiconductor, or CMOS, circuits. CMOS circuits are by far the dominant circuits used today in digital and computer circuits. (Incidentally, the **Metal-Oxide-Semiconductor** name refers to older technologies where the gate material was made of **m**etal and the insulator beneath the gate made of silicon **oxide**). These basic logic circuits form the basis for all digital and computer circuits.

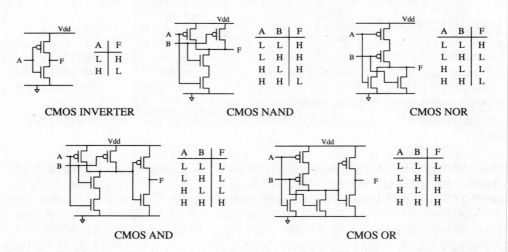

CMOS INVERTER   CMOS NAND   CMOS NOR

CMOS AND   CMOS OR

When these circuits are used in schematic drawings, the well-known symbols shown below are used rather than the FET circuit diagrams (it would simply be too tedious to draw the FET circuits). A straight edge on the input side of a symbol and smoothly curved output side means AND, while a curved edge on the input side and pointed output side means OR. A bubble on an input means that input must be at LLV to produce the indicated logic function output, and a bubble on the output means that a LLV output signal is produced as a result of the logic function. The lack of a bubble on inputs means that signals must be at LHV to produce the indicated function, and the lack of a bubble on the output means that a LHV signal is produced as a result of the logic function.

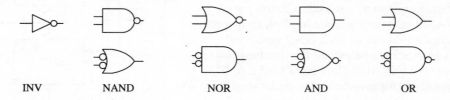

INV   NAND   NOR   AND   OR

Note that each of the symbols above has two appearances. The symbols on the top may be considered the primary symbols, and those on the bottom may be considered the conjugate symbols (properly, each symbol is the conjugate of the other). Conjugate symbols swap AND and OR shapes, and input and output assertion levels. The reader should verify that both symbols are appropriate for the underlying CMOS circuit. For example, the AND shaped symbol for the NAND circuit shows that if two inputs A and B are at LVH, then the output is at LLV. The OR shaped symbol for the NAND circuit shows that if either of two input A and B are at LLV, then the output is at LHV. Both statements are true, illustrating that any logic gate can be thought of in conjugate forms. (Why conjugate forms? In certain settings, it can be easier for humans to follow circuit schematics if the appropriate symbol is used—more on this later).

Logic Circuit Schematics

Digital logic circuits can be built from individual logic chips, or from resources available on larger chips (like the user-programmable Xilinx chip on the Basys board). Regardless of how logic circuits are implemented, they can be fully specified by truth tables, logic equations, or schematics. This section will present the preparation and reading of logic circuit schematics. A later lab will explore the relationships between circuits and truth tables.

A circuit schematic for any logic equation can be easily created by substituting logic gate symbols for logical operators, and by showing inputs as signal wires arriving at the logic gates. Perhaps the only step requiring some thought is in deciding which logic operation (and therefore, which logic gate) drives the output signal, and which logic operations drive internal circuit nodes. Any confusion can be avoided if parenthesis are used liberally in logic equations to show operator precedence, of if rules of precedence are established. For example, a schematic for the logic equation "F <= A • B + C • B" might use an OR gate to drive the output signal F, and two AND gates to drive the OR gate inputs, or it might use a three-input AND gate to drive F, with AND inputs coming from the A and B signals directly and a "B + C" OR gate. If no parentheses are used, then NAND/AND has the highest precedence, followed XOR, then NOR/OR, and finally INV. In general, it is easiest to sketch circuits from logic equations if the output gate is drawn first.

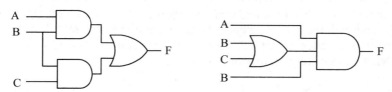

"F = A·B + C·B" can be interpreted in two different ways as shown

Inverters can be used in logic equations to show that an input signal must be inverted prior to driving a logic gate. For example, a schematic for "F <= A'B + C" would use an inverter on the A input prior to a 2-input AND gate. Equations may also show that the output of a logic function must be inverted—in this case, an inverter can be used, or the preceding circuit symbol can show an inverted output (i.e., the preceding symbol can show an output bubble). The figure below shows an example.

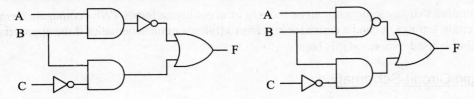

"$F = (A \cdot B)' + C'B$" can be implemented in two different ways as shown

Reading logic equations from schematics is straightforward. The logic gate that drives the output signal defines the "major" logic operation, and it can be used to determine how other terms must be grouped in the equation. An inverter, or an output bubble on a logic gate, requires that the inverted signal or function output be shown in the output of the "downstream" gate (see example below). A bubble on the input of a logic gate can be thought of as an inverter on the signal leading to the gate.

Two "back-to-back" signal inversions cancel each other. That is, if a signal is inverted, and immediately inverted again before it is used anywhere else, then the circuit would perform identically if both inversions were simply removed. This observation can be used to simplify circuits, or to make them more efficient. As an example, consider the circuits below, both of which perform identical logic functions. The circuit on the right has been simplified by removing the two inverters on signal C, and made more efficient by adding inversions on internal nodes so that NAND gates (at four transistors each) could be used instead of AND/OR gates (at 6 transistors each).

26

Exercise 1: Digital Circuits and the Basys Board

Problem 1. Below are some circuit elements from a simple digital system.

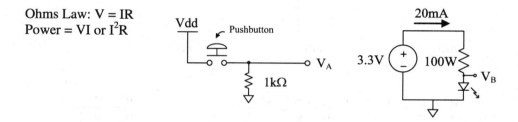

Ohms Law: V = IR
Power = VI or I²R

When the pushbutton is not pressed, what is the voltage at V_A? _____

When the pushbutton is pressed, what is the voltage at V_A? _____

When the pushbutton is pressed, how much current flows in the 1kΩ resistor?

_____

What voltage V_B is required so that 20mA flows in the LED circuit as shown?

_____

Problem 2. An LED requires 20mA of current to show the presence of a "1" output in a 3.3V system. The LED has a 1.3V threshold voltage (this voltage

---

must be present across the LED in order for it to emit light). What size of current-limiting resistor should be used? Sketch the circuit.

Problem 3.   How much power is dissipated in the resistor in the problem 2 above?

Problem 4.   Complete the truth tables below.

A	B	F

AND

A	B	F

OR

A	B	F

XOR

A	F

INV

A	B	C	F
0	0	0	
0	0	1	
0	1	0	
0	1	1	
1	0	0	
1	0	1	
1	1	0	
1	1	1	

$F = A'B + C$

A	B	C	F
0	0	0	
0	0	1	
0	1	0	
0	1	1	
1	0	0	
1	0	1	
1	1	0	
1	1	1	

$F = ABC' + BC$

A	B	C	F
0	0	0	
0	0	1	
0	1	0	
0	1	1	
1	0	0	
1	0	1	
1	1	0	
1	1	1	

$F = BC' + B'C$

Problem 5. Complete the truth tables for the circuits in Figures 1 and 2 in Chapter 1 using 1's and 0's to indicate Vdd and GND.

SW1	SW2	F	SW1	SW2	F
Figure 1 Truth Table			Figure 2 Truth Table		

Problem 6. Sketch a circuit similar to figure to the right that asserts logic 1 only when both switches are closed.

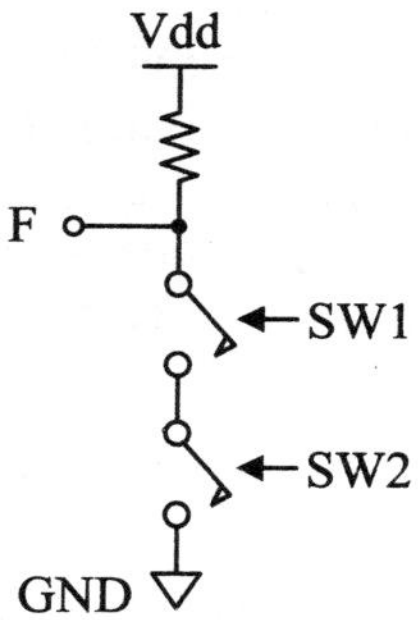

Describe how your sketch can be interpreted as an AND relationship:

Describe how your sketch can be interpreted as an OR relationship:

Sketch a circuit similar to the figure to the right that asserts logic 0 only when either switch is closed.

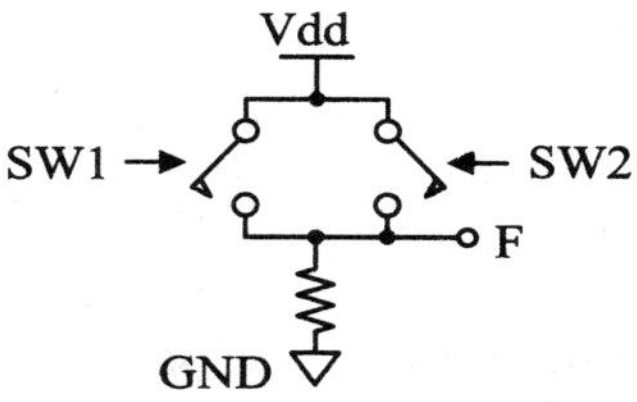

Describe how your sketch can be
interpreted as an AND relationship:

Describe how your sketch can be
interpreted as an OR relationship:

Problem 7.   Sketch a circuit using just switches and resistors that can drive an output
F to LHV if two signals A and B are at "0", or if a third signal C is at "1"
regardless of the state of A and B (assume a "1" closes a switch, and '0'
opens a switch). Then, state an alternate interpretation of the circuit
sketched in problem 5.

Problem 8.   Complete the truth tables below (enter "on" or "off" under each transistor
entry), and enter the gate name and schematic shapes in the tables.

30

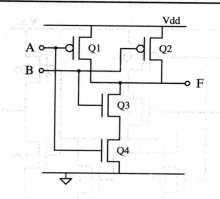

A	B	Q1	Q2	Q3	Q4	F
0	0					
0	1					
1	0					
1	1					

Gate Name	
AND shape	OR shape

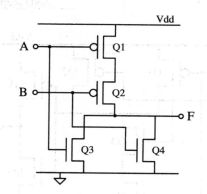

A	B	Q1	Q2	Q3	Q4	F
0	0					
0	1					
1	0					
1	1					

Gate Name	
AND shape	OR shape

31

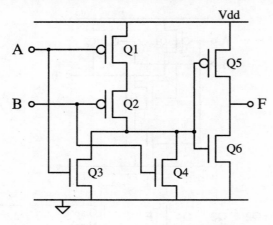

A	B	Q1	Q2	Q3	Q4	F
L	L					
L	H					
H	L					
H	H					

Gate Name	
AND shape	OR shape

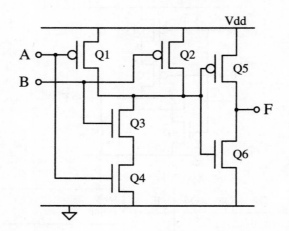

A	B	Q1	Q2	Q3	Q4	F
L	L					
L	H					
H	L					
H	H					

Gate Name	
AND shape	OR shape

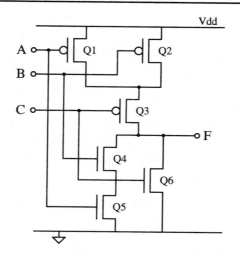

A	B	C	Q1	Q2	Q3	Q4	Q5	Q6	F
L	L	L							
L	L	H							
L	H	L							
L	H	H							
H	L	L							
H	L	H							
H	H	L							
H	H	H							

Enter the logic equation for the 3-input circuit above: | F = |

Problem 9:   Complete the following.

A. A pFET turns [ON / OFF] with LLV and conducts [LHV / LLV] well (circle one in each bracket).
B. An nFET turns [ON / OFF] with LLV and conducts [LHV / LLV] well (circle one in each bracket).

C. Write the number of transistors used in each gate:

NAND: _____   OR: _____   INV: _____   AND: _____   NOR: _____

Problem 10. In a logic function with n inputs, there are 2^n unique combinations of inputs and 2^{2^n} possible logic functions. The table below has four rows that show the four possible combinations of two inputs ($2^2 = 4$), and 16 output columns that show all possible two-input logic functions ($2^{2^2} = 16$). Six of these output columns are associated with common logic functions of two variables. Circle the six columns, and label them with the appropriate logic gate name. Draw the circuit symbols for the functions represented

INPUTS		ALL POSSIBLE OUTPUTS															
A	B	1	2	3	4	5	6	7	8	9	10	11	12	13	14	15	16
0	0	0	1	0	1	0	1	0	1	0	1	0	1	0	1	0	1
0	1	0	0	1	1	0	0	1	1	0	0	1	1	0	0	1	1
1	0	0	0	0	0	1	1	1	1	0	0	0	0	1	1	1	1
1	1	0	0	0	0	0	0	0	0	1	1	1	1	1	1	1	1

A table like the one above for 3 inputs would need _____ rows and _____ columns.

A table like the one above for 4 inputs would need _____ rows and _____ columns.

A table like the one above for 5 inputs would need _____ rows and _____ columns.

Problem 11. Sketch circuits for the following logic equations (a′ following a variable means the variable should be inverted).

$$F = A' \cdot B \cdot C + A \cdot B' \cdot C' + A' \cdot C$$

$$F = (A' \cdot B \cdot C')' + (A + B)'$$

$$F = (A + B') \cdot ((B + C)' \cdot A')'$$

Problem 12.   Write logic equations for the following circuits.

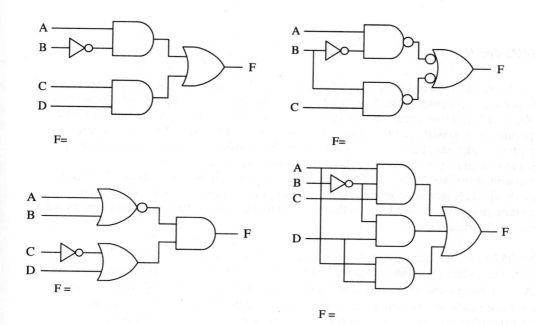

F=

F=

F =

F =

Chapter 2: Introduction to Digilent FPGA-based Boards

Overview

This chapter introduces Digilent's FPGA-based circuit boards and the Adept™ software that is used to program them. In tutorial fashion, Adept is used to download a logic circuit to the board, and that circuit is used in an experiment with basic logic circuits. In future experiments, you will use the Xilinx CAD tools, Digilent board and Adept software to design and implement a wide range of circuits, from basic logic devices through more advanced digital systems. Digilent boards are built around a chip called a "Field Programmable Gate Array" (or FPGA) produced by the Xilinx corporation. The boards include all necessary support circuits (including power supplies, clock sources, resets, programming circuits, and I/O), so that you can focus on your designs, without worrying about the hardware itself.

The FPGA can be configured many thousands of times into a virtually unlimited number of circuits, making it an ideal tool for learning about digital circuits and systems. In fact, FPGA's have gained wide acceptance in the electronics industry for the same reason—they can quickly be configured into virtually any circuit (and even entire computer systems), allowing engineers to thoroughly study designs before they are built commercially. In recent years, FPGA costs have decreased to the point where a large and growing number of customers design them into their final products; such products get the added benefit of allowing in-the-field system hardware upgrades. In the years to come, it is likely FPGA's will continue to find their way into a larger number of products, perhaps eventually replacing microprocessors and a host of other special purpose chips in the majority of designs.

Before beginning this chapter, you should…	After completing this chapter, you should…
• Obtain the reference manual and schematic for your Digilent board;	• Know that your Digilent board functions correctly;
• Be familiar with the basic concepts of electronic circuits and power supplies;	• Be able to use Adept™ to program your board;

- Know the definitions of voltage, current, resistance, power, and energy;
- Be familiar with basic circuit components such as resistors, capacitors, diodes, LEDs, switches, transistors, and simple integrated circuits;
- Be able to apply Ohm's law to basic circuits;
- Be familiar with the basic logic operations AND, OR, NOT, NAND, NOR, XOR, and XNOR (or EQV).

- Be able to recognize electronic components such as resistors, capacitors, and logic chips.

This chapter requires:

- A Windows PC running the Xilinx ISE/WebPack software;
- A Digilent FPGA-based circuit board.

After power-on, an FPGA on a Digilent board must be configured (or programmed) by the user before it can perform any useful functions. During configuration, a "bit" file is transferred into memory cells within the FPGA to define a circuit's logical functions and interconnections. The free ISE/WebPack CAD software from Xilinx can be used to create bit files from VHDL, Verilog, or schematic-based source files. After a programming file has been created, it can be downloaded to the board using Digilent's Adept software (the Xilinx iMPACT software can also be used, but a Digilent JTAG3 programming cable is required). Once programmed, the FPGA will retain its configuration only as long is power is applied.

All Xilinx chips can be programmed using a special built-in interface known as the "JTAG" port (JTAG in an acronym for the "Joint Test Action Group", which is group composed of member companies interested in ensuring that test and programming ports evolve to use a common interface). JTAG ports are commonly used for moving test data between computers and integrated circuits, and they are increasingly used for transferring configuration data as well. All JTAG ports follow published signal definition, timing, and control specifications, but data formatting is largely left up to individual companies. Xilinx has developed programming algorithms for their devices, and programming software (like Digilent's Adept or Xilinx's iMPACT) must drive the JTAG ports in accordance with JTAG specifications and the programming algorithms.

FPGA's on Digilent boards can be programmed in two ways: directly from a PC via a USB cable, and from an on-board Platform Flash ROM that is also user-programmable. Once programmed, the Platform Flash can automatically transfer a stored bit file to the FPGA at a subsequent power-on or reset event. A "Mode Jumper" is available on Digilent boards to select between JTAG/PC-based programming and ROM based programming. Whereas JTAG/PC-based programming can occur at any time, ROM-based programming can only occur after a power-cycle or reset event (a reset-event occurs when the "FPGA reset" button on the Digilent board is pressed). The FPGA will remain configured until the next power-cycle or reset event, but the Platform Flash ROM will retain a bit file until it is reprogrammed, regardless of power-cycle events.

To program a Digilent board using Adept, attach the USB cable to the board (if USB power will not be used, attach a suitable power supply to the power jack or battery connector on the board, and set the power switch to VEXT). Start the Adept software, and wait for the FPGA and the Platform Flash ROM to be recognized. Use the browse function to associate the desired .bit file with the FPGA, and/or the desired .mcs file with the Platform Flash ROM. Right-click on the device to be programmed, and select the "program" function. The configuration file will be sent to the FPGA or Platform Flash, and the software will indicate whether programming was successful. The "configuration done" LED will also illuminate after the FPGA has been successfully configured. Further information on using Adept is available in the appendix and in documentation available at the Digilent website.

Board Reference Materials

Digilent boards contain from hundreds to thousands of components, depending on the number and complexity of circuits they contain. Each component is chosen specifically for some intended function, and during manufacturing each must be correctly sourced from the manufacturer. The printed circuit board (PCB) itself must be properly designed and manufactured, and every component must be loaded onto the board to exact tolerances (typically less than 1/1000 of an inch). A single incorrect or bad component, or a single good component loaded incorrectly during manufacturing can cause the board to malfunction or fail completely. Even a relatively simple board (like the Basys) must be carefully manufactured and tested thoroughly prior to being released for sale. Ultimately, development boards (like the Digilent boards) are sophisticated engineering tools, and at one time or another, users need to understand all the components, circuits, and functions in order to use the board productively.

Three documents are available for users to fully understand a Digilent board and its functions: the reference manual, the schematic, and the parts list. It is prudent to have copies of all of these documents handy for reference, and to learn something about them prior to actually needing them.

The reference manual essentially explains the schematic. It is a good introduction for new users, but experienced engineers may not use it at all. For experienced engineers, the most concise, accurate, and unambiguous reference document is the schematic. The schematic is the engineering source document from which the board was produced, and as such, it contains all pertinent data anyone might need to use the board.

The schematic shows all components on the board, their values, and their connections to all other components. Each component on the schematic and on the PCB is identified by a unique alpha-numeric string called a reference designator. If you examine the schematic, you will see the reference designator text strings (e.g., "R21" or "C37") near every component. The contents of designators are not really significant, although in general resistors start with he letter "R", capacitors with "C", inductors with "L", chips with "IC", diodes with "D", LEDs with "LD", transistors with "Q", and connectors with "J". The number following the letter can represent either the order in which parts were added to the schematic, the order in which they appear in the schematic, or some combination of the two. All that really matters is that each component be identified with a unique test string. If you examine the board, you will see the same reference designators spread around both sides of the board.

Before using your board, you should verify that it is functioning properly. All boards with a simple test program loaded in the Flash ROM that can be used to quickly check many of the connections and device on the board.

Exercise 2: Introduction to Digilent FPGA-based Boards

Problem 1. Obtain and read the board's reference manual, paying close attention to the Power Supply and Configuration Sections. Complete the following.

How many LED's are on the board? ____ Are they illuminated with a logic "1" or "0"? ____

How many pushbuttons on the board? ____ Do they output logic "1" or "0" when pressed? ____

How many slideswitches on board? ____ Do they output constant logic levels (yes or no)? ____

Which signals turn on the seven-segment displays? _____ _____ _____ _____

Problem 2. Obtain and print the board schematic, and identify the following components by circling and labeling them, both in the schematic and on the photo below. Write the reference designator in the spaces following the components.

1. Pushbutton number 2   Reference Designator: _____
2. 3.3V voltage regulator   Reference Designator: _____
3. JTAG programming header   Reference Designator: _____
4. The FPGA   Reference Designator: _____
5. The Platform Flash ROM   Reference Designator: _____
6. "CLK1" oscillator   Reference Designator: _____

---

7. The Mode Select jumper   Reference Designator: _____
8. Any LED   Reference Designator: _____
9. The FPGA reset pushbutton   Reference Designator: _____
10. Capacitor C71   What is C71's value?_____
11. Resistor R62   What is R62's value?_____

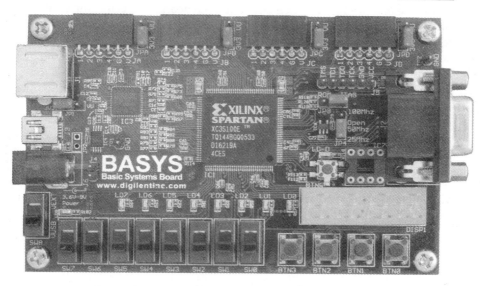

Problem 3.   Perform a basic inspection and test of the board.

- Understand the definition of voltage, electric current, and resistance, and be able to apply Ohm's law to basic circuits.
- Inspect the board and note any components that appear to be missing, damaged, or otherwise compromised. When inspecting the board, you can compare it to the picture on the Digilent website (or the picture in this document).
- Set the programming mode jumper to ROM.
- Apply power to the board, and ensure the power-on LED illuminates and glows brightly.
- The automated test, stored in the on-board Flash ROM at manufacturing time, will automatically configure the FPGA with a circuit that can be used to test all circuits. If the automated test does not automatically load, the ROM image may have been overwritten. Obtain the appropriate "Board Verification Project" from the Digilent website, and re-load the Flash ROM (see Appendix A the Lab Project 2 document for a brief tutorial on using Adept).

Complete the check-off sheet below. If any item has been checked "N" in the table, consult the lab assistant for help in resolving the issue.

All required components present (board, programming cable, etc.)	Y	N
Visual inspection reveals no obvious problems	Y	N
"Power On" LED glows brightly when power supply attached	Y	N
All segments on all seven-segment digits are functional	Y	N
All slide switches function correctly by illuminating/extinguishing LEDs	Y	N
All LED's illuminate properly	Y	N
All pushbuttons function correctly	Y	N

Lab Project 2: Board Verification and Basic Logic Circuits

Introduction

In this lab project, you will download a .bit file to your board to configure the FPGA with eight different logic circuits. The circuits use buttons and switches for inputs, and LEDs for outputs. You must probe the logic circuits by applying all possible combinations of input signals, and from the results write logic equations that describe the circuit's behavior.

Problem   Obtain the file "lab1_boardname.bit" from the class website, and download it to your Digilent board following the procedure in Appendix A below. Your board will be configured with eight logic circuits that drive the eight on-board LEDs. You must find logic equations to describe the circuits. After the FPGA is configured with the bit file, apply all combinations of relevant inputs (hint: see the input variable names on the top row of each truth table), and use the output LED status to complete the following truth tables. Have the lab assistant inspect your work.

swt7	btn3	LED7
L	L	
L	H	
H	L	
H	H	

LED7 <=

swt6	btn3	LED6
L	L	
L	H	
H	L	
H	H	

LED6 <=

swt7	swt6	swt5	LED5
L	L	L	
L	L	H	
L	H	L	
L	H	H	
H	L	L	
H	L	H	
H	H	L	
H	H	H	

LED5 <=

btn3	btn2	LED4
L	L	
L	H	
H	L	
H	H	

LED4 <=

swt4	swt3	btn1	LED3
L	L	L	
L	L	H	
L	H	L	
L	H	H	
H	L	L	
H	L	H	
H	H	L	
H	H	H	

LED3 <=

swt2	btn0	LED2
L	L	
L	H	
H	L	
H	H	

LED2 <=

btn1	btn0	LED1
L	L	
L	H	
H	L	
H	H	

LED1 <=

swt2	swt1	swt0	LED0
L	L	L	
L	L	H	
L	H	L	
L	H	H	
H	L	L	
H	L	H	
H	H	L	
H	H	H	

LED0 <=

Appendix: Programming Digilent Boards Using Adept

Adept™ is a suite of Windows-based applications that can transfer programming files and other data between a PC and Digilent boards. Adept typically uses a USB2 port for communications, but Ethernet, Serial, and Parallel ports are also supported.

Applications in the Adept suite include ExPort for transferring programming files, TransPort for moving user-data to and from devices on Digilent boards, USB Administrator for modifying USB port settings, and Ethernet Administrator for modifying Ethernet port settings. Although Adept is flexible enough to support many specific end-user requirements, most users can install Adept with default settings and immediately begin programming devices using a USB port.

This document provides a brief tutorial demonstrating the installation and basic use of Adept. For more complete information, please visit our website at www.digilentinc.com.

Installing Adept

Adept Suite is compatible with Windows 2000, XP, and Vista. The Adept Suite installer will install the ExPort, TransPort, Ethernet Administrator, and USB Administrator applications as well as the USB driver. To install the Adept Suite, you must log on to your PC as an Administrator, disconnect any USB devices connected to the PC, and run the DASV1-9-1.msi file. Then, follow the instructions below.

(1) When the installer application opens, click "Next" button.

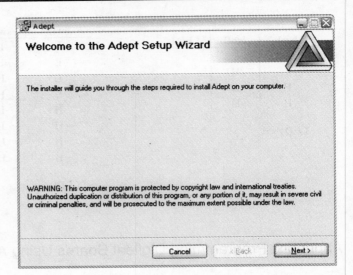

(2) Read the EULA, click the "I Agree" radio button and click "Next" button.

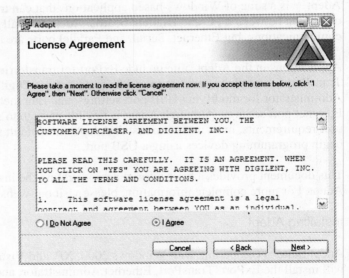

(3) We recommend installing Adept Suite for "Everyone".

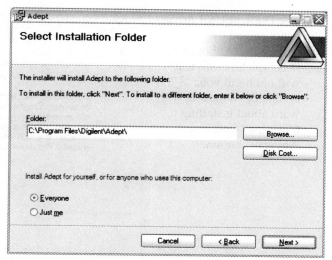

(4) Click "Next" button to start the installation.

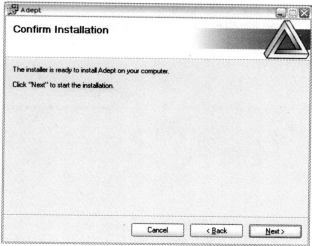

(5) The Digilent USB driver is not signed by Microsoft. Although it is completely safe and will not harm your computer, Windows will warn about installing it. Click the "Continue Anyway" button.

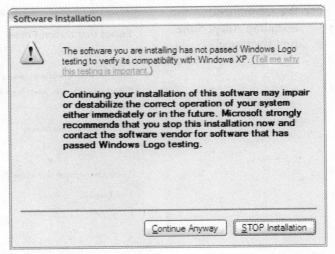

(6) Click the "OK" button to finish installation.

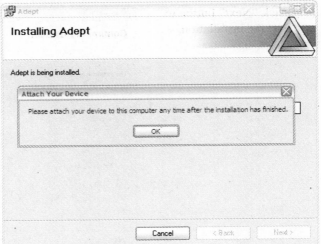

(7) Connect board to PC via USB cable. Windows should recognize the device.

(8) The Found New Hardware Wizard will appear. Select "No, not this time" and click the "Next" button.

(9) Set the wizard to "Install the software automatically". Click the "Next" button.

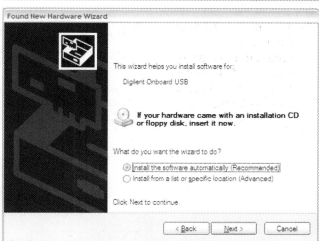

(10) Windows will again prompt you with the warning about the unsigned USB driver. Once again, click "Continue Anyway" button to allow the installation to complete.

Using ExPort

(1) Open ExPort.

(2) To Initialize the Scan
Chain for
programming, make
sure the "Auto-Detect
USB" box is checked
and Click "Initialize
Chain" button.

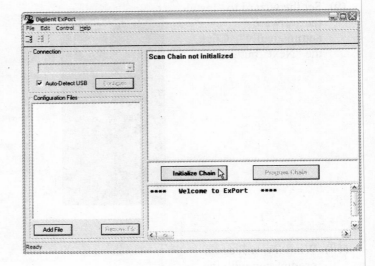

(3) After scan-chain
initialization, devices
can be programmed,
erased, and verified.
To program a device,
assign a configuration
file to the device in the
pull-down box. To
add a file, click the
"Browse..." button
and navigate to the
desired file.

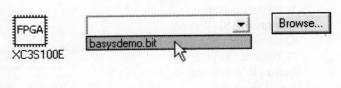

(4) After the programming file has been selected, right-click on the device icon and select "Program Device".

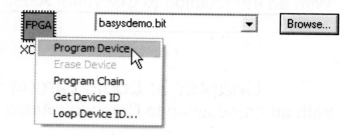

(5) An on-screen message will tell you if programming was successful. If programming is not successful, ensure the board is properly powered and that all cable connections are intact, and try again.

For more information on ExPort and all other Adept applications, please see the Digilent Adept Suite Users Manual.

Chapter 3: Logic Circuit Structure
With an Introduction to Computer Aided Design (CAD) Tools

1. Overview

This chapter presents the basic structure of combinational logic circuits, and introduces the use of computer aided design (CAD) tools in modern circuit design. Combinational logic circuits use networks of logic gates to produce outputs that change in strict relation to input changes; that is, an output can only change state immediately after an input changes state. In a combinational circuit, some input signal changes propagate through the logic gates and interconnections and produce output signal changes, while some input changes may have no effect on outputs; further, the same input patterns will always produce the same outputs. In contrast, outputs from a "sequential circuit", or a circuit that contains memory devices, can change irrespective of input signal changes, and the same input patterns applied at different times can produce different outputs (memory containing circuits are covered in a later chapter). All combinational circuits can be expressed in two forms: an OR'ing of AND'ed terms, or an AND'ing of OR'ed terms. Since these general forms, called "Sum of Products" (or SOP) and "Product of Sums" (or POS), can be used to express any combinational logic requirement, we will examine them in some detail.

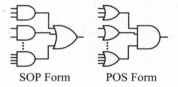

SOP Form   POS Form

CAD tools are an indispensable design resource used by electrical engineers on a daily basis. They allow engineers to easily create picture-based or text-based circuit definitions, perform circuit simulations, and implement circuits in a variety of technologies. Because CAD tools allow engineers to work with "virtual" circuits before constructing them, more time can be spent studying different solution methods and circuit architectures, and less time on building and rebuilding prototypes. Although CAD tools have been used for generations, they are still being modified and improved on a regular basis. As technologies and methodologies advance, new tools are being developed to take advantage of them. It is safe to say that practicing engineers will need to learn and apply many different CAD tools over their career. This chapter provides some general discussion about CAD tools, and then introduces the use of Xilinx ISE/WebPack tools. The Xilinx tools can be used to design, test, and implement (in a programmable chip) virtually any digital circuit. They allow circuits to be defined using several different graphical and text-based methods. The graphical method known as "schematic capture" will be covered first, together with a simulation tool that can be used to verify a circuit's performance. A later chapter will introduce text-based methods.

Before beginning this chapter, you should…	After completing this chapter, you should…
• Be familiar with reading and constructing basic logic circuits;	• Construct a logic circuit from a logic equation;
• Be familiar with logic equations and their relation to logic circuits;	• Understand CAD tool use in basic circuit design;
• Know how to operate Windows computers and Windows programs.	• Be able to implement any given combinational circuit using the Xilinx ISE schematic editor;
	• Be able to simulate any logic circuit;
	• Be able to use a logic simulator to verify a given circuit's behavior.

This chapter requires:

- A Windows PC running the Xilinx ISE/WebPack software;
- A Digilent circuit board.

2. Introduction to Basic Structure of Logic Circuits

Schematics and Prototypes

A schematic is a pictorial representation of a circuit that directly defines circuit structure, and indirectly defines circuit behavior (that is, behavior must be deduced from circuit structure). A schematic is composed of shapes that represent electronic components, lines that represent interconnecting wires, and connector symbols that show external connections. Labels are used to uniquely identify every component, wire, and connector. Symbols used in digital logic circuits are typically restricted to the AND, OR, NAND, NOR, XOR, XNOR, and INV logic gates. Most digital schematics use symbols without Vdd and GND connections, because it is understood that all logic gates require electric power to operate, and showing the power supply connections add no value.

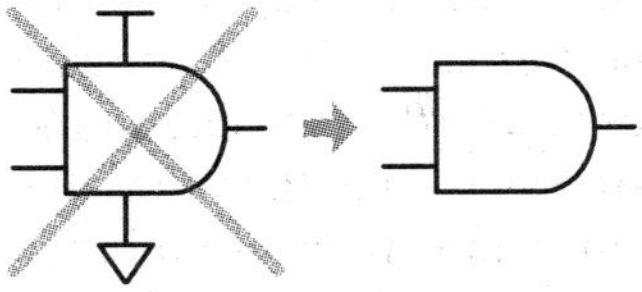

A schematic shows how input signals are combined in logic gates to drive one or more outputs. In the example circuit shown below, the output Z is driven to a logic "1" if B is a "0" or C is a "0", or if B and D are a "1" at the same time that C is a "0". No information is provided to indicate where the inputs originated, or what function the outputs will perform; this is typical in logic circuit schematics, where such details are left for a higher level system description. In the example shown, inputs might arise from switches, sensors, or other logic circuits, and outputs might drive indicators or other circuits.

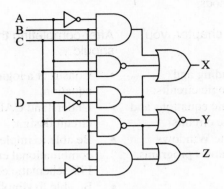

In a schematic editor, circuits can readily be constructed by assembling graphical shapes that describe logic gates, interconnections, and I/O ports. The completed schematic defines a virtual circuit model, and such models serve two primary purposes: they can be *simulated* so that a circuit's behavior can be analyzed before it is built; and they can be *synthesized*, or automatically implemented in a real, physical circuit device. The widespread use of simulation and synthesis CAD tools has defined a new and powerful design approach used by virtually all digital design engineers. But it is important to remember that CAD tools work with virtual circuit models, and not with real, physical circuits. Even the most powerful circuit simulators cannot fully model all circuit behaviors, and much about circuit function can only be learned through building and interacting with a physical circuit.

The use of CAD tools greatly simplifies the job of creating a circuit definition that meets the needs of any given design problem. Design problems are typically expressed as a "behavioral" requirement—for example, a design requirement might be to illuminate a warning light if a measured temperature exceeds 90℃ for 10 seconds, or if coolant level is too low. This worded description describes how a circuit should behave, but it provides no information about circuit structure. A circuit model can be developed to meet the needs of such a behavioral problem statement, and that circuit model can be simulated so that its performance can be compared to the problem requirements. But note that the assumptions used to create the circuit model are verified against the assumptions in the problem statement, and therefore the overall solution is only as good as the assumptions. In any environment or discipline, assumptions are used in place of rigorous knowledge, and they are usually lacking. When circuits are implemented in real, physical devices, their behavior and performance can be thoroughly checked and validated, leaving no room for faulty assumptions—the circuit either works properly in its intended environment or it does not. It is fair to say that a solution to a given problem is only "proven" after a real circuit has been built and verified. In fact, most design work is performed, and most knowledge is gained, after a virtual circuit model seems complete, and the process of implementing and validating a circuit has begun. Restated, there is no substitute for implementing and working with a real circuit.

Once a design has been proven, it can be implemented in some final target technology. A design destined for an electronic device that might sell millions of units would probably be implemented in a fully custom chip; a design that may sell in the tens of thousands might be implemented in a programmable device; and a design for a low-end, inexpensive toy or novelty might be implemented using discrete components and paper-based circuit boards. In any case, if a circuit prototype is defined in a CAD tool, it is easy to reuse any or all of the source files in the final design.

Beginning with this module and continuing in all subsequent modules, you will learn to use the features of the Xilinx CAD tools to define, simulate, and synthesize circuits. Many of the circuits will be implemented in a Digilent board for validation and verification. In later modules, after you have achieved a level of proficiency with the tools, more information will be presented about CAD tool methods and their use in modern designs.

Combinational Circuit Structure

Combinational logic circuits produce outputs that are some logical function (i.e., AND, OR, NOT, etc.) of their inputs. Any given pattern of inputs to a combinational circuit will always produce the same outputs, regardless of when the inputs are applied. The behavior of combinational logic circuits is most typically identified and specified by a logic equation or by a truth table. Either of these methods provides a clear, concise, and unambiguous definition of how input signals are combined to drive outputs signals.

Logic equations arise naturally when a given worded problem is stated in a more rigorous engineering formalism. For example, the worded problem statement "the latch should be released when the EAST and WEST buttons are pressed simultaneously, or when the NORTH button is pressed provided the WEST button is not pressed at the same time, or whenever the SOUTH button is pressed all by itself" could be cast in a logic equation as:

L <= (E and W) or (N and not W) or (S and not E and not W and not N)

A logic equation states behavioral requirements in a concise, unambiguous fashion. Often, for simple equations (as with the example), a structural circuit can be constructed directly from the equation.

Truth tables are perhaps the most rigorous expression of a combinational logic system, because they define output behavior under all possible combinations of inputs. A truth table for N variables contains 2^N rows, with each row showing a unique pattern of inputs. The rows are typically

E	W	N	S	L
0	0	0	0	0
0	0	0	1	1
0	0	1	0	1
0	0	1	1	1
0	1	0	0	0
0	1	0	1	0
0	1	1	0	0
0	1	1	1	0
1	0	0	0	0
1	0	0	1	0
1	0	1	0	1
1	0	1	1	1
1	1	0	0	1
1	1	0	1	1
1	1	1	0	1
1	1	1	1	1

arranged so that each successive N-bit row is the next binary number in sequence from the preceding row. The truth table on the right shows the input-output behavior of the logic system example above. A circuit schematic can readily be defined from either a logic equation or from a truth table.

A schematic for a logic equation can be created by substituting logic gate symbols for logical operators, and by showing inputs as signal wires arriving at the logic gates. Perhaps the only step requiring some thought is in deciding which logic operation (and therefore, which logic gate) drives the output signal, and which logic operations drive internal circuit nodes. Any confusion can be avoided if parenthesis are used in logic equations to show operator precedence, of if rules of precedence are followed. For example, a schematic for the logic equation "F <= A • B + C • B" might use an OR gate to drive the output signal F, and two AND gates to drive the OR gate inputs, or it might use a three-input AND gate to drive F, with AND inputs coming from the A and B signals directly and a "B + C" OR gate.

If no parentheses are used in a logic equation, then INV has the highest precedence, followed by NAND/AND, followed by XOR, and then NOR/OR. In general, it is easiest to sketch circuits from logic equations if the output gate is drawn first. In the figure, the left-most schematic is correct for F <= A • B + C • B.

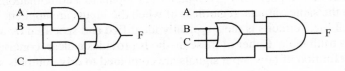

Inversions in logic equations show when an input signal must be inverted prior to driving a logic gate, and also when an output from a logic gate must be inverted. These inversions can map directly to inverters in schematics. For example, in the schematic for the equation F <= (A • B)' + B • C' below left, an inverter is placed on the C input prior to a 2-input

NAND gate and on the output of the A·B gate as required by the equation. It is common practice to "absorb" an inverter

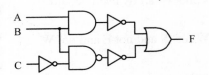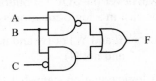

that follows a logic gate into the gate itself, by placing an inverting "bubble" on the gate output (if one did not exist), or removing an output bubble if one was already present. In fact, using an output bubble instead of an inverter often results in a more minimal CMOS circuit. For example, an inverter following an AND gate represents 8 transistors, while a NAND gate performing the same logic uses only 4 transistors. It is also common to absorb an input inverter into a subsequent logic gate, particularly if the inverted signal only drives one single logic input. The figure on the right above shows an example of absorbing inverters into gate symbols. The meaning of the one-bubble AND gate symbol for B • C' is clear: drive the gate output to a "1" if B is a "1" and C is a "0".

Two "back-to-back" signal inversions cancel each other. That is, if a signal is inverted, and immediately inverted again before it is used anywhere else, then the circuit would perform identically if both inversions were simply removed. This observation can be used to simplify circuits, or to make them more efficient. As an example, consider the circuits below, both of which perform identical logic functions. The circuit on the right has been simplified by removing the two inverters on signal C, and made more efficient by adding inversions on internal nodes so that NAND gates (at four transistors each) could be used instead of AND/OR gates (at 6 transistors each).

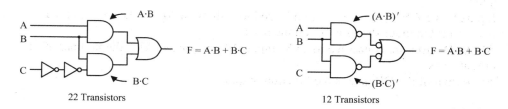

Reading logic equations from schematics is also straightforward. The logic gate that drives the output signal defines the "major" logic operation, and it can be used to determine how other terms must be grouped in the equation. An inverter, or an output bubble on a logic gate, requires that the inverted signal or function output be shown in the output of the "downstream" gate (see example below). A bubble on the input of a logic gate can be thought of as an inverter on the signal leading to the gate.

SOP and POS Circuits

The terms "product" and "sum" have long been borrowed from mathematics to describe AND and OR logic operations. A product term is defined as an AND relationship between any number of variables, and a sum term is defined as an OR relationship between any number of logic variables. Any logic system can be represented in two logically equivalent ways: as the OR'ing of AND'ed terms, known as the Sum Of Products (SOP) form; or as the AND'ing of OR'ed terms, known as the Product of Sums (POS) form. The two forms are interchangeable, and one form can be transformed to the other following a few basic rules. As an example, consider the XOR relationship $Y_{SOP} <= $ (not A and B) or (A and not B). This SOP relationship can be expressed in POS form as $Y_{POS} <= $ (A or B) and (not A or not B). In this example, the POS and SOP forms are equally simple, but this is not always the case. For circuits with more than two inputs, it may turn out that one form is simpler that the other. If a circuit is to be constructed, it makes sense to evaluate both forms so that the simplest one can be constructed.

A logic equation (and therefore a logic circuit) can easily be constructed from any truth table by applying the rules presented below.

For SOP circuits:

- A circuit for a truth table with N input columns can use AND gates with N inputs, and each row in the truth table with a "1" in the output column requires one N-input AND gate;
- Inputs to the AND gate are inverted if the input shows a "0" on the row, and not inverted if the input shows a "1" on the row;
- All AND terms are connected to an M-input OR gate, where M is the number of "1" output rows;
- The output of the OR gate is the function output.

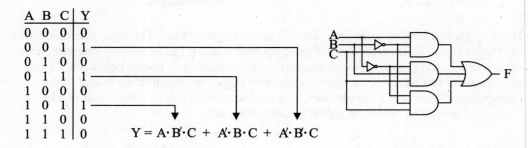

A	B	C	Y
0	0	0	0
0	0	1	1
0	1	0	0
0	1	1	1
1	0	0	0
1	0	1	1
1	1	0	0
1	1	1	0

$$Y = A \cdot B' \cdot C + A' \cdot B \cdot C + A' \cdot B' \cdot C$$

And for POS circuits:

- A circuit for a truth table with N input columns can use OR gates with N inputs, and each row in the truth table with a "0" in the output column requires one N-input OR gate;
- Inputs to the OR gate are inverted if the input shows a "1" on the row, and not inverted if the input shows a "0" on the row;
- All OR terms are connected to an M-input AND gate, where M is the number of "1" output rows;
- The output of the AND gate is the function output.

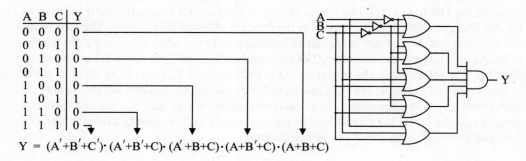

A	B	C	Y
0	0	0	0
0	0	1	1
0	1	0	0
0	1	1	1
1	0	0	0
1	0	1	1
1	1	0	0
1	1	1	0

$$Y = (A' + B' + C') \cdot (A' + B' + C) \cdot (A' + B + C) \cdot (A + B' + C) \cdot (A + B + C)$$

In the SOP circuit shown above, every product term contains all three input variables. Likewise, in the POS circuit, every sum term contains all three input variables. Product terms that contain all input variables are known as minterms, and sum terms that contain all input variables are known as maxterms. A minterm or maxterm number can be assigned to each row in a truth table if the input 1's and 0's on a given row are interpreted as a binary number. Thus, the SOP equation above (and in the truth table to the right) contains minterms 1, 3, and 5, and the POS equation contains maxterms 0, 2, 4, 6, and 7. In an SOP equation, an input value of "1" creates a non-inverted variable in the minterm (and "0" creates an inverted variable). This defines a minterm code that associates each minterm with a corresponding truth table row. In a POS equation, an input value of "1" creates an inverted variable (and "0" creates a non-inverted variable). This defines a maxterm code that associates every maxterm with a particular truth table row.

A	B	C	#	Minterm	Maxterm	F
0	0	0	0	$A' \cdot B' \cdot C'$	$A + B + C$	0
0	0	1	1	$A' \cdot B' \cdot C$	$A + B + C'$	1
0	1	0	2	$A' \cdot B \cdot C'$	$A + B' + C$	0
0	1	1	3	$A' \cdot B \cdot C$	$A + B' + C'$	1
1	0	0	4	$A \cdot B' \cdot C'$	$A' + B + C$	0
1	0	1	5	$A \cdot B' \cdot C$	$A' + B + C'$	1
1	1	0	6	$A \cdot B \cdot C'$	$A' + B' + C$	0
1	1	1	7	$A \cdot B \cdot C$	$A' + B' + C'$	0

Using minterm and maxterm codes, it is possible to write a new, compact form of SOP and POS equations that follow directly from a truth table. The SOP equation uses the summation symbol Σ to suggest the summing of terms, and the POS equation uses the symbol Π to suggest taking the product of terms. Both equations simply list the minterms or maxterms present in a given truth table after the initial symbol. Every truth table output row that contains a "1" defines a minterm, and every row that contains a "0" defines a maxterm. Minterm and maxterm equations are shown for the truth table above.

$$F = \sum m(1, 3, 5) \qquad F = \prod M(0, 2, 4, 6, 7)$$

XOR Functions

The Exclusive OR (or XOR) relationship F $<= A$ XOR B is defined by the truth tables shown and the equivalent two-variable logic expressions:

$$F_{SOP} <= A \cdot B' + A' \cdot B \quad F_{POS}$$
$$<= (A + B) \cdot (A' + B')$$

A	B	F
0	0	0
0	1	1
1	0	1
1	1	0

2-input XOR

A	B	C	F
0	0	0	0
0	0	1	1
0	1	0	1
0	1	1	0
1	0	0	1
1	0	1	0
1	1	0	0
1	1	1	1

3-input XOR

The $\oplus$ symbol is also used frequently for XOR functions, for example, F <= A $\oplus$ B or F <= A $\oplus$ B $\oplus$ C. The XOR function is frequently used in digital circuits to manipulate signals that represent binary numbers—these circuits will be presented in a later module. For now, note the XOR output is asserted whenever an odd number of inputs are asserted. This "odd detector" nature of the XOR relationship holds for any number of inputs.

Compound XOR functions like F <= A $\oplus$ (B $\cdot$ C) can always be written in an equivalent SOP or POS forms: F_{SOP} <= A' $\cdot$ (B $\cdot$ C) + A $\cdot$ (B $\cdot$ C)' and F_{POS} <= (A + (B $\cdot$ C))(A' + (B $\cdot$ C)').

The XNOR function is the inverse of the XOR function. Since the output of a 2-input XNOR is asserted when both inputs are the same, it is sometimes referred to as the Equivalence function (EQV), but this name is misleading, because it does not hold for three or more variables (i.e., the output of a 3-input XNOR is not asserted whenever all three inputs are the same) Truth tables for 2 and 3 input XNOR functions are shown, and it can be seen that for each combination of inputs, the output is the inverse of the XOR truth tables above. The Exclusive NOR (or XNOR) relationship F <= A XNOR B shown in the truth tables has the equivalent two-variable logic expressions:

A	B	F
0	0	1
0	1	0
1	0	0
1	1	1

2-input XNOR

A	B	C	F
0	0	0	1
0	0	1	0
0	1	0	0
0	1	1	1
1	0	0	0
1	0	1	1
1	1	0	1
1	1	1	0

3-input XNOR

$$F_{SOP} <= A' \cdot B' + A \cdot B \quad F_{POS} <= (A' + B) \cdot (A + B').$$

The $\oplus$ symbol is also used frequently for XNOR functions, with the entire expression inverted: F <= (A $\oplus$ B)' or F <= not (A $\oplus$ B); or F <= (A $\oplus$ B $\oplus$ C)' or F <= not (A $\oplus$ B $\oplus$ C).

If either the A or B inputs are in the XNOR truth table are inverted, then XOR outputs are produced; that is, F <= (A $\oplus$ B)' produces the same logic output as F <= A' $\oplus$ B or F <= A $\oplus$ B'. If both the A and B inputs are inverted, XNOR outputs are still produced: F <= (A $\oplus$ B)' produces the same output as F <= A' $\oplus$ B'. This same property holds for the XOR function—inverting any single input variable will result in XNOR function, and inverting two inputs will again produce the XOR function. In fact, this property can be generalized to XOR/XNOR functions of any number of inputs: any single input inversion changes the function output between the XOR and XNOR functions; any two input signal inversions does not change function outputs; any three input signal inversions changes the function output between the XOR and XNOR functions, etc. More succinctly, inverting an odd number of inputs changes an XOR to an XNOR and vice-versa, inverting an even number of inputs changes nothing, and inverting the entire function has the same effect as inverting a single input. Some representative cases are shown.

F=A xnor B xnor C $\Leftrightarrow$ F <= (A $\oplus$ B $\oplus$ C)' $\Leftrightarrow$ F <= A' $\oplus$ B $\oplus$ C $\Leftrightarrow$ F <= (A' $\oplus$ B' $\oplus$ C)' etc.
F=A xor B xor C $\quad$ $\Leftrightarrow$ F <= A $\oplus$ B $\oplus$ C $\Leftrightarrow$ F <= A' $\oplus$ B' $\oplus$ C $\Leftrightarrow$ F <= (A $\oplus$ B' $\oplus$ C)' etc.

An even more succinct description of the XOR and XNOR function outputs can be drawn from the properties discussed. The XOR output is asserted whenever an odd number of inputs are asserted, and the XNOR is asserted whenever an even number of inputs are asserted: the XOR is an *odd* detector, and the XNOR, an *even* detector. This very useful property will be exploited in data error detection circuits discussed in a later module.

XOR and XNOR gate symbols are shown. CMOS circuits for either function can be can built from just 6 transistors, but those circuit have some undesirable features. More typically, XOR and XNOR logic gates are built from three NAND gates and two inverters, and so take 16 transistors.

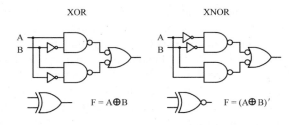

An useful application of the XOR function is the "controlled inverter" circuit illustrated below. The truth table, derived directly from the XOR truth table, uses an XOR gate with one input tied to a signal named "control". When control is a "1", the input A is inverted, but when control is a "0", A is simply passed through the logic gate without modification. This controlled inversion function will be useful in later work.

A	B	F	Control	A	F
0	0	0	0	0	0
0	1	1	0	1	1
1	0	1	1	0	1
1	1	0	1	1	0
XOR truth			Controlled INV		

} ← Pass

} ← Invert

3. Introduction to Computer Aided Design Tools

An idea for a new circuit design rarely proceeds directly from concept to flawless implementation. Rather, during the design phase, several potential circuits are considered, and some of them are implemented and evaluated. These prototype circuits help the designer build a greater understanding of the design requirements and possible solutions before a final design is selected. In the early days of digital design, prototype circuits were sketched on paper and then constructed from discrete components or simple integrated circuits. More recently, CAD tools are used to specify and design digital circuits, rendering pencil-and-paper techniques all but obsolete. With the onset of the computer age, engineers learned they could be far more productive by designing a virtual circuit on a computer instead of actually building it. Now, after several generations of engineers have completed countless designs using CAD tools, they are accepted as a basic and irreplaceable design resource. Their prolific use across all engineering disciplines has allowed new concepts and new technologies to be developed and exploited at an incredible pace. Without their use, it is fair to say technological progress would be crippled. In recent

years, CAD tools have become powerful enough to usher in a whole new class of design
methods and engineering processes. At the same time, they have become so affordable that
virtually any engineer can use them.

The Product Design Process

A new product or circuit design process begins with an idea that might arise from any one
of several sources, including customers, sales and marketing personnel, or engineers. A
new idea that survives the scrutiny and challenges of various
feasibility studies typically results in a proposal that describes
high level product features, presents target budgets, defines
schedules, outlines marketing plans, and generally discusses
any useful information. Ideas that make it through the proposal
stage enter the engineering design process (indicated by the
shaded area of the flowchart). The engineering design process
typically starts with a specification. A product specification is
an engineering document that contains enough information to
guide skilled engineers through the design process. Based on
the specification, a behavioral description, a structural
description, or some combination of both can be prepared. A
behavioral description is essentially a highly detailed
specification that states only how a new design is to behave,
without providing any information as to how it might actually
be built (this is the job of a structural description). For example,
a specification for a status indicator on an automobile might be
"a *fuel_low* warning light shall be illuminated whenever the
fuel tank indicator reads less than 2 gallons for 10 continuous
seconds". A behavioral description might be "*fuel_warning_
light* <= check_2s(*under_2_gallons*)". This behavioral
description is written in an easily readable format that clearly indicates a signal named
"*fuel_warning_light*" gets assigned a logic value based on the output of a process that
evaluates the input signal "*under_2_gallons*". This behavioral description makes the basic
design requirement perfectly clear, but it provides no information to indicate how a circuit
might be constructed. In fact, before the circuit can be constructed, this behavioral
description must be transformed into a structural description. A structural description, such
as a circuit schematic showing all components and their interconnections, conveys not
only a circuit's behavior, but the information needed to actually construct the circuit as
well.

This progression from a more abstract behavioral description to a more detailed structural
description is a required part of any design process, and may in fact be *defined* as the
design process. Even in this simple "warning light" example, the structural definition
might take any one of several forms, including a circuit based on a microprocessor, a
circuit based on discrete components, or a circuit based on a programmable device. Which
form the structural design takes depends on many factors, including the designer's skills,

the cost of various components, the amount of power required by different approaches, etc.

CAD tools are useful throughout the engineering design process, and they benefit simple logic designs and complex system designs alike. In the early stages of a design, CAD tools allow designers to capture circuit definitions on a computer using any one of several different entry modes. Some text-based modes, such as those using a "Hardware Definition Language" or HDL editor, allow highly behavioral descriptions. Other picture-based modes, such as those using a schematic editor, require highly structural descriptions. Any given circuit can be described by a behavioral or structural source file, but significant differences exist. For example, a schematic description that shows all components and interconnections can take significant effort to create, but it yields a description that can be accurately simulated and directly implemented. A behavioral HDL definition can be quickly entered, but since it contains no information about the structure of a circuit, it must be transformed to a structural representation before a circuit can be implemented.

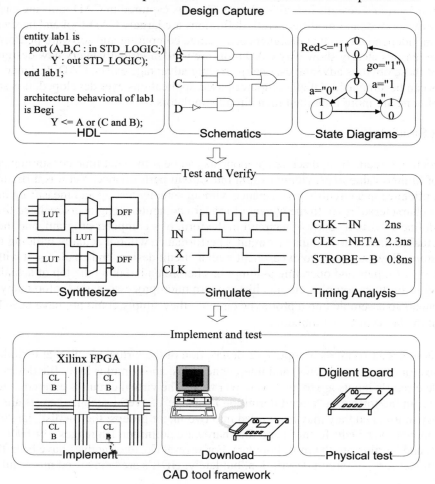

CAD tool framework

Much of the work in generating a structural description lies in *drawing* a circuit, and not in *defining* a circuit to meet a given need (i.e., its one thing to sketch a house to meet a family's needs, but another thing to actually build it). Likewise, transforming a behavioral circuit description to a structural description can require significant work, and this work may not add significant value to the ultimate solution. A class of computer programs called synthesizers can perform this work, thereby freeing design engineers to focus on other design tasks. Although synthesizers use rules and assumptions that allow for a wide range of behavioral definitions, several studies have shown that they are nevertheless able to produce structural descriptions that are better than most engineers can produce. HDL editors and synthesizers will be examined in a later lab exercise.

CAD tools allow designers to capture circuits in a convenient manner, using highly evolved tools that significantly reduce labor. They allow captured circuits to be simulated and thoroughly studied before they are actually constructed. They also allow a circuit definition to be implemented in a given technology, so that engineers can readily interact with their "virtual" designs in real hardware. Circuits captured in CAD tools are easily stored, transported, and modified. HDL definitions are largely CAD-tool and hardware platform independent, so that designers can change computing and software platforms. All of these reasons clearly show why CAD tools are used in virtually every new design. But of all of these obvious advantages, one overriding advantage exists: CAD-designed circuits can be simulated. Of all computer-based applications ever developed, it is safe to say that none are more important than circuit simulators.

Circuit Simulators

Constructing circuits from discrete components can be somewhat time consuming, and often of limited value in providing insight into circuit performance. Yet it is difficult to gain confidence in a circuit's performance without actually testing and measuring its various characteristics. With the advent of modern computers, engineers realized that they could define a "virtual" copy of a circuit in the form of a computer program, and then use that virtual definition to simulate a circuit's performance without actually building it. Simulators allow engineers to experiment with a circuit design, and challenge it with a wide array of inputs and operating assumptions before undertaking the job of actually building it. Further, complex circuits like modern microprocessors use far too many components to assemble into a prototype circuit—they simply could not have been built without the heavy use of simulators.

Simulators need two kinds of inputs—a description of the virtual circuit that includes all of the gates (or other components) and interconnections, and stimulus input file describing how the circuit's inputs are to be driven over time. The virtual circuit is entered in to the computer in the form of a "circuit definition language". Several such languages are currently in use, and they may be divided into two major groups: the "netlist" languages (most popular is the edif format); and the "hardware definition languages", or HDL's (VHDL and Verilog are the most popular). For several decades, netlists have been the predominant form of circuit description, but lately, HDL's are being used more and more.

In this module, we'll look at netlists and the tools used to create, simulate, and download them to programmable devices. HDLs will be examined in a later module.

A netlist is simply a textual description of the components and interconnections in a given circuit. A netlist for a simple circuit might appear as shown to the right. The first entry in each line of the netlist (before the colon) is a label that uniquely identifies a given logic gate or circuit. Next comes the name of the gate and a list of all the inputs and outputs in some predetermined order—in this netlist, the logic gate output is last in the list. Line 2, for example, describes a 2-input NAND gate labeled G2 with inputs *net1* and *a* and output *net2*.

> *G1: INV(sel,net1)*
> *G2: NAND2(net1,a,net2)*
> G3: NAND2(sel,b,net3)
> G4: NAND2(net2,net3,y)
>
> **Example netlist**

Netlists use many different formats, with the "electronic data interchange format" (or edif) being the most popular. Although edif-fomatted netlists look somewhat different than this example, they contain the same essential information. Whatever the appearance, the entries in a netlist provide a simulation program with all information needed to simulate the described circuit. In the example shown, you can think of each line as a subroutine call, where the logic function name refers to a particular subroutine and the input/output list provides the subroutine parameters. At each simulation time step, any subroutines whose inputs have changed are executed to compute a new output value. Each newly computed output value might be the input of some other subroutine, and that subroutine would then be executed in a later time step.

To simulate a circuit, a set of stimulus inputs is also required. Often, a sequential list of stimulus commands are collected into a text file, and then given to the simulator (along with the netlist) for a "batch" run. But it is also possible to enter the simulation commands one at a time, and watch the circuit respond in real-time. A set of stimulus inputs may look like those shown in the box to the right.

> Force a,b,sel to '0 '
> *simulate 100ns*
> Force a to '1 '
> *simulate 100ns*
> Force sel to '1 '
> simulate 100ns
> Force b to '1 '
> Simulate 100ns
>
> **Example stimulus**

Schematic Capture

A netlist could be created by hand and typed directly into a computer. But this would be a tedious and laborious practice, even for a moderately complex circuit. First, an accurate and complete circuit sketch would need to be created, then all logic gates and interconnecting nets in a circuit would need to be assigned unique names, and finally the netlist itself, with all components together with a list of all interconnects could be prepared. Note that once a sketch of the circuit is prepared, the remaining tasks are straightforward, repetitious, and time consuming—characteristics that make them well suited to a computer.

A sketch (or a computer-based graphical drawing) of a circuit, with symbols representing logic functions and lines representing interconnecting wires, is commonly referred to as a schematic. A schematic is simply graphical rendition of a netlist, and it is much easier to draw a schematic on a computer than to create a netlist by hand. Computer programs known as "schematic capture tools" allow designers to draw circuits on a computer using a graphical interface. The schematic drawing tool allows symbols representing logic gates (or logic functions) and lines representing wires to be added to a computer-based drawing.

Basic symbols take the shape of recognizable logic gates and functions (NAND's, OR's, INV's, etc.), and more complex functions may appear as simple boxes. Users may also create their own custom symbols to represent logic circuits that they design themselves. Whether a symbol comes from a standard parts library, or whether it is designed by an user, it will have several protruding lines about its periphery representing inputs (generally on the left of the symbol) and outputs (generally on the right of the symbol). Referred to as pins or ports, these inputs and outputs provide connection points for the lines that represent wires. Although symbols usually do not show ports for power and ground connections, their presence is always assumed.

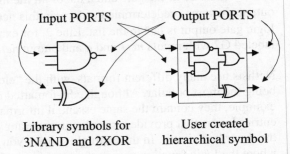

Input PORTS   Output PORTS

Library symbols for 3NAND and 2XOR   User created hierarchical symbol

A circuit is defined in the schematic capture tool by adding symbols and wires until all required components and interconnections are present. Once the schematic is complete, a program called a "netlister" processes the graphical information to produce (or "extract") the netlist. A schematic must be transformed into netlist representation before it can be simulated. Although the netlist and schematic descriptions of a given circuit look very different from one another, they contain exactly the same information. A one-to-one relationship exists between the schematic and netlist, and it is always possible to convert from one to the other using a simple replacement algorithm. Since it is generally easier for humans to read a circuit schematic than a netlist, circuits are more often shown in schematic form. The process of defining and entering a circuit using a graphical computer tool, and extracting a netlist from the schematic is known as schematic capture.

Each circuit symbol has an outline shape and several pins that act as connection points. Many symbols represent common logic functions that can be readily identified due to shape association (and, or, xnor, etc.). Many symbols also appear as rectangular boxes that give no clue as to their function. These non-shape-specific symbols are "wrappers" around circuit blocks that have been designed from more basic logic gates. Circuits grouped into such symbols are commonly called macros, and they are frequently used by designers to hide the details of more basic circuits. In this sense, circuit macros are used in schematics in the same way that subprograms are used in computer programs. Circuit macros are most useful when used as building blocks for larger, more complex circuits. Macros are more complex than simple logic gates or circuits, but they are smaller, simpler and easier to understand than the overall circuit. A circuit built from macros is said to be a hierarchical circuit, and many levels of hierarchy can be used (i.e., macros can contain other macros as circuit elements). Once designed, macro components can be stored in a project library so that they can be recalled and reused as needed. "I/O markers" are used to identify signals in hierarchical circuits that are meant to be inputs or outputs (as opposed to signals that are limited to internal nodes).

Hierarchical schematic editors allow design complexities to be abstracted away, and hidden inside macros. Macros can be designed and verified independently, often before the overall design is started. Then, they can be used as trusted building blocks for a more complex design. Hierarchical editors allow a "divide and conquer" approach to complex design problems. A primary challenge, and one of the more important design tasks, is to partition a design appropriately. A good partition can make a complex task flow relatively smoothly, and a poor partition can create additional work or cause a design to fail.

Associated with each symbol in a schematic, hidden from view, are computer routines that tell a logic simulator program exactly how to model the circuit. A netlister translates the shapes and lines of a schematic into a netlist, and the netlist is essentially a list of calls to these computer routines. Thus, when a schematic is drawn on the screen, the source for a netlist (and therefore, the input to a simulator) is being created as well.

Schematic Design Flow

A detailed schematic design flow is shown in the flowchart to the right. The design flow starts with a clear specification, and the specification is used to generate a schematic (and therefore a netlist). The process of generating an error-free schematic and netlist can be somewhat challenging based on the complexity of the design and the features of the CAD tool. Once the netlist is complete, stimulus input can be generated to test the design. In a schematic flow, stimulus inputs can typically be generated using a simple graphical interface called a waveform

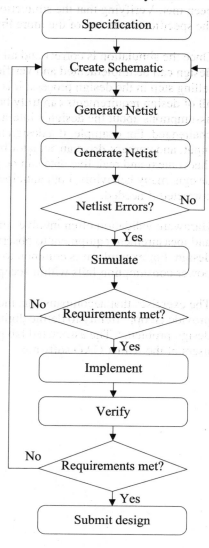

Schematic design flow

editor. A waveform editor allows signals to be assigned different logic values over time. When all input values have been assigned, the simulation can be executed, and the simulator will produce output values based on the inputs. The output values are typically shown in the same graphic interface window so it is easy to match circuit inputs with the resulting outputs. In general, the simulator inputs should drive the circuit with all possible input conditions so that the designer can verify that the output is correct for every possible combination of inputs. Once the simulation has been executed, the designer must determine whether the simulation results demonstrate that the design requirements have been met. Verifying that the simulation outputs indicate a working design consistent with the specification is one of the more important and challenging process in the design flow.

Once the simulation is correct and all design requirements have been confirmed, the design can be implemented and verified in hardware. This is the most important and telling step in the design process; it is not until the design is made "real" in hardware that all of design requirements can truly be validated. And as importantly, all of the assumptions about the design's interaction with its intended physical environment can be challenged. For example, if a design is intended to process signals acquired from a sensor input, and perhaps drive an actuator based on the acquired data, the circuit can be placed in this context and real, live data can be processed. In this ultimate proving ground of the design, many behaviors, both anticipated and unexpected, can be observed, validated, and corrected if needed.

Hardware validation often involves the use of various meters, oscilloscopes, and other test and measurement equipment to observe and measure various electronic signals in the design. For example, it is common to check that signal timings meet requirements, that power consumption falls within acceptable limits, or that electronic noise is well contained.

The exercises that accompany this module will reinforce many of the topics presented and provide an opportunity to define digital circuits to meet the requirements of some basic design problems. The associated lab project provides a basic tutorial targeted at first-time users of the Xilinx CAD software.

Exercise 3: Logic Circuit Structure

STUDENT	
I am submitting my own work, and I understand penalties will be assessed if I submit work for credit that is not my own.	
Print Name	ID Number
Sign Name	Date

Estimated Work Hours

2	3	4	5	6	7	8	9	10

2	3	4	5	6	7	8	9	10

Overall Weight

GRADER

#	*Points*	*Score*
1	8	
2	6	
3	6	
4	9	
5	4	
6	10	
7	8	
8	6	
9	6	

Total Score

Weeks late

Adjusted Score

Adjusted Score:
Deduct 20% from score for each week late

Problem 1. Sketch circuits for the following logic equations.

$Y <= (A \cdot B \cdot C) + ((A \cdot B' \cdot C \cdot D')+(B + D)')'$

$X <= (A \oplus B \cdot C \oplus D') + (B \oplus C)' \cdot (C + D)'$

Problem 2. Sketch circuits for the following equations.

$$F = \sum m(1, 2, 6) \qquad F = \prod M(0, 7)$$

Problem 3. Write logic equations for the following circuit.

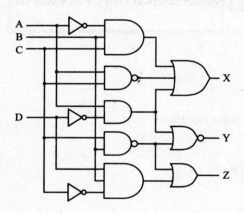

Problem 4. Sketch circuits defined by the truth tables below.

A	B	C	F
L	L	L	1
L	L	H	0
L	H	L	1
L	H	H	0
H	L	L	1
H	L	H	1
H	H	L	1
H	H	H	1

70

A	B	C	F
L	L	L	1
L	L	H	1
L	H	L	0
L	H	H	0
H	L	L	0
H	L	H	0
H	H	L	1
H	H	H	1

A	B	C	F
L	L	L	1
L	L	H	0
L	H	L	0
L	H	H	1
H	L	L	1
H	L	H	0
H	H	L	0
H	H	H	1

Problem 5.   Sketch POS circuits for the 2XOR and 2XNOR functions.

Problem 6. Sketch the circuit described by the netlist shown, and complete the timing diagram for the stimulus shown to document the circuit's response to the example stimulus. Use a 100ns vertical grid in your timing diagram, and show all inputs and outputs.

G1: INV(sel,net1)
G2: NAND2(net1,a,net2)
G3: NAND2(sel,b,net3)
G4: NAND2(net2,net3,y)

Netlist

Force a,b,sel to '0'
simulate 100ns
Force a to '1'
simulate 100ns
Force sel to '1'
simulate 100ns
Force b to '1'
Simulate 100ns

Stimulus

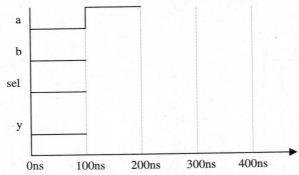

Timing diagram showing input/output changes over time

Problem 7. Create a truth table that corresponds to the simulation shown below. Show all input and output values in the truth table, and sketch a logic circuit that could have been used to create the waveform.

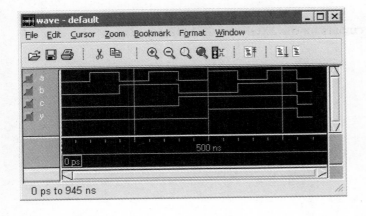

A	B	C	Y
0	0	0	
0	0	1	
0	1	0	
0	1	1	
1	0	0	
1	0	1	
1	1	0	
1	1	1	

Problem 8.   The Seattle Mariners haven't had a stolen base in 6 months, and the manager decided it was because the other teams were reading his signals to the base runners. He came up with a new set of signals (pulling on his EAR, lifting one LEG, patting the top of his HEAD, and BOWing) to indicate when runners should attempt to steal a base. A runner should STEAL a base if and only if the manager pulls his EAR and BOWs while patting his HEAD, or if he lifts his LEG and pats his HEAD without BOWing, or anytime he pulls his EAR without lifting his LEG. Sketch a minimal circuit that could be used to indicate when a runner should steal a base.

Problem 9.   A room has four doors and four light switches (one by each door). Sketch a circuit that allows the four switches to control the light—each switch should be able to turn the light on if it is currently off, and off if it is currently on. Note that it will not be possible to associate a given switch position with "light on" or "light off"—simply moving any switch should modify the light's status.

Lab Project 3: Introduction to Schematic Capture

Estimated Work Hours

1	2	3	4	5	6	7	8	9	10

1	2	3	4	5	6	7	8	9	10

Overall Weight

Point Scale

4: Exemplary
3: Complete
2: Incomplete
1: Minor effort
0: Not submitted

20% will be deducted from scores for each week late
Score=Points awarded (Pts)×Weight (Wt)

LAB ASSISTANT

#	Demonstration	Wt	Pts	Late	Score	Lab Asst Signature	Date	Total In-Lab Score
2	Inspect source & sim files	2						
2	Circuit demo	3						
3	Circuit demo	3						

GRADER

#	Attachments	Wt	Pts	Score	Weeks late	Total Grading Score	_Total score is In-lab score plus grading score_	Total Score
1	Schematic and simulation	3						
2	Schematic	3						
3	Schematic	3						

Introduction

This Lab project introduces the Xilinx ISE/WebPack schematic capture and simulation tools. A few basic designs are presented as vehicles to illustrate tool use.

Modern CAD tools like ISE/WebPack have a top-level graphical interface called a "framework" from which all individual CAD tools can be launched. This top-level interface, called the Project Navigator, is used to set up new projects, load existing projects, and start programs like the schematic capture, simulation, and synthesizer tools. The Project Navigator shows the status of all individual tools, and keeps track of all work in progress so that no required steps are omitted.

Appendix provides a detailed tutorial of all steps needed to create, simulate and implement a circuit.

Problem 1. Use the Xilinx schematic capture and simulation tools to enter and simulate the following three individual circuits. Be sure to add I/O markers to both inputs and outputs (and be sure to change the output signals to *output*). Drive the circuit simulation with all possible combinations of inputs. Print and submit a copy of the schematic and simulation waveform files. You do not need to download these circuits to the Digilent board.

(1) $Y = A \cdot C + B \cdot C'$ (2) $F = A \cdot B' + A' \cdot C + B \cdot C'$

(3) $G = (A+B+C) \cdot (A'+B'+C')$

Problem 2. Design and implement a circuit that meets the following requirement. Use the Xilinx CAD tools to capture a schematic and simulate the design, and then implement the circuit on the Digilent board. Print and submit the schematic, and have the lab assistant inspect your work. When your circuit is complete, demonstrate its function to the lab assistant.

Amy, Baker, Cathy, and David are responsible for buying new beans for the "Overhead Coffee Company". Each of them casts a vote to determine if a given lot of beans should be purchased. They sometimes use questionable criteria when deciding to vote, but they have learned through experience that certain combinations of votes yield good results. Design and implement a logic circuit that they can use to indicate whether they should buy new beans. Use slide switches for vote entry (either "buy" or "not buy"), and an LED to indicate when beans should be purchased. A "buy" order is placed if:

David and Baker votes YES,
or   Amy votes NO while Cathy vote YES,
or   Amy and Baker vote YES and the rest vote NO,
or   Cathy and David vote NO,
or   they all vote YES.

Problem 3. Design and implement a circuit that can illuminate an LED whenever an odd number of the eight slide switches outputs a logic "1". Download this circuit to the Digilent board, and demonstrate your circuit to the lab assistant. Print and submit your schematic.

Appendix: WebPack schematic design entry tutorial

The Xilinx WebPack CAD software includes schematic capture, simulation, implementation, and device programming tools, all of which can be started from a single "navigator" tool that coordinates the files and processes associated with a given design project. The navigator shows all source files, all CAD tools that can be used with the source files, and any output or status messages and files that result from running a given tool.

Project Navigator

The entry point to the Xilinx ISE or WebPack tool is the **Project Navigator**. The Project Navigator provides an user interface that organizes all files and programs associated with a given design. The main screen is divided into four main panels. The **sources** panel shows all source files associated with a given design. Double-clicking on a file name shown in this panel will open the file in the appropriate CAD tool. The **processes** panel shows all processes that are available for a given source file (different source files have different process options). Double-clicking on any process name will cause that process to run. The **status** panel shows process status, including all warnings and errors that result from running a given process on a given source file. The **editor** panel shows the HDL source code for any selected HDL source file. The project navigator will also open other windows as needed for some applications (for example, the schematic capture tool opens in a separate window). Most designs can be completed without ever leaving the project navigator window.

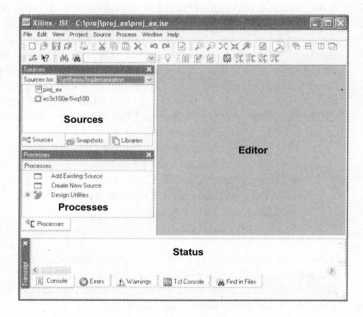

Starting a New Project

New projects can be defined and existing projects can be reopened from within the project navigator window (project navigator can be started from the windows Start menu, or by double-clicking the desktop icon). In general, a new project should be created for each new lab exercise or each new design. The project navigator can be configured to automatically load the last project used, or to not load any project (see the "properties" dialog box).

Selecting "new project" from the File pull-down menu will open the **New Project** dialog box, where all information for a new project can be entered. Enter a descriptive name (such as *lab2*) in Project Name box, and choose an appropriate directory in the Location box. This directory will store all design files and all intermediate files, so you will want to choose a directory that is protected, backed-up, and accessible from different locations (if applicable). The Top-Level Source Type box is not critical—here, typically, you will simply choose the default "HDL" as shown.

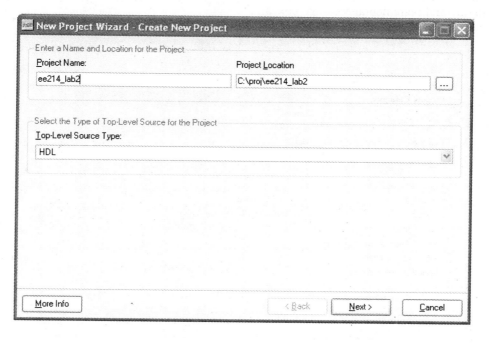

Clicking Next will bring up the Device Properties box. This box can be used to identify several parameters associated with a given design. The **Product Category** field is provided to help organize your projects. The entry in this field is not critical—typically, you will simply choose the default "All". The **Family** and **Device** fields let the CAD tools know what chip you are targeting—this information is required for several of the CAD tools to work properly. For the Basys board, choose Spartan3E and XC3S100E, and for the Nexys, Spartan3 and XC3S200. For other boards, choose the family and device corresponding to the device loaded on the board (you can typically get this information by inspecting the chip itself). The **Package** field lets the CAD tools now what chip carrier (or chip package) you are targeting—this information is required so that physical pins can be properly assigned to circuit networks in the chip. The **Speed** field is required so that timing models used by the simulator can accurately model the actual timings in the physical chip itself. This field is only critical if you need very precise simulations of your design.

The **Top-Level Source Type** field can change the user interface display for certain tools. This information is not critical and you will typically choose the default "HDL". For the **Synthesis Tool**, accept the default XST (there are no other choices unless you have loaded other synthesis tools on your PC). For the **Simulator**, you can use either the included ISE simulator, or the ModelSim-SE simulator if you have downloaded and installed it (for know, use the included ISE simulator). Finally, accept the defaults for the lower three check boxes (check the box for Enhanced Design Summary, and uncheck the Message Filtering and Incremental Message boxes).

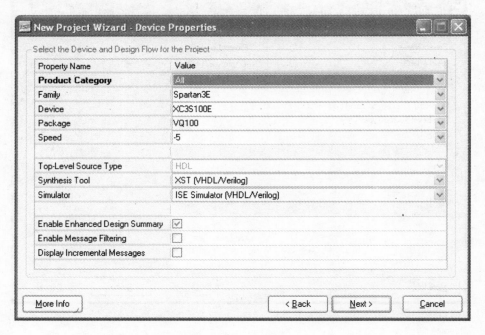

Click "Next" button to bring up the "Create New Source" dialog box. It is easy to create new source files at any point in the project— this box makes it convenient to create new source files right at the start. In some later designs, you may find this convenient. But for now, hit "Next" button without adding any information to this box.

The "Add Existing Sources" dialog box appears allowing you to add existing source files to the project. Again, it is easy to add existing source files at any later stage in the project. This box makes it convenient to define new source files right at the start, and you may wish to do this in later designs. For now, hit "Next" button without adding any information to this box.

This brings up a project summary screen showing all information entered so far. Hit "Finish" button to accept the information and launch the new project. Any of the information entered so far can easily be changed later in the project simply by double-clicking on the project name in the Sources window.

The screen shot below shows how the screen should look at this point. You can now define source files that will be used with the project.

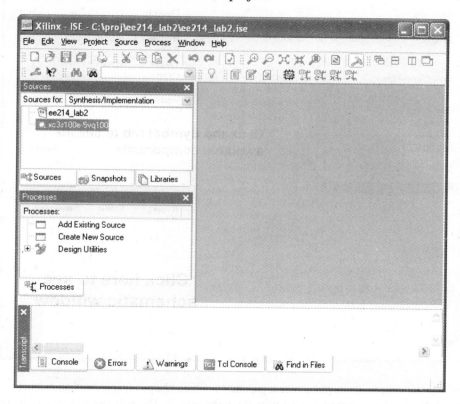

In this tutorial, we will start by defining schematic-based projects. Later, we will define VHDL-based projects.

Basic Schematic Capture

To create a new schematic, double-click on the "Create New Source" process in the

Processes window. This brings up the "Select Source Type" dialog box allowing you to define the new source file. Select "Schematic" from the list of source types, and enter a file name and directory in the provided boxes, check the "add to project" box, and click "Next" button to bring up the New Source summary box. Click "Finish" button to bring up the schematic editor window (if the Design Summary window opens, click on the *filename.sch* tab at the bottom of the editor window—see figure below).

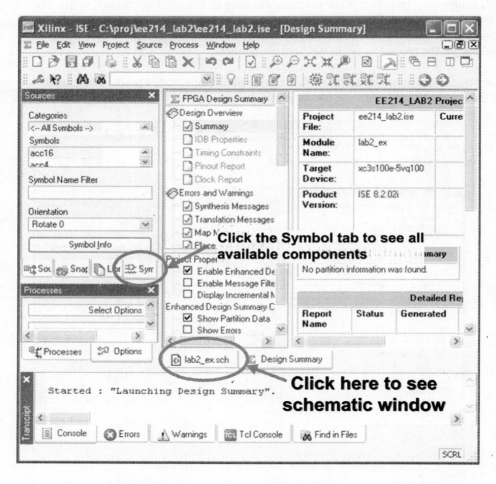

The schematic editor is simply a blank palette to which shapes (representing circuit components) and lines (representing wires) can be added. The schematic tool can be used effectively using tool-bar buttons or pull-down menu choices. In general, the tool-bar buttons and pull-down menus offer the same functions, but the pull-down menus offer some unique features; you are encouraged to experiment with them.

To draw a schematic, components must be added and interconnected with wires. To add components, click the *Add Symbol (or component)* tool-bar button to cause the component library to be displayed in a menu on the left of the schematic entry window. The components shown in the menu depend on which *device family* was selected in the new project setup window—different families use different schematic symbol libraries. Under *Categories,* select "Logic", which restricts the *Symbol* menu to displaying only the more basic logic components like AND and OR gates. To add a particular component, scroll through the menu to locate it, or type its name in the box at the bottom of the menu. Components can be moved after they have been added, so it's generally a good idea to add all needed components first, and then to rearrange them into a neater circuit once they are all present. Selected components can be "dragged and dropped" onto the schematic drawing palette.

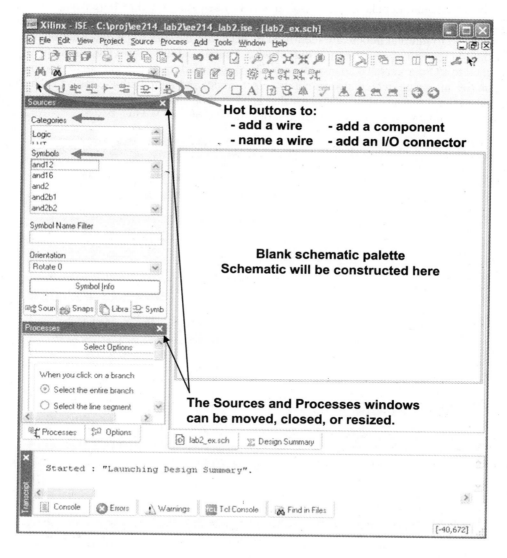

In this example, we'll create the circuit specified by: $Y = A \cdot B + B' \cdot C$. This circuit requires two **AND2** gates, an **OR2** gate, and an **INV** gate. These components can be added the schematic by selecting them from the component menu as described, and then dragging-and-dropping them to place them on the schematic palette. Once the needed components are in place, wires can be added by pressing the *add wire* tool button, and then clicking on the source and destination component pins. When connecting components with wires, be sure some amount of wire exists between all component pins. Note that it is difficult to tell whether a wire segment exists between the inverter and the AND gate. In general, enough wire should be used so that it is obvious that the pins are not directly touching. Wires can be ended in "space" by double clicking the screen area where the wire is to be terminated. Labels can be added to wires by selecting the *Add Wire Name* button, and then selecting the wire, or by double-clicking on the wire. Circuit inputs and outputs (as opposed to internal nodes) are identified by selecting the *Add I/O marker* button and clicking on the end of each input or output wire. Unique default names are automatically assigned to I/O markers. To change the default names, click on the *select cursor* toolbar button (or hit escape, which always enters *select* mode) and then double-click on each I/O marker in the schematic. In the window that appears, you can enter a new name in the name field. Save your schematic when it looks like the picture below.

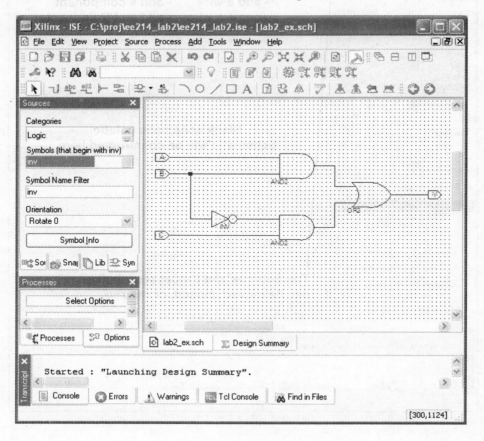

Hierarchical Design

For all but the simplest circuits, schematics can be made much more readable if certain well-defined parts of the circuit are grouped inside of a "wrapper" called a **macro** or **symbol** (just like in computer programming, where often-used code is placed inside of a subroutine). When creating a macro, it is important to make sure all inputs and outputs have I/O markers, and that all I/O markers are named. These names will appear as pin labels on the macro symbol. A macro can be created from any schematic page, and everything on the schematic page will be placed inside the macro symbol. To create a macro for a given schematic source, select *Synthesis/Implementation* in the Sources Process Menu at the top of the Sources window, and select the *Sources* tab at the bottom of that same window. In the Processes window, select the process tab, and then double-click the "Create Schematic Symbol" process. The screen below shows the key points.

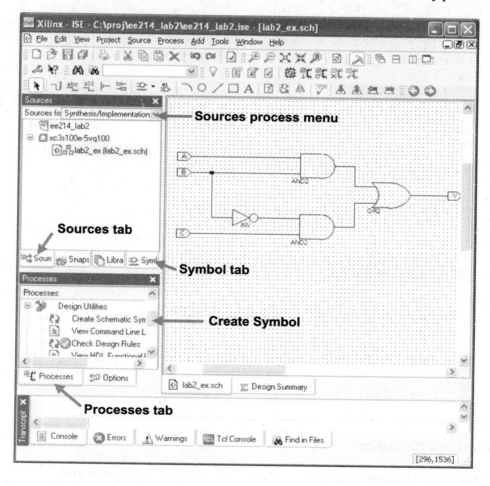

After a macro has been created, it is added to your project and it can be added as a component to any new schematics. To see your symbol, you must create a new schematic and add your symbol to it. Click on the sources tab of the Sources window, and click on the processes tab of the Processes window. Double-click on Create New Source, and create a new schematic as before. When the schematic opens, click on the Symbol Tab at the bottom of the sources window. The directory where you stored your project will appear in the Categories pull-down menu. Select your directory, and all schematic symbols you have made will be available in the symbols list. Select the circuit macro name in the symbols pull-down menu and select the Add Symbol hot button. You can now drop your new symbol into the schematic. Add I/O ports and wires to the schematic, and save your work. Using just these basic methods, schematics for circuits of arbitrary complexity can be created.

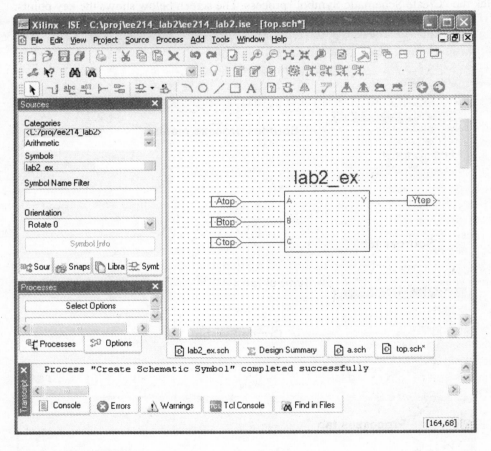

Basic Logic Simulation

A logic simulator allows a designer to observe circuit outputs in response to all combinations of inputs before the circuit is implemented in hardware. Simulating a circuit is perhaps the best technique an engineer can use to ensure that all required features are present, and that no unintended behaviors are present. For larger designs, simulation is far cheaper and far less error prone than designing and testing a hardware prototype. If errors are observed in the simulator's output, the circuit can easily be corrected and re-simulated as often as necessary.

The simulator requires two kinds of inputs: the circuit description source file, and a set of stimulus values that define all input logic inputs for the duration of the simulation. The circuit description source must be an HDL file; if a schematic source is created, an HDL file is automatically generated whenever the schematic is saved. No matter what type of source file is used to describe a circuit, the designer must define the stimulus inputs.

The simulator functions by dividing the overall simulation into very small time steps (typically 10 ps, but this value can be changed by the user). At each time step, the simulator finds all signals that have changed during the preceding time step, and processes those signals as dictated by the circuit's HDL source file. If output signals must change as a result of that processing, then changes to these signals are "scheduled" for a later time step (signal changes are scheduled for a later time step because signals can't change voltage values instantaneously).

Different simulators provide various methods for designers to define input signals over time. Most simulators provide at least three methods, including a graphical interface, a text file based interface, and a command line interface. Any of these methods can be used with the ISE simulator included with the Xilinx ISE/WebPack CAD tools. Graphical interfaces are most useful when defining small numbers of inputs (up to 20 or so) that require relatively few changes over time (e.g., each of the 20 signals might need 20 or 30 changes between "0" and "1"). When dealing with a greater number of input signals (possibly numbering in the hundreds), or a greater number of signal changes over time (possibly in the tens of thousands), a graphical interface is too cumbersome. In this case, a text file based interface is used. The third method using the command line interface is most useful when changing a few signals once or twice to make some quick adjustments to the end of a graphical or text file based simulation.

The ISE simulator is a state-of-the-art tool that has many features to assist engineers in creating stimulus inputs, editing circuit descriptions, and analyzing circuit outputs. Only the most basic features of the ISE graphical interface are presented here—more involved features will be introduced later. A later section of this document (dealing with creating HDL source files) will present creation of text-based stimulus files.

ISE Simulator Graphical User Interface

The ISE tool uses a graphical interface to show the input waveforms you define, and the output signals generated by the simulator. Input waveforms can be created using a "point and click" interface to set logic levels on input signals. Once the input signals are defined, you can run the simulator to compute and display output signals based on your inputs.

Before running a simulation, input waveforms must be defined. To define input waveforms, create a new "Test Bench Waveform" source file by double-clicking "Create New Source" from the processes window (you may need to click on the Sources Tab in the Sources window, and on the Processes tab in the Process window to see the Create New Source process option).

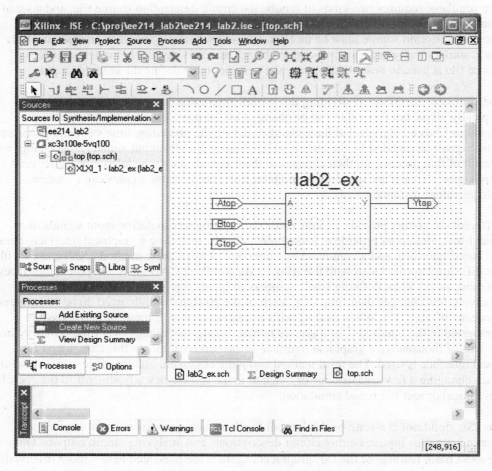

From the New Source dialog box, choose "Test Bench WaveForm", enter a suitable filename, select your current directory, and be sure the "Add to project" box is checked. Click "Next" button, and in the dialog box that opens, choose the name of the schematic file you wish to simulate—in this case, choose the name of the top-level schematic that contains the macro you build earlier. Click Finish to bring up the Initialize Timing box (shown below). The Initialize Timing box sets several values that govern the simulation run, and most are not of interest here. Simply check the "Combinatorial (or internal clock)" radio button and click "Finish" button. This will bring up the Waveform Viewer window.

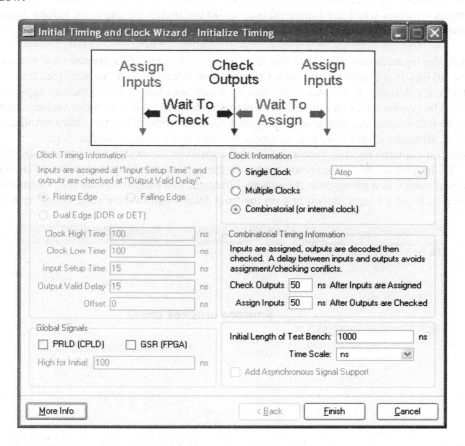

When the waveform editor window opens, all "top level" signals are shown on the left of the window (top-level signals, by definition, are those to which input or output connectors have been attached). Input signal names are shown next to a waveform icon with a blue-green arrow pointing to the right, and output signal names are shown next to a waveform icon with a yellow arrow pointing to the left. A time scale is shown across the top of the window, and the current logic level of each signal (a "0" or "1") is shown in a column between the signal names and waveforms. To the right of the signal names, stretching to the far end of the window, are grid positions underneath a time base—in this area, input signals can be defined, and "expected values" can be defined for output signals.

Values for each input signal can be defined in the waveform viewer simply by clicking on the waveform at a given point in time. Each click will toggle the waveform to the opposite state. Using this interface, you can create input waveforms on the three input signals to drive the inputs with all possible combinations (see figure below). You can also enter the expected values for output signals in the same way. Output logic levels, however, are used only to check the outputs generated by the simulator—they do not drive values on to output signals. Expected values define the expected outputs, and the simulator can issue warnings or errors when the simulated outputs do not match the expected values. Leaving the expected output values at the default "0" level will not cause any errors.

Inspect the figure below, and note that the "Atop" signal defines a regular time window where all inputs are stable. Each such time window is known as a "vector" (or "test vector"). By definition, a vector is defined by a time window during which all inputs are stable. The border between consecutive vectors is defined by one or more signals changing state, so that vectors are non-overlapping and seamless throughout the entire simulation. In general, all vectors have the same duration, but this is not a requirement. A good simulation contains enough vectors so that all signals in the design are driven to both "0" and "1". In general, the term vector applies to the collection of input signals and output expected values in a given time slice (note, however, that output signals may change state in the middle of a vector, depending on the time delays within the circuit being simulated).

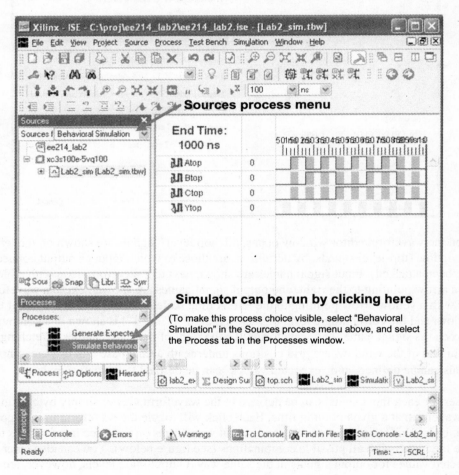

Running a Simulation

After the waveforms are defined, you can run the simulation by double-clicking the "Simulate Behavioral Model" process (see image above). After the simulation completes, two new windows are added to the Project Navigator. The "simulation" window shows simulation outputs together with "error" signals that show when the expected values were different than the simulation outputs. This window allows panning and zooming, so you can focus on the details of any signal transition.

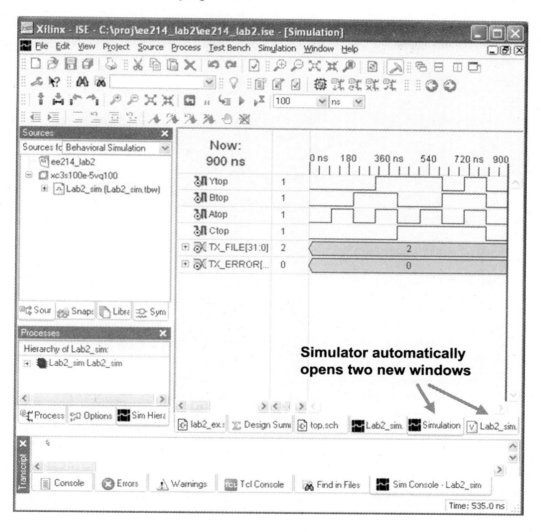

The other window, available by clicking the tab named *filename.tfw*, shows the source file that was automatically generated by the waveform editor. This source file is simply a translation of the waveform graphical display into Verilog, which is the language used by the simulator. For now, you can ignore this window.

Any circuit can be simulated using these basic tools and methods. The simulator contains many more features than have been discussed here. You are encouraged to experiment with the simulator, and to read the extensive documentation available both from within the tool and on the Xilinx website.

The final step in the design process is to download the .bit file for your completed design as discussed in Chapter 2.

Chapter 4: Logic Minimization

1. Overview

The requirements for new logic circuit designs are often expressed in some loose, informal manner. For an informal behavioral description to result in an efficient, well designed circuit that meets the stated requirements, appropriate engineering design methods must be developed. As an example, the following statement might serve as the starting point for a new design: "a warning light, running from a circuit powered by a back-up battery, should be illuminated if the main power is disconnected, or if main power is OK but the reserve power source falls below 48 V, or if the current exceeds 2 amps, or if the current exceeds 1 amp and the reserve falls below 48 V". An initial engineering task is to state this requirement more concisely: WL <= (not P) or (P and not R) or C2 or (C1 and R). This equation removes all ambiguity from the worded description, and it can also be directly implemented as a logic circuit using two 2-input AND gates and one 4-input OR gate. But a simpler 4-input OR circuit that behaves identically under all input conditions could also be constructed (WL <= not R or not R or C1 or C2). Clearly, it would be faster, easier, less costly and less error prone to build the simpler circuit. Another engineering task involves analyzing the requirements of a logic design, with the goal of finding a minimal expression of any logic relationship.

Before beginning this chapter, you should…	After completing this chapter, you should…
• Be familiar with reading and constructing basic logic circuits; • Understand logic equations, and how to implement a logic circuit from a logic equation; • Know how to operate Windows computers and Windows programs.	• Be able to minimize any given logic system; • Understand CAD tool use in basic circuit design; • Be able to implement any given combinational circuit using the Xilinx ISE schematic editor; • Be able to simulate any logic circuit; • Be able to examine the output of a logic simulator to verify whether a given circuit has been designed correctly.

This chapter requires:
• A Windows PC;
• The Xilinx ISE/WebPack software;
• A Digilent circuit board.

2. Background

A digital logic circuit consists of a collection of logic gates, the input signals that drive them, and the output signals they produce. The behavioral requirements of a logic circuit are best expressed through truth tables or logic equations, and any design problem that can be addressed with a logic circuit can be expressed in one of these forms. Both of these formalisms define the behavior of a logic circuit—how inputs are combined to drive outputs—but they do not specify how to build a circuit that meets these requirements. One goal of this module is to define engineering design methods that can produce optimum circuits based on behavioral descriptions.

Only one truth table exists for any particular logic relationship, but many different logic equations and logic circuits can be found to describe and implement the same relationship. Different (but equivalent) logic equations and circuits exist for a given truth table because it is always possible to add unneeded, redundant logic gates to a circuit without changing its logical output. Take for example the logic system introduced in the previous module (reproduced in the figure below). The system's behavior is defined by the truth table in the center of the figure, and it can be implemented by any of the logic equations and related logic circuits shown.

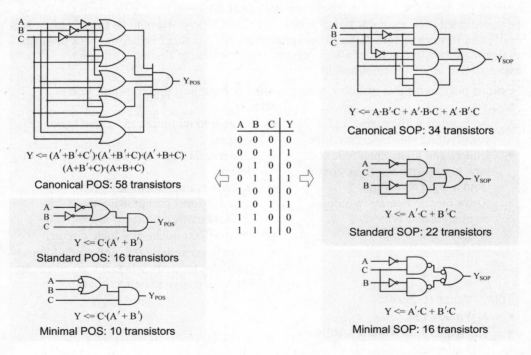

$$Y \leq (A'+B'+C')\cdot(A'+B'+C)\cdot(A'+B+C)\cdot$$
$$(A+B'+C)\cdot(A+B+C)$$

Canonical POS: 58 transistors

$$Y \leq C\cdot(A'+B')$$

Standard POS: 16 transistors

$$Y \leq C\cdot(A'+B')$$

Minimal POS: 10 transistors

A	B	C	Y
0	0	0	0
0	0	1	1
0	1	0	0
0	1	1	1
1	0	0	0
1	0	1	1
1	1	0	0
1	1	1	0

$$Y \leq A\cdot B'\cdot C + A'\cdot B\cdot C + A'\cdot B'\cdot C$$

Canonical SOP: 34 transistors

$$Y \leq A'\cdot C + B'\cdot C$$

Standard SOP: 22 transistors

$$Y \leq A'\cdot C + B'\cdot C$$

Minimal SOP: 16 transistors

All six circuits shown are equivalent, meaning they share the same truth table, but they have different physical structures. Image a black box with three input buttons, two LEDs, and two independent circuits driving the LEDs. Any of the six circuits shown above could drive either LED, and an observer pressing buttons in any combination could not identify which circuit drove which LED. For every possible combination of button presses, the LEDs would be illuminated in exactly the same manner regardless of which circuit was used. If we have a choice of logic circuits for any given logic relationship, it follows we should first define which circuit is the best, and develop a method to ensure we find it.

The circuits in the blue boxes above are said to be "canonical" because they contain all required minterms and maxterms. Canonical circuits typically use resources inefficiently, but they are conceptually simple. Below the canonical circuits are standard POS and SOP circuits—these two circuits behave identically to the canonical circuits, but they use fewer resources. Clearly, it would be less wasteful of resources to build the standard POS or SOP circuits. And further, replacing logic gates in the standard circuits with transistor-minimum gate equivalents (by taking advantage of NAND/NOR logic) results in the minimized POS and SOP circuits shown in the green boxes.

As engineers, one of our primary goals is to implement circuits efficiently. The most efficient circuit can use the fewest number of transistors, or it can operate at the highest speeds, or it can use the least amount of power. Often, these three measures of efficiency cannot all be optimized at the same time, and designers must trade-off circuit size for speed of operation, or speed for power, or power for size, etc. Here, we will define the most efficient circuit as the one that uses the minimum number of transistors, and leave speed and power considerations for later consideration. Because we have chosen the minimum-transistor measure of efficiency, we will look for "minimum" circuits. The best method of determining which of several circuits is the minimum is to count the needed transistors. For now, we will use a simpler method—the minimal circuit will be defined as the one that uses the fewest number of logic gates (or, if two forms use the same number of gates, then the one that uses the fewest number of total inputs to all gates will be considered the simplest). The following examples show circuits with the gate/input number shown below. Inverters are not included in the gate or input count, because often, they are absorbed into the logic gates themselves.

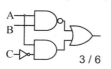 3 / 6

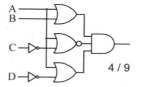 4 / 9

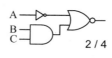 2 / 4

A minimal logic equation for a given logic system can be obtained by eliminating all non-essential or redundant inputs. Any input that can be removed from the equation without changing the input/output relationship is redundant. To find minimal equations, all redundant inputs must be identified and removed. In the truth table above, note the SOP terms generated by rows 1 and 3. The A input is "0" in both rows, and the C input is "1" in both rows, but the B input is "0" in one row and "1" in the other. Thus, for these two rows, the output is a "1" whether B is a "0" or "1" and B is therefore redundant.

The goal in "minimizing" logic systems is to find the simplest form by identifying and removing all redundant inputs. For a logic function of N inputs, there are 2^{2^N} logic functions, and for each of these functions, there exists a minimum SOP form and a minimum POS form. The SOP form may be more minimal than the POS form, or the POS form may be more minimal, or they may be equivalent (i.e., they may both require the same number of logic gates and inputs). In general, it is difficult to identify the minimum form by simply staring at a truth table. Several methods have evolved to assist with the minimization process, including the application of Boolean algebra, the use of logic graphs, and the use of searching algorithms. Although any of these methods can be employed using pen and paper, it is far easier (and more productive) to implement searching algorithms on a computer.

3. Boolean Algebra

Boolean algebra is perhaps the oldest method used to minimize logic equations. It provides a formal algebraic system that can be used to manipulate logic equations in an attempt to find more minimal equations. It is a proper algebraic system, with three set elements {"0", "1", and "A"} (where "A" is any variable that can assume the values "0" or "1"), two binary operations (*and* or *intersection*, *or* or *union*), and one unary operation (*inversion* or *complementation*). Operations between sets are closed under the three operations. The basic laws governing and, or, and inversion operations are easily derived from the logic truth tables for those operations. The associative, commutative, and distributive laws can be directly demonstrated using truth tables. Only the distributive law truth table is shown in the truth table below, with colors used to highlight the columns that show the equivalency of both sides of the distributive law equations. Truth tables to demonstrate the simpler associative and commutative laws are not shown, but they can be easily derived.

AND operations		OR operations		INV operations	
Truth table	Laws	Truth table	Laws	Truth table	Laws
$0 \cdot 0 = 0$	$A \cdot 0 = 0$	$0 + 0 = 0$	$A + 0 = A$	$0' = 1$	$A'' = A$
$1 \cdot 0 = 0$	$A \cdot 1 = A$	$1 + 0 = 1$	$A + 1 = 1$	$1' = 0$	
$0 \cdot 1 = 0$	$A \cdot A = A$	$0 + 1 = 1$	$A + A = A$		
$1 \cdot 1 = 1$	$A \cdot A' = 0$	$1 + 1 = 1$	$A + A' = 1$		

Associative Laws	Commutative Laws	Distributive Laws
$(A \cdot B) \cdot C = A \cdot (B \cdot C) = A \cdot B \cdot C$	$A \cdot B \cdot C = B \cdot A \cdot C = \dots$	$A \cdot (B+C) = (A \cdot B) + (A \cdot C)$
$(A+B)+C = A+(B+C) = A+B+C$	$A+B+C = B+C+A = \dots$	$A+(B \cdot C) = (A+B) \cdot (A+C)$

A	B	C	A+B	B+C	A+C	A·B	B·C	A·C	A·(B+C)	(A·B)+(A·C)	A+(B·C)	(A+B)·(A+C)
						Truth tables to verify distributive laws						
0	0	0	0	0	0	0	0	0	0	0	0	0
0	0	1	0	1	1	0	0	0	0	0	0	0
0	1	0	1	1	0	0	0	0	0	0	0	0
0	1	1	1	1	1	0	1	0	0	0	1	1
1	0	0	1	0	1	0	0	0	0	0	1	1
1	0	1	1	1	1	0	0	1	1	1	1	1
1	1	0	1	1	1	1	0	0	1	1	1	1
1	1	1	1	1	1	1	1	1	1	1	1	1

AND'ing operations take precedence over OR'ing operations. Parenthesis can be used to eliminate any possible confusion. Thus, the following two sets of equations show equivalent logic equations.

$$A \cdot B + C = (A \cdot B) + C \qquad\qquad A + B \cdot C = A + (B \cdot C)$$

DeMorgan's Law provides a formal algebraic statement for the property observed in defining the conjugate gate symbols: the same logic circuit can be interpreted as implementing either an AND or an OR function, depending how the input and output voltage levels are interpreted. DeMorgan's law, which is applicable to logic systems with any number of inputs, states

$$(A \cdot B)' = A' + B' \quad \text{(NAND form)}$$
$$(A+B)' = A' \cdot B' \quad \text{(NOR form)}$$

The laws of Boolean algebra generally hold for XOR functions as well, except that DeMorgan's law takes a different form. Recall from the pervious module that the XOR function output is asserted whenever an odd number of inputs are asserted, and that the XNOR function output is asserted whenever an even number of inputs are asserted. Thus, inverting a single input to an XOR function, or inverting its output, yields the XNOR function. Likewise, inverting a single input to an XNOR function, or inverting its output, yields the XOR function. Inverting an input together with the output, or inverting two inputs, changes an XOR function to XNOR, and vice-versa. These observations lead to a version of DeMorgan's Laws that hold for XOR functions of any number of inputs:

XOR Conjugates

XNOR Conjugates

95

F=A xnor B xnor C $\Leftrightarrow$ F<=$(A \oplus B \oplus C)'$ $\Leftrightarrow$ F<=$A' \oplus B \oplus C$ $\Leftrightarrow$ F <= $(A' \oplus B' \oplus C)'$ etc.
F=A xor B xor C $\Leftrightarrow$ F<=$A \oplus B \oplus C$ $\Leftrightarrow$ F<=$A' \oplus B' \oplus C$ $\Leftrightarrow$ F <= $(A \oplus B' \oplus C)'$ etc.

Note that a single input inversion can be moved to any other signal in a multi-input XOR circuit without changing the logical result. Note also that any signal inversion can be replaced with a non-inverted signal and an XNOR function. These properties will be useful in later work.

The circuits below also serve illustrate the laws of Boolean Algebra.

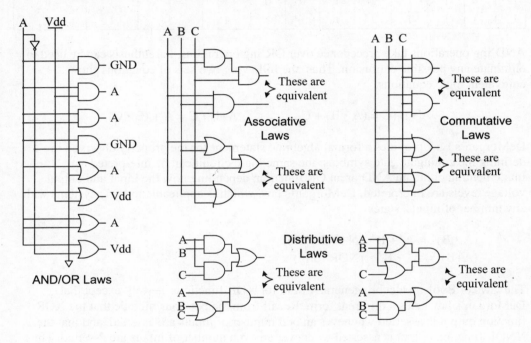

The following examples illustrate the use of Boolean Algebra to find simpler logic equations.

$F = A \cdot B \cdot C + A \cdot B \cdot C' + A' \cdot B \cdot C + A' \cdot B$

$F = A \cdot B \cdot (C + C') + A' \cdot B \cdot (C + 1)$	Factoring
$F = A \cdot B \cdot (1) + A' \cdot B \cdot (1)$	OR law
$F = A \cdot B + A' \cdot B$	AND law
$F = B \cdot (A + A')$	Factoring
$F = B \cdot (1)$	OR law
$F = B$	AND law

$F = (A + B + C) \cdot (A + B + C') \cdot (A + C')$

$F = (A + B + C) \cdot (A + C') \cdot (B + 1)$	Factoring
$F = (A + B + C) \cdot (A + C') \cdot (1)$	OR law
$F = (A + B + C) \cdot (A + C')$	AND law
$F = A + ((B + C) \cdot (C'))$	Factoring
$F = A + (B \cdot C' + C \cdot C')$	Distributive
$F = A + (B \cdot C' + 0)$	AND law
$F = A + (B \cdot C')$	OR law

$F = (A \cdot B \cdot C)' + A' \cdot B \cdot C + (A \cdot C)'$

$F = (A' + B' + C') + A' \cdot B \cdot C + (A' + C')$	DeMorgan's
$F = A' + A' + (A' B C) + B' + C' + C'$	Commutative
$F = A' \cdot (1 + 1 + B \cdot C) + B' + C'$	Factoring
$F = A' \cdot (1) + B' + C'$	OR law
$F = A' + B' + C'$	AND law

$F = (A \oplus B) + (A \oplus B')$

$F = A' B + A B' + A' B' + A B$	XOR expansion
$F = A' B + A' B' + A B + A B'$	Commutative
$F = A' \cdot (B + B') + A \cdot (B + B')$	Factoring
$F = A' \cdot (1) + A \cdot (1)$	OR law
$F = A' + A$	AND law
$F = 1$	

$F = (A \oplus B)' + A \cdot B \cdot C + (A \cdot B)'$

$F = A' B' + A B + A \cdot B \cdot C + (A' + B')$	DeMorgan's
$F = A' B' + A' + B' + A B + A \cdot B \cdot C$	Commutative
$F = A' \cdot (B + 1) + B' + A \cdot B \cdot (1 + C)$	Factoring
$F = A' + B' + A \cdot B$	OR law
$F = A' + (B' + A) \cdot (B' + B)$	Factoring
$F = A' + (B' + A) \cdot (1)$	OR law
$F = A' + B' + A$	AND law
$F = 1$	OR law

$F = (A' + B')' + (A + B)' + (A + B')'$

$F = (A')' \cdot (B')' + (A' \cdot B') + (A' \cdot B)$	DeMorgan's
$F = A \cdot B + A' B' + A' B$	NOT law
$F = A \cdot B + A' \cdot (B' + B)$	Factoring
$F = A \cdot B + A' \cdot (1)$	OR law
$F = A \cdot B + A'$	AND law
$F = (A + A') \cdot (B + A')$	Factoring
$F = (1) \cdot (B + A')$	OR law
$F = A' + B$	AND/Commutative

$F = A + A' \cdot B$	$= A + B$
$F = (A + A') \cdot (A + B)$	Factoring
$F = (1) \cdot (A + B)$	OR law
$F = A + B$	AND law

$F = A \cdot (A' + B)$	$= A \cdot B$
$F = (A \cdot A') + (A \cdot B)$	Distributive
$F = (0) + (A \cdot B)$	AND law
$F = A \cdot B$	OR law

$F = A \cdot B' + B' \cdot C + A' \cdot C$	$= A \cdot B' + A' \cdot C'$
$F = A \cdot B' + B' \cdot C \cdot 1 + A' \cdot C$	AND law
$F = A \cdot B' + B' \cdot C \cdot (A + A') + A' \cdot C$	OR law
$F = A \cdot B' + A \cdot B' \cdot C + A' \cdot B' \cdot C + A' \cdot C$	Distributive
$F = A \cdot B' \cdot (1 + C) + A' \cdot C \cdot (B' + 1)$	Factoring
$F = A \cdot B' \cdot (1) + A \cdot C' \cdot (1)$	OR law
$F = A \cdot B' + A \cdot C'$	AND law

The last two examples on the left (with the blue boxes) shows relationships that are sometimes called the "absorptive" laws, and the example on the right (with the green box) is often called the "consensus" law. The so-called absorptive laws are easily demonstrated with other laws, so it is not necessary or even convenient to use these relationships as laws —particularly because different forms of equations can make it difficult to identify when the law might apply. The consensus law is also easily derived, if the "trick" of AND'ing a "1" into the equation, and then expanding that AND into an OR relationship is used (this trick is perfectly acceptable, if not entirely obvious).

4. Logic Graphs

Truth tables are not very useful for minimizing logic systems, and Boolean algebra has limited utility. Logic graphs offer the easiest and most useful pen-and-paper method of minimizing a logic system. A logic graph and truth table contain identical information, but patterns that indicate redundant inputs can be readily identified in a logic graph. A logic graph is a two (or even three) dimensional construct that contains exactly the same information that a truth table does, but arranged in an array structure so that all logic domains are contiguous, and logic relationships are therefore easy to identify. Information in a truth table can easily be recast into a logic graph. The figure below shows how a three-input truth table is mapped to an 8-cell logic graph; the numbers in the logic graph cells are the numbers in the truth table rows.

A 1-to-1 correspondence exists between the cells in the logic graph and the rows in a truth table, and that the cell numbers have been arranged so that each logic variable domain is represented by a group of four connected cells (the A domain is a row of four cells, and the B and C domains are squares of four cells). This particular arrangement of cells in the logic graph isn't the only one possible, but it has the useful property of having each domain overlap the others in exactly two cells. As can be seen in the figure, the logic domains are contiguous in the logic graph, but they are not contiguous in the truth table. It is the contiguous logic domains in the logic graphs that make them so useful.

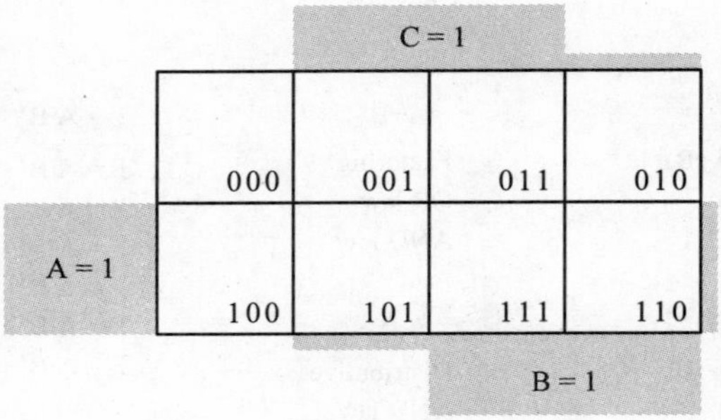

Logic graphs are typically shown with variable names near the graph borders, and 1's and 0's near cell rows and columns to indicate the value of the variables for the rows and columns. The logic graph below shows a typical appearance. Note that the variable values on the logic graph edges can be read from left to right to find the truth table row that corresponds to a given cell. For example, the A = 1, B = 0, C= 1 row in the truth table below is shaded, and that row corresponds to the shaded cell in the logic graph.

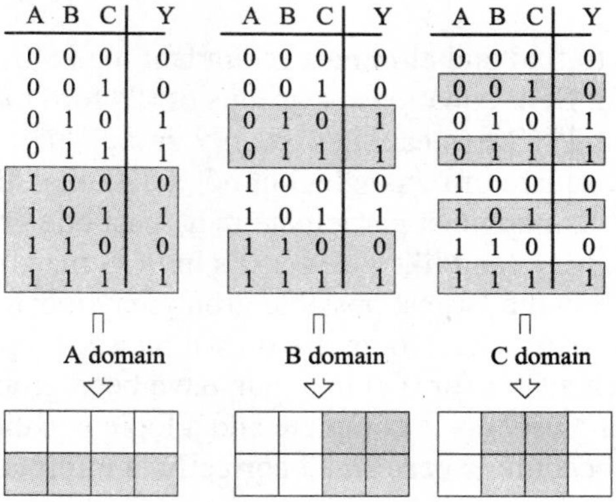

A	B	C	Y		A	B	C	Y		A	B	C	Y
0	0	0	0		0	0	0	0		0	0	0	0
0	0	1	0		0	0	1	0		0	0	1	0
0	1	0	1		0	1	0	1		0	1	0	1
0	1	1	1		0	1	1	1		0	1	1	1
1	0	0	0		1	0	0	0		1	0	0	0
1	0	1	1		1	0	1	1		1	0	1	1
1	1	0	0		1	1	0	0		1	1	0	0
1	1	1	1		1	1	1	1		1	1	1	1

A domain   B domain   C domain

The information in the output column of the truth table below has been transferred row-for-cell into the cells of the logic graph, and so the truth table and logic graph contain identical information. In the logic graph, 1's that appear adjacent to one another (either vertically or horizontally) are said to be "logically adjacent", and these adjacencies represent opportunities to find and eliminate redundant inputs. Logic graphs used in this manner are called Karnaugh Maps (or just K-Maps) after their inventor.

A	B	C	Y
0	0	0	0
0	0	1	1
0	1	0	0
0	1	1	1
1	0	0	0
1	0	1	1
1	1	0	0
1	1	1	0

A \ BC	00	01	11	10
0	0	1	1	0
1	0	1	0	0

The figure below shows a four-input truth table mapped to a 16-cell K-map.

A	B	C	D	Y
0	0	0	0	0
0	0	0	1	1
0	0	1	0	0
0	0	1	1	1
0	1	0	0	0
0	1	0	1	1
0	1	1	0	0
0	1	1	1	0
1	0	0	0	1
1	0	0	1	1
1	0	1	0	1
1	0	1	1	1
1	1	0	0	0
1	1	0	1	1
1	1	1	0	0
1	1	1	1	0

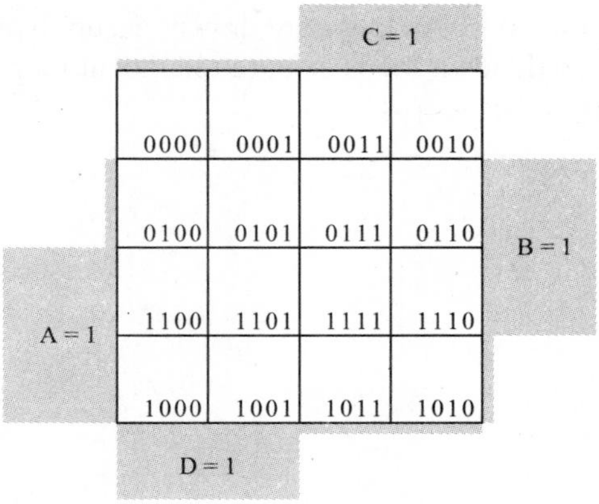

C = 1

	0000	0001	0011	0010
	0100	0101	0111	0110
A = 1	1100	1101	1111	1110
	1000	1001	1011	1010

B = 1

D = 1

AB \ CD	00	01	11	10
00	0	1	1	0
01	0	1	0	0
11	0	1	0	0
10	1	1	1	1

99

The key to using K-maps to find and eliminate redundant inputs from a logic system is to identify "groups" of 1's for SOP equations or groups of 0's for POS equations. A valid group must be a "power of 2" size (meaning that only groups of 1, 2, 4, 8, or 16 are allowed), and it must be a square or rectangle, but not a diagonal, dogleg, or other irregular shape. Each "1" in a SOP K-map must participate in at least one group, and each "1" must be in the largest possible group (and likewise for 0's in POS maps). The requirement that all 1's (or 0's) are grouped in the largest possible group may mean that some 1's (or 0's) are part of several groups. In practice, loops are drawn on a K-map to encircle the 1's (or 0's) in a given group. Once all 1's (or 0's) in a map have been grouped in the largest possible loops, the grouping process is complete and a logic equation can be read directly from the K-map. If the procedure is performed correctly, a minimal logic equation is guaranteed.

SOP logic equations are read from a K-map by writing product terms defined by each loop, and then OR'ing the product terms together. Likewise, POS logic equations are read from a K-map by writing sum terms defined by each loop, and then AND'ing all the sum terms together. A loop term is defined by the logic variables on the periphery of the K-map. SOP loop terms use minterm codes (i.e., the "0" domain of a variable results in that variable being complemented in the product term for the loop), and POS loop terms use maxterm codes (i.e., the "1" domain of an input variable results in that variable being complemented in the sum term for the loop). If a loop spans across both the "1" and "0" domain of a given logic variable, then that variable is redundant and it does not appear in the loop term. Restated, a logic variable is included in a loop term only if the loop is contained entirely in the "1" or "0" domain of that variable. The edges of maps are continuous with the opposite edges, so loops can span from one edge to the other without grouping 1's or 0's in the middle (the examples below illustrate this process).

K-maps can be used for finding minimal logic expressions for systems of 2, 3, 4, 5, or 6 input variables (beyond 6 variables and the technique becomes unwieldy). For systems of 2, 3, or 4 variables, the technique is straightforward, and it is illustrated in several examples below. In general, the looping process should be started with 1's (or 0's) that can only be grouped in one possible loop. As loops are drawn, ensure that all 1's (or 0's) are in at least one loop, and that no redundant loops exist (a redundant loop contains 1's or 0's that are *all* already grouped in other loops).

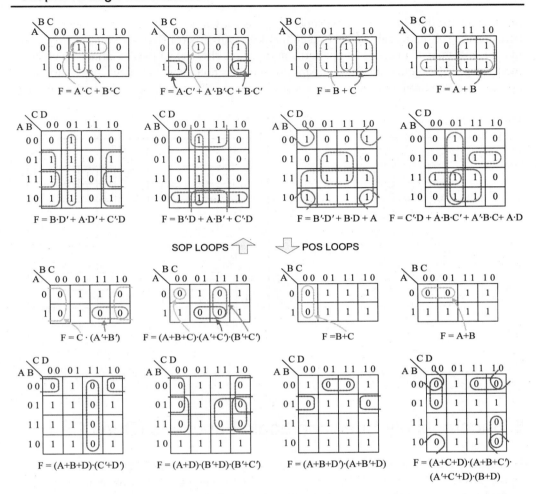

Minterm SOP equations and maxterm POS equations can be readily transferred into K-maps by simply placing 1's (for SOP equations) and 0's (POS) in the cells listed in the equation. For SOP equations, any cell not listed as receiving a "1" gets a "0", and vice-versa for POS equations. The figures below illustrate the process.

$F = \Sigma m(1, 3, 5, 6)$ ⇒

A \ B C	00	01	11	10
0	0	1	1	0
1	0	1	0	1

$F = \Pi m(0, 3, 7)$ ⇒

A \ B C	00	01	11	10
0	0	1	0	1
1	1	1	0	1

For systems of 5 or 6 variables, two different methods can be used. One method uses 4-variable K-maps nested in 1 or 2 variable "super maps", and the other method uses "map entered variables". The super-map technique for finding minimum equations for 5 or 6 variables closely follows the technique used for 2, 3, or 4 variables, but 4-variable maps

101

must be nested into 1 or 2-variable super-maps as shown below. Logic adjacencies between the sub-maps can be discovered by identifying 1's (or 0's) in like-numbered cells in adjacent super-map cells. The patterns in the maps show examples of adjacent cells in the K-maps. SOP equations for the maps are shown—note that the "super map" variables do not appear in product terms when 1's are located in like-numbered cells in the sub maps.

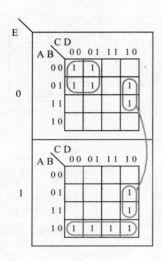

$$F = A'{\cdot}C'{\cdot}E' + B{\cdot}C{\cdot}D' + A{\cdot}B'{\cdot}E$$

$$F = A'{\cdot}C'{\cdot}E' + B{\cdot}C{\cdot}D' + A{\cdot}B'{\cdot}E{\cdot}F + A{\cdot}B{\cdot}C'{\cdot}E{\cdot}F'$$

5. Incompletely Specified Logic Functions (Don't Cares)

Situations can arise where a circuit has N input signals, but not all 2^N combinations of inputs are possible. Or, if all 2^N combinations of inputs are possible, some combinations might be irrelevant. For example, consider a television remote control unit that can switch between control of a television, VCR, or DVD. Some remotes might have operational modes where buttons like "fast forward" are physically switched out of the circuit; other remotes may use modes where such buttons are left in the circuit, but their functions are irrelevant. In either case, some combinations of input signals are completely inconsequential to the proper operation of the circuit. It is possible to take advantage of these situations to further minimize logic circuits.

Input combinations that cannot possibly effect the proper operation of a logic system can be allowed to drive circuit outputs high or low—literally, the designer doesn't care what the circuit response is to these impossible or irrelevant inputs. This information is encoded by using a special "don't care" symbol in truth tables and K-maps to indicate that the signal can be a "1" or a "0" without effecting circuit operation. Some sources use an "X" to indicate a don't care, but this can be confused with a signal named "X". It is perhaps a better practice to use a symbol that is not normally associated with signal names—here, we choose the " φ " symbol.

A	B	C	F	G
0	0	0	0	1
0	0	1	1	φ
0	1	0	φ	1
0	1	1	0	φ
1	0	0	1	1
1	0	1	0	0
1	1	0	0	0
1	1	1	φ	0

BC \ A

A \ BC	00	01	11	10
0	0	1	1	φ
1	0	1	φ	0

F

A \ BC	00	01	11	10
0	1	φ	φ	1
1	1	0	0	0

G

The truth table on the right shows two output functions (F and G) for the same three inputs. Both outputs have two rows where the output is a don't care. This same information is also shown in the associated K-maps. In the "F" K-map, the designers "don't care" if the output is a "1" or a "0" for minterms 2 and 7, and so cells 2 and 7 in the K-map can be looped as either a "1" or a "0". Clearly, looping cell 7 as a "1" and cell 2 as a "0" results in a more minimal logic circuit. In this case, both an SOP and POS looping would result in identical circuits.

In the "G" K-map, the don't cares in cells 1 and 3 can be looped as either a "1" or a "0". In an SOP looping, both don't cares would be looped as 1's, giving a logic function of "G = $A' + B' \cdot C'$". In a POS looping, however, cells 1 and 3 would be looped as 0's, giving the logic function "G = $C' \cdot (A' + B')$". A little Boolean algebra reveals these two equations are not algebraically equal. Often, the SOP and POS forms of equations looped from K-maps that contain don't cares are not algebraically equal (although they would perform identically in the circuit). The following examples illustrate the use of don't cares in K-maps.

103

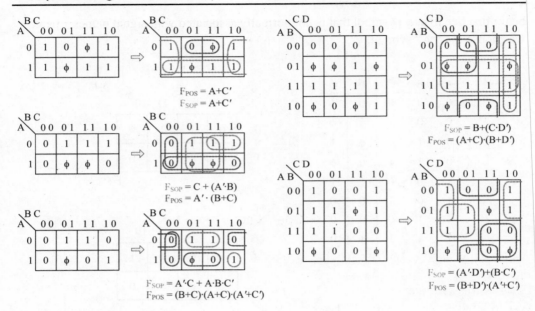

$F_{POS} = A + C'$
$F_{SOP} = A + C'$

$F_{SOP} = C + (A' \cdot B)$
$F_{POS} = A' \cdot (B + C)$

$F_{SOP} = A' \cdot C + A \cdot B \cdot C'$
$F_{POS} = (B + C) \cdot (A + C) \cdot (A' + C')$

$F_{SOP} = B + (C \cdot D')$
$F_{POS} = (A + C) \cdot (B + D')$

$F_{SOP} = (A' \cdot D') + (B \cdot C')$
$F_{POS} = (B + D') \cdot (A' + C')$

6. Entered Variables

Truth tables provide the best mechanism for completely specifying the behavior of a given combinational logic circuit, and K-maps provide the best mechanism for visualizing and minimizing the input-output relationships of digital logic circuits. So far, we have shown input variables across the top left of a truth table and around the periphery of K-maps. This allows every state of an output signal to be defined as a function of the input patterns of 0's and 1's on a given row in a truth table, or as the binary coding for a given K-map cell. Without any loss of information, truth tables and K-maps can be translated into a more compact form by moving input variables from the top-left of a truth table to the output column, or from outside the K-map to inside the cells of a K-map. Although it will not be clear until later modules, the use of entered variables and compressed truth tables and K-maps often makes a multi-variable system much easier to visualize and minimize.

The translation mechanics are illustrated in the figures below, where a 16-row truth table is compressed into both 8-row and 4-row truth tables. In the 8-row truth table, the variable D is no longer used to identify an input column. Instead, it appears in the output column, where it encodes the relationship between two rows of output logic values and the D input. In the 4-row truth table, variables C and D are no longer used to identify an input column, but rather in the output column where they encode the relationship between four rows of the output logic values and the C and D inputs.

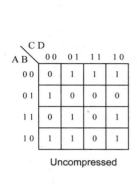

Uncompressed

A	B	C	D	Y	
0	0	0	0	0	D
0	0	0	1	1	
0	0	1	0	1	1
0	0	1	1	1	

} C+D

A	B	C	D	Y	
0	1	0	0	1	D'
0	1	0	1	0	
0	1	1	0	0	0
0	1	1	1	0	

} (C+D)'

A	B	C	D	Y	
1	0	0	0	1	1
1	0	0	1	1	
1	0	1	0	1	D'
1	0	1	1	0	

} (C·D)'

A	B	C	D	Y	
1	1	0	0	0	D
1	1	0	1	1	
1	1	1	0	1	D'
1	1	1	1	0	

} C⊕D

A	B	C	Y
0	0	0	D
0	0	0	1
0	0	1	D'
0	0	1	0
0	1	0	1
0	1	0	D'
0	1	1	D
0	1	1	D'

A\BC	00	01	11	10
0	D	1	0	D
1	1	D	D	D

Compressed one time

A	B	Y
0	0	C+D
0	1	(C+D)'
1	0	(C·D)'
1	1	C⊕D

A\B	0	1
0	C+D	(C+D)'
1	(C·D)'	C⊕D

Compressed two times

The 4-cell K-map is reproduced to the right, this time showing the implied sub-maps that illustrate the relationship between C and D for each of the four unique values of the A and B variables. For any entered variable K-map, thinking of (or actually sketching) the sub-maps can help identify the correct encoding for the entered variables. Note that truth table row numbers can be mapped to cells in the sub-maps by reading the K-map index codes, starting with the super-map code, and appending the sub-map code. For example, the shaded box in the sub-map is in box number 1110.

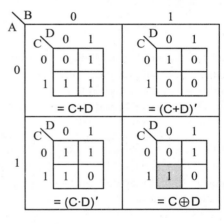

This same map compression is illustrated below, showing the mapping from non-compressed K-maps directly to compressed K-maps. The colors show how cells in the uncompressed map are translated to the cells in the compressed map. Note that two cells in the 16-cell map are compressed into a single cell in the 8-cell map, and that four cells in the 16-cell map are compressed into a single cell in the 4-cell map.

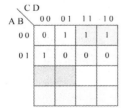

A\BC	00	01	11	10
0	D	1	0	D
1	1	D	D	D

AB\CD	00	01	11	10
00	0	1	1	1
01	1	0	0	0

A\B	0	1
0	C+D	(C+D)'
1	C·D'	C D

Minterm SOP equations and maxterm POS equations can also be translated directly into entered variable K-maps as shown in the illustration below (the smaller numbers at the bottom of K-map cells show the minterm or maxterm numbers assigned to that cell). The minimum number of input variables is assumed when encoding minterms or maxterms into the K-maps. For example, if the largest minterm present is 14, four input variables are assumed.

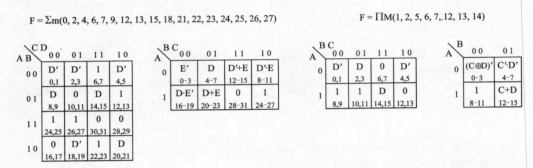

$$F = \Sigma m(0, 2, 4, 6, 7, 9, 12, 13, 15, 18, 21, 22, 23, 24, 25, 26, 27)$$

$$F = \Pi M(1, 2, 5, 6, 7, 12, 13, 14)$$

Looping entered variable K-maps follows the same general principles as looping "1-0" maps—optimal groupings of 1's and entered variables (EVs) are sought for SOP circuits, and optimal groupings of 0's and EVs are sought for POS circuits. The rules are similar: all EVs and all 1's (or 0's) must be grouped in the largest possible "power of 2" sized rectangular or square grouping, and the process is complete when all EV's and all 1's (or 0's) are included in an optimal loop. The differences are that similar EVs can be included in loops by themselves or with 1's (or 0's), and care must be taken when looping cells with 1's (or 0's), because a "1" (or "0") indicates that all possible combinations of EV's are present in that map cell, and loops that include 1's (or 0's) together with EV's often include only a subset of the possible combinations of the EV's (this is illustrated in the figures below). Looping an EV K-map is complete when all minterms or maxterms are contained in an adequate group. Perhaps the most challenging aspect is to ensure that all possible combinations of EV's have been accounted for in cells that contain 1's (or 0's).

To help understand looping in EV K-maps, it may be helpful to think of the sub-maps implied by every K-map cell. As shown in the figures below, the variables in K-map cells can arise from looping the "1-0" information entered into cells in the implied sub-maps. A looping of information in adjacent cells in the EV K-map can include 1's (or 0's) in the sub-maps that appear in the same positions in the sub-maps.

When reading the loop equations, the SOP product terms (or POS sum terms) for each loop must include the variables that define the loop domain and the EVs contained within the loop. For example, in the first example below, the first SOP term $A' \cdot B' \cdot D$ includes the loop domain $A' \cdot B'$ and the entered variable D.

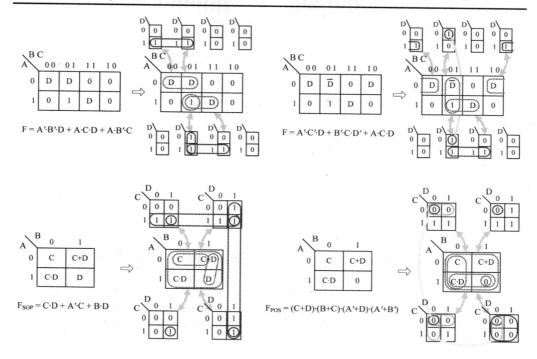

F = A'·B'·D + A·C·D + A·B'·C

F = A'·C'·D + B'·C·D' + A·C·D

F_{SOP} = C·D + A'·C + B·D

F_{POS} = (C+D)·(B+C)·(A'+D)·(A'+B')

Cells in entered variable maps might contain a single entered variable or a logic expression of two or more variables. When looping cells that contain logic expressions, it helps to recognize the differences in SOP and POS looping mechanics. As compared to a single EV in a K-map cell, a product term in a cell represents a smaller SOP domain, because the more AND'ed variables in a product term, the smaller the defined logic domain. A sum term in a cell represents a larger SOP domain, because the more OR'ed variables in a sum term, the larger the defined logic domain. When looping SOP equations from an EV map, cells containing product terms have fewer 1's in their sub-maps than cells that contain single EV's, and cells with sum terms contain more 1's. Similarly, when looping POS equations from an EV map, cells containing sum terms have fewer 0's in their sub-maps than cells that contain single EV's, and cells with product terms contain more 0's.

Don't cares in entered variable K-maps serve the same purpose as they did in "1-0" maps; they indicate input conditions that cannot occur or that are irrelevant, and they can be included in groupings of 1's, 0's, or entered variables as needed to minimize logic. As shown in the examples below, a given don't care can be taken as a "1", "0", or entered variable as needed for any particular loop.

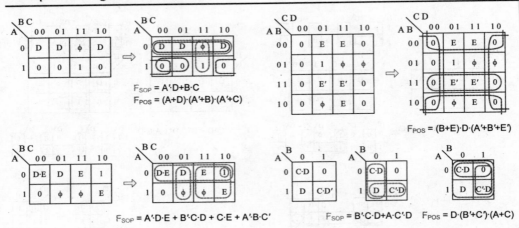

$F_{SOP} = A' \cdot D + B \cdot C$
$F_{POS} = (A+D) \cdot (A'+B) \cdot (A'+C)$

$F_{POS} = (B+E) \cdot D \cdot (A'+B'+E')$

$F_{SOP} = A' \cdot D \cdot E + B' \cdot C \cdot D + C \cdot E + A' \cdot B \cdot C'$

$F_{SOP} = B' \cdot C \cdot D + A \cdot C' \cdot D$ $F_{POS} = D \cdot (B'+C') \cdot (A+C)$

7. Computer-based Logic Minimization Algorithms

Several logic minimization algorithms have been developed over the years, and many of them have been incorporated into computer-based logic minimization programs. Some of these programs, such as those based on the Quine-McCluskey algorithm, find a true minimum by exhaustively checking all possibilities. Programs based on these exhaustive search algorithms can require long execution times, especially when dealing with large numbers of inputs and outputs. Other programs, such as the popular Espresso program developed at UC Berkeley, use heuristic (or rule-based) methods instead of exhaustive searches. Although these programs run much faster (especially on moderate to large systems), they terminate upon finding a "very good" solution that may not always be minimal. In many real-world engineering situations, finding a greatly minimized solution quickly is often the best approach.

Espresso is by far the most widely used minimization algorithm, followed by Quine-McCluskey. These two algorithms will be briefly introduced, but not explained. Many good references exist in various texts and on the web that explain exactly how the algorithms function—you are encouraged to seek out and read these references to further your understanding of logic minimization techniques.

The Quine-McCluskey logic minimization algorithm was developed in the mid-1950's, and it was the first computer-based algorithm that could find truly minimal logic expressions. The algorithm finds all possible groupings of 1's through an exhaustive search, and then from that complete collection finds a minimal set that covers all minterms in the on-set (the on-set is the set of all minterms for which the function output is asserted). Because this method searches for all possible solutions, and then selects the best, it can take a fair amount of computing time, In fact, even on modern computers, this algorithm can execute for minutes to hours on moderately sized logic systems. Many free-ware programs exist that use the Q-M algorithm to minimize a single equation or multiple equations simultaneously.

Espresso was first developed in the 1960's, and it has become the most commonly used logic minimization program used in industry. Espresso is strictly "rule-based", meaning that it does not search for a guaranteed minimum solution (although in many cases, the true minimum is found). An espresso input file must be created before espresso can be run. The input file is essentially a truth table that lists all the minterms in the non-minimized function. Espresso returns an output file that shows all the terms required in the output expression. Espresso can minimize a single logic function of several variables, or many logic functions of several variables. Espresso makes several simplifying assumptions about a logic system, and it therefore runs very quickly, even for large systems.

Digimin is a windows wrapper that allows both Boozer and Espresso to be run in a Windows environment. Digimin also provides an easy to use truth-table entry mechanism and provides output in the form of SOP and POS equations. Digimin, available from the class website, is easy and intuitive to use—simply run it, add functions (by selecting Action → add function), and then add variables to the functions (by selecting Action → add variables). When all functions and variables have been added, simply choose the MIN function and the Espresso or Boozer algorithm.

Since the1990's, Hardware Definition Languages (HDLs) and their associated design tools and methods have been replacing all other forms of digital circuit design. Today, the use of HDLs in virtually all aspects of digital circuit design is considered standard practice. We will introduce the use HDLs in a later module, and as we will see, any circuit defined in an HDL environment is automatically minimized before it is implemented. This feature allows a designer to focus strictly on a circuit's behavior, without getting slowed down in the details of finding efficient circuits. Although it is important to understand the structure and function of digital circuits, experience has shown that engineers can be far more productive by specifying only a circuit's behavior, and relying on computer-based tools to find efficient circuit structures that can implement those behaviors.

Exercise 4: Logic Minimization

Estimated Work Hours

| 1 | 2 | 3 | 4 | 5 | 6 | 7 | 8 | 9 | 10 |

| 1 | 2 | 3 | 4 | 5 | 6 | 7 | 8 | 9 | 10 |

Overall Weight

GRADER

#	Points	Score
1	6	
2	12	
3	14	
4	12	
5	19	
6	9	
7	14	

Total Score

Weeks late

Adjusted Score

Adjusted Score:
Deduct 20% from score for each week late

Problem 1.   Show the total transistor count and gate/input number for the circuits below.

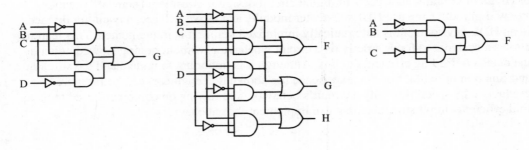

Problem 2.   Use Boolean algebra to minimize the logic equations below.

$$F = (A \oplus B' \cdot C) + A \cdot (B+C')$$
$$F = A \cdot B' \cdot C + A' \cdot B' \cdot C \cdot D + (A \cdot B \cdot D)' + A' \cdot B \cdot C \cdot D$$

$$F = ((A \oplus B') \cdot C) + A \cdot B' \cdot C + A \cdot B \cdot C + (A'+C')' \quad F = ((A \cdot (A \cdot B))')' \cdot (B \cdot (A \cdot B))')')'$$

$$F = (A \cdot B)' \oplus (B+C)'$$

$$F = A' \cdot (B \cdot C + (A \cdot (((B \cdot C \cdot D)' + A \cdot B \cdot D) \oplus ((A' \cdot B \cdot C)' + A \cdot B' \cdot C)))'$$

Hint: Think before you work!

Problem 3. Find minimal equations for the systems shown.

A\B	0	1
0	0	1
1	1	1

$F_{SOP}=$
$F_{POS}=$

A\B	0	1
0	1	1
1	1	0

$F_{SOP}=$
$F_{POS}=$

A\B	0	1
0	0	1
1	1	0

$F_{SOP}=$
$F_{POS}=$

A\B	0	1
0	1	0
1	0	1

$F_{SOP}=$
$F_{POS}=$

A\BC	00	01	11	10
0	1	0	0	1
1	1	1	0	1

$F_{SOP}=$
$F_{POS}=$

A\BC	00	01	11	10
0	0	1	1	1
1	0	1	0	1

$F_{SOP}=$
$F_{POS}=$

A\BC	00	01	11	10
0	1	0	1	0
1	1	1	1	1

$F_{SOP}=$
$F_{POS}=$

AB\CD	00	01	11	10
00	1	0	0	1
01	1	1	1	1
11	1	1	0	0
10	1	0	0	1

$F_{SOP}=$
$F_{POS}=$

AB\CD	00	01	11	10
00	0	1	1	1
01	0	1	1	1
11	0	1	1	0
10	0	1	0	0

$F_{SOP}=$
$F_{POS}=$

AB\CD	00	01	11	10
00	0	1	1	0
01	1	0	1	1
11	1	0	1	1
10	0	1	1	0

$F_{SOP}=$
$F_{POS}=$

E, F map

F = 0, E = 0

AB\CD	00	01	11	10
00	0	0	1	1
01	0	0	1	1
11	0	1	1	1
10	0	1	1	1

F = 1, E = 0

AB\CD	00	01	11	10
00	1	1	0	0
01	1	1	0	0
11	0	1	1	1
10	0	1	1	1

F = 0, E = 1

AB\CD	00	01	11	10
00	0	0	1	1
01	1	0	1	1
11	1	1	0	1
10	0	1	0	1

F = 1, E = 1

AB\CD	00	01	11	10
00	1	1	0	1
01	1	1	0	0
11	1	1	0	0
10	0	1	1	1

$F_{SOP}=$
$F_{POS}=$

E = 0

AB\CD	00	01	11	10
00	1	1	0	0
01	1	1	0	1
11	1	1	1	1
10	0	0	0	0

E = 1

AB\CD	00	01	11	10
00	1	1	0	1
01	0	0	0	1
11	1	1	1	1
10	0	1	1	1

$F_{SOP}=$
$F_{POS}=$

$$F = \sum m(0, 1, 4, 5)$$

$$G = \prod M(0, 1, 3, 4, 5, 7, 13, 15)$$

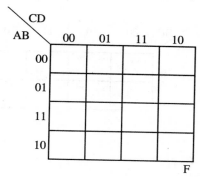

$F_{SOP} =$

$F_{POS} =$

$F_{SOP} =$

$F_{POS} =$

Problem 4. Find minimal equations for the systems shown below. Circle the equation of the simplest form (SOP or POS), and circle both if they are equal.

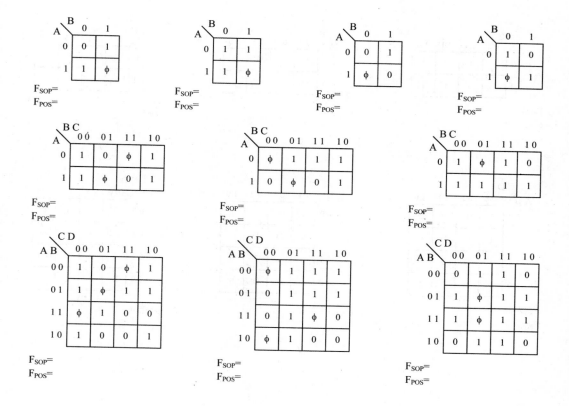

$F_{SOP} =$
$F_{POS} =$

$F_{SOP} =$
$F_{POS} =$

$F_{SOP} =$
$F_{POS} =$

$F_{SOP} =$
$F_{POS} =$

$F_{SOP} =$
$F_{POS} =$

$F_{SOP} =$
$F_{POS} =$

$F_{SOP} =$
$F_{POS} =$

$F_{SOP} =$
$F_{POS} =$

$F_{SOP} =$
$F_{POS} =$

$$F = \sum m(0, 1, 4, 5) + \Phi(2, 7) \qquad G = \prod M(0, 1, 4, 5, 7, 13, 15) + \Phi(2, 3, 11, 12, 14)$$

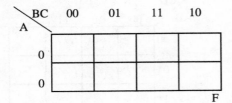

A \ BC	00	01	11	10
0				
0				

F

$F_{SOP} =$

$F_{POS} =$

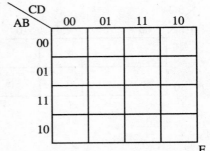

AB \ CD	00	01	11	10
00				
01				
11				
10				

F

$F_{SOP} =$

$F_{POS} =$

Problem 5. Find minimal SOP and POS equations for the systems shown.

A \ BC	00	01	11	10
0	1	1	D	1
1	1	D'	0	1

$F_{SOP}=$
$F_{POS}=$

A \ BC	00	01	11	10
0	D	1	D'	0
1	D	1	D'	0

$F_{POS}=$

A \ BC	00	01	11	10
0	D	D+E	E	0
1	D'·E	E	D·E	1

$F_{SOP}=$

AB \ CD	00	01	11	10
00	1	1	D	D
01	1	D	D	D
11	1	D	D	0
10	1	1	0	0

$F_{SOP}=$
$F_{POS}=$

AB \ CD	00	01	11	10
00	1	1	1	1
01	0	D	D	D
11	0	1	1	0
10	0	D'	D'	0

$F_{POS}=$

AB \ CD	00	01	11	10
00	D'	1	1	E
01	D'·E	D'	1	D·E
11	E	0	D	D+E
10	D'	1	1	E

$F_{SOP}=$

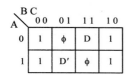

A \ BC	00	01	11	10
0	1	φ	D	1
1	1	D′	φ	1

$F_{SOP}=$
$F_{POS}=$

A \ BC	00	01	11	10
0	D	1	D′	0
1	φ	φ	D′	φ

$F_{POS}=$

A \ BC	00	01	11	10
0	D	D+E	E	φ
1	D′E	E	φ	1

$F_{SOP}=$

AB \ CD	00	01	11	10
00	φ	1	D′	D
01	1	D	φ	D
11	1	φ	D′	0
10	1	φ	1	φ

$F_{SOP}=$
$F_{POS}=$

AB \ CD	00	01	11	10
00	1	φ	φ	1
01	0	D	D	D
11	φ	1	1	0
10	0	D′	D′	0

$F_{POS}=$

AB \ CD	00	01	11	10
00	D′	1	φ	E
01	D′E	D′	1	D·E
11	φ	0	φ	1
10	D′	1	1	E

$F_{SOP}=$

$F=\sum m(0,2,7,9,10,11,14) + \Phi(4,5)$

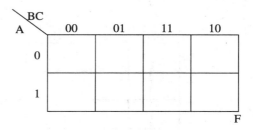

$F_{SOP} =$

$F_{POS} =$

$F= \sum m(0, 2, 3, 7, 8, 15) + \Phi(4, 5, 12, 13)$ (Map and loop this equation in all three maps below)

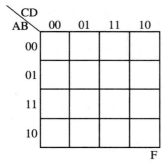

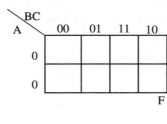

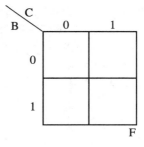

$F_{SOP} =$

$F_{POS} =$

$Y = \sum m\,(0,2,4,8,9,10,14,22,31) + \Phi\,(6,7,12,13,24,25)$

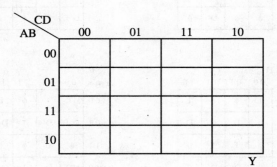

$F_{SOP} =$

$F_{POS} =$

$Y = \Pi M\,(0,2,4,8,9,10,14,22,31) + \Phi\,(6,7,12,13,24,25)$

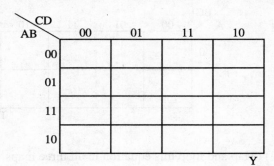

$F_{SOP} =$

$F_{POS} =$

Problem 6. Find global minimum circuits for the following three logic signal outputs that are all functions of the same three inputs. Show all work.

$$F1 = \sum m\,(0, 3, 4) \qquad F2 = \sum m\,(1, 6, 7) \qquad F3 = \sum m\,(0, 1, 3, 4)$$

Problem 7.   The following problems are not unlike those found in industry. They are too large to easily complete using pencil-and-paper methods, but they are relatively easy with computer-based tools. Use DigiMin to minimize the following systems. Select the "create VHDL" option when minimizing, and print and submit the VHDL file.

(1) Six judges are scoring a particular event, and they need a device to indicate particular judgments. Each judge can enter "good" or "bad" with a single switch. Design a circuit that can indicate three separate conditions: A strong majority (i.e., 5 or 6 "good" votes); a simple majority (4 or more "good" votes), and a tie (exactly 3 "good" votes).

(2) A thermometer produces a continuously varying voltage signal between 0V and 5V, where 0V represents 0 degrees, and 5V represents 100 degrees. The signal is fed to an analog-to-digital converter (ADC). The ADC produces an 8-bit binary number that is directly proportional to the temperature—"00000000" represents 0 degrees, each increasing binary number from "00000000" represents a temperature increase of 100/256 degrees, and "11111111" represents 100 degrees. Design a circuit that outputs a logic high signal whenever the temperature is between 50 and 60 degrees.

Lab Project 4: Logic Minimization

STUDENT

I am submitting my own work, and I understand penalties will be assessed if I submit work for credit
that is not my own.

Print Name

ID Number

Sign Name

Date

Estimated Work Hours

1	2	3	4	5	6	7	8	9	10

1	2	3	4	5	6	7	8	9	10

Overall Weight

Point Scale

4: Exemplary
3: Complete
2: Incomplete
1: Minor effort
0: Not submitted

20% will be deducted from scores for each week late
Score = Points awarded (Pts) × Weight (Wt)

LAB ASSISTANT

#	Demonstration	Wt	Pts	Late	Score	Lab Asst Signature	Date	Total In-Lab Score
1	Inspect source & sim files	2						
1	Circuit demo	2						
2	Circuit demo	3						
E1	Circuit demo	3						
4	Circuit demo	4						

GRADER

#	Attachments	Wt	Pts	Score
1	Schematic and simulation	2		
2	Schematic and simulation	2		
E1	Schematic and simulation	3		
3	Schematic and simulation	3		
4	Worksheet	4		

Weeks late	Total Grading Score		Total Score
		Total score is In-lab score plus grading score	

Introduction

This lab project presents several worded problems that serve as behavioral specifications for digital circuits. Your job is to design, simulate, and download those circuits to the Basys board.

Problem 1.   Amy, Baker, Cathy, and David, the bean buyers for the "Overhead Coffee Company", have designed a more complex voting system to decide when to buy new beans. Design and implement a logic circuit that they can use to indicate whether they should buy new beans. Use slide switches for vote entry (either "buy" or "not buy"), and an LED to indicate when beans should be purchased. A "buy" order is placed if:

	Amy, Cathy, and David vote NO and Baker votes YES,
or	Amy and David vote NO and the rest vote YES,
or	Baker and David vote YES and the rest vote NO,
or	Amy votes NO and the others vote YES,
or	Baker votes NO and the others vote YES,
or	Baker and Amy vote YES and the others vote NO,
or	Cathy votes NO and the others vote YES,
or	David votes NO and the others vote YES,
or	Amy and Cathy vote YES and the others vote NO,
or	they all vote YES.

After you have designed and implemented your circuit, demonstrate it to the TA, and print and submit your source files for credit.

Problem 2.   (12 points) Use the schematic capture tool to implement and simulate a circuit that can detect all prime numbers less than 15. Assume that the four inputs to your circuit ($B_3B_2B_1B_0$) are used to form a four-bit binary number in the range 0 to 15. Your circuit should illuminate an LED whenever the input binary number is a prime number. Begin by completing the K-map (or, if you wish, start with a truth table), then extract minimum SOP and POS circuits, and then implement the circuit that requires the fewest number of transistors. After you have verified the circuit through simulation, download it to the Basys board, using four slide switches as inputs, and a single LED as output. Note that this circuit can co-reside in the Basys board with the previous problem if you use a different LED for the output.

After you have designed and implemented your circuit, demonstrate it to the lab assistant, and print and submit your source files for credit.

Extra Credit. Design and implement a circuit that can detect all prime numbers less than 64. After you have designed and implemented your circuit, demonstrate it to the lab assistant, and print and submit your source files for credit.

Problem 3. (15 points) Use the K-map below to specify a 5-input, one output circuit to serve as your K-map battleship field. You may want to print additional copies of the K-map to practice designing a circuit that you think will be the hardest to guess. Find a minimum circuit, and enter and simulate it using the Xilinx CAD tools. Name the inputs A,B,C,D, and E, and name the output OUT. Print and submit the circuit schematic and simulator output.

Problem 4. (15 points) Download the circuit to your board, test it, and demonstrate it to the lab assistant. Then have a neighboring student attempt to locate all the minterms in your circuit. Before starting, the visitor can request that the five input switches be set to any initial pattern. The visitor hunts for your minterms by sliding the input switches one at a time to new positions. The visitor should record their path through your K-maps in the "offense" K-map in their submission form, and you should also record the path in your "defense" K-map. The visitor keeps changing the input pattern until all the 1's have been discovered. After all 1's have been discovered, enter the total number of moves the visitor required in the "defense" blank below. Then change roles, and probe your neighbor's map. Enter the total number of moves required in the "offense" blank below.

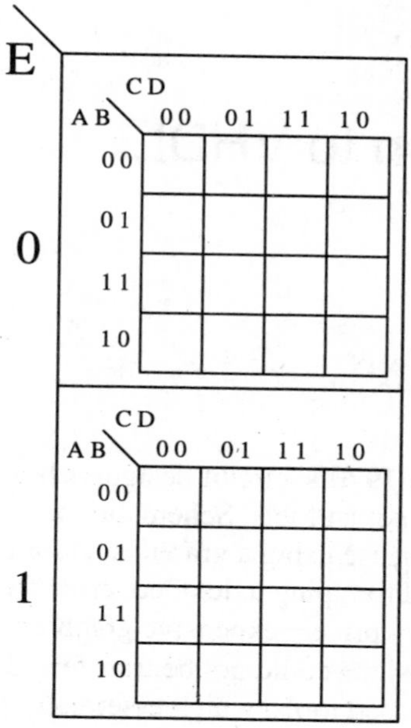

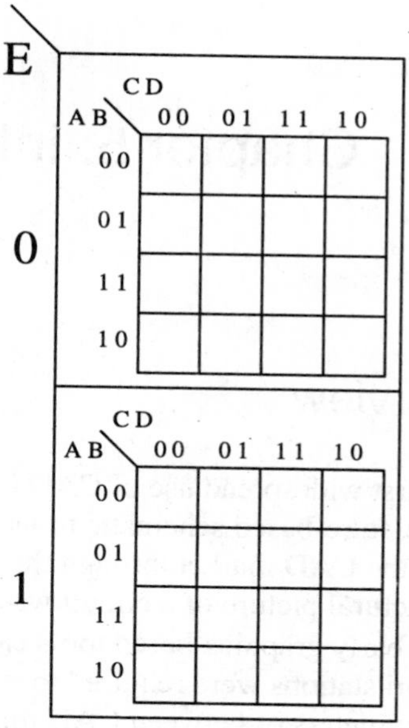

E 0

A B \ C D	00	01	11	10
0 0				
0 1				
1 1				
1 0				

1

A B \ C D	00	01	11	10
0 0				
0 1				
1 1				
1 0				

E 0

A B \ C D	00	01	11	10
0 0				
0 1				
1 1				
1 0				

1

A B \ C D	00	01	11	10
0 0				
0 1				
1 1				
1 0				

"Defensive" moves:_____

"Offensive" moves:_____

Use this map when probing another's circuit

Use this map when someone else is
probing your circuit

Total score: (Equals Offensive Moves$+$(100$-$Defensive Moves)) _____

Chapter 5: Introduction to VHDL

1. Overview

Since the first widespread use of CAD tools in the early 1970's, circuit designers have used both picture-based schematic tools and text-based netlist tools. Schematic tools dominated the CAD market through the mid-1990's because using a graphics editor to build a structural picture of a circuit was easy compared to typing a detailed, error-free netlist. But early graphics-based tools came with a heavy price—expensive graphics-capable workstations were required to run them, and designs could not be transferred between computers or between CAD tools. Early text-based tools, which essentially just allowed designers to type netlists directly, gained momentum because the tools weren't tied to high-end computers.

As progress in IC fabrication technologies made it possible to place more and more transistors on a chip, it became apparent that schematic methods were not scaling very well to the more complex design environments. A single designer could specify the behavior of a circuit that required several thousand logic gates, but it took several layout engineers many weeks or months to transfer that behavior to patterns of transistors. As designs increased in complexity, more engineers were employed on larger teams, and a much larger volume of detailed technical data had to be shared between workers.

Technology advances created new bottlenecks—it was proving difficult to keep large numbers of designers and layout engineers all up to date with precise specifications in complex and evolving design environments. In response, the US Department of Defense began a program to develop a method by which designers could communicate highly specific technical data. In 1981, the DOD brought together a consortium of leading technical companies, and asked them to create a new "language" that could be used to precisely specify complex, high-speed integrated circuits. The language was to have a wide range of descriptive capability, so that detailed behaviors of any digital circuit could be specified. This work resulted in the advent of VHDL, an acronym for "Very-high-speed-integrated-circuit Hardware Description Language". This chapter presents several of the basic concepts involved in using VHDL as a design tool for digital circuits. In subsequent modules, further discussions of the VHDL language will keep pace with circuit descriptions.

Before beginning this chapter, you should...

- Be familiar with the structure of logic circuits;
- Know how to use the WebPack schematic tools to enter and simulate circuits;
- Know how to download circuits to the Digilent circuit board;
- Understand logic systems and minimization techniques.

This chapter requires:

- A Windows PC;
- The Xilinx ISE/WebPack software;
- A Digilent circuit board.

After completing this chapter, you should...

- Be able to enter a VHDL description of a combinational logic circuit;
- Be able to synthesize, simulate, and download a VHDL-based circuit;
- Understand the role of VHDL and circuit synthesizers, and the difference between structural and behavioral designs.

2. Background

VHDL was introduced as a means to provide a detailed design specification of a digital circuit, with little thought given to how a circuit might be implemented based on that specification (the assumption was the requirements in the source file would be captured as a schematic by a skilled engineer). At the time, the creation of a design specification, although involved, was almost trivial in comparison to the amount of work required to translate the specification to a schematic-based structural description needed to fabricate a device. Over several years, it became clear that a computer program could be written to automatically translate a VHDL behavioral specification to a structural circuit, and a new class of computer programs called synthesizers began appearing. A synthesizer produces a low-level, structural description of a circuit based on its HDL description. This automated behavioral-to-structural translation of a circuit definition greatly reduced the amount of human effort required to produce a circuit, and the VHDL language matured from a specification language to a design language.

The use of HDLs and synthesizers has revolutionized the way in which digital engineers work, and it is important to keep in mind how rapidly this change has come about. In 1990, very few new designs were started using HDLs (the vast majority were schematic based). By the mid 1990's, roughly half of all new designs were using HDLs, and today, all but the most trivial designs use HDL methods. Such rapid change demonstrates that engineers overwhelmingly recognize the advantages of using HDLs. But such rapid change also means that tools, methods, and technologies are still evolving, and that CAD tools are continuing to be developed and improved.

Digital design CAD tools can be placed in two major categories—the "front-end" tools that allow a design to be captured and simulated, and "back-end" tools that synthesize a design, map it to a particular technology, and analyze its performance (thus, front-end tools work mostly with virtual circuits, and back-end tools work mostly with physical circuits). Several companies produce CAD tools, with some focusing on front-end tools, some on back-end tools, and some on both. Two major HDLs have emerged—one developed by and for private industry (called Verilog), and the other fueled by the government and specified by the IEEE (VHDL). Both are similar in appearance and application, and both have their relative advantages. We will use VHDL, because a greater number of educational resources have been developed for VHDL than for Verilog. It should be noted that after learning one of the two languages, the other could be adopted quickly.

HDLs have allowed design engineers to increase their productivity many fold in just a few years. It is fair to say that a well-equipped engineer today is as productive as a small team of engineers just a few years ago. Further, hardware specification is now within the reach of a wider range of engineers; no longer is it the domain of only a few with highly specialized training and experience. But to support this increased level of productivity, engineers must master a new set of design skills: they must be able to craft behavioral circuit definitions that provably meet design requirements; they must understand synthesis and other CAD tool processes so that results can be critically examined and interpreted; and they must be able to model external interfaces to the design so that it can be rigorously tested and verified. The extra degree of abstraction that HDL allows brings many new sources of potential errors, and designers must be able to recognize and address such errors when they occur.

Structural vs. Behavioral Design

A behavioral circuit design is a description of how a circuit's outputs are to behave when its inputs are driven by logic values over time. A purely behavioral description provides no information to indicate how a circuit might be constructed—that information must inferred from the definition through application of several pre-designed rules. As an example, consider the following behavioral definition written in proper VHDL syntax: *GT <= "1" if A > B else "0"*. The GT ("greater than") output could be formed by a processor circuit doing a comparison under the control of software, or by the "borrow out" of a hardware subtractor circuit, or by a custom-designed logic circuit. Any of these implementation methods would meet the behavioral requirements contained in the VHDL statement.

A structural circuit definition is essentially a plan, recipe, or blueprint of how a circuit is to be constructed, and it is required before a circuit can be constructed. In its most detailed and basic form, a structural definition provides no information to indicate how a circuit might behave. Consider the structural circuit definition (schematic) shown. To discover the high-level behavior of this circuit (assuming no prior knowledge of the design), a time consuming and detailed analysis would need to be performed. But its behavior can be stated rather succinctly: assert LT if the 4-bit input number A is less than B, and GT if A is greater than B.

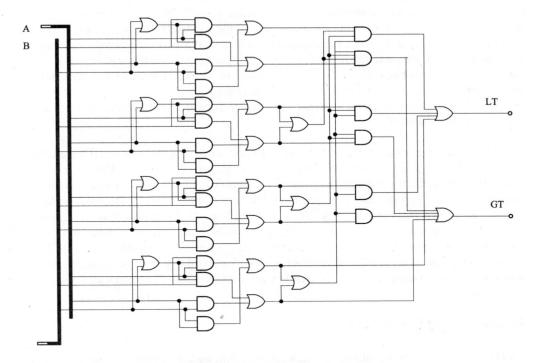

Schematic for a 4-bit magnitude comparator circuit

HDL source files can be written to define circuits using behavioral methods or structural methods (or more commonly, a mixture of the two). In any case, an HDL source file must be synthesized into a structural description before a circuit can be implemented. When a behavioral circuit is synthesized, the synthesizer must search through a large collection of template circuits, and apply a large collection of rules to try to create a structural circuit that matches the behavioral description. The synthesis process can result in any one of several alternative circuits being created due to the variability inherent in generating rule-based solutions. But when a structural description is synthesized, the synthesizer's job is a relatively straightforward, involving far fewer rules and inferences. A post-synthesis structural circuit will closely resemble the original structural definition. For this reason, many designers prefer to use a "mostly structural" approach, even though this approach does not capitalize on one of the major benefits of using VHDL (i.e., the ability to quickly and easily create behavioral designs).

In general, it is far easier and less time consuming to define a given circuit using behavioral methods than to define the same circuit using structural methods. Behavioral descriptions allow engineers to focus on high-level design considerations, and not on the details of circuit implementation. But while behavioral methods allow engineers to design more complex systems more quickly, they don't allow engineers to control the structure of their final circuit. Synthesizers must use rules that are applicable to a wide range of circuits, and they cannot be optimized for a particular circuit. In some situations, engineers must have greater control over the final structure of their circuits. In these cases, structural methods are more appropriate. Often, engineers might start a new design with a behavioral description so that they can readily study the circuit and possible alternatives. Then, once a particular design has been chosen, it can be recoded in structural form so that the synthesis process becomes more predictable. Structural descriptions read rather like a netlist, and although they are more difficult to create, it is straightforward to sketch circuit from a structural HDL source file.

Instead of using a graphics interface to add gates and wires to a schematic, HDLs editors use a text editor to add structural or behavioral descriptions to a text file. Behavioral descriptions describe the conditions required for a given signal to take on a new value. For example, the VHDL statement Y <= (A and B) or (not A and B and C) or (not A and not C), read as "Y gets assigned AB + A$'$BC + A$'$C$'$", describes only how Y is to behave, and not how a circuit that performs the operation is to be built. Structural descriptions use components interconnected by signal names to create a netlist (see problem 1 above for an example). Whether a circuit is coded structurally or behaviorally, it must be synthesized before it can be implemented, and the synthesizer automatically minimizes all logic equations.

Synthesis and Simulation

A VHDL design can be simulated to check its behavior, and/or synthesized so that it can be implemented. These two functions, simulation and synthesis, are really separate functions that do not need to be related. In a typical flow, a new design would be simulated, then synthesized, and then simulated again after synthesis to ensure the synthesizer did not introduce any errors. But it is possible to eliminate either (or both) simulation steps altogether, and proceed directly to synthesis. It is also possible to simulate a new design many, many times prior to synthesis so that various design alternatives can be investigated. In either case, a typical first step is to use a CAD tool called an analyzer to check the VHDL source for any grammar or syntax errors. Code that analyzes successfully can be routed to the simulator or synthesizer.

Although the simulator used in HDL environments is similar to the simulator used in schematic environments, there are a few key differences. One difference is that a schematic must be rendered into a netlist before it can be simulated, but a VHDL source file can be simulated directly (or, restated, a VHDL source file can be simulated before synthesis). This difference results from the fact that in a schematic environment, symbols added to a circuit are really just graphical placeholders for simulation routines. In an HDL environment, no such simulation routines exist—the user must define each circuit's behavior in proper VHDL syntax, and the simulator directly uses these definitions. Another difference is that VHDL environments are more tightly integrated with their

126

simulation environments, and several VHDL language features exist solely for use in circuit simulations (more on this later).

A VHDL circuit description must be synthesized before it can be implemented in a given device or technology. A typical synthesis process transforms a behavioral description to basic logic constructs such as AND, OR and NOT operations (or perhaps NAND and NOR operations), and these basic operations are then mapped to the targeted implementation technology. For example, a given design might be mapped to a programmable device like an FPGA, or it might be mapped to a fully custom design process at a semiconductor foundry. The desired target technology is specified during the synthesis step, which means that the same VHDL source file can be used to create a prototype design that will be downloaded to an FPGA, or it can be used to create a custom chip. This ability to use the same source file to implement a design in vastly different technologies is a key strength to using HDL design methods.

The design flow on the right shows the steps involved with HDL based designs. Note that two simulation steps occur—one just after the HDL code is entered, and the other after the design has been synthesized. The first simulation step allows designers to quickly check the logical behavior of their design, before any thought or effort is applied to implementing a physical circuit. This early simulation allows several architectural alternatives to be compared and contrasted early in the design cycle, before decisions are "locked in" to a particular hardware solution. The second simulation step allows designers to verify the design still works after it has been synthesized and mapped to a given hardware device.

A VHDL source file contains no information to direct how a given circuit might be implemented. Most designs must meet stringent timing requirements, or power consumption limits, or size specifications. During the synthesis operation, the designer can constrain the synthesizer to optimize the process for power consumption, for area, or for operating speed. The post-synthesis simulation allows a designer to check that the synthesis process created a

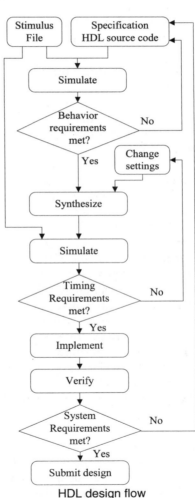

HDL design flow

physical circuit that meets the original design specifications. If the specifications are not met, the designer can re-run the synthesis process with new constraints.

In the recent past, the majority of the engineering effort required for a new design was applied to transferring high-level specifications into low-level structural descriptions—the exact function that synthesizers perform today. Although this very detailed process required much effort, it also allowed designers to gain a very detailed understanding of the actual, physical circuit. Using synthesizers to perform these tasks alleviates designers from some involved chores, but it also removes a potentially valuable source of design information. To help offset this loss of information, designers must understand the synthesis process very well, and they must be able to thoroughly analyze the post-synthesis circuit to make sure that all required specifications are met. This, in turn, requires rigorous use of simulators and other tools to recheck the design. These tools will be investigated in later labs.

3. Introduction to VHDL

In a schematic capture environment, a graphical symbol defines a given logic circuit by showing a "bounding box" as well as input and output connections. In VHDL, this same concept is used, only the bounding box must be explicitly typed into the text editor. The format for describing this bounding box requires an *entity* block with a corresponding *port* statement. The entity block (as shown in the example) gives the circuit a name and defines all input and output ports. Thus, the entity block in VHDL plays the same role as a symbol in a schematic capture environment. A VHDL circuit description also requires an *architecture* statement. The architecture statement defines circuit performance in the same manner as the "behind the scenes" simulation models define circuit performance in schematic capture programs. When VHDL code is simulated, these architecture statements are executed instead of the library-based simulation subroutines used in the schematic capture environment.

General Structure of a VHDL Source File

```
library ieee;
use ieee.std_logic_1164.all;

entity circuit_name is
  port (list of inputs, outputs and type);
end circuit_name;

architecture arch_name of circuit_name is
begin
   (statements defining circuit go here);
end arch_name;
```

The general format for a VHDL circuit description is shown in the figure above. Required keywords have been shown in boldface, and text strings that the user must supply are shown in italics. The example below shows a schematic and corresponding VHDL code. The first two lines of the VHDL code establish the location of needed library elements. The actual function of these two lines will be explained later—for now, you can simply be type them as shown. By referring to the format and the following example, you can prepare VHDL code to describe the circuits required in this lab project that accompanies this chapter. In particular, you will need to define your circuit's input and output signal names in a port statement, and provide a description of circuit behavior in the architecture statement.

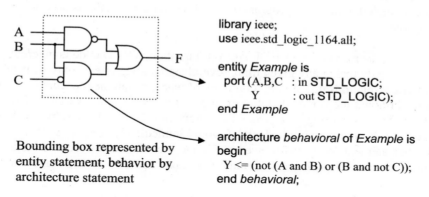

```
library ieee;
use ieee.std_logic_1164.all;

entity Example is
   port (A,B,C  : in STD_LOGIC;
         Y      : out STD_LOGIC);
end Example

architecture behavioral of Example is
begin
   Y <= (not (A and B) or (B and not C));
end behavioral;
```

Bounding box represented by entity statement; behavior by architecture statement

The port statement in the example code above defines the inputs A, B, and C, and the output Y as being of type std_logic. In VHDL, the std_logic type models signals that use wires in physical circuits. VHDL allows other data types (such as integers, characters, Boolean, etc.), but these more abstract types do not directly correspond to voltages on signals on wires. Rather, they are included so that a designer can think more about data flow than about electronics in the early stages of a design. These more abstract data types must be resolved to a std_logic type before the HDL description can be implemented. It is always possible to create a design using nothing but the std_logic type. In some cases, using only std_logic types can make the early stages of the design more time consuming, but in return, no translation of other data types is needed. For the next several labs, we use the std_logic type exclusively for all inputs and outputs.

Signal Assignments

The act of designing a digital circuit can be simply described as creating new output signals based on some combination of input signals. From a computer system, to a controller inside of an appliance, to a media playback device, digital circuits process inputs from some source and produce useful outputs. Thus, the signal assignment operator in VHDL is the most fundamental operator.

The signal assignment operator ("<=") is used to indicate how an output signal is to be driven. Simple examples include A <= "1", meaning that the signal A gets assigned the logic value "1" (assumed to be LHV). Or, A <= B means the signal A gets assigned the signal B. Whenever a signal gets assigned a new value, the VHDL simulator requires that some amount of time passes before the signal is allowed to take the new value. This is because VHDL models circuits that use wires to carry signals—because the voltage on a wire cannot change instantaneously, a signal assignment in VHDL cannot happen instantaneously. This property differentiates VHDL from a computer language like "C".

When a VHDL program is being executed, it is simulating a circuit that operates in real time. But "real time" to a computer is simply a count value stored in a memory location. In VHDL, if the time counter is at "430ns" when the assignment A <= "1" occurs, then A will not change to a "1" until the time value is incremented from 430ns. This is fundamentally different than a C program, where information transfer is not forced to occur over time.

Because time is a factor in every VHDL signal transaction, VHLD code is inherently *concurrent*, meaning that at any given time, several signal assignments may be pending. Cause-and-effect relationships are not a function of where a statement occurs in the VHDL code, but rather how time is modeled. For example, if in a C program variable X is storing a "1" and variable Y is storing a "2" when the statements X = Y followed by Z = X are encountered, Z = Y would be implied, and Z would immediately store a "2". Not so in VHDL: if the statement A<=B is followed by C<=A, then C would store a "1" until enough time had passed to allow A to assume B's value, and then more time to allow C to assume A's value.

Signal assignment operators can assign an output signal a new value based on a *function* that operates on input signals (the signal on the left of the "<=" operator is the output, and those to the right are inputs). The basic logic operations are included as standard functions in VHDL tools, so that signal assignments such as "A <= C or D;" can be written (*and, or, nand, nor, xor, xnor,* and *not* may all be used). Thus, it is trivial to write VHDL code for basic logic circuits. VHDL contains other more powerful signal assignment operators, and more "built-in" functions, but these will be explored in later exercises. Note that all signal assignment statements in VHDL must be terminated with a semicolon.

Before beginning the lab procedure, you should follow the VHDL portion of the ISE/WebPack tutorial on the class website. Although the tutorial presents only the most basic features needed to design logic circuits using VHDL, it is sufficient for the needs of this lab. Later exercises will explore more features of the VHDL language, as well as more features available in WebPack.

Using the ISE/WebPack VHDL Tools

To implement VHDL designs in the WebPack environment, a text editor is required to create the VHDL source file, a simulator is needed to check the results, and a synthesizer is needed to translate the source file to a form that can be downloaded to a chip. Other tools, like a floor-planner and/or timing analyzer, might also be needed for more complex designs (these tools will be discussed later). Any text editor can be used to create a VHDL source file. Xilinx supplies an editor with WebPack, and this editor uses colors and auto-indents to make the source file more readable (the WebPack editor is highly recommended). The lab project that accompanies this chapter provides a brief tutorial on creating VHDL designs, and then all subsequent labs will present further features of the VHDL language and Xilinx tool set. For now, we will start with a few simple projects to create a basic logic circuits like "Y<= (not A and B) or C".

Lab Project 5: Introduction to VHDL

Estimated Work Hours

| 1 | 2 | 3 | 4 | 5 | 6 | 7 | 8 | 9 | 10 |

| 1 | 2 | 3 | 4 | 5 | 6 | 7 | 8 | 9 | 10 |

Overall Weight

Point Scale

4: Exemplary
3: Complete
2: Incomplete
1: Minor effort
0: Not submitted

20% will be deducted from scores for each week late
Score = Points awarded (Pts) × Weight (Wt)

LAB ASSISTANT

Total In-Lab Score

#	Demonstration	Wt	Pts	Late	Score	Lab Asst Signature	Date
6	LED function	3					

GRADER

#	Attachments	Wt	Pts	Score	Weeks late	Total Grading Score		Total Score
1	Annotated schematic and VHDL	3						
2	Schematic, VHDL, sketch, comments	2						
3	VHDL source and simulation	3					*Total score is In-lab score plus grading score*	
4	VHDL source, test bench and simulation	3						
5	VHDL source, schematic and simulation	4						
6	VHDL source	2						
EC	Simulation source and output	3						

Overview

This lab project presents a brief tutorial (in Appendix 1) on the use of the Xilinx
ISE/Webpack VHDL design environment. After completing the tutorial, you should be
able to design and implement the basic logic circuits presented in the problems below.

Problem 1. Use WebPack tool to create a schematic for $Y = A'BC + B'C' + AB'$.
Save the schematic, and then double-click on the "View VHDL
Functional Model" entry in the Sources in Project" panel of the Project
Navigator. This creates a structural VHDL file from the schematic. Print
and attach the schematic and VHDL file, and then label the gates and
wires in the schematic with the labels generated in the VHDL file.

Problem 2. Use WebPack to create a schematic for $Y = AB + A'BC + A'C'$. Save
the schematic, double-click on the "View VHDL Functional Model"
entry in the "Sources in Project" panel of the Project Navigator, and view
the results. Print and attach the schematic and VHDL file, and sketch a
circuit that corresponds to the VHDL listing. Comment below on the
differences between the original schematic and the sketched circuit.

Problem 3. Use the Xilinx HDL tool to enter, simulate, and synthesize a 4-input, 2-
output logic system that behaves according to the two logic equations
shown. Simulate the source file by creating a stimulus file using the
waveform editor in the same manner as you did with schematic-based
circuits in previous modules. Print and submit your VHDL source file
and simulation output.

$$RED = A'D + AB'C' + ACD + AB' + BD$$
$$YELLOW = AB + AC + BC + A'B$$

Problem 4. Use the Xilinx HDL tool to enter, simulate, and synthesize the two logic
circuits shown below. Simulate the source file by creating and running a
VHDL test bench. Print and submit your VHDL source file, your VHDL
test bench, and simulation output.

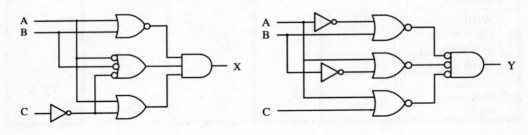

Problem 5.	Use the Xilinx HDL tool to enter and simulate a 3-input, 2-output circuit that behaves according to the truth table shown. Create a macro symbol for the circuit, and add that symbol to a newly-created schematic page. Simulate the schematic using the waveform editor simulation interface. Print and submit your VHDL source file, your schematic, and your simulation output.

A	B	C	F	G
0	0	0	1	1
0	0	1	0	1
0	1	0	1	0
0	1	1	0	1
1	0	0	0	1
1	0	1	1	1
1	1	0	0	0
1	1	1	1	1

Hint: You can implement these truth-table functions in any way you choose—you can simply type non-minimized logic equations, or you can type minimized logic equations, or you can write VHDL code that uses a "selected assignment" statement to implement the truth table directly (see appendix 2 of this document for an example).

Problem 6.   Use the Xilinx HDL tool to create a circuit that can perform the logical AND of two 4-bit numbers represented as two 4-bit busses. Implement the circuit on your Digilent board by connecting four switches to one 4-bit bus, four switches to a second 4-bit bus, and the outputs to 4 LED's. Demonstrate your project to the TA, and print and submit your source file for credit.

Extra Credit.   Simulate your circuit for problem 6 using a VHDL test bench that includes the use of bus assignment statements. Print and submit your test bench and simulator output for credit.

Appendix 1: An Introductory Tutorial for the ISE/WebPack VHDL Tool

A new VHDL project can be started following the methods used to start a new schematic project as discussed Chapter 3. When the new project is created, click on the "Create New Source" process as before. In the Select Source Type window that opens, select VHDL Module, enter an appropriate file name, choose an appropriate directory, and ensure the "Add to project" box is checked. Click "Next" button to bring up the Define Module dialog box. The optional Define Module box is provided as a convenient way for you to generate part of the contents required in any VHDL source file. You can choose to enter information into this box, or proceed without entering anything and type the information directly into the VHDL editor at a later time. Here, we will enter information in the Define Module box to save time and effort. We will create a VHDL circuit defined by the equation "Y <= (not A and B) or C". This circuit uses three inputs labeled A, B, and C, and a single output Y, and this information can be entered into the dialog box as shown below (be sure to change the direction of Y to "out"). The entity name must be entered in the top-most field in the box using any alphanumeric text string. You can choose any name you like, but as always, it is a good idea to choose a name that will help you identify the file later. The architecture name can be any valid alphanumeric string. For now, accept the default name "Behavioral". Click "Next" button to bring up the summary window, and "Finish" button to start the VHDL editor. When the VHDL editor opens, a file is automatically opened that contains the information you entered in the New Source Wizard, together with some additional items.

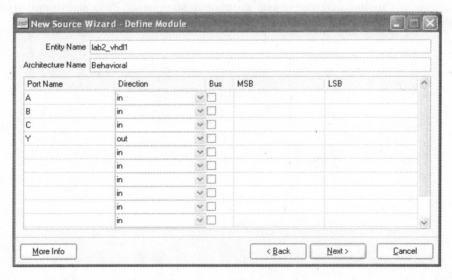

Comments in VHDL source files are shown in green, they always start with a double-dash, and they must be defined on a line-by-line basis. Anything between a double-dash and the end of a line is considered a comment, and will be ignored by all VHDL tools. Libraries and packages are always defined near the top of the source file. The "library" and "use" statements make vital information visible to your project—for now, simply leave them in the source file. Their functions will be explained in a later project.

The "entity" block defines the externally visible ports for the design. Every entity in a project must have a unique name, and once defined, every entity can be used as a component in another design. The "port" statement is the main statement of the entity block—the port statement defines all input and output signals, their direction ("in", "out", or "inout"), and their type. Types will be discussed in more detail at a later time. For now, and in fact for almost any design you encounter, the "std_logic" type is preferred (std_logic is the VHDL type that is meant to model a wire in a real circuit, and so it is the most generally applicable data type).

The window below shows an example of a VHDL source file. All of the code shown, except the code between the "begin" and "end" statements in the architecture block, was generated by the Define Module wizard. The "library" and "use" statements shown will appear at the top of virtually every source file. The entity block and port statement can also be seen in the code.

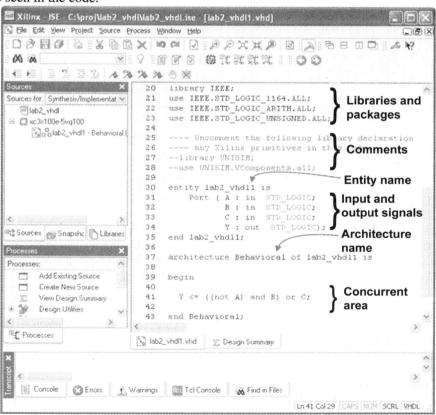

The "architecture" statement defines the behavior of the circuit—you must enter valid VHDL assignment statements between the "begin" and "end" statements in the architecture block to define your circuit. Note the area between the begin/end statements in the figure above is referred to as the "concurrent area". This is because all assignment statements in this area are treated as concurrent by the VHDL simulator ("concurrent" means the statements are not executed by the simulator in sequence as they appear in the source file, but rather in parallel whenever the simulator detects that an input signal has changed). Concurrency is required when modeling physical circuits. This concept will be more fully explained later.

To complete this VHDL source file, you must type the VHDL assignment statement "Y<= ((not A) and B) or C;" into the concurrent area to defines the circuit's behavior. The completed source file can now be simulated or synthesized, and then downloaded to the Digilent board.

To simulate the source file, the simulation procedures used for schematics can be followed (namely, create a new source file to define input stimulus using WebPack's waveform editor, then run the simulator using that stimulus file to check the results). But a more effective method exists for creating simulator input for VHDL source files. A separate source file, called a "VHDL test bench" can be created as described below. Once a VHDL test bench is created, it is easy to execute in the simulator, and it is easy maintain, modify, and adapt for other VHDL designs.

To synthesize a VHDL source, highlight its name in the *Sources* window in the Project navigator, and then double-click the "Synthesize" process in the *Processes* window. If synthesis completes without errors, a green check mark will be displayed by the synthesize process, and a "process completed successfully" message will appear in the status window at the bottom of the Project Navigator window. If errors are present, error messages in the status window will guide you towards appropriate corrective action. Note that if error messages are related to problems in the source file, double-clicking the red "error" icon in the status window will automatically jump to the offending line in the source file.

It is possible (and sometimes desirable) to add VHDL modules into schematics. To create a schematic symbol for the VHDL module, select the VHDL source file name in the *Sources* window, and double-click on the "Create Schematic Symbol" process in the Design Utilities section of the *Processes* window. This will create a symbol that can be added to any schematic.

In future modules, we will discuss more VHDL language features, and show VHDL code examples for many new circuits. In addition to the material presented in these modules, you will find a wealth of reference material in the ISE/Webpack tool (see for example the "language assistant" available from the light bulb icon in the ISE VHDL editor toolbar), and in many websites.

VHDL Test Benches

A test bench can be created and added to a project in the same manner as any other source file (i.e., add a new source to the project, but select "VHDL test bench" as the source type). Once created, a test bench can be used to run a simulation by selecting the test bench source file, and then selecting the simulation process in the process window. Defining stimulus inputs in a test bench makes it easier to create a wider range of stimulus inputs, particularly with respect to the timing of input signals. In the exercises that accompany this chapter, you will need the ability to create specific input signal timings. An example of a test bench suitable for use in the exercises is presented on the following page.

A test bench is an entity-architecture pair that looks similar to any other VHDL source file, except that the entity statement is empty (see example below), and the VHDL source file that is to be simulated must be "instantiated" as a component. By following the example below, you can create a test bench suitable for simulating the exercise problems for this module. In later modules, more information will be presented about test benches, their use, and their capabilities.

```
Library ieee;
use ieee.std_logic_1164.all;
use ieee.std_logic_unsigned.all;
use ieee.numeric_std.all;
```
Standard file header containing library and package definitions

```
entity lab5test_bench is
end lab5test_bench;
```
An "empty" entity statement required for all test bench source files. The entity name can be any legal string.

```
architecture test of lab5test_bench is

    component ex1
        port( a, b, c  : in std_logic;
                     y  : out std_logic);
    end component;
```
The entity under test (EUT) must be declared as a component. The port must exactly match the port statement from the EUT.

```
    signal a, b, c, y : std_logic;

begin
```
All signals that attach to entity port pins must be declared as signals.

```
    EUT: ex1 port map(a => a,
              b => b,
              c => c,
              y => y);
```
The EUT must be instantiated. The port map statement maps the declared signals to the port pins of the EUT. It is common to use matching signal and port pin names.

```
process begin

  a <= '0';
  b <= '0';
  c <= '0';
  wait for 100 ns;
  a <= '1';
  wait for 100 ns;
  b <= '1';
  wait for 100 ns;
  c <= '1';
  wait for 100 ns;
  a <= '0';
  wait for 100 ns;
  b <= '0';
  wait for 100 ns;
  c <= '0';

end process;
end test;
```

Statements to define input stimulus are placed in a process statement so that the "wait" statement can be used to control the passage of time.

Assigning Physical Pins

Appendix 2: VHDL Example Source File for Implementing a Truth Table Directly

```
library IEEE;
use IEEE.std_logic_1164.all;

-- Implement the following truth table in VHDL
--
--        A  B  C  X  Y
--        0  0  0  1  0
--        0  0  1  0  1
--        0  1  0  0  0
--        0  1  1  0  1
--        1  0  0  1  0
--        1  0  1  0  1
--        1  1  0  1  1
--        1  1  1  0  1

entity ttable is
    port (ABC:    in  STD_LOGIC_VECTOR(2 downto 0);
          X,Y:    out STD_LOGIC);
end ttable;

architecture behavioral of ttable is

signal OUTS : STD_LOGIC_VECTOR(1 downto 0)

begin
  with ABC select
        OUTS <= "10" when "000",
                "01" when "001",
                "00" when "010",
                "01" when "011",
                "10" when "100",
                "01" when "101",
                "11" when "110",
                "01" when others;    -- the "others" clause is used in place
                                     -- of "111" for reasons explained later
  X <= OUTS(1); Y<= OUTS(0);

end behavioral;
```

Chapter 6: Combinational Circuit Blocks

1. Overview

This chapter introduces several combinational circuits that are frequently used by digital designers, including a data selector (also called a multiplexor or just "mux"), a binary decoder, a seven-segment decoder, an encoder, and a shifter. Each of these circuits can be used by themselves in the solution of some simpler logic problems, but they are more often used as building blocks in the creation of larger, more complex circuits. In this module, these circuits will be developed from first principles following a general design procedure that will serve as a model for all later designs. In later modules, these circuits will be used as modular (or "macro") building blocks in larger designs.

This general design procedure has five main steps. First, you must gain a clear understanding of the design intent of each circuit before any design activities start. When you are doing original design work, this understanding comes from many sources, including other persons, previous or competing designs, research papers, or your own insightful thinking. For now, the discussion that leads the presentation of each new circuit is intended to impart that clear understanding to you. Second, a block diagram that shows all circuit inputs and outputs will be developed. A block diagram is an indispensable part of any design, especially when dealing with complex circuits. In conceiving and capturing a block diagram, you are committing to a set of input and output signals, and those signals define the context and boundaries of your design. Third, the design requirements will be captured in an engineering formalism like a truth table or logic equations. This formalism removes all ambiguity from the design, and establishes a solid specification for the circuit. Fourth, the formally stated requirements will be used to find minimal circuits that meet the specifications. And finally, those minimal circuits will be created and implemented using the ISE/WebPack tool and a Digilent board, and verified in hardware to ensure they meet their behavioral requirements.

Before beginning this chapter, you should…	After completing this chapter, you should…
• Be able to specify, design, and minimize combinational logic systems;	• Understand the application, function, and structure of decoder, multiplexor, encoder, and shifter circuits;

- Be able to create schematic-based or VHDL-based designs in the Xilinx WebPack environment;
- Be able to download designs created in WebPack to the Digilent circuit board.

- Know how to use these circuits in the solution of larger problems;
- Be able to quickly implement these circuits in the Xilinx CAD tool environment.

This chapter requires...

- A Windows computer running Xilinx WebPack;
- A Digilent board.

2. Background

Binary Numbers as Signals (Busses)

In a digital system, all information must be encoded as signals that carry either a logic high voltage (a "1") or logic low voltage (a "0"). Individual signals are often grouped together to form logical units called "buses" for the purpose of representing a binary number. For example, a group of four signals can be viewed as a logical grouping that can represent the first ten 4-bit binary numbers (0000 –1001), or all 16 hexadecimal digits (0000–1111). In the block diagram above, the two inputs A and B and the output Z are shown as bold lines with hash marks cutting them, and the number "8" near the hash mark. This notation is used to show groups of logic signals that are to be considered as a bus carrying a binary number. In this case, A and B are 8-bit busses, meaning they each are composed of 8 wires that, when taken together, represent a single 8-bit binary number. The output bus Z is a 16-bit bus that can transport a 16-bit number, and the outputs X and Y are simply 1-bit signal wires.

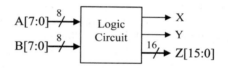

Nearly all schematic capture tools represent busses in the same way. The bus is given a name, followed by two numbers enclosed in parenthesis and separated by a colon. For example, a bus labeled "A[7:0]" would apply to an 8-bit bus named "A". Each wire in the bus has a unique name that is formed by concatenating the bus "root" name with a number in the indicated range. For instance, A0 would refer to the 0th wire in the bus, and A4 would refer to the 4th wire in the bus. Note that although the use of buses makes it easier to refer to collections of similar signals, it is always possible to represent those signals as

141

individual wires (and note also that if you were to construct the circuit on a circuit board, you'd need 8 individual wires for each bus).

In the Xilinx schematic capture tool, a bus can be added to a schematic in much the same way as a wire. To add a bus to a schematic, first draw a wire using the wire add tool, and then select "Add→Net Name". Naming a wire using the bus naming convention of "bus_name (MSB:LSB)" will automatically create a bus (typically, the MSB is 7 or 15, and the LSB is 0). For example, naming a wire A[7:0] will make an 8-bit bus named "A". Busses can be used to connect components that have been designed to consume and/or produce bussed signals (i.e., busses can be used to connect signals that use bus pins instead of logic signal pins). Individual wires from the bus can be accessed by adding a "bus tap" and labeling the tap with the signal name (for example, if the 5th signal of bus A must be accessed, a bus tap with label A5 can be added). In VHDL, busses can be defined using the "std_logic_vector" type. For example, an 8-bit input bus named A can be defined in a VHDL port statement by typing "A: in std_logic_vector (7 downto 0)". The entire bus can be referred to as simply "A", and signal number 5 can be referred to as A5.

Minimizing Circuits with Multiple Outputs

In a previous exercise, we examined methods for minimizing circuits that produced a single output based on some number of inputs. They circuits were simple enough that Boolean algebra or K-maps could be used to find suitable minimal descriptions for the required circuits. In a more general case, logic systems produce more than one output from the same set of inputs. In these more general and more complex designs, "pencil and paper" methods become unwieldy, and the use of computer-based methods becomes more imperative. In particular, logic systems involving more than 5 or 6 inputs and/or two or more outputs are best minimized using computer-based methods. And further, the use of computer-based tools can relieve designers from many tedious and labor-intensive design chores, thereby allowing more time to be spent investigating design requirements and experimenting with various design approaches. After various high-level design approaches have been analyzed, the best can be readily implemented using computer tools like minimizers, synthesizers, and optimizers.

An example of a four-input, three-output logic system is shown below. A design problem like this could be attacked as if it were composed of three unique, independent logic circuits, all of which just happen to use the same four inputs. Optimal solutions for each of the three circuits have been found independently of the others, and they are shown below labeled with the "LM" subscript (for local minimum). This "one at a time" solution method is certainly the simplest, but it ignores any global optimization opportunities that may exist. Specifically, it may turn out that a more optimal overall solution can be found if all of the logic functions are analyzed at once, and (possibly) if one or two of the individual functions are allowed to be sub-optimal. This multi-output analysis starts by listing all possible product terms (including non-minimal terms) that could be used to define each function, and then from that list finding all product terms that could be used in more than one equation. Each shared product term is then algorithmically inserted into every equation it could be used in, to see if a more minimal set of equations result. After this process is complete, a true global minimum can be found.

The loops below show the sub-optimal groupings in individual maps used to arrive at a true global minimum. Equations with the "GM" subscript (for global minimum) show their unique product terms in shaded boxes (shared terms are not shaded). The local minimum requires 12 gates and 37 inputs, but the global minimum requires just 10 gates and 34 inputs. Computer-based algorithms like espresso automatically search for global minimum solutions for multi-output logic systems, and these methods are far more practicable than the lengthy and error-prone pencil-and-paper methods.

$X = \Sigma m(1, 2, 5, 9, 11, 12, 13, 14, 15)$ $Y = \Sigma m(3, 9, 11, 14, 15)$ $Z = \Sigma m(2, 3, 9, 11, 12, 13)$

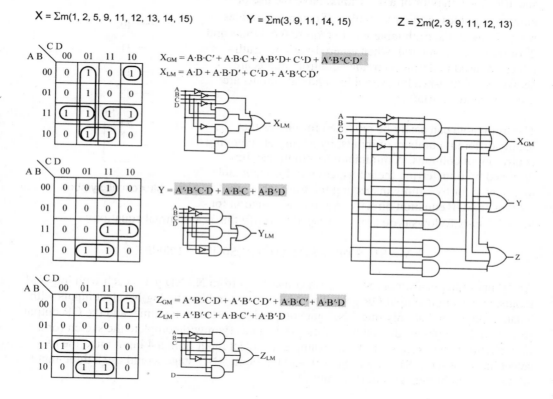

$X_{GM} = A{\cdot}B{\cdot}C' + A{\cdot}B{\cdot}C + A{\cdot}B'{\cdot}D + C'{\cdot}D + A'{\cdot}B'{\cdot}C{\cdot}D'$
$X_{LM} = A{\cdot}D + A{\cdot}B{\cdot}D' + C'{\cdot}D + A'{\cdot}B'{\cdot}C{\cdot}D'$

$Y = A'{\cdot}B'{\cdot}C{\cdot}D + A{\cdot}B{\cdot}C + A{\cdot}B'{\cdot}D$

$Z_{GM} = A'{\cdot}B'{\cdot}C{\cdot}D + A'{\cdot}B'{\cdot}C{\cdot}D' + A{\cdot}B{\cdot}C' + A{\cdot}B'{\cdot}D$
$Z_{LM} = A'{\cdot}B'{\cdot}C + A{\cdot}B{\cdot}C' + A{\cdot}B'{\cdot}D$

3. Combinational Circuit Blocks

Data Selectors (Multiplexors)

Data selectors, more commonly called multiplexors (or just muxes), function by connecting one of their input signals to their output signal as directed by their "select" or

143

control input signals. Muxes have N data inputs and $\log_2$N select inputs, and a single output. In operation, the select inputs determine which data input drives the output, and whatever voltage appears on the selected input is driven on the output. All non-selected data inputs are ignored. As an example, if the select inputs of a 4 : 1 mux are "1" and "0", then the output Y will be driven to the same voltage present on input I2.

S1	S0	Y
0	0	I0
0	1	I1
1	0	I2
1	1	I3

4 : 1 mux truth table

Common mux sizes are 2 : 1 (1 select input), 4 : 1 (2 select inputs), and 8 : 1 (3 select inputs). The truth table shown specifies the behavior of a 4 : 1 mux. Note the use of entered variables in the truth table—if entered variables were not used, the truth table would require 6 columns and 2^6 or 64 rows. In general, when entered-variable truth tables are used to define a circuit, "control" inputs are shown as column-heading variables, and data inputs are used an entered variables.

The truth table can easily be modified for muxes that handle different numbers of inputs, by adding or removing control input columns. A minimal mux circuit can be designed by transferring the information in the truth table to a K-map, or by simply inspecting the truth table and writing an SOP equation directly. A minimal equation for the 4 : 1 mux follows (you are encouraged to verify this is a minimal equation):

Mux circuit symbol

$$Y = S1'\cdot S0'\cdot I0 + S1'\cdot S0\cdot I1 + S1\cdot S0'\cdot I2 + S1\cdot S0\cdot I3$$

An N-input mux is a simple SOP circuit constructed from NAND gates each with $\log_2$N+1 inputs, and a single output OR gate. The AND gates combine the $\log_2$N select inputs with a data input such that only one AND gate output is asserted at any time, and the OR output stage simply combines the outputs of the AND gates (you will complete the sketch for a mux circuit in the exercises). As an example, to select input I2 in a 4 input mux, the two select lines are set to S1 = 1 and S0 = 0, and the input AND stage would use a three input AND gate combining S1, not (S0), and I2.

Often, mux circuits use an enable input in addition to the other inputs. The enable input functions as a sort of global on/off switch, driving the output to logic "0" when it is de-asserted, and allowing normal mux operation when it is asserted.

Larger muxes can easily be constructed from smaller muxes. For example, an 8 : 1 mux can be created from two 4 : 1 muxes and one 2 : 1 mux if the outputs from the 4 : 1 muxes drive the data inputs of the 2 : 1 mux, and the most-significant select input drives the select input of the 2 : 1 mux.

144

Muxes are most often used in digital circuits to transfer data elements from a memory array to data processing circuit in a computer system. The memory address is presented on the mux select lines, and the contents of the addressed memory location are presented on the mux data inputs (this application of muxes will be presented in later labs that deal with memory systems). Since most data elements in computer systems are bytes or words consisting of 8, 16, or 32 bits, muxes used in computer circuits must switch 8, 16, 32 or more signals all at once. Muxes that can switch many signals simultaneously are called "bus muxes". A block diagram and schematic for a bus mux that can select one of four 8-bit data elements is shown below.

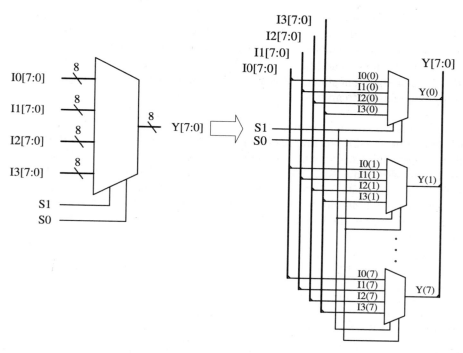

Since this most common application of multiplexors is beyond our current presentation, we will consider a less common, somewhat contrived application. Consider the K-map representation of a given logic function, where each K-map cell contains a "0", "1", or an entered variable expression. Each unique combination of K-map index variables selects a particular K-map cell (e.g., cell 6 of an 8 cell K-map is selected when A=1, B=1, C=0). Now consider a mux, where each unique combination of select inputs selects a particular data input to be passed to the output (e.g., I6 of an 8 input mux can be selected by setting the select inputs to A=1, B=1, C=0). It follows that if the input signals in a given logic function are connected to the select inputs of a mux, and those same input signals are used as K-map index variables, then each cell in the K-map corresponds to a particular mux data input. This suggests a mux can be used to implement a logic function by "connecting" the K-map cell contents to the data lines of the mux, and connecting the K-map index variables to the select lines of the mux. Mux data inputs are connected to: "0" (or ground) when the corresponding K-map cell contains a "0"; "1" (or Vdd) when the corresponding K-map cell contains a "1"; and if a K-map cell contains an entered variable expression, then a circuit implementing that expression is connected to the corresponding mux data input. Note that when a mux is used to implement a logic circuit directly from a truth table or K-map, logic minimization is not performed. This saves design time, but usually creates a less efficient circuit (however, a logic synthesizer would remove the inefficiencies before such a circuit was implemented in a programmable device).

A mux can easily be described in behavioral VHDL using a selected signal assignment statement as shown below. The statement functions by comparing the value of the *sel* input to the value shown in the *when* clause: the output variable Y gets assigned I0, I1, I2, or I3 depending on whether sel = "00", "01", "10", or "11" (in a selected signal assignment statement, the "when others" clause is used for the final case for reasons that will be explained later). In addition to assigning values to individual signals or busses, the selected signal assignment statement can also be used to assign the result of arithmetic and/or logic operations to an output.

The example code on the left below is for a mux that switches logic signals, and the code on the right is for an 8-bit bus mux. Note the only difference in the code is in the port statement, where the data elements for the bus mux are declared to be vectors instead of signals. Note also that the assignment statement in the bus mux example assigns vector quantities just like signals. When you examine the code examples, particularly the bus mux, look again at the previous figure and consider the amount of effort required to create a bus mux schematic vs. the bus mux VHDL code.

```
entity mux_select is
  port ( I3, I2, I1, I0: in std_logic;
         sel   : in std_logic_vector (1 downto 0);
         Y     : out std_logic);
end mux_select;

architecture behavioral of mux_select is
Begin
  with sel select
    Y <= I0 when "00";
         I1 when "01";
         I2 when "10";
         I3 when others;
end behavioral;
```

```
entity busmux_select is
  port ( I3, I2, I1, I0: in std_logic_vector (7 downto 0);
         sel    : in std_logic_vector (1 downto 0);
         Y      : outstd_logic_vector (7 downto 0));
end busmux_select;

architecture behavioral of busmux_select is
Begin
  with sel select
    Y <= I0 when "00";
         I1 when "01";
         I2 when "10";
         I3 when others;
end behavioral;
```

VHDL source code for implementing a more complex mux'ing circuit, such as one that might select any one of four logic function outputs to pass through to the output, is shown below. This example code uses a "conditional assignment" statement. Conditional assignment statements and selected signal assignments both allow more complex logic requirements to be succinctly described, and they can generally be used interchangeably.

In most cases, a synthesizer will produce the same circuit regardless of whether a selected or conditional assignment statement is used. There are subtle differences between the statements, and these differences will be discussed later. For now, it is a matter of personal taste as to which one is used.

```
entity mux_cond is
    port (  A, B, C : in std_logic_vector (7 downto 0);
            Sel     : in std_logic_vector (1 downto 0);
            Y       : outstd_logic_vector (7 downto 0));
end mux_cond;

architecture behavioral of mux_cond is
Begin
    Y <=    (A or not C) when  (Sel = "00") else
            (A xor B) when     (Sel = "01") else
            not A when         (Sel = "10") else
            (B nand C);
end behavioral;
```

VHDL code for a mux using a conditional assignment

A conditional assignment statement uses the "when-else" language feature to describe compound logic statements. By following the example code shown, conditional assignments can be written to describe a wide variety of assignments.

Decoders

Decoder circuits receive inputs in the form of an N-bit binary number and generate one or more outputs according to some requirement. Decoder inputs are typically viewed as a binary number representing some encoded quantity, and outputs typically drive some other circuit or device based on decoding that quantity. For example, a PS/2 keyboard decoder decodes the "scan codes" that are generated each time a given key is pressed (scan codes are unique binary numbers that are assigned to individual keys on a PS/2 keyboard). Most scan codes are simply sent to the host computer for parsing, but some perform specific functions. If the "Capslock" key is pressed, a signal is generated to illuminate an LED on the keyboard, and if "Ctrl-Alt-Del" is pressed, a signal is generated to interrupt PC operations.

Here, we will examine two different types of decoders—a simple binary decoder, and a seven-segment decoder that can drive a common numeric data display.

A binary decoder has N inputs and 2^N outputs. It receives N inputs (often grouped as a binary number on a bus) and then asserts one and only one of its 2^N outputs based on that input.

3 : 8 binary decoder

147

If the N inputs are taken as an N-bit binary number, then only the output that corresponds to the input binary number is asserted. For example, if a binary 5 (or "101") is input to a 3 : 8 decoder, then only the 5th output of the decoder will be asserted and all other outputs will be de-asserted. Practical decoder circuits are usually built as 2 : 4 decoders with 2 inputs and 2^2 (4) outputs, 3 : 8 decoders with 3 inputs and 2^3 (8) outputs, or 4 : 16 decoders with 4 inputs 2^4 (16) outputs. A decoder circuit requires one AND gate to drive each output, and each AND gate decodes a particular binary number. For example, a 3 : 8 decoder requires 8 AND gates, with the first AND gate having inputs $A' \cdot B' \cdot C'$, the second $A' \cdot B' \cdot C$, the third $A' \cdot B \cdot C'$, etc.

If a binary decoder larger than 4 : 16 is needed, it can be built from smaller decoders. Only decoders with an enable input can be used to construct larger decoder circuits. As with the mux, the enable input drives all outputs to "0" when de-asserted, and allows normal decoder operation when asserted.

Decoders are most often used in more complex digital systems to access a particular memory location based on an "address" produced by a computing device. In this application, the address represents the coded data inputs, and the outputs are the particular memory element select signals. A typical memory circuit contains a decoder to select which memory element to write, the memory elements themselves, and a mux to select which element to read.

As with multiplexors, this most common application of decoders is beyond our current presentation, so instead we will consider a less common, somewhat contrived application. Consider the function of a decoder and the truth table, K-map, or minterm representation of a given function. Each row in a truth table, each cell in a K-map, or each minterm number in an equation represents a particular combination of inputs. Each output of a decoder is uniquely asserted for a particular combination of inputs. Thus, if the inputs to a given logic function are connected to the inputs of a decoder, and those same inputs are used as K-map input logic variables, then a direct one-to-one mapping is created between the K-map cells and the decoder outputs. It follows that any given function represented in a truth table or K-map can be directly implemented using a decoder, by simply by OR'ing the decoder outputs that correspond to a truth table row or K-map cell containing a "1" (decoder outputs that correspond to K-map cells that contain a zero are simply left unconnected). In such a circuit, any input combination with a "1" in the corresponding truth table row or K-map cell will drive the output OR gate to a "1", and any input combination with a "0" in the corresponding K-map cell will allow the OR gate to output a "0". Note that when a decoder is used to implement a circuit directly from a truth table or K-map, no logic minimization is performed. Using a decoder in this fashion saves time, but usually results in a less efficient implementation (here again, a logic synthesizer would remove the inefficiencies before such a circuit was implemented in a programmable device).

A decoder can easily be described in behavioral VHDL using a selected signal assignment statement as shown below. In the example, both the inputs and outputs are grouped as busses so that a selected assignment statement can be used. In this example, the inputs can be individually referred to as I(1) and I(0), and the outputs as Y(0) through Y(3). The code can easily be modified to describe a decoder of any size.

```
entity decoder is
  port ( in:  in std_logic_vector (1 downto 0);
          Y:  out std_logic_vector (7 downto 0));
end decoder;

architecture behavioral of decoder is
Begin
 with in select
  Y <=   "0001" when "00";
         "0010" when "01";
         "0100" when "10";
         "1000" when others;
end behavioral;
```

VHDL code for a 2:4 decoder

De-multiplexor

Our use of the word "multiplexor" has its origins in telecommunications, defining a system where one signal is used to transmit many different messages, either simultaneously or at different times. "Time-multiplexing" describes a system where different messages use the same physical signal, with different messages being sent at different times. Time multiplexing works if a given signal can carry more traffic than any one message needs. For example, if ten messages each require that 1Kbit of information be sent every second, and if a communication signal is available that can carry 10Kbits per second, then time-multiplexing can be used to provide ten 1Kbit time windows each second, one for each signal. A multiplexor can be used as a simple time multiplexor, if the select inputs are used to define the time window, and the data inputs are used as the data sources.

A decoder with an enable can be used as a de-multiplexor. Whereas a multiplexor selects one on N inputs to pass through to the output, a de-multiplexor takes a single input and routes it to one of N outputs. A multiplexor/de-multiplexor (or more simply, mux/de-mux) circuit can be used to transmit the state of N signals from one place to another using only Log_2N+1 signals. Log_2N signals are used to select the data input for the mux and to drive the decoder inputs, and the rate at which these signals change define the time-window length. The data-out of the mux drives the enable-in of the decoder, so that the same logic levels that appear on the mux inputs also appear on the corresponding decoder outputs, but only for the mux input/decoder output currently selected. In this way, the state of N

149

signals can be sent from one place to another using only Log_2N+1 signals, but only one signal at a time is valid.

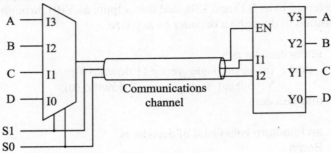

Seven-Segment Displays and Decoders

Seven-segment displays (7sd) are some of the most common electronic display devices in use. They can be used to display any decimal digit by illuminating particular segments and leaving other segments dark. 7sd devices are constructed from seven LEDs that have been arranged in a figure "8" pattern as shown in the figure below. These LEDs function identically to the individual LEDs—they emit light when a small current passes through them. The 7sd device can display a particular digit if certain LED segments are illuminated while others remain dark. As examples, if only segments b and c are illuminated, then the display will show a "1", and if segments a, b and c are illuminated then the display will show a "7". To cause an illuminating current to flow through any given LED segment, a logic signal must be impressed across the segment LED. In a typical 7sd circuit, a current-limiting resistor is placed on the cathode lead, and a transistor is used on the anode lead to provide additional current (most signal pins on digital ICs— like the FPGA on the Digilent board—cannot provide enough current to light all the display segments, so a transistor is used to provide more current).

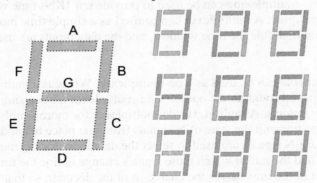

An un-illuminated seven-segment display, and nine
illumination patterns corresponding to decimal digits

In order that all 10 decimal digits can be displayed, a 7sd device requires seven logic signals, one for each segment. By asserting particular combinations of these signals, all ten decimal digits can be displayed.

The Digilent board uses a common anode display, which means that all the anode connections for a given digit are tied together into a common circuit node as shown below. To illuminate a given segment in a given digit, a "1" must be applied to the digit's anode, and "0" must be applied to the segment's cathodes (Note: With Digilent boards, a "1" is applied to a digit's anode by applying a "0" to the circuit node that drives the transistor; thus, the anode signals AN3 – AN0 are "active low").

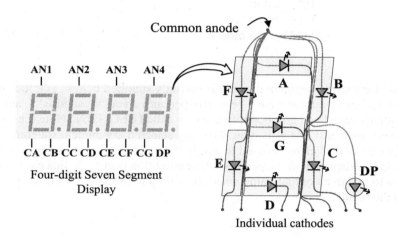

Four-digit Seven Segment
Display

Individual cathodes

A seven-segment decoder (SSD) receives four signals that represent the four bits of a binary number, and produces seven output signals that can drive the seven segments in the seven-segment display. Thus, for example, if "0000" is input to the SSD, all outputs except "g" should be asserted (to cause a "0" to be displayed on the 7sd). And if "1000" is input to the SSD, then all outputs should be asserted (to cause an "8" to be displayed). Typically, the input signals are named B3–B0, and the output signals are given a letter to indicate which segment they must drive (A–F). As discussed above, each of the seven outputs could be thought of as a separate 4-input logic design problem, and optimal circuits for each output could easily be found using the techniques developed in previous labs. In lab project that accompanies this module, various methods will be used to optimize (or minimize) the system as a whole, considering all seven outputs at the same time.

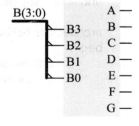

A 7sd can easily be described in VHDL using a selected signal assignment statement. In fact, a selected assignment statement can be used to implement any truth table by listing the function inputs on the right of the "when" clause, and the associated outputs on the left. In the example shown below, the input and output variables are both vectors—the *ins* represents a 2-bit binary number, and the *outs* represent a 4-bit binary number. As discussed in the "muxes" section above, the output variable *outs* gets assigned the binary values shown in quotes when *ins* is equal to the value in the "when" clause. Thus, if *ins* is "01", then *outs* gets assigned "1010".

ins		outs			
A	B	F1	F2	F3	F4
0	0	0	0	1	0
0	1	1	0	1	0
1	0	1	1	0	0
1	1	1	1	1	0

```
With ins select
    outs <= "0010" when "00";
            "1010" when "01";
            "1100" when "10";
            "1110" when others;
```

VHDL code for a seven-segment decoder is partially supplied below. The four inputs (representing a binary number) have been grouped into a vector called BIN, and the seven segment outputs have been grouped into a vector called SEG_OUT. Note the "when others" clause in the last line as is typical for any selected assignment statement. This catch-all "when others" clause is used to assign the value "0000001" to the seven segment decoder outputs whenever an unspecified input condition occurs. In this case, this clause can be used to assign an output value when the binary numbers 1010 through 1111 are present on the inputs.

```
entity seven_seg_dec is
        port (bin: in STD_LOGIC_VECTOR (3 downto 0);
              segout : out STD_LOGIC_VECTOR (6 downto 0));
end seven_seg_dec;

architecture behavioral of seven_seg_dec is
begin
        with bin select
            segout <=    "1111110" when "0000";
                         "0110000" when "0001";
                            ⋮

                         "0000001" when others;
end behavioral;
```

Example VHDL code for a Seven-Segment Decoder

Priority Encoders

A priority encoder is, in a sense, the dual (or opposite) of the decoder circuit—it receives N inputs (where N is typically 4, 8 or 16), and asserts an output binary code of $M=\log_2 N$ bits (so the M-bit binary code is typically 2, 3, or 4 bits). The M-bit binary code indicates which input was asserted (i.e., in a 4 : 2 binary encoder, binary code 00 would be output if the 0th input line was asserted, binary code 01 would be output of the 1st input line was asserted, etc.). Since more than one input line to the encoder might be asserted at any given time, the priority encoder asserts an output code corresponding to the highest numbered input that is asserted (i.e., if both input line 0 and input line 2 were asserted in a 4 : 2 encoder, then binary code 10 would be output indicating that input line 2 is the highest line number—or highest priority input—currently asserted).

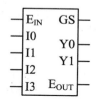

Priority Encoder

At first thought, a four input encoder circuit should require just two outputs. In such a circuit, asserting the 3rd input signal would cause a "11" output, asserting the 2nd input signal would output a "10", asserting the 1st input signal would output a "01", and asserting the 0th input would output "00". But what if no inputs are asserted? Again, a "00" would be appropriate. To avoid creating an ambiguous "00" output, encoders typically use an "Enable In" (E_{IN}) signal and an "Enable Output" (E_{OUT}) signal. E_{IN} functions like other enable signals—when it is de-asserted, all outputs are driven to logic "0", and when it is asserted, the encoder outputs can be driven by the inputs. E_{OUT} is asserted only when E_{IN} is asserted and no input signals are asserted. Thus, E_{OUT} can be used to distinguish between no inputs asserted and the 0th input asserted.

Larger encoders can be built from smaller encoder modules in much the same way that larger decoders can be built from smaller decoder modules. An encoder module that can be used as a building block for larger encoders must have one additional output called group-signal (GS). GS is asserted whenever E_{IN} is asserted along with any other input signal, and it is used to form the most significant bit of the encoded output data element.

Encoder circuits are typically used in digital systems when a binary number that corresponds to a given input must be generated. For example, individual "call attendant" signals arising from passengers seated on an airplane could be encoded into a seat number. Priority encoders are also used when certain input signals must be dealt with in a special manner. For example, if inputs from several sources can all arrive simultaneously, a priority encoder can indicate which signal should be dealt with first. Behavioral VHDL code for an encoder is shown below.

```
entity encoder is
    port (ein :              in std_logic;
          I :                in std_logic_vector (3 downto 0);
          eout, gs :         out std_logic;
          Y :                out std_logic_vector (1 downto 0));
    end encoder;

    architecture Behavioral of encoder is
    Begin
      eout <=ein and not I(3) and not I(2) and not I(1) and not I(0);
      gs <= ein and (I(3) or I(2) or I(1) or I(0));
      Y(1) <= I(3) or I(2);
      Y(0) <= I(3) or I(1);
    end Behavioral;
```

VHDL code for a priority encoder

Shifters

A shifter is a circuit that produces an N-bit output based on an N-bit data input and an M-bit control input, where the N output bits are place-shifted copies of the input bits, shifted some number of bits to the left or right as determined by the control inputs. As an example, the function of an 8-bit shifter capable of shifting one, two, or three bits to the right or left is illustrated in the top row of the figure below. The control signals enable several different functions: two bits (A_1 and A_0) to determine how many bit positions to shift (0, 1, 2, or 3); a Fill signal (F) determines whether bits vacated by shift operations receive a "1" or a "0"; a Rotate signal (R = "1" for rotate) determines whether shifted-out bits are discarded or recaptured in vacated bits; and a Direction signal (D = "1" for right) determines which direction the shift will take.

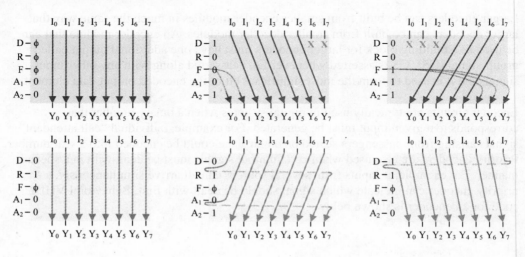

When bits are shifted left or right, some bits "fall off" one end of the shifter, and are simply discarded. New bits must then be shifted in from the opposite side. If no Fill input signal exists, then 0's are shifted in (otherwise, the Fill input defines whether 1's or 0's are shifted in to vacated bits). Shifters that offer a Rotate function recapture shifted-out bits in vacated bits as shown in the lower row of the figure above.

Based on the shifter functions Shift, Rotate, Direction, Fill, and Number of Bits, many different shifter circuits could be designed to operate on any number of inputs. As an example of a simple shifter design, the truth table on the right shows input/output requirements for a four-bit shifter that can shift or rotate an input value left or right by one bit (R=0 for shift, R=1 for rotate, D=0 for left, D=1 for right). Note the truth table uses entered variables to compress the number of rows that would otherwise be required. A minimal circuit can be found from this truth table using pencil-and-paper methods or a computer-based minimization program.

EN	R	D	Y_3	Y_2	Y_1	Y_0
0	ϕ	ϕ	0	0	0	0
1	0	0	I_2	I_1	I_0	0
1	0	1	0	I_3	I_2	I_1
1	1	0	I_2	I_1	I_0	I_3
1	1	1	I_0	I_3	I_2	I_1

Truth table for 4-bit shifter with shift/rotate left/right functions

Shifters are most often found in circuits that work with groups of signals that together represent binary numbers, where they are used to move data bits to new locations on a data bus (i.e., the data bit in position 2 could be moved to position 7 by right shifting five times), or to perform simple multiplication and division operations (exactly why a bit might want to be moved from one location to another on a data bus is left for a later module). A shifter circuit can multiply a number by 2, 4, or 8 simply by shifting the number right by 1, 2, or 3 bits (and similarly, a shifter can divide a number by 2, 4, or 8 by shifting the number left by 1, 2, or 3 bits).

A behavioral VHDL design of a simple 8-bit shifter that can shift or rotate left or right by one bit is shown below. A conditional assignment statement is used in this example as the only statement in the architecture body. The "when-else" clause evaluates the state of enable (en), rotate (r), and direction (d) to distinguish between the possible output vector signal assignments. The first assignment in the conditional assignment statement assigns all zero's to the dout bus when en="0". The remaining four assignments make use of the concatenation operator (&) to assign shifted or rotated versions of the input data bus to the output bus, depending on the states of r and d.

```
entity my_shift is
  port (din:      in std_logic_vector (7 downto 0);
        r, d, en: in std_logic;
        dout:     out std_logic_vector (7 downto 0));
end my_shift;

architecture my_shift_arch of my_shift is
begin
  dout <= "00000000" when en = '0' else
          din(6 downto 0) & din(7) when (r = '1' and d = '0') else
          din(0) & din(7 downto 1) when (r = '1' and d = '1') else
          din(6 downto 0) & '0' when (r = '0' and d = '0') else
          '0' & din(7 downto 1);
end my_shift_arch;
```

156

Exercise 6: Combinational Circuit Blocks

Problem 1. Explain why the stated LM circuit gate/input count of 12/37 for the figure in the module document is different than the sum-total number of gates and inputs for three LM circuits shown in the figure.

Problem 2. Complete the 4 : 1 mux circuit by sketching the missing wires.

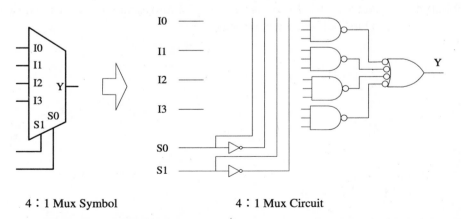

4 : 1 Mux Symbol   4 : 1 Mux Circuit

Contains material © Digilent, Inc.

Problem 3. Complete the truth table and circuit sketch for a 4 : 1 mux. When completing the truth table, make use of don't care's to reduce the number of required rows.

EN	S1	S0	Y

4 : 1 mux with enable truth table

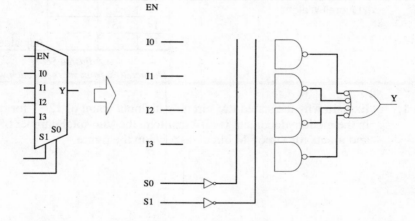

4 : 1 Mux with enable

Problem 4. Sketch an 8 : 1 mux using two 4 : 1 muxes and one 2 : 1 mux. Be sure to label all inputs and outputs.

158

Problem 5.   Compete a circuit sketch to show how

$$F = \sum m(0, 2, 4, 5, 6)$$

can be implemented using the mux shown.
(Hint: prepare an entered-variable K-map).

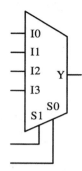

Problem 6.   Complete the 3 : 8 decoder schematic below by sketching the missing wires.

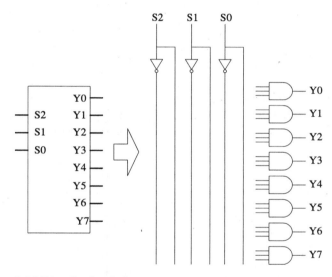

3 : 8 Decoder Symbol

3 : 8 Decoder Circuit

159

Problem 7. Complete the 3 : 8 decoder with enable schematic by sketching the missing wires.

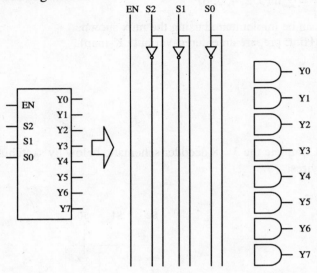

Problem 8. Complete the 4 : 16 decoder built from 4 2 : 4 decoders below by sketching the missing wires. Label all inputs and outputs.

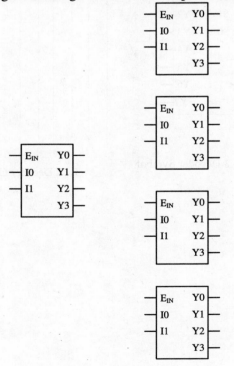

Problem 9.   Complete a sketch to show how the 3 ∶ 8 decoder can be used to implement the logic equation

$$F = \sum m(1, 2, 4, 6)$$

Decoder inputs and outputs are all asserted HIGH.

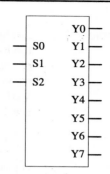

Problem 10.   Complete the truth table. The table shows the nine decimal digits, their binary equivalents, and seven columns labeled A–G. The columns labeled A–G can be used to record when a segment must be illuminated to display a given digit. For example, in the first row corresponding to the digit "0", segments A, B, C, D, E, and F must be illuminated, so a "1" must be placed in those columns. When completed, the table can serve as a truth table for the seven-segment controller—it shows the required logic relationship between the four inputs and seven outputs. Note that in the truth table, the last six input patterns (1010 through 1111) are not associated with a decimal digit. They are therefore "illegal" inputs, so outputs can receive a "don't care" for those rows.

Digit	Inputs 4-bit numbers				Outputs Segment-drive functions						
	B3	B2	B1	B0	A	B	C	D	E	F	G
0	0	0	0	0							
1	0	0	0	1							
2	0	0	1	0							
3	0	0	1	1							
4	0	1	0	0							
5	0	1	0	1							
6	0	1	1	0							
7	0	1	1	1							
8	1	0	0	0							
9	1	0	0	1							
NA	1	0	1	0							
NA	1	0	1	1							
NA	1	1	0	0							
NA	1	1	0	1							
NA	1	1	1	0							
NA	1	1	1	1							

Problem 11. Design a 7sd controller circuit using pencil-and-paper/schematic capture methods, or by creating a VHDL source file, your choice. If you have lots of spare time and choose schematic capture, complete the K-maps below, create a schematic in WebPack, and submit it. If you are sane and choose VHDL, leave the K-maps blank, and create and submit a VHDL source file.

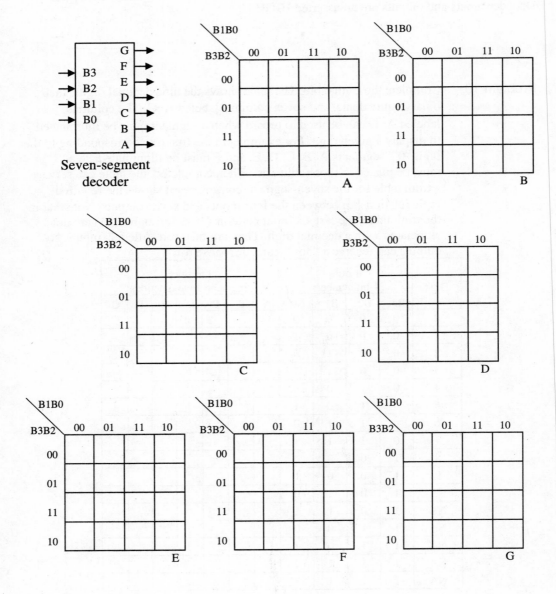

Problem 12. Complete the truth table below for a three-input priority encoder. When completing the truth table, note that if I3 is a "1", it DOES NOT matter what I2, I1, or I0 are—the encoded output will be "11". This information can result in don't cares in the truth table, which makes the design much easier (note that X's have been used in the truth table to indicate don't care input conditions). When the truth table is complete, transfer the information to the K-maps using E_{IN} as the entered-variable. Then use the K-maps to find minimal SOP equations. Note that although this is a five input, four output system, you may be able to find minimal circuits by inspecting the K-map, without resorting to the Digimin minimizer.

E_{IN}	I3	I2	I1	I0	GS	Y1	Y0	E_{OUT}
0	X	X	X	X	0	0	0	0
1	1	X	X	X				
1	0	1	X	X				
1	0	0	1	X				
1	0	0	0	1				
1	0	0	0	0	0	0	0	1

Priority encoder truth table

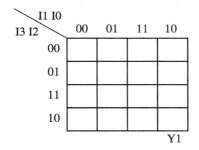

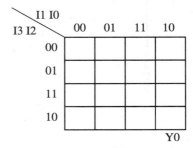

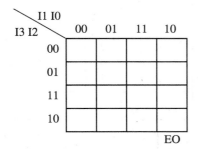

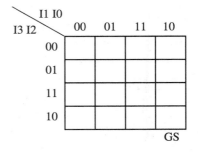

$Y1_{SOP}=$_____ $EO_{SOP}=$_____

$Y0_{SOP}=$_____ $GS_{SOP}=$_____

163

Problem 13. Complete the truth table for a 4-bit shifter that has no enable input, no rotate input, two inputs that dictate whether the input is to be shifted 0, 1, 2, or 3 bits, a direction input, and a fill input.

A1	A0	F	D	Y3	Y2	Y1	Y0

Problem 14. Complete the table below to show the numerical results from applying the indicated operation to the data shown. Opcodes are 6-bit numbers defined as shown below. R = 1 for Rotate; D = 1 for Right; F is fill, and A2–A0 define the number of bits. Show all work to be eligible for partial credit.

R	D	F	A2	A1	A0

Input$_{(Base10)}$	Input$_{(Base2/8-bit)}$	Op Code	Output$_{(Base10)}$	Output$_{(Base2/8-bit))}$
47	00101111	000011	188	10111100
96		110111		
16		011001		
111		100011		
63		001111		
188		110001		

Problem 15.   Modify only two characters in the code below to add a Fill bit.

```
entity my_shift is
    port (din:          in std_logic_vector (7 downto 0);
          r, d, f, en:  in std_logic;
          dout:         out std_logic_vector (7 downto 0));
end my_shift;

architecture my_shift_arch of my_shift is
begin
  dout <= "00000000" when en = '0' else
     din(6 downto 0) & din(7) when (r = '1' and d = '0') else
     din(0) & din(7 downto 1) when (r = '1' and d = '1') else
     din(6 downto 0) & '0' when (r = '0' and d = '0') else
     '0' & din(7 downto 1);
end my_shift_arch;
```

Lab Project 6: Combinational Circuit Blocks

STUDENT

I am submitting my own work, and I understand penalties will be assessed if I submit work for credit that is not my own.

Print Name ______________ ID Number ______________

Sign Name ______________ Date ______________

Estimated Work Hours

1	2	3	4	5	6	7	8	9	10

1	2	3	4	5	6	7	8	9	10

Overall Weight

Point Scale

4: Exemplary
3: Complete
2: Incomplete
1: Minor effort
0: Not submitted

20% will be deducted from scores for each week late
Score=Points awarded (Pts)× Weight (Wt)

LAB ASSISTANT

#	Demonstration	Wt	Pts	Late	Score	Lab Asst Signature	Date
2	Circuit demo	3					
3	Circuit demo	3					
5	Circuit demo	3					

Total In-Lab Score: NA

GRADER

#	Attachments	Wt	Pts	Score
1	VHDL source, test bench, and simulation	2		
2	VHDL source, test bench, and simulation	3		
3	VHDL source, test bench, and simulation	3		
4	VHDL source, test bench and simulation	3		
5	VHDL source, test bench and simulation	3		

Weeks late	Total Grading Score		Total Score
		Total score is In-lab score plus grading score	

Lab Project 6: Combinational Circuit Blocks

Problem 1.   Create a VHDL source file for a circuit that behaves according to the requirements shown by the K-map below. Simulate the circuit using a VHDL test bench, and print and submit the VHDL source files and the simulation output.

A \ BC	00	01	11	10
0	D	D or E	E xor F	E xnor F
1	not D	D nand E	1	0

Problem 2.   Design and implement mux/de-mux circuit using the Xilinx tools and the Digilent board that can communicate 8 data signals using only 4 wires. Use three slide switch inputs to select the data channel, four buttons to form the eight required data channel inputs, and 8 LEDs to show the output. The eight inputs are formed from the four buttons as follows: I0 = BTN1; I1 = BTN2; I2 = BTN3; I3 = BTN4; I4 = BTN1 and BTN2; I5 = BTN2 and BTN3; I6 = BTN3 and BTN4; and I7 = BTN4 and BTN1. After the circuit design is complete, simulate the circuit, download it to the Digilent board, and demonstrate it to the lab assistant. Print and submit the source and simulation files.

Problem 3.   Design and implement a "bin2hex" seven-segment decoder circuit that can drive a single digit on the 4-digit 7sd device on the Digilent board. Your decoder should display the decimal digits 0–9 for bit patterns 0000–1001, and A–F for bit patterns 1010–1111 (you will need to get a little bit creative to show all the hex digits—think about lower-case letters). Use four slide switches as inputs to select the pattern to be displayed. Recall you will need to drive the anode signal of the digit you wish to use to GND (you can drive the others to Vdd to ensure they are off—note that if you drive all anode signals to GND, then all four digits will show the same pattern). Demonstrate your circuit to the lab assistant, and print and submit the VHDL source files. (Note: The circuits for parts a and b can both be loaded into the board at the same time, if you wish).

Problem 4.   Use the Xilinx tools to define and simulate a 8-3 priority encoder with Enable In, Enable Out, and Group Signal. Submit your source and simulation files.

Problem 5. Use the Xilinx tools to define and simulate an 8-bit shifter in VHDL that can shift or rotate left or right by 0, 1, 2, or 3 bit positions. Implement this circuit in the Digilent board, Use the 8 slide switches as inputs to the shifter, and 8 LEDs as outputs from the shifter. Use the pushbuttons to control the functions of the shifter. Demonstrate your circuit to the lab assistant, and print and submit your source and simulation files.

Chapter 7: Combinational Arithmetic Circuits

1. Overview

This chapter examines several combinational circuits that perform arithmetic operations on binary numbers, including adders, subtractors, multipliers, and comparators. Arithmetic circuits typically combine two or more data busses of 8, 16 or 32 bits to produce outputs that use similar sized busses. They present special design challenges, because there are simply too many inputs to list all possible combinations in a truth table (for example, a circuit combining two 8-bit busses would require a truth table with 2^{16} or 650,000 rows). This chapter introduces a divide-and-conquer design method known as the "bit slice" method that is well suited to arithmetic circuit design, as well as to any other circuit that operates on binary number inputs. In applying this method, bus-wide operations are broken into simpler bit-by-bit operations that are more easily defined by truth-tables, and more tractable to familiar design techniques. The major challenge lies in discovering just how a given problem can be decomposed into bit-wise operations.

This lab also introduces structural VHDL design, which closely parallels schematic-based design in concept and in method. Structural VHDL designs are hierarchical, with high-level designs constructed from smaller, independently designed VHDL entity-architecture design units. As with schematic design, signals from lower-level design units can connect to overall circuit input and output signals, or to internal signals that are not visible outside the current level of hierarchy. Special VHDL statements are used to declare and instantiate components, and to define internal signals. Structural methods are often used on larger designs where pre-existing circuit blocks might already exist, or when detailed simulation studies are required.

Special attention is focused on a circuit that combines many previously encountered designs and techniques. This circuit, known as an "arithmetic and logic unit", or ALU, is found at the core of computing circuits. At first glance, an ALU design seems complex and involved, but as you will see, the design is actually a straightforward application of circuits and methods already encountered. The challenge lies in thoroughly understanding the design problem before beginning any design activities, and in following a disciplined, step-by-step design approach.

Before beginning this chapter, you should:	After completing this chapter, you should:

Before beginning this chapter, you should:

- Be able to add, subtract, and multiply binary numbers;
- Be able to enter and simulate circuits using schematic and VHDL methods in the ISE/WebPack tool;
- Be able to download circuits to the Digilent board;
- Be familiar with design of basic combinational circuit blocks.

After completing this chapter, you should:

- Know how to design circuits using structural VHDL methods;
- Know when and how to apply the bit-slice design method;
- Understand how comparators, adders, subtractors, and multipliers work, and be able to design them using schematics or VHDL.

This chapter requires:

- A windows computer running the Xilinx WebPack tools;
- The Digilent circuit board.

2. Background

The Bit-Slice Design Method

When designing circuits with bussed inputs that represent binary numbers, it is often easier to consider a circuit designed for a single pair of bits, rather than for the entire binary number. The reason is straightforward—a truth table describing a circuit operating on two 8-bit busses requires 65K rows, whereas a circuit operating on a single pair of bits requires only four rows. When considering a design for a single pair of bits, the goal is to create a circuit that can simply be replicated N times—once for each bit.

Many circuits that operate on binary numbers can be easily broken down into smaller, bit-wise operations. Some circuits defy this approach, and a bit-by-bit requirements analysis does not indicate any

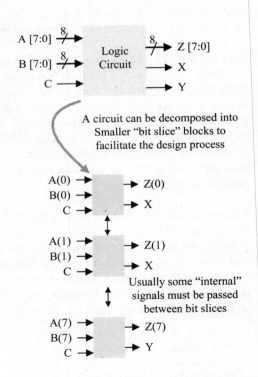

A circuit can be decomposed into Smaller "bit slice" blocks to facilitate the design process

Usually some "internal" signals must be passed between bit slices likely bit-slice solutions (e.g., some circuits that convert one type of data code to another fall in this category). Thus, the first goal in applying the bit-slice design method is to determine whether it is possible to express a given problem as an assemblage of bit-wise operations.

In a typical bit slice design, information must be passed between adjacent bits. For example, in a circuit that can add two binary numbers, any pair of bits may generate a "carry out" to the next more significant bit pair. Any such inter-slice dependencies must be identified and included in the design of the bit-slice module. Dealing with these additional "internal" signals may require some additional gates that would not have been needed in a non-bit slice design. But most often, the additional gates are a very small price to pay for enabling a more practicable design approach. All of the designs in this lab will use the bit-slice design approach.

Comparators

A magnitude comparator is device that receives two N-bit inputs and asserts one of three possible outputs depending on whether one input is greater than, less than, or equal to the other (simpler comparators, called equality comparators, provide a single output that is

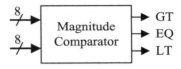

asserted whenever the two inputs are equal). Comparators are readily described in behavioral VHDL, but they are somewhat more difficult to design using structural or schematic methods. In fact, comparator design is an excellent vehicle to showcase the power of behavioral design, and the relative tedium of structural design.

Comparators are described in behavioral VHDL using the greater-than and less-than operators (> and <, respectively) as shown in the code below. Note the "inout" mode used in the port statement for the GT and LT output port signals. The inout mode is required whenever an output port signal also must be used within the architecture on the *right side* of an assignment statement. In next-to-last line in the example, both the GT and LT

outputs are used on the right side of the assignment operator to form the EQ output, and thus, the GT and LT signals are *inputs* to the EQ assignment statement. If GT and LT were simply declared as "out" mode types, the VHDL analyzer would generate an error.

A structural comparator design is best attacked using the bit-slice method. Consider an 8-bit magnitude comparator circuit that creates the GT, LT, and EQ

```
entity my_comp is
  port ( A, B : in std_logic_vector (7 downto 0);
         gt, lt : inout std_logic;
         eq    : out std_logic);
end my_comp;


architecture behavioral of my_comp is
Begin
  Y <=   gt <= '1' when  A > B else '0';
         lt <= '1' when A < B else '0';
         eq <= not gt and not lt;
end behavioral;
```

output signals for two 8-bit operands. In the illustration below, if A=159 and B=155 are presented to the comparator, then the GT output should be asserted, and the LT and EQ outputs should be de-asserted. The operand bits are equal in all slices except the bit 2 slice. Somehow, the inequality in the bit 2 slice must influence the overall circuit outputs, forcing GT to a "1" and LT and EQ to a "0". Any bit pair could show an inequality, and any bit-slice module design must work in any bit position.

Clearly, a bit-slice design cannot work in isolation, using only the two data bits as inputs. A bit-slice design must take into account information generated from neighboring bit-slices. Specifically, each comparator bit-slice must receive not only the two operand input bits, but also the GT, LT, and EQ outputs of its less-significant bit neighbor. In the present example, the bit 3 slice in isolation would assert the EQ output, but the inequality in the bit 2 slice should force the bit 3 slice to assert GT and de-assert both EQ and LT. In fact, the outputs from any stage where the operand bits are equal depend on the inputs arising from the neighboring stage.

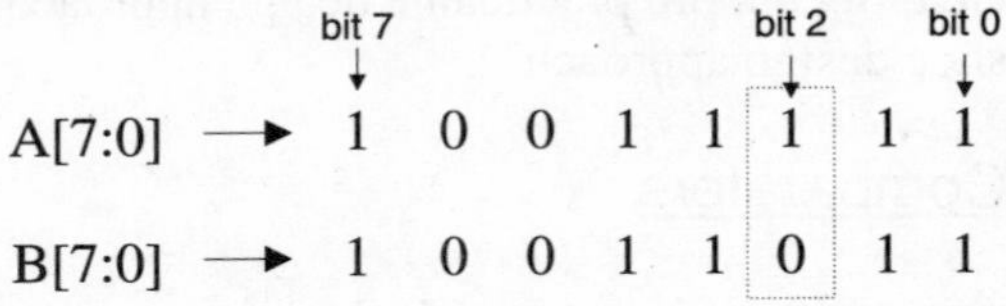

$$\begin{array}{c} \text{bit 7} \\ \downarrow \end{array} \qquad \begin{array}{c} \text{bit 2} \\ \downarrow \end{array} \quad \begin{array}{c} \text{bit 0} \\ \downarrow \end{array}$$

A[7:0] $\longrightarrow$ 1 0 0 1 1 1 1 1

B[7:0] $\longrightarrow$ 1 0 0 1 1 0 1 1

A bit-slice magnitude comparator circuit must have five inputs and three outputs as shown in the truth table. As with any combinational design, the truth table completely specifies the required comparator bit-slice behavior. Normally, a truth table for a five-input function would require 32 rows. The 8-row truth table on the right is adequate because certain input combinations are not

Operand inputs		Inputs from neighboring slices			Bit-slice outputs		
An	Bn	GTI	LTI	EQI	GTO	LTO	EQO
0	0	1	0	0	1	0	0
0	0	0	1	0	0	1	0
0	0	0	0	1	0	0	1
0	1	φ	φ	φ	0	1	0
1	0	φ	φ	φ	1	0	0
1	1	1	0	0	1	0	0
1	1	0	1	0	0	1	0
1	1	0	0	1	0	0	1

possible (i.e., the inputs from the neighboring slice are mutually exclusive), and others are immaterial (i.e., if the current operand inputs show A > B, the neighboring slice inputs do not matter). You are encouraged to examine the truth table in detail, and convince yourself that you agree with the information it contains.

The truth table can be used to find a minimal bit-slice comparator circuit using pencil-and-paper methods or computer-based methods. Either way, a bit-slice circuit with the block diagram shown in the figure below can be designed. Once designed, a bit slice circuit can be used in an N-bit comparator as shown. Note that for the N-bit comparator, no neighbor bit-slice exists for the least-significant bits—those non-existent bits are assumed to be equal. Note also that the overall comparator output arises from the outputs from the most-significant bit pair. In the exercises and lab project that accompany this chapter, you are asked to design a comparator bit-slice design as well as an 8-bit comparator circuit.

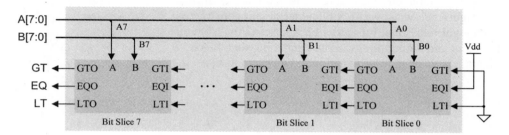

Adders

Adder circuits add two N-bit operands to produce an N-bit result and a carry out signal (the carry out is a "1" only when the addition result requires more than N bits). The basic adding circuit is one of the cornerstones of digital system design, and it has been used in countless applications since the earliest days of digital engineering. The simplest adding circuit performs addition in much the same way that humans do, performing the operation "right to left", bit-by-bit from the LSB to the MSB. Like any circuit that deals with signals grouped as binary numbers, the simplest adding circuit can most easily be designed using the bit-slice approach. By focusing on the requirements for adding a single pair of bits from two N-bit binary numbers, an otherwise complex design challenge can be divided into a more tractable problem. Once a circuit that can add any pair of bits has been designed, that circuit can be replicated N times to create an N-bit adder.

The logic graph below shows the eight different cases that may be encountered when adding two binary numbers. The highlighted bit pairs and the associated carries show that a bit-slice adder circuit must process three inputs (the two addend bits and a carry-in from the previous stage) and produce two outputs (the sum bit and a carry out bit). In the exercises and lab project, you are asked to create a truth table and circuit for various adding circuits.

Cin \ A B	0 0	0 1	1 1	1 0	
0	**0 0** ↑ ↑ …0 0 1 0… +…1 0 0 0… …1 0 1 0…	**0 0** ↑ ↑ …0 0 1 0… +…1 1 0 0… …1 1 1 0…	**1 0** ↑ ↑ …0 1 1 0… +…1 1 0 0… …0 0 1 0…	**0 0** ↑ ↑ …0 1 1 0… +…1 0 0 0… …1 1 1 0…	Inputs ▨ Outputs ▨
1	**0 1** ↑ ↑ …0 0 1 0… +…1 0 1 0… …1 1 0 0…	**1 1** ↑ ↑ …0 0 1 0… +…1 1 1 0… …0 0 0 0…	**1 1** ↑ ↑ …0 1 1 0… +…1 1 1 0… …0 1 0 0…	**1 1** ↑ ↑ …0 1 1 0… +…1 0 1 0… …0 0 0 0…	

A block diagram for the bit-slice circuit is shown on the right, and it is called a Full Adder (FA). Full adders can be used to assemble circuits that can add any number of bits. The figure below shows an 8-bit adder circuit constructed from eight individual full-adder bit-slice circuits. Note that the input and output pin locations on the bit-slice block diagram have been re-arranged in the diagram to make the drawing more convenient.

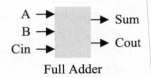

Full Adder

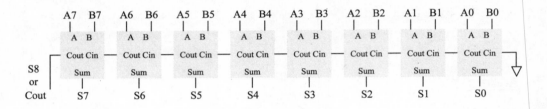

The carry-out generated in the very first stage of an 8-bit adder must "ripple" through all seven higher-order stages before a valid 9-bit sum can be produced. It is this need to ripple carry information from one bit-slice to the next that gives the adder its name—the Ripple Carry Adder (RCA). This slice-by-slice processing of carry information severely limits the speed at which an RCA can run. Consider for example an 8-bit RCA adding A = "11111010" and B = "10001110", and then consider that the least-significant-bit (LSB) of the B operand switches from a "0" to a "1". In order for all nine bits of the adder to show the correct answer, carry information from the LSB must ripple through all eight full adders. If each full adder requires, say, 1 nanosecond (ns) to create the sum and carry-out bits after an input changes, then an 8-bit RCA will require up to 8ns to create an accurate answer (8ns is the worst-case situation, which occurs when an operand LSB change requires the S8 output bit to change). If an 8-bit addition in a computer circuit requires 8ns, then the computer's maximum operating frequency would be the reciprocal of 8ns, or 125MHz. Most computers today are 32bits—a 32bit addition using an RCA would require 32ns, limiting the computers operating frequency to no more than about 33MHz. An RCA circuit is too slow for many applications—a faster adder circuit is needed.

Note the carry-in of the RCA LSB is connected directly to ground, because (by definition) the carry-in to the LSB of any adder must be logic 0. It is possible to capitalize on this observation, and create a smaller bit-slice circuit for use in the LSB position that does not have a carry-in input. Called a Half-Adder (HA), this reduced-function adder circuit is often used in the LSB position.

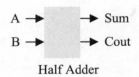

Half Adder

The carry-look-ahead adder (CLA) overcomes the speed limitations of the RCA by using a different circuit to determine carry information. The CLA uses a simpler bit-slice module, and all carry-forming logic is placed in a separate circuit called the "Carry Propagate/Generate (CPG) circuit. The CPG circuit receives carry-forming outputs from all bit-slices in parallel (i.e., at the same time), and forms all carry-in signals to all bit-slices at the same time. Since all carry signals for all bit positions are determined at the same time, addition results are generated much faster.

Since a CLA also deals with signals grouped as binary numbers, the bit slice approach is again indicated. Our goal is to re-examine binary number addition to identify how and where carry information is generated and propagated, and then to exploit that new knowledge in an improved circuit.

The figure below shows the same eight addition cases as were presented in the first figure. Note that in just two of the cases (3 and 7), a carry out is generated. Also note that in four cases, a carry that was previously generated will propagate through the current pair of bits, asserting a carry out even though the current bits by themselves would not have created a carry.

A B	0 0	0 1	1 1	1 0	
Cin					Inputs
	0 0	**0 0**	**1 0**	**0 0**	
0	...0 0 1 0...	...0 0 1 0...	...0 1 1 0...	...0 1 1 0...	No carry out
	+...1 0 0 0...	+...1 1 0 0...	+...1 1 0 0...	+...1 0 0 0...	possible
	...1 0 1 0...	...1 1 1 0...	...0 0 1 0...	...1 1 1 0...	
					Propagates
	...0 0 1 0...	...0 0 1 0...	...0 1 1 0...	...0 1 1 0...	carry-in to
	...1 0 1 0...	...1 1 1 0...	...1 1 1 0...	...1 0 1 0...	carry-out
	...1 1 0 0...	...0 0 0 0...	...0 1 0 0...	...0 0 0 0...	
					Generates

Based on these observations, we can define two intermediate signals related to the carry out: carry generate (or G); and carry propagate (or P). G is asserted whenever a new carry is generated by the current set of inputs (i.e., when both operand inputs are a "1"), and P is asserted whenever a previously generated carry will be propagated through the current pair of bits (whenever either operand is a "1"). Based on this discussion, a truth table for the CLA bit-slice module can be completed (and you are asked to do so in the exercises).

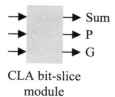

CLA bit-slice
module

The CLA bit-slice module generates the P and G outputs instead of a carry out bit. Note that a carry-out from the ith stage in an RCA, written as $C_{i+1} = C_i \cdot (A_i \text{ XOR } B_i) + A_i \cdot B_i$, can be written as

$C_{i+1} = C_i \cdot P_i + G_i$ in the CLA. Since the carry-ins to each bit-slice in a CLA arise from the carry out (in terms of P and G) from the previous stage, the carry-ins to each stage can be written as:

0th stage: Cin = C0   (C0 is the carry-in to the 0th stage)
1st stage: C1   = C0·P0 + G0

2rd stage: C2 = C1·P1 + G1

                        = (C0·P0 + G0) · P1 + G1

                        = C0·P1·P0 + G0·P1 + G1

3rd stage: C3 = C2·P2 + G2

                        = ((C0·P0 + G0) · P1 + G1) · P2 + G2

                        = C0·P2·P1 ·P0 + G0·P2·P1 + G1·P2 + G2

4th stage: = etc. –   the equations can be expanded to any number of stages.

Restated in written form, carry-ins to the first few CLA bit-slices are formed as follows:

0th stage: Cin is simply connected to the overall, global carry in (called C0).

1st stage: Cin is "1" if a carry is generated in stage 0, or if a carry is propagated in stage 0 and C0 is "1".

2nd stage: Cin is "1" if a carry is generated in stage 1, or if a carry is propagated in stage 1 and generated in stage 0, or if a carry is propagated in stages 1 and 0 and C0 is a "1".

3rd stage: Cin is "1" if a carry is generated in stage 2, or if a carry is propagated in stage 2 and generated in stage 1, or if a carry is propagated in stages 2 and 1 and generated in stage 0, or if a carry is propagated in stages 2, 1, and 0 and C0 was a "1".

4th stage: The pattern continues for any number of stages.

The carry-in logic equations for each stage are implemented in the CPG circuit block shown below. A complete CLA adder requires the CLA bit-slice modules and the CGP circuit. This complete CLA circuit involves a bit more design work than the RCA, but because the CGP circuit drives the carry-in of each CLA bit-slice module in parallel, it avoids the excessive delays associated with the RCA. You have the opportunity to design and implement a CLA circuit in the lab project.

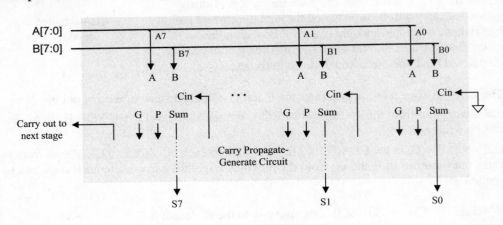

Subtractors

Subtracting circuits use two N-bit operands to produce an N-bit result and a borrow out signal. Subtractor circuits are rarely encountered in digital systems (for reasons that will be explained later), but they nevertheless provide an interesting design opportunity. Like adders, the simplest subtracting circuits perform subtraction bit-by-bit from the LSB to the MSB, and they are most easily designed using the bit-slice approach. The design process closely follows adder design, in that sample subtraction problems can be studied to gain insight into subtractor requirements, a truth table can be prepared based on the observations, and then a circuit can be designed from the truth table. Once a bit-slice subtractor circuit has been designed, it can be replicated N time to create an N-bit subtractor.

The full-subtractor circuit differs only slightly from the full-adder, in that the subtractor requires two inverters that are not needed by the adder. The full-subtractor can be used to build a "Ripple Borrow Subtractor" that can subtract any two N-bit numbers, but RBS circuits suffer from the same slow operation as RCA circuits. Other, more efficient subtractor architectures are possible. But it is also possible to make a slight modification to an adder circuit, and then to use the modified adder as a subtractor. Following this method, if the number to be subtracted (the subtrahend) is made negative, then it can simply be added to the minuend (the minuend is number from which the subtrahend is to be subtracted). As an example, the operation "5−3" can be written as "5 + (−3)". This, of course, requires a method of representing negative numbers in a digital circuit.

Negative Numbers

Digital systems have a fixed number of signals that can be used to represent binary numbers. Smaller, simpler systems might use 8-bit buses that can only represent 256 different binary numbers, while larger systems might use 16, 32, or even 64 bit busses. Whatever the number of bits, all systems have a finite number of wires, storage elements, and processing elements to represent and manipulate digital data. The number of available bits determines how many different numbers can be represented in a given system. Digital circuits that perform arithmetic functions often must deal with negative numbers, so a method of representing negative numbers must be defined. An N-bit system can represent 2^N total numbers, so an useful encoding would use half the available codes (i.e., $2^N/2$) to represent positive numbers, and half negative numbers. A single bit can be designated as a "sign bit" to distinguish positive and negative numbers—if the sign bit is "1", the number is negative; if the sign bit is "0", positive. The most-significant-bit (MSB) is a good choice for the sign bit, because if it is a "0" (indicating a positive number), then it can simply be ignored when figuring the number's magnitude.

Of all possible encodings of negative numbers, two have been used most often: signed magnitude, and 2's compliment. Signed magnitude representations simply designate the MSB as the sign bit, and the remaining bits as magnitude. In an 8-bit signed-magnitude system, "16" would be represented as "00010000", and "−16" as "10010000". This system is easy for humans to interpret, but it has a major disadvantage for digital circuits: if the 0 to 2^N count range is traversed from smallest to largest, then the largest positive number appears halfway through the range, followed immediately by the smallest negative number. Further, the largest negative number appears at the end of the range (at binary number 2^N), and counting once more results in "rollover", since the number 2^N+1 cannot be represented. Thus, 0 follows 2^N in the count range, so the largest negative number is immediately adjacent to the smallest positive number. Because of this, a simple operation like "2−3", which requires counting backwards from two three times, will not yield the expected result of "−1", but rather the largest negative number in the system. A better system would place the smallest positive and negative numbers immediately adjacent to one another in the count range, and this is precisely what the 2's compliment representation does. The number wheels below illustrate signed-magnitude and 2's compliment encodings for 8-bit numbers.

In 2's compliment encoding, the MSB still functions as a sign bit—it is always "1" for a negative number, and "0" for a positive number. The 2's compliment code has a single "0"

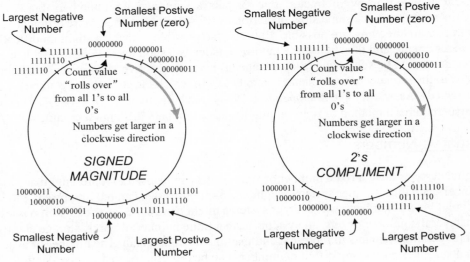

Number wheels illustrating signed magnitude and 2's complement encodings for negative numbers

value, defined by a bit pattern containing all 0's (including the leading "0"). This leaves 2^N-1 codes to represent all non-zero numbers, both positive and negative. Since 2^N-1 is an odd number, we end up with $(2^N-1)/2$ negative numbers, and $(2^N-1)/2-1$ positive numbers (since "0" uses one of the available codes for a positive number). In other words, we can represent one more non-zero negative number than positive, and the magnitude of the largest negative number is one greater than the magnitude of the largest positive number.

The disadvantage to 2's compliment encoding is that negative numbers are not easily interpreted by humans (e.g., is it clear that "11110100" represents a−12?). A simple algorithm exists for converting a positive number to a 2's compliment-encoded negative number of the same magnitude, and for converting a 2's compliment-encoded negative number to a positive number of the same magnitude. The algorithm, illustrated in examples below, requires inverting all bits of the number to be converted, and then adding "1" to the resulting bit pattern. The algorithm can be visualized in the 2's compliment number wheel above by noting that "inverting all bits" reflects a number around an axis drawn through "0" and the largest negative number, and "adding one" compensates for the 2's compliment code containing one more negative code than positive code.

$$0\ 0\ 0\ 1\ 0\ 0\ 0\ 1\ =\ 17\ \rightarrow \textit{Convert to}-17$$

$$1\ 1\ 1\ 0\ 1\ 1\ 1\ 0 \quad \text{(1) Invert all bits}$$

$$+\ 0\ 0\ 0\ 0\ 0\ 0\ 0\ 1 \quad \text{(2) Add one}$$

$$\boxed{1\ 1\ 1\ 0\ 1\ 1\ 1\ 1}\ =\ -17$$

$$1\ 1\ 0\ 1\ 1\ 1\ 0\ 1\ =\ -35\ \rightarrow \textit{Convert to +35}$$

$$0\ 0\ 1\ 0\ 0\ 0\ 1\ 0 \quad \text{(1) Invert all bits}$$

$$+\ 0\ 0\ 0\ 0\ 0\ 0\ 0\ 1 \quad \text{(2) Add one}$$

$$\boxed{0\ 0\ 1\ 0\ 0\ 0\ 1\ 1}\ =\ 35$$

$$1\ 0\ 0\ 0\ 0\ 0\ 0\ 1\ =\ -127\ \rightarrow \textit{Convert to +127}$$

$$0\ 1\ 1\ 1\ 1\ 1\ 1\ 0 \quad \text{(1) Invert all bits}$$

$$+\ 0\ 0\ 0\ 0\ 0\ 0\ 0\ 1 \quad \text{(2) Add one}$$

$$\boxed{0\ 1\ 1\ 1\ 1\ 1\ 1\ 1}\ =\ 127$$

$$0\ 0\ 0\ 0\ 0\ 0\ 0\ 1\ =\ 1\ \rightarrow \textit{Convert to }-1$$

$$1\ 1\ 1\ 1\ 1\ 1\ 1\ 0 \quad \text{(1) Invert all bits}$$

$$+\ 0\ 0\ 0\ 0\ 0\ 0\ 0\ 1 \quad \text{(2) Add one}$$

$$\boxed{1\ 1\ 1\ 1\ 1\ 1\ 1\ 1}\ =\ -1$$

Adder/Subtractors

An adder circuit can easily be modified with a combinational logic circuit that can selectively implement the 2's compliment encoding of one of the input binary numbers. Recall that a two-input XOR gate can be used as a "controlled inverter", where one of the inputs is passed through to the output either inverted or unchanged, based on the logic level of the second "control" input. If XOR gates are included on all bits of one of the operand inputs to an adder, then driving the XOR "control" input to a "1" will invert all bits. If that same control input is also

Control	Y
0	A
1	$\overline{A}$

179

connected to the Cin input to the adder, then a "1" is added to the inverted bits, which results in that input being converted to a 2's compliment-encoded number. Thus, the adder is summing a positive number with a negative number, which is the same as subtraction. you are asked to implement an adder subtractor in the lab project.

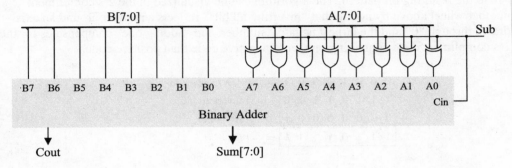

When designed from truth-tables and K-maps, a full subtractor is very similar to a full adder, but it contains two inverters that a full adder does not. When configured to subtract, an adder/subtractor circuit adds a single inverter (in the form of an XOR gate) to one input of a full adder module. A ripple borrow subtractor performs the same function as an adder/subtractor in subtract mode, but the two circuits are different as shown below. The differences can be explained by noting the carry-in to the LSB of the adder/subtractor must be set to a "1" to form the 2's complement coding of the operand, but it takes some thought to convince yourself. In the exercises, you are asked to demonstrate how the circuit structures of a ripple-carry adder circuit configured as a 2's compliment subtractor and a ripple-borrow subtractor perform identical functions.

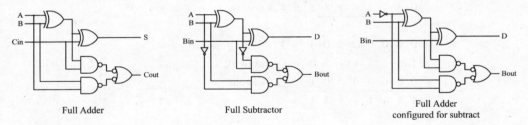

| Full Adder | Full Subtractor | Full Adder configured for subtract |

Adder Overflow

When performing arithmetic operations on numbers that must use a fixed number of bits, it is possible to create a result that requires more bits than are available. For example, if the two 8-bit numbers 240 and 25 are added, the result 265 cannot be represented as an 8-bit binary number. When numbers are combined and the result requires more bits than are available, overflow (for positive results) or underflow (for negative results) errors occur. Although underflow and overflow errors cannot be prevented, they can be detected.

The behavioral requirements for an overflow/underflow detect circuit can be defined by examining several examples of addition overflow and subtraction underflow. In the simplest case, the carry-in to the MSB can be compared to the carry out of the same bit. But it is also possible to detect an overflow/underflow condition without needing access to the carry-in of the MSB. In the exercise and lab project, you are asked to design circuits that can output a "1" whenever an addition or subtraction result is incorrect due to underflow or overflow.

Hardware Multipliers

Hardware multipliers, based directly on adder architectures, have become indispensable in modern computers. Multiplier circuits are modeled after the "shift and add" algorithm as shown below. In this algorithm, one partial product is created for each bit in the multiplier—the first partial product is created by the LSB of the multiplier, the second partial product is created by the second bit in the multiplier, etc. Partial products are a copy of the multiplicand if the corresponding multiplier bit is a "1", and all 0's if the corresponding multiplier bit is "0". Each successive partial product is shifted one bit position to the left.

```
        1 0 0 1      Multiplicand
      × 1 0 1 1      Multiplier
      ---------
        1 0 0 1  ⎫
      1 0 0 1    ⎬   Partial
    0 0 0 0      ⎪   Products
  1 0 0 1        ⎭
  -------------
  1 1 0 0 0 1 1      Result
```

This specific multiplication example is recast in a generalized example on the left below. Each input, partial product digit, and result have been given a logical name, and these same names are used as signal names in the circuit schematics. By comparing the signal names in the multiplication example with the schematics, the behavior of the multiply circuit can be confirmed.

```
                 A3  A2  A1  A0
               × B3  B2  B1  B0
               ----------------
                P03 P02 P01 P00
            P13 P12 P11 P10
        P23 P22 P21 P20
    P33 P32 P31 P30
--------------------------------
R3  R2  R1  R0  R3  R2  R1  R0
```

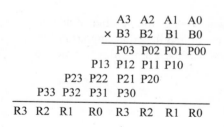

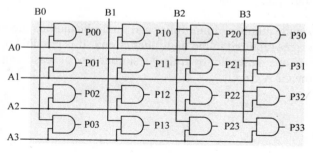

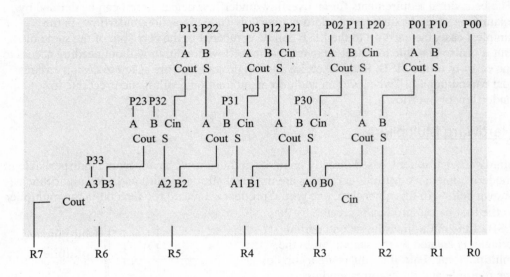

In the circuit above, each bit in the multiplier is AND'ed with each bit in the multiplicand to form the corresponding partial product bits. The partial product bits are fed to an array of full adders (and half adders where appropriate), with the adders shifted to the left as indicated by the multiplication example. The final partial products are added with a CLA circuit. Note that some full-adder circuits bring signal values into the carry-in inputs (instead of carry's from the neighboring stage). This is a valid use of the full-adder circuit; the full adder simply adds any three bits applied to its inputs. You are encouraged to work through a few examples on your own to confirm the adder array and CLA work together to properly sum the partial products. In the lab project, you are asked to implement a multiplier circuit.

As the number of multiplier and multiplicand bits increase, so does the number of adder stages required in the multiplier circuit. It is possible to develop a faster adding array for use in a multiplier by follow a similar line of reasoning as was used in the development of the CLA circuit.

ALU Circuits

Arithmetic and Logic Units (or ALUs) are found at the core of microprocessors, where they implement the arithmetic and logic functions offered by the processor (e.g., addition, subtraction, AND'ing two values, etc.). An ALU is a combinational circuit that combines many common logic circuits in one block. Typically, ALU inputs are comprised of two N-bit busses, a carry-in, and M select lines that select between the 2^M ALU operations. ALU outputs include an N-bit bus for function output and a carry out.

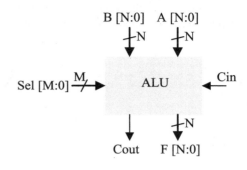

ALUs can be designed to perform a variety of different arithmetic and logic functions. Possible arithmetic functions include addition, subtraction, multiplication, comparison, increment, decrement, shift, and rotate; possible logic functions include AND, OR, XOR, XNOR, INV, CLR (for clear), and PASS (for passing a value unchanged). All of these functions find use in computing systems, although a complete description of their use is beyond the scope of this document. An ALU could be designed to include all of these functions, or a subset could be chosen to meet the specific needs of a given application. Either way, the design process is similar (but simpler for an ALU with fewer functions).

As an example, we will consider the design of an ALU that can perform one of eight functions on 8-bit data values. This design, although relatively simple, is not unlike many of ALUs that have been designed over the years for all sizes and performance ranges of processors. Our ALU will feature two 8-bit data inputs, an 8-bit data output, a carry-in and a carry out, and three function select inputs (S2, S1, S0) providing selection between eight operations (three arithmetic, four logic, and a clear or "0").

Targeted ALU operations are shown in the operation table. The three control bits used to select the ALU operation are called the "operation code" (or Op Code), because if this ALU were used in an actual microprocessor, these bits would come from the "opcodes" (or machine codes) that form the actual low-level computer programming code. (Computer software today is typically written in a high-level language like "C", which is compiled into assembler code. Assembler code can be directly translated into machine codes that cause the microprocessor to perform particular functions).

Op Code	Function
000	A PLUS B
001	A PLUS 1
010	A MINUS B
011	0
100	A XOR B
101	A'
110	A OR B
111	A AND B

Since ALUs operate on binary numbers, the bit-slice design method is indicated. ALU design should follow the same process as other bit-slice designs: first, define and understand all inputs and outputs of a bit slice (i.e., prepare a detailed block diagram of the bit slice); second, capture the required logical relationships in some formal method (e.g., a truth table); third, find minimal circuits (by using K-maps or espresso) or write VHDL code; and fourth, proceed with circuit design and verification.

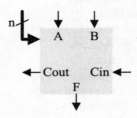

Op Code	Function	F	Cout
000	A PLUS B	A XOR B XOR CIN	(A AND B) OR (Cin AND (A XOR B))
001	A PLUS 1	A XOR CIN	A AND Cin
010	A MINUS B	A XOR B XOR CIN	(A$'$ AND B) OR (Cin AND (A XOR B)$'$)
011	Zero	0	0
100	A XOR B	A XOR B	0
101	A$'$	A$'$	0
110	A OR B	A OR B	0
111	A AND B	A AND B	0

A block diagram and operation table for our ALU example is shown above. Note in the operation table, entered variables are used to define the functional requirements for the two outputs (F and Cout) of the bit-slice module. If entered variables were not used, the table would have required 64 rows. Since Cout is not required for logic functions, it can be assigned "0" or a don't care for those rows. A circuit diagram for an 8-bit ALU based on the developed bit slice is shown below.

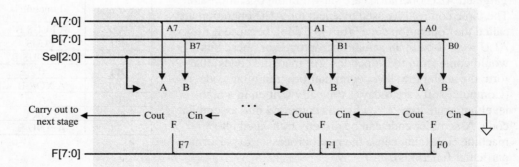

Once the ALU operation table is complete, a circuit can be designed following any one of several methods: K-maps can be constructed and minimal circuits can be looped; muxes can be used (with an 8 ∶ 1 mux for F and a 4 ∶ 1 mux for Cout); the information could be entered into a computer-based minimizer and the resulting equations implemented directly; or we could bypass all the difficult and error-prone structural work and create a VHDL description.

Behavioral VHDL ALU Description

As mentioned in the previous module, when circuit outputs are assigned a value based on some number of select inputs, a *selected signal assignment* statement can be used to minimize and clarify VHDL code. A selected signal assignment can assign one of 2^N possible outputs based on the state of N select bits. Simple multiplexor circuits can easily be coded using a selected assignment, and so can more complex multiplexors that assign the result of an arithmetic or logic function to the output.

```
entity ALU is
   port (A, B : in std_logic_vector (7 downto 0);
        Sel   : in std_logic_vector (1 downto 0);
        Y     : out std_logic_vector (7 downto 0));
end ALU;

architecture behavioral of ALU is
Begin
   With sel select
      Y <=  (A + B) when "00",
            (A + "00000001") when "01",
            (A or B) when "10",
            (A and B) when others;
end behavioral;
```

The example code to the right shows an example of an 8-bit, four function ALU based on a selected signal assignment statement. By following this example, you can easily define any ALU or similar circuit.

An 8-bit, four-function ALU example

This example code can easily be modified to create a more complex ALU. For example, more sel bits (and therefore more ALU functions) can be added, and/or different ALU functions can be coded.

3. More about VHDL

Structural vs. Behavioral Designs

The VHDL language can be used to define circuits in many different ways, with different levels of abstraction. Behavioral descriptions describe only the input and output relationships of a circuit, with no attention given to the ultimate structure of the circuit. Behavioral designs are abstract descriptions that are relatively easy to read and understand, and they rely on synthesizer software to define structural details. At the other end of the spectrum, structural descriptions define circuit blocks and interconnections. They are rigorous descriptions and full of detail, and they can be difficult for other engineers to read and understand. Often, the circuit's behavior gets lost in the volume of structural detail. Both methods have advantages and disadvantages. Behavioral designs can proceed quickly, since it is usually much easier to describe how something behaves rather than how it is built. Because behavioral designs can be completed relatively quickly, designers can spend more time studying various alternative design approaches, and more time ensuring all design requirements are properly implemented. But in trade, behavioral designs hide many important details, making it difficult to model and simulate circuits with a high degree of fidelity.

In our brief exposure to the VHDL language so far, we have focused on basic behavioral descriptions of circuits. For example, in an earlier lab, you were asked to create a VHDL description for a circuit that could detect the first seven prime numbers. The circuit was implemented using a signal assignment statement, and no concern was given to the actual structure of the circuit—those details were left to the synthesizer. It would have been a much more time consuming project if you were required to first find the circuit structure, and then implement it.

In some situations, designers choose to use structural VHDL to define a circuit instead of (or in addition to) defining its behavior. More work is required to create a structural VHDL definition, because a larger amount of detail must be described. But in return for that greater effort, far more accurate and powerful simulation models can be created. For example, consider a circuit to add two 4-bit numbers. A behavioral description would read "Y <= A + B;" (assuming Y, A, and B are all four-bit standard logic vectors). After synthesis, this circuit might be composed of four full adders connected in an RCA configuration. But the simulator would not have access to the internal nodes (like the carry signals), and so timing or other problems with those signals could not easily be discovered. Contrast this behavioral statement with the structural description in the example code below. In the structural description, internal signals are explicitly named and are therefore readily available to the simulator.

In a given design, an engineer may elect to first capture a design relatively quickly using high-level behavioral VHDL to study its behavior and validate its performance against the design requirements. At this stage, different solutions can easily be coded and simulated, and their relative advantages brought to light. Once a preferred solution is discovered, some or all of the design might be recoded in structural VHDL so that more detailed simulations could occur, giving the designer a more complete understanding of hardware behavior. As a further advantage of using structural methods, completed design blocks can be reused in subsequent designs.

Structural VHDL methods are similar to schematic-based methods—individual components are designed and saved into a project library, and then added to the higher-level design as needed. Component signals can be connected directly to I/O ports in the higher-level design, or interconnected to other components using locally declared signals. Any valid VHDL entity/architecture pair can be used as a component in another VHDL source file, just like any circuit schematic can be made into a macro and then used in another schematic. In a schematic environment, a component can be added to the design by adding its graphic symbol to the schematic page. In VHDL, a component is added to a source file by first declaring it in the "declaration area", and then by instantiating it. A component *declaration* statement informs the VHDL analyzer that a given component may be used in the current source file. When the analyzer finds a component declaration statement, it checks to be sure the component is available in a project library. A component *instantiation* statement is used to actually add the component to the design. Instantiation statements provide unique names for each component instance, and then list all port signal connections in a *port map* statement. Examples of both of these statements are provided in the example source code for a 4-bit RCA below.

```
entity RCA is
    port ( A, B    : in std_logic_vector (3 downto 0);
           S       : out std_logic_vector (3 downto 0);
           Cout    : out std_logic);
end RCA;

architecture structural of RCA is

    component HA
        port (A, B    : in std_logic;
               S, Cout : out std_logic);
    end component;

    component FA
        port (A, B    : in std_logic;
               S, Cout : out std_logic);
    end component;

    signal CO : std_logic_vector (3 downto 0);

Begin

    C0: HA port map (A=>A(0), B=>B(0), S=>S(0), Cout=>CO(0));
    C1: FA port map (A=>A(1), B=>B(1), Cin=>CO(0), S=>S(1), Cout=>CO(1));
    C2: FA port map (A=>A(2), B=>B(2), Cin=>CO(1), S=>S(2), Cout=>CO(2));
    C3: FA port map (A=>A(3), B=>B(3), Cin=>CO(2), S=>S(3), Cout=>CO(3));

end behavioral;
```

Components and signals are declar the *Declaration* between the Architecture and Begin statements

Components can instantiated anyw within the Architecture statement

Components are connected to signals in the higher-level design using a *port map* statement. Component signals may be connected directly to I/O ports in the higher-level design, or they may connect to other components using locally declared signals. Every component instantiation statement must include a port map statement to establish all required signal connections. In the example code above, some component signals are connected to I/O port signals in the higher-level design, and some are connected to other components using the locally declared CO signals.

The component instantiation statement starts with a unique alphanumeric label terminated with a colon. Labels can use any legal characters (generally, letters and numbers), and they can be descriptive of the component, or just a sequential place holder as in the example above. The component entity name follows the label, and then the key words "port map". The port map statement contains a list of all component signals named exactly as they were in the earlier declaration statement. Component signals are listed one by one, followed by the "assigned to" operator => and the name of the higher-level signal to which they are assigned. All port map signal assignments are contained in a list demarked by parenthesis, and the close parenthesis is followed by a semicolon.

The 4-bit RCA example above shows two component declaration statements (one for the half-adder named HA and one for the full-adder named FA) and four component instantiations. The component declaration statements will generate errors if the half-adder and full-adder entities are not named "HA" and "FA" (i.e., the HA entity statement must read "entity *HA* is"). Often, new VHDL programmers mistakenly use the windows *filename* for a component rather than the entity name. You can choose to give the source file the same name as the entity if you wish.

In a typical structural VHDL design, some components must be connected to other components using locally declared signals. The 4-bit RCA example is no exception—local signals are needed to connect the carry-out of one bit slice to the carry-in of the next. In the example, four new signals (in the form of a bus named CO) are declared. Since these signals are not included in the higher-level entity port statement, they are not "visible" outside of the entity and can only be used locally, within the entity. If such signals must be accessed outside of the entity, then their declaration must be removed from the declaration area and placed in the higher-level entity's port statement.

In summary, a structural VHDL source file uses other, pre-designed VHDL modules as components. Any pre-existing VHDL entity/architecture pair can be used as a component by first declaring the entity as a component and then by instantiating the component. An instantiation is comprised of a unique alphanumeric label, the entity name, and a port map statement that connects component signals to higher-level signals (either locally declared signals or directly to I/O port signals).

Modular Design in VHDL

The VHDL language includes several ways to reuse previously written code in other source files. In the method discussed above, you can write circuit descriptions as entity/architecture pairs and then include that code as a component in another design. In another method, you can write circuit descriptions in subprograms like functions and procedures. Subprograms encapsulate often-used descriptions in a single piece of code that can be parameterized for use in different contexts within a source file.

The creation of subprograms is beyond our current scope, but you have already used several subprograms (in the form of functions) without knowing. The VHDL language does not contain any intrinsic facilities to evaluate logic expressions in assignment statements, so logic functions like AND, OR, NAND, etc. are defined as functions, and those functions are included in a library that is distributed with every VHDL tool set.

A VHDL library is a collection of "design units" that have be prewritten and analyzed, and stored in a directory in the host computer's file system. Any design unit stored in a library can be used in any other source file. The VHDL language defines five types of design units, including entities, architectures, packages, package bodies, and configurations. You are familiar with entity and architecture design units. Packages are used for defining and storing commonly used declarations for components, types, constants, global signals, etc., and package bodies contain functions and procedures. Configurations associate an entity with a particular architecture, and are only needed in the somewhat rare case that more than one architecture is written for a given entity (configurations are occasionally used in larger or more complex designs and will be dealt with in a later module).

The std_logic type you have been using is defined in the "std_logic_1164" package that was written long ago, stored in a library named "IEEE", and transferred to your computer when you installed the ISE/WebPack tool. Logic functions like AND, OR, NAND, NOR, XOR, XNOR, etc., are stored in the 1164 package body. If the 1164 package were not available in the IEEE library, you couldn't use the std_logic types, and you couldn't write assignment statements like "Y <= A and B;".

In fact, several types and functions have been standardized by the IEEE, and they are included in packages within the IEEE library. As mentioned, the std_logic_1164 package in the IEEE library contains definitions for common data types (like std_logic and std_logic_vector) as well as common logic functions like AND, OR, NAND, NOR, XOR, etc. Another common package called "std_logic_arith" contains a collection of arithmetic functions like addition ($+$), subtraction ($-$), multiplication ($*$). Still other packages contain further collections of useful functions.

Libraries and packages must be declared in a source file before their contents can be accessed. Libraries are identified in a source file using a "logical name"; a library manager tool associates a logical library name with the library's physical location in the computer's file system. This way, VHDL source files need only know the logical names. The keywords *library* (followed by the library's logical name) and *use* (followed by the package name) must be included in a source file to make their contents available. When the VHDL analyzer encounters a word or symbol that is doesn't recognize, it will look inside the available libraries and packages for suitable definitions. For example, when the analyzer finds the "and" in "Y<= A and B;", or the "+" in "Y <= A + B;", it will look for "and" and "+" definitions in the packages that have been declared. It is common practice to include the library and use statements shown to the right in every VHDL source file so that common types and functions can be used.

```
library IEEE;
use IEEE.std_logic_1164.all;
use IEEE.std_logic_arith.all;
```

Arithmetic Functions in VHDL

The std_logic_arith package in the IEEE library defines several arithmetic functions that can be performed on std_logic and std_logic_vector data types. If the "library IEEE" and "use std_logic_arith" statements are included in your source file, addition (+), subtraction (−), multiplication (∗), and division (/) operators (as well as some other operators) can be used with std_logic types. For example, the binary numbers carried by two std_logic_vectors can be summed by writing a statement like "Y<=A + B;".

When using arithmetic operators on std_logic_vectors, the output vector must be sized correctly or the VHDL analyzer will flag an error, or data will be lost. For our purposes in the accompanying lab module, ensure the output logic vector used to capture arithmetic function outputs is no smaller than the input vectors. In general, if smaller logic vectors are combined through arithmetic operations into larger vectors, the results will be right-justified in the larger output vector. If larger vectors are combined into vectors that are too small to contain all required output bits, the results will still be right justified and the more significant bits will be lost.

Exercise 7: Combinational Arithmetic Circuits

Problem 1. Sketch a block diagram for a magnitude comparator bit-slice circuit. Create K-maps to define the bit-slice circuit, and use them to find optimal logic equations. Sketch the circuit.

Problem 2. Modify the block diagram and circuit of problem 1 by removing the logic gates and signals that form the EQ output. Sketch a circuit diagram for a 4-bit comparator that uses the modified bit slice blocks, and add a single gate to form the EQ output from the LT and GT outputs from the MSB (most significant bit). Comment on the differences in the new circuit (i.e., which circuit is more efficient? Which is easier to design and implement? Which might run faster? Anything else?)

Could you make the bit-slice modules even more efficient by leaving in the EQ logic and removing some other logic? Explain.

Problem 3. Complete truth tables and K-maps for HA and FA circuits, using XOR patterns where appropriate. Loop minimum SOP equations, and sketch the circuits (assume all inputs and outputs are active high).

Half Adder	A	B	S	Cout
	0	0		
	0	1		
	1	0		
	1	1		

A \ B	0	1
0		
1		

S

S =

A \ B	0	1
0		
1		

Cout

Cout =

192

Full Adder

A	B	Cin	S	Cout
0	0	0		
0	0	1		
0	1	0		
0	1	1		
1	0	0		
1	0	1		
1	1	0		
1	1	1		

A \ B Cin	00	01	11	10
0				
1				

S =   S

A \ B Cin	00	01	11	10
0				
1				

Cout =   Cout

Problem 4. Sketch a circuit for a full adder using two half-adder blocks and an OR gate.

Problem 5. Complete the truth table and K-maps for a CLA adder bit-slice module, and sketch a minimal SOP circuit (be sure to use XOR's where appropriate!).

A	B	Cin	S	G	P
0	0	0			
0	0	1			
0	1	0			
0	1	1			
1	0	0			
1	0	1			
1	1	0			
1	1	1			

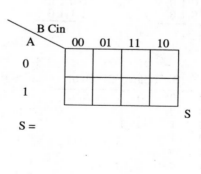

A \ B Cin	00	01	11	10
0				
1				

S =   S

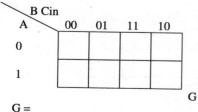

A \ B Cin	00	01	11	10
0				
1				

G =   G

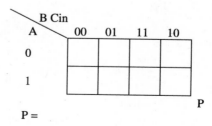

A \ B Cin	00	01	11	10
0				
1				

P =   P

Problem 6. Sketch a Carry-Propagate-Generate circuit that can form the carry-ins for a 4-bit CLA.

Problem 7. Design a full-subtractor bit-slice circuit. Label the inputs A, B, and Bin, and label the outputs D and Bout. Start by completing the subtraction examples, then complete the truth table and K-maps, and then sketch the circuit.

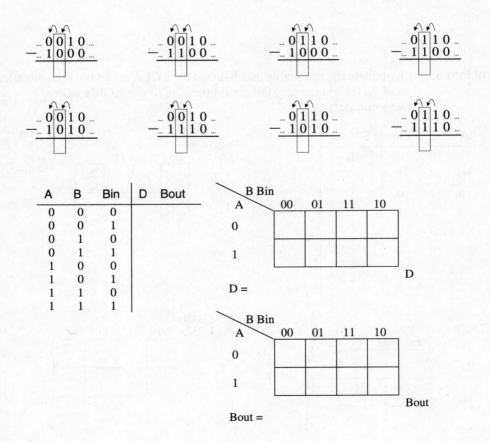

A	B	Bin	D	Bout
0	0	0		
0	0	1		
0	1	0		
0	1	1		
1	0	0		
1	0	1		
1	1	0		
1	1	1		

D =

Bout =

Problem 8.   Complete the number conversions indicated.

$-19 =$ _____ $10011010 =$ _____

$10000000 =$ _____ $-101 =$ _____

Problem 9.   Complete the four 2's compliment arithmetic problems below, showing both the decimal and binary numbers in each case.

```
    17    0 0 0 1 0 0 0 1 0        -22
  - 11    1 1 1 1 1 0 1 0 1      +  6    _____
```

```
          0 1 0 1 0 0 1 1 0         35
  -       1 1 1 1 1 0 1 0 1       - 42    _____
```

```
    19
  - -7    _____
```
Is the above answer correct in 8 bits? Explain.

Problem 10.   Sketch a circuit to convert a 4-bit binary number to its 2's complement representation. (Hint: can you use only 3 XOR/XNOR gates and 2 AND or OR gates?)

Problem 11.   Explain how the circuit structures of a ripple-carry adder circuit configured as a 2's compliment subtractor and a ripple-borrow subtractor perform identical functions.

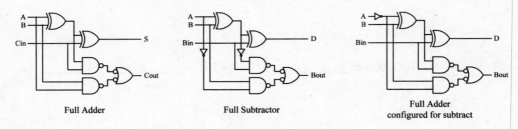

Full Adder   Full Subtractor   Full Adder
                                                                     configured for subtract

Problem 12.   Examine several examples of addition overflow and subtraction underflow, and sketch a circuit below that can output a "1" whenever an addition or subtraction result is incorrect due to underflow or overflow. (Hint: compare the carry in and carry out signals of the most-significant bit.)

Problem 13. Fill in the squares below to show all signal values when "1101" and "1010" are multiplied.

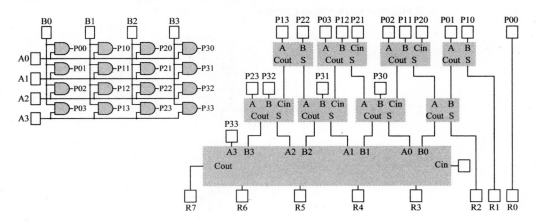

Problem 14. Sketch a block diagram for a 4-bit ALU built from bit-slice ALU circuits that can implement the functions shown in the table. Label all signals, and recall that inputs to the bit slices must come from the A and B input busses as well as from neighboring bit slices (and outputs must drive the F output bus as well as neighboring bit slices). To design the signals that communicate information between slices, you must understand the ALU operations and the implications for information transfer (e.g., does the operation A PLUS B require that information be transferred between slices? If so, what? Does the operation A OR B require that information be transferred?).

Operation Code	ALU function
000	A PLUS B
001	A PLUS 1
010	A MINUS B
011	A MINUS 1
100	A XOR B
101	A'
110	A OR B
111	A AND B

Problem 15. In the ALU example in the module it was stated that an 8 : 1 mux could be use for the F output and a 4 : 1 mux could be used for the Cout output. Sketch the mux-based circuit.

Problem 16. Transfer the ALU operation table from the module has been reproduced below, but opcode 3 has been redefined as "decrement". Complete the F and Cout table entries to define the decrement logic functions.

Op Code	Function	F	Cout
000	A PLUS B	A xor B xor Cin	(A and B) or (Cin and (A xor B))
001	A PLUS 1	A xor Cin	A and Cin
010	A MINUS B	A xor B xor Cin	(A' and B) or (Cin and (A xor B)')
011	A MINUS 1		
100	A XOR B	A xor B	0
101	A'	A'	0
110	A OR B	A or B	0
111	A AND B	A and B	0

Problem 17.   Use the operation table above to complete the K-maps for the functions F and Cout.

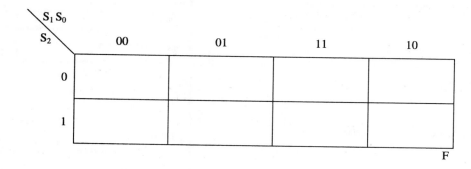

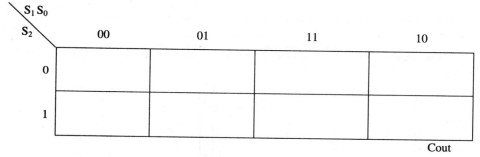

Problem 18.   Loop the K-maps above, finding minimal expression in each case (Hint: note the points awarded for this exercise, and spend your time accordingly).

$F_{SOP} =$

$Cout_{SOP} =$

Lab Project 7: Combinational Arithmetic Circuits

STUDENT

I am submitting my own work, and I understand penalties will be assessed if I submit work for credit that is not my own.

Print Name ______________ ID Number ______________

Sign Name ______________ Date ______________

Estimated Work Hours

1	2	3	4	5	6	7	8	9	10

1	2	3	4	5	6	7	8	9	10

Overall Weight

Point Scale

4: Exemplary
3: Complete
2: Incomplete
1: Minor effort
0: Not submitted

20% will be deducted from scores for each week late

Score = Points awarded (Pts) × Weight (Wt)

LAB ASSISTANT

#	Demonstration	Wt	Pts	Late	Score	Lab Asst Signature	Date	Total In-Lab Score
3	VHDL source code inspection	2						
4	Circuit demo	3						
E1	Circuit demo	3						NA
5	Circuit demo	4						
5	Circuit demo	5						
7	Circuit demo	5						

GRADER

#	Attachments	Wt	Pts	Score	Weeks late	Total Grading Score	Total Score
1	VHDL source, test bench, and simulation	2					
2	VHDL source, test bench, and simulation	3					
3	VHDL source, test bench, and simulation	3					
4	Source and simulation files	3					*Total score is In-lab score plus grading score*
E1	VHDL or schematic source and simulation	3					
5	VHDL or schematic source and simulation	4					
6	Source and simulation files	5					
7	VHDL source and simulation files	5					

Problem 1.   Design and simulate an 8-bit comparator using the WebPack VHDL environment. Submit the source and simulation files for credit (Hint: you may use behavioral design methods).

Problem 2.   Design and simulate an 8-bit RCA using structural methods and the WebPack VHDL environment (Hint: the FA and HA bit-slice modules can be designed as behavioral modules and used as components in a separate structural VHDL source file). Submit the source and simulation files for credit.

Problem 3.   Design and simulate an 8-bit CLA using structural VHDL methods. Have the lab assistant inspect your work, and submit the source and simulation files for credit.

Problem 4.   Use the Xilinx tools (schematic or VHDL, your choice) to design, simulate and implement a 4-bit adder/subtractor module. Download the design to the Digilent board, using four slide switches to set the A operand, four slide switches to set the B operand, and a pushbutton to select add or subtract. Use five LEDs for circuit output. Check enough cases to be sure your circuit works, demonstrate your circuit to the lab assistant, and print and submit your source and simulation files for credit.

Extra Credit: Display the output from problem 4 on a seven-segment digit. Demonstrate your circuit to the lab assistant, and print and submit your source files for credit.

Problem 5.   Design an underflow/overflow detect circuit that does not need to access the carry-in signal to the most-significant bit, and add that circuit to your design from problem 4. Drive a LED to show when a output is in error. Demonstrate your circuit to the lab assistant, and print and submit your source files for credit.

Problem 6.   Using your HA, FA, and 8-bit CLA components, implement a 4-bit multiplier using the Xilinx tools. Simulate the multiplier using several representative cases stored in a test bench waveform file. Implement the multiplier in the Digilent board using the eight slide switches as inputs (four switches per input) and the eight LED's as outputs, and demonstrate your circuit to the lab assistant. Submit your source and simulation files for credit.

Problem 7.   Design and implement a 4-bit ALU using the Xilinx VHDL tools and the Digilent board. The ALU must perform the operations shown in the operation table presented earlier. Assign inputs to slide switches and pushbuttons as you see fit, and assign outputs to LEDs or the 7sd. Demonstrate your circuit to the assistant and submit your source and simulation files for grading.

Chapter 8: Signal Propagation Delays

1. Overview

This chapter considers the time-course of logic signals as they pass through logic circuits. Until now, we have not considered the time required for logic signals to propagate through logic gates and along signal wires. Instead, we have been assuming that logic gate outputs change from "0" to "1" or "1" to "0" immediately (i.e., in zero time). Further, we have assumed that in response to input changes, logic circuit outputs either remain constant or change immediately to new values. This simplifying approach was justified because it allowed us to focus on the logical properties of circuits. But now, it is time to examine the behavior of real logic circuits, where voltage levels cannot change immediately.

Before beginning this chapter, you should:	After completing this chapter, you should:
<ul><li>Be familiar with combinational logic circuits of all sorts, from basic SOP and POS circuits through more complex; arithmetic and logic designs;</li><li>Be able to design and simulate structural and behavioral circuits using VHDL and/or schematic capture in the Xilinx ISE/WebPack tool;</li><li>Be able to download circuits to the Digilent board;</li><li>Be familiar arithmetic circuits and the bit-slice design method.</li></ul>	<ul><li>Be comfortable in approaching more complex design problems;</li><li>Understand the value of partitioning a design properly;</li><li>Appreciate the utility and trade-offs in top-down vs. modular design methods;</li><li>Understand where circuit delays come from;</li><li>Be able to analyze a combinational circuit to determine whether its outputs will suffer from logic noise (or "glitches").</li></ul>

This chapter requires:

- A windows computer running the Xilinx ISE/WebPack tools.

2. Propagation Delays in Logic Circuits

Electronic signals travel along conductors at about 8cm per nanosecond (the actual speed depends on the conductor material, dimensions, and other external factors). Electronic switches, like the FETs used in logic circuits, typically require up to several hundred picoseconds to turn on and off. When a switch does turn on, it must transfer charge to or from the capacitance at its output node, and again, this takes time. All of these factors contribute to the simple fact that time is required for electric signals to propagate through logic circuits. Restated, time is required to process information in digital circuits. This processing time is divided between the less significant signal transmission time, and the more significant propagation delays associated with switching logic circuits. If not managed properly, propagation delays can result logic circuits that run too slowly to meet their requirements, or that fail altogether.

A simple logic circuit, its equivalent CMOS circuit, and a timing diagram are shown below with a particular intra-gate node (N1) highlighted. Note that if B changes from low to high when C is high as shown, the circuit node N1 changes from high to low after a time $\tau 1$ has elapsed. The time $\tau 1$ is the "propagation delay" associated with the NAND gate. Referring to the CMOS circuit, the propagation delay $\tau 1$ models transistor Q1 turning on and discharging node N1 from Vdd to GND. Although there is no actual capacitor at the output node, all the signal wires and FET connections associated with the circuit node N1 behave like a single capacitor, and this "parasitic" accumulated capacitance is shown lumped into a single component labeled C1. As is the case with any capacitor, C1 cannot transition from Vdd to GND immediately; the propagation delay $\tau 1$ models the time required to discharge this capacitance.

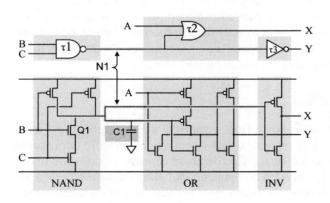
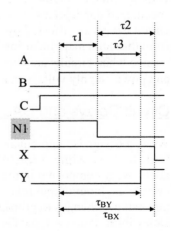

As the C1 capacitance discharges, the voltage at N1 decreases below the input switching threshold of the inverter, the inverter drives its output Y to a "1" after the propagation delay τ3. The propagation delay of the OR gate (τ2) is longer than the delay for the inverter —in general, different gates will have different propagation delays. Further, since the delay through a given gate depends on the number of other gates and wires that it must drive, different instances of the same type of gate in a given circuit will have different propagation delays as well. In a given digital circuit, a designer is typically interested in the system response time rather than individual gate delays. For this circuit, the system response times τ$_{BX}$ and τ$_{BY}$ that show the time required for signals X and Y to change in response to a change on signal B are shown at the bottom of the timing diagram.

The amount of time required to drive an output from "0" to "1" (or vice-versa) depends on how much capacitance is present on the output node. In a CMOS circuit, the capacitance on a given output node is determined by how many "downstream" gate inputs are connected to the output node (for example, in the circuit above, node A is driving a single gate input, while node N1 is driving two gate inputs). As a first approximation, it is reasonable to assume a linear relationship between the number of downstream gates driven by an output node and the amount of time required to transition the output node. That is, if an output node connected to 2 downstream gate inputs can transition from "0" to "1" in time X, the same gate driving 4 downstream gate inputs can transition in time 2X.

Different circuit implementation technologies have different typical delays. For example, a circuit implemented in a modern FPGA will typically have delays that are much smaller than a circuit implemented in a five-year-old FPGA, and in turn, both FPGA circuits would have far smaller delays than a similar circuit built from discrete gates. The smallest delay times (on the order of 10's of picoseconds) are available in the most expensive technologies, and these are reserved for "fully custom" chip designs that sell in high-volumes (like Pentium processors), or for designs that require the best performance for specialized applications (like sensitive scientific instruments). Whatever the technology, circuit delays are affected by variations in the manufacturing process, so no two devices from the same manufacturing line will exhibit exactly the same delay. Further, delays can change when circuits are exposed to different operating environments—both temperature and power supply voltage can greatly alter delays on various circuit nodes.

Circuit Delays and CAD Tools

When a design is "implemented" (i.e., translated and mapped to a given technology) in a CAD tool like Xilinx's ISE/Webpack, a separate database containing specific information about every component in the design is created. This database contains information that defines the input/output relationships for each component, including the time required for input signal changes to propagate through the component to cause output signal changes. Delay information is typically stored separately for rising-edge transitions (i.e., a 0-to-1 transition) and for falling-edge transitions. Different delay values are used for rising and falling edges to account for the differences in the FETs that are used to drive an output node to "0" or "1". In a falling transition, nFETs are responsible for driving the output node to "0", while in a rising transition, pFETs are responsible for driving an output node to "1" (see the circuit example above). In CMOS circuits, nFETs can typically pass twice the amount of current as similarly sized pFETs, so driving an output node to "1" typically takes twice as long as driving an output to "0". Some simpler CAD tools ignore this phenomenon, and use a single number to define "gate delay". This single gate delay number is applied to all inputs for both rising and falling transitions.

In general, the delays encountered in a given circuit cannot be precisely known until the circuit is transformed into its most basic structural representation. The most basic representation depends on the technology that will be used to implement the circuit. When circuits are synthesized to a given device like an FPGA or CPLD, all the "logical" components and interconnections specified in the source file are mapped to particular physical devices in the chip. Once this mapping happens, it is possible to calculate the delays for every circuit node in the design with a high degree of accuracy. Prior to this mapping, it is only possible to estimate the delays. Whether calculated or estimated, all useful logic simulators must accommodate delay values so that designers can simulate the behavior of physical circuits. In fact, it is fair to say that accurate delay modeling is the most important and most useful feature of a simulator. Designers have learned that they must know the effects of all delays on all circuit nodes prior to releasing a design to manufacturing.

In a modern design flow, a circuit is initially designed without paying much attention to delays. In this early stage, a simulator is used only to check that the circuit logic has been correctly defined. When the design is synthesized to a given technology, the CAD tools can automatically calculate accurate delays for every single circuit node. Then, the circuit can be re-simulated, and the designer can study the circuit's behavior with accurate node delays included. Delay information is typically stored in a file called a "standard delay format", or .sdf file. In a post-synthesis simulation, the .sdf file is used by the simulator along with the circuit definition and the stimulus file to create a highly accurate output.

Many schematic-based CAD tools, and all VHDL tools, allow designers to include delays at the time a circuit is initially specified. These delays are by definition "best guesses", but they are nevertheless useful in studying a given circuit's performance. These delay values can easily be modified to simulate a circuit's behavior under different operating conditions that might arise. For example, best-case or worst-case delays could be used to model circuit performance at different operating temperatures or supply voltages.

In problems and exercises up to this point, the focus has been on creating functionally correct circuits, and the effects of gate delays have been ignored. Going forward, you will come to appreciate that creating a "functionally correct" circuit is the simplest part of solving a given problem. The greater challenge often lies in creating a circuit that will always work in a given physical environment, with all the attendant gate delay and timing issues, and in validating circuit performance through testing.

Circuit Delays Specified in VHDL Source Files

The time-behavior of any VHDL
assignment statement can be
specified using the keyword "after"
and a time definition as shown in
the example code. In the simplest
case, a single delay value is
provided to define the time between
any input change and a resulting
output change. For example, in the
second code example for the circuit
on the right, Y won't assume a new
value until 3ns after A, B, or C
changes.

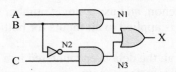

architecture *simple* of *example* is begin
  Y <= (A and B) or (not B and C);
end *simple*;

The example above treats the entire
circuit as one entity, and assigns a
single delay value to the entire
circuit. Although this is a simple
way to assign delays, a great deal of
potentially useful information is
hidden. In general, if you are
attempting to model delays in a
circuit, it is better to assign delays
to each logic gate, including those
that drive intermediate nodes
between the inputs and outputs.
Then, more detailed simulations
can demonstrate whether circuit
delays resulting from individual
gates are likely to cause problems.

architecture *simple* of *example* is begin
  Y <= (A and B) or (not B and C) after 3ns;
end *simple*;

architecture *gates* of *example* is
  signal N1, N2, N3 : std_logic;
begin
  N1 <= (A and B) after 2ns;
  N2 <= not B after 1ns;
  N3 <= (N2 and C) after 2ns;
  X <= (N1 or N3) after 3ns;
end *gates*;

The third architecture example provides a more detailed description by assigning delay
values to each individual circuit node. When more complex assignment statements are
broken into their constituent parts like this, more detailed (and therefore more useful)
delay values can be assigned. Further, when this VHDL code is simulated, every signal
node can be examined in the waveform viewer.

Glitches

Propagation delays not only limit the speed at which a circuit can operate, they can also
cause unexpected and unwanted transitions in outputs. These unwanted transitions, called
"glitches", result when an input signal changes state, provided the signal takes two or more

paths through a circuit and one path has a longer delay than the other. The increased delay on one path can cause a glitch when the signal paths are recombined at an output gate. Asymmetric path delays commonly arise when an input signal drives an output through two or more paths, with one path containing an inverter and one not. The figures below illustrate a glitch being formed by an inverter. Note the glitch (the 1−0−1 transition on Y) has the same duration as the delay in the inverter.

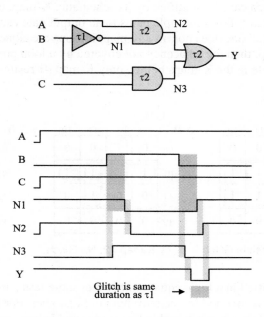

All logic gates add some delay to logic signals, with the amount of delay determined by their construction and output loading. In the figure to the right, the inverter is shown with a larger delay (identified by time T1) than the other gates (T2). This contrived example uses an over-long inverter delay to clearly show its role in creating an output glitch, but a glitch would appear no matter what the delay time. By carefully studying the timing diagram, it is clear how the inverter delay is related to the output glitch.

Glitches occur when an input is used in two product terms (or two sum terms for a POS equation), and inverted in one term but not in the other. This is illustrated in the figure, the logic equation, and in the K-map to the right. In the K-map, two loops define a minimal logic expression. The B·C term is independent of A; that is, if B and C are both "1", the output will be a "1" regardless of changes on A. Likewise, the term A·B′ is independent of C, so that if A and B are "1" and "0", the output is a "1" regardless of how C might change. But note if A is a "1" and C is a "1", the output should always be a "1" regardless of B, but no single

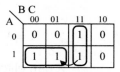

$$Y = AB' + BC$$

B is a "coupled" variable

term is driving the output independent of B. This is the situation that gives rise to the problem: two different product terms keep the output at a "1" when A and C are both "1"—one when B is a "1" (B·C), and one when B is a "0" (A·B′). Thus, as B changes, two different product terms must recombine at the output to keep the output high, and this is what gives rise to the glitch.

A circuit that can glitch can be identified by its schematic, K-map, or logic equation. In a schematic, an input that follows multiple paths to an output gate can create a glitch, if one path has an inverter and one does not. In a K-map, if loops are adjacent but not joined by an "overlapping" loop, then the adjacency not covered by a loop presents the opportunity for a glitch. In example in the K-maps below, only K-map #1 results in a circuit that can glitch.

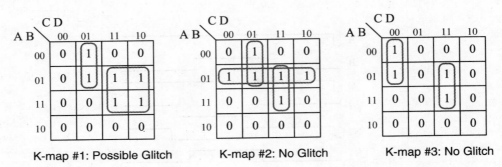

K-map #1: Possible Glitch   K-map #2: No Glitch   K-map #3: No Glitch

A glitch can be identified in a logic equation if two or more terms include the same logic signal, and the signal is inverted in one term but not in another. For this discussion, each pair of terms that contain a single variable that is inverted in one term but not the other are called "coupled terms", the inverted/non-inverted variable the "coupled variable", and the set of all other variables in both terms the "residue". The examples below illustrate.

$$X = (A + B') (A + C) (B' + C)$$

No glitch possible
No coupled terms

$$X = A \cdot B' + A' \cdot C$$

X can glitch when A changes
Both terms are coupled
A is the coupled variable
B′ and C are the residue

$$X = A' \cdot C' + A \cdot B + B' \cdot C$$

X can glitch when A, B or C changes
A′ · C′ & A · B are coupled terms
A · B & B′ · C are coupled terms
A′ · C′ & · B′·C are coupled terms

In some applications, it may be desirable to remove the glitch so that the output remains steady when a coupled variable changes state. Note that in the solution to Problem 1, the glitch on Y is only possible if B and C are held high. This observation can be generalized: for a glitch to occur, a logic circuit must be "sensitized" to a coupled variable by driving all inputs to appropriate levels so that only the coupled variable can affect the output. In an SOP circuit, this means that all inputs other than the coupled input must be driven to a "1" so that they have no effect on the outputs of the first-level AND gates.

This observation leads directly to the method for removing a glitch from a logic circuit: combine all residue input signals in a new first-level logic gate (i.e., an AND gate for an SOP circuit), and add the new gate to the circuit. For example, in the equation $X = A' \cdot B + A \cdot C$, the coupled term is A, the residue signals would combine to form the term $B \cdot C$, and that term would be added to the circuit to form $X = A' \cdot B + A \cdot C + B \cdot C$. This is shown in the K-map—note that the original equation is minimal (blue loops), and that the glitch-free equation adds a redundant term (red loop).

A \ B C	00	01	11	10
0	0	0	1	1
1	0	1	1	0

This is always the case—removing glitches requires a larger circuit with redundant logic. In practice, it is almost always preferable to design minimal circuits and deal with glitches in another manner (discussed in a later module). Perhaps the best lesson is to be aware that in general, whenever an input to a combinational circuit changes, glitches are possible (at least, until proven otherwise).

The loops for the original SOP equation in problem 1 did not overlap, and this is the hallmark of a potential glitch. When a loop for the redundant term is added, every loop overlaps with at least one other, and no glitches are possible.

If non-overlapping (or isolated) loops are located in non-adjacent K-map cells (see K-map #3 above), there are no coupled terms, no coupled variables, and it is not possible to add a loop (or loops) to cause all loops to overlap with at least one other. In such a case, no single input change can cause a glitch. In this type of circuit, two or more inputs might be directed to change state "at the same time", with the desired outcome of having the output remain at some stable state. For example, in the circuit $Y = A' \cdot C' \cdot D' + B \cdot C \cdot D$ from K-map #3 above, it might be desired that all inputs go from "0" to "1" simultaneously, and that in response, the output stay constantly at "1". In practice, it is impossible to change all inputs simultaneously (at least, on a scale of picoseconds), and as a result, the output will show a glitch-like transition equal in duration to the time difference between input signal changes. Such unwanted transitions cannot be eliminated by adding redundant gates; rather, they must be dealt with by redefining the circuit or with sampling and pipelining (these topics are discussed in a later module). We will not deal further with unwanted output transitions resulting from multiple input changes here.

Most of the glitch discussion so far has focused on SOP circuits, but the same phenomenon is present in POS circuits as well. POS circuits suffer from glitches for the same reasons as SOP circuits (asymmetric path delays for an input arriving at multiple input gates). As you might expect, the conditions required are similar, but not identical to the SOP case.

These simple experiments demonstrate the basic effects of gate delays on digital circuits —namely, output glitches are possible in response to input transitions, provided the input passes through asymmetric circuit path delays in forming the output. In the more general case, any time an input passes through two different circuit branches, and those two branches are recombined at a "downstream" point in the circuit, timing problems like glitches are possible. Again, the lesson is to be aware that signals take time to propagate through logic circuits, and different circuit paths have different delays. And in certain cases, those differential delays can cause problems.

Using CAD-tool Generated Delays

The Xilinx ISE simulator can model delays for circuits that may be programmed into a Xilinx device. The simulator contains a "post-route simulation" feature that automatically generates and includes accurate delays for all circuit nodes. The delays are calculated after the circuit has been mapped to the physical devices in the target chip, and so they are quite accurate. Any source file can be simulated with delays by first "implementing" the design in the Xilinx project navigator, and then by running the simulator in the post-route mode (or, simply run the simulator in the post-route mode, and if the circuit has not yet been implemented, it will be implemented automatically). A brief appendix in the lab project document shows how to run the simulator in post-route mode.

Lab Project 8: Signal Propagation Delays

STUDENT	
I am submitting my own work, and I understand penalties will be assessed if I submit work for credit that is not my own. Print Name ____ ID Number ____ Sign Name ____ Date ____	Estimated Work Hours 1 2 3 4 5 6 7 8 9 10 1 2 3 4 5 6 7 8 9 10 Overall Weight Point Scale 4: Exemplary 3: Complete 2: Incomplete 1: Minor effort 0: Not submitted *20% will be deducted from scores for each week late* *Score = Points awarded (Pts) × Weight (Wt)*

LAB ASSISTANT

#	Demonstration	Wt	Pts	Late	Score	Lab Asst Signature	Date	Total In-Lab Score
6	Simulator output inspection	5						NA

GRADER

#	Attachments	Wt	Pts	Score	Weeks late	Total Grading Score		Total Score
1	Worksheet	2					*Total score is In-lab score plus grading score*	
2	Worksheet	1						
3	Worksheet, source, annotated simulation	3						
4	Worksheet	1						
5	Worksheet, source, annotated simulation	2						
6	Worksheet, source, annotated simulation	4						
7	Worksheet, source, annotated simulation	5						

Problem 1. Implement the function $Y = A'\cdot B + A\cdot C$ in the VHDL tool. Define the INV, OR and two AND operations separately, and give each operation a 1ns delay. Simulate the circuit with all possible combinations of inputs. Watch all circuit nets (inputs, outputs, and intermediate nets) during the simulation. Answer the questions below.

Observe the outputs of the AND gates and the overall circuit output when B and C are both high, and A transitions from H to L and then from L to H (you may want to create another simulation to focus on this behavior). What output behavior do you notice when A transitions?

What happens when A transitions and B or C are held a "0"?

How long is the output glitch? _______ Is it positive ( ) or negative ( ) (circle one)?

Change the delay through the inverter to 2ns, and resimulate. Now how long is output glitch? ______

What can you say about the relationship between the inverter gate delay and the length of the timing glitch?

Based on this simple experiment, an SOP circuit can exhibit positive/negative glitches (circle one) when an input that arrives at one AND gate in a complemented form and another AND gate in uncomplemented form transitions from a _____ to a _____.

Problem 2. Enter the logic equation from problem 1 in the K-map below, and loop the equation with redundant term included. Add the redundant term to the Xilinx circuit, re-simulate, and answer the questions.

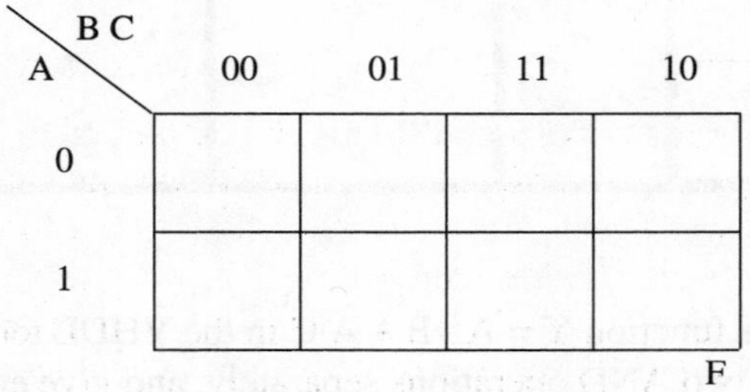
B C
A
00
01
11
10
0
1
F

F_{SOP} (original):

F_{SOP} (new):

Did adding the new gate to the circuit change the *logical* behavior of the circuit?

What effect did the new gate have on the output, particularly when A changes and B and C are both held high?

Problem 3. Create a three-input POS circuit to illustrate the formation of a glitch. Drive the simulator to illustrate a glitch in the POS circuit, and answer the questions below.

A POS circuit can exhibit a positive/negative glitch (circle one) when an input that arrives at one OR gate in a complemented form and another OR gate in un-complemented form transitions from a _____ to a _____.

Write the POS equation you used to show the glitch:

Enter the equation in the K-map below, loop the original equation with the redundant term, add the redundant gate to your Xilinx circuit, and resimulate.

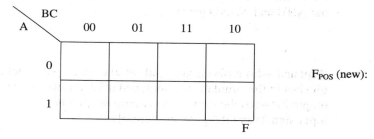

F_{POS} (new):

How did adding the new gate to the circuit change the *logical* behavior of the circuit?

What effect did the new gate have on the output, particularly when A changes and B and C are both held high?

Print and submit the circuits and simulation output, label the output glitches in the simulation output, and draw arrows on the simulation output between the events that caused the glitches (i.e., a transition in an input signal) and the glitches themselves.

Problem 4. Copy the SOP circuit above to a new VHDL file, and increase the delay of the output OR gate. Simulate the circuit and answer the questions below.

How did adding delay to the output gate change the output transition?

Does adding delay to the output gate change the circuit's glitch behavior in any way?

Problem 5. Create a circuit for $Z = (A \cdot B) \cdot (A \cdot C)'$. Change the delay of the AND gate to 1ns and the NAND gate to 2ns. Simulate the circuit, inspect the output, and answer the questions below.

What kind of glitch did you observe?

What input conditions are required for the glitch to form?

How long was the glitch, and how is its length related to timing delays in the AND and NAND gates?

Print and submit the circuits and simulation output, label the output glitches in the simulation output, and draw arrows on the simulation output between the events that caused the glitches (i.e., a transition in an input signal) and the glitches themselves.

Problem 6. Design and implement an 8-bit adder using behavioral VHDL. Use a VHDL test-bench to simulate the circuit in post-route mode, have the Lab Assistant inspect your simulation output, and print and submit the source and simulation files. Annotate the simulation output to show the "settling" time of the adder (i.e., the time the outputs are in flux).

How long does it take for the adder result to be valid after the inputs change? _____

What is the maximum frequency this circuit could run at? _____

Problem 7. Simulate your 8-bit RCA and CLA from the previous lab in post-route mode using the test bench from problem 6 above. Print and submit the source file and simulation outputs. Annotate the simulation outputs to show the "settling" time of the adders. How long does it take for the adder results of each to be valid after the inputs change?

RCA: CLA:

Appendix 1: Running the ISE/WebPack simulator in the Post-Route mode

To run the simulator in the post-route simulation mode, choose "post-route simulation" from the "Sources for:" pull-down menu in the Source window of the project navigator, and run the simulator as before (note the only process available in the "Processes" window is "Simulate Post-Place & Route Model). The figure below shows a screen-shot with the appropriate choices highlighted.

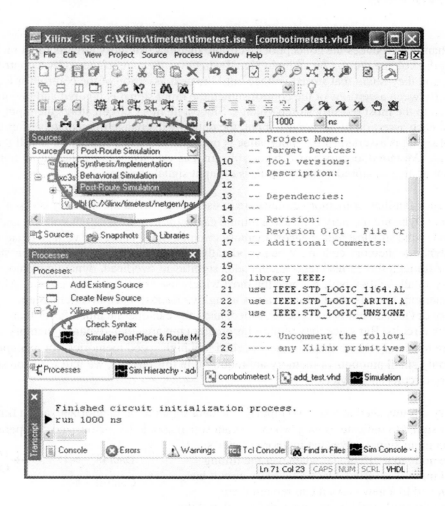

Chapter 9: Basic Memory Circuits

1. Overview

This chapter introduces the concept of electronic memory. Memory circuits function by storing the voltage present on an input signal whenever they are triggered by a control signal, and they retain that stored voltage until the next assertion of the control (or trigger) signal. Between assertions of the control signal, the input signal is ignored and the output is driven to the most recently stored voltage. Since a memory circuit stores the input signal level at each assertion of the control input, the output will change immediately after the control signal is asserted (if the input value is opposite to what is stored), or it will remain constant. "Memory" occurs between control signal assertions, because the output remains constant at the last stored value, regardless of input signal changes.

Two major families of memory circuits are in use today—dynamic memory and static memory. Dynamic memory cells use a minute capacitor to store a signal voltage, and they are used in the smallest and cheapest memory circuits. Since capacitor voltage decays over time, dynamic memory cells must be periodically refreshed or they will loose their stored value. Although this refresh requirement adds significant overhead, dynamic memory cells are very small, so they have become the most widely used of all memory circuits. Most static memory circuits store a logic values using two back-to-back inverters. Static memory devices do not need to be refreshed, and they can operate much faster than dynamic circuits. But since they require far greater chip area than dynamic memory cells, they are used only where they are most needed—in high speed memories, for example—or when only small amounts of memory are required. In this chapter, we will focus on static memory circuits and devices.

Memory circuits need at least two inputs—the data signal to be memorized, and a timing control signal to indicate exactly when the data signal should be memorized. In operation, the data input signal drives the memory circuit's storage node to a "1" or "0" whenever the timing control input is asserted. Once a memory circuit has transitioned to a new state, it can remain there indefinitely until some future input changes direct the memory to a new state. This lab examines basic

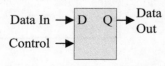

Basic Memory Device

circuits that can be used to create electronic memory.

Before beginning this chapter, you should...	After completing this chapter, you should...
• Be well practiced in the design of various combinational circuits; • Be familiar with the Xilinx WebPack design tools.	• Understand the design and function of basic memory circuits; • Be aware of the potential problems that might arise when memory circuits sample an input signal; • Be familiar with the various memory devices in use today.

This chapter requires:

- A Digilent board
- A PC running the Xilinx ISE/WebPack CAD tools.

2. Background

Introduction to Memory Circuits

Memory circuits can largely be seperated into two major groups: dyanamic memories that store data for use in a computer system (such as the RAM in a PC); and static memories that store information that defines the operating state of a digital system. Dynamic memory circuits for computer systems have become very specialized, and they will be covered in a later lab. This exercise will present memory circuits that are used to store information about the operating state of a digital system.

Many electronic devices contain digital systems that use memory circuits to define their operating state. In fact, any electronic device that can create or respond to a sequence of events must contain memory. Examples of such devices include watches and timers, appliance controllers, gaming devices, and computing devices. If a digital system contains N memory devices, and each memory device stores a "1" or a "0", then the system's operating state can be defined by an N-bit binary number. Further, a digital system with N memory devices must be in one of 2^N states, where each state is uniquely identified by a binary number created from the collective contents of all memory devices in the system.

At any point in time, the binary number stored in its internal memory devices defines the current state of a digital system. Inputs that arrive at the digital system may cause the contents of one or more memory devices to change state (from a "1" to a "0" or vice-versa), thereby causing the digital system to change states. Thus, a digital system state change or state transition occurs whenever the binary number stored in internal memory changes. It is through directed state-to-state transitions that digital systems can create or respond to sequences of events. The next lab will present digital systems that can store and change states according to some algorithm; this lab will examine the circuits that can be used to form memory.

In digital engineering, we are concerned with two-state or bistable memory circuits. Bistable circuits have two stable operating states—the state where the output is a logic "1" (or Vdd), and the state where the output is a "0" (or GND). When a bistable memory circuit is in one of the two stable states, some amount of energy is required to force it out of that state and into the other stable state. During the transition between states, the output signal must move through a region where it is astable. Memory circuits are designed so that they cannot stay in the astable state indefinitely—once they enter the astable state, they immediately attempt to regain one of the two stable states.

The figure on the right provides an adequate analogy. Here, the ball represents the value stored in memory, and the "hill" represents the astable region that must be crossed before the memory circuit can transition to storing the opposite value. Note that a third potential stable state exists in this analogy—with just the right amount of energy, it would be possible to balance the ball directly on top of the hill. Likewise, memory circuits also have a third potential stable state, somewhere between the two stable states. When memory circuits transition between their two stable states, it is important to ensure that enough energy is imparted to the circuit to ensure that the astable region is crossed.

Both the "0" and "1" states in a bistable circuit are easily maintained once they are attained. A control signal that causes the circuit to change states must deliver some minimal amount of energy to move the circuit through the astable state. If the input that causes transition from one stable state to the next delivers more than the minimum required energy, then the transition happens very quickly. If the control signal delivers less than the minimum required energy, then the circuit returns to its original stable state.

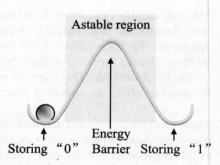

Astable region

Storing "0"   Energy Barrier   Storing "1"

But if the input delivers just the wrong amount of energy—enough to start the transition but not quite enough to force it quickly through the astable region—then the circuit can get temporarily "stuck" in the astable region. Memory circuits are designed to minimize this possibility, and to decrease the amount of time that a circuit is likely to remain in the astable state if in fact it gets there (in the analogy, imagine a very pointed summit in the astable region, with very steep slopes). If a memory device were to get stuck in an astable state for too long, its output could oscillate, or stay midway between "0" and "1", thereby causing the digital system to experience unintended and often unpredictable behavior. A memory device that gets stuck in the astable region is said to be metastable, and all memory devices suffer from the possibility of entering a metastable state (more will be said about metastability later).

A static memory circuit requires feedback, and any circuit with feedback has memory (to date, we have dealt only with feed-forward, combinational circuits without memory). Any logic circuit can have feedback if an output signal is simply "fed back" and connected to an input. Most feedback circuits will not exhibit useful behavior—they will either be monostable (i.e., stuck in an output "1" or "0" state), or they will oscillate interminably. Some feedback circuits will be bistable and controllable, and these circuits are candidates for simple memory circuits. Simple feedback circuits are shown below, and they are labeled as controllable/not controllable and bistable/not bistable.

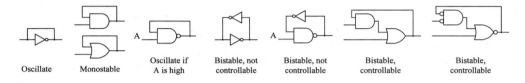

| Oscillate | Monostable | Oscillate if A is high | Bistable, not controllable | Bistable, not controllable | Bistable, controllable | Bistable, controllable |

The rightmost two circuits above are both bistable and controllable, and either could be used as a memory element. Timing diagrams for these circuits are shown below.

Basic Cells

Both circuits below use two inputs named S (for set) and R (for reset), and both use an output named Q (by convention, Q is nearly always used to label the output signal from a memory device). The S input, when asserted, "sets" the output to a "1", and the R input "resets" the output to a "0".

In the AND/OR circuit on the left below, S must be driven to "1" to drive Q to "1", and R must be driven to "0" to drive Q to "0" (so S is active high and R is active low). The output Q is set by the positive pulse on S at time 2, and Q remains set until it is reset at time 3. Thus, Q exhibits memory by remaining at "1" after the input S is deasserted, and during the time between point 2 and point 3 the circuit memorized a logic "1". Likewise, when R is asserted (as a negative pulse), Q is reset to logic "0" and it remains there until it is set sometime in the future, and the circuit memorized a logic "0".

In the NOR circuit on the right below, S must be driven to "1" to drive Q to "0", and R must also be driven to "1" to drive Q to "1" (so both S and R are active high). Because the AND/OR circuit requires more transistors, and because its inputs have opposite active levels, it is not used as a memory circuit. The reader is highly encouraged to examine the circuits and timing diagrams below, and ensure that the behaviors shown are well understood.

The figure below shows the same NOR circuit and a similar NAND circuit. Both of these circuits are very commonly used as memory circuits, and they are both called "basic cells". The timing diagram for the NAND basic cell can be easily derived, and it is similar to the NOR diagram shown above.

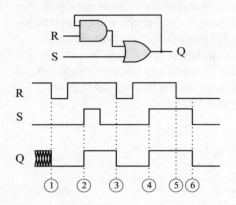
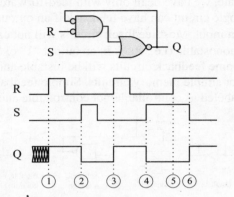

① Q is undefined until R is asserted
② Q → "1" when S is asserted
③ Q → "0" when R is asserted
④ Q → "1" when S is asserted
⑤ Q stays at "1" when S & R asserted
⑥ Q → "0" when R asserted, S de-asserted

① Q is undefined until R is asserted
② Q → "0" when S is asserted
③ Q → "1" when R is asserted
④ Q → "0" when S is asserted
⑤ Q stays at "0" when S & R asserted
⑥ Q → "1" R when asserted, S de-asserted

The NAND and NOR circuits are symmetric, so either input can be labeled S or R. By convention, the output that S drives to "1" is called Q, and the output that S drives to "0" is called QN (and thus the NOR-based circuit above is mislabeled, while the one below is correctly labeled). In the NOR circuit, a "1" on S drives Q to "1" (provided R is at "0"), and so the NOR circuit inputs are active high. In the NAND circuit, a "0" on S drives Q to "1", and so the NAND inputs are active low.

In the figure below, the basic cells have been redrawn as a cross-coupled circuit, with the feedback path emboldened for emphasis. In the NOR basic cell, the Q output is derived from the gate driven directly by R, and so R can determine the output Q regardless of S: if R is driven to a "1", Q will be a "0" regardless of S. Thus, a NOR basic cell is said to be "reset dominant". In the NAND basic cell, the input S can determine the output regardless of R: if S is driven to a "0", Q will be "1" regardless of R. The NAND basic cell is said to be "set-dominant". The difference between set and reset dominance are evident in the truth table rows where both inputs are asserted. In the reset-dominant NOR cell, Q is forced to "0" when R is asserted (last row), and in the set-dominant NAND cell Q is forced to "1" when S is asserted (first row).

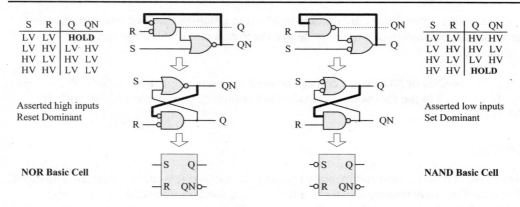

S	R	Q	QN
LV	LV	**HOLD**	
LV	HV	LV	HV
HV	LV	HV	LV
HV	HV	LV	LV

Asserted high inputs
Reset Dominant

NOR Basic Cell

S	R	Q	QN
LV	LV	HV	HV
LV	HV	HV	LV
HV	LV	LV	HV
HV	HV	**HOLD**	

Asserted low inputs
Set Dominant

NAND Basic Cell

Examining the truth tables and figure above yields the following observations:

- The middle two rows of the truth tables are similar for both circuits (i.e., both Q and QN are driven opposite from one another when either just S is asserted or just R is asserted).
- When both inputs are asserted, Q and QN are driven to the same logic level (i.e., they are no longer inverses of one another).
- When neither input is asserted, the logic level present on the feedback loop determines the circuit output.

Based on these observations, we can state the following behavioral rules for a basic cell (remembering that SET and RESET are active high for the NOR cell and low for the NAND cell):

- When just SET is active, Q is driven to "1" and QN is driven to "0";
- When just RESET is active, Q is driven to "0" and QN is driven to "1";
- When both SET and RESET are active, Q and QN are both driven to "0" (NOR cell) or "1" (NAND cell);
- When neither SET or RESET are active, the output is determined by the logic value "stored" in the feedback loop.

If both inputs to a basic cell are de-asserted at exactly the same time, the feedback loop can become astable, and the memory device can get temporarily stuck in the astable region. This results from the fact that two different logic levels are introduced into the feedback loop at the same time, and these values "chase" each other around the loop creating an oscillation. The oscillation shown in the simulator results from the fact that gate delays can be set to exactly the same value, and inputs can be changed at exactly the same time. In a real circuit, gate delays are not identical and input values cannot change (to the picosecond) at exactly the same time. Thus, oscillations may be seen, but only for a short while. Equally likely is an output that "floats" temporarily between "1" and "0". Either behavior represents metastability, where the output from the memory circuit is temporarily not in one of the two stable operating states. Metastable states are highly unlikely in a real circuit, and if they are entered, they are quickly resolved to a stable state. But it is important to note that the possibility of a memory device entering a metastable state can never be eliminated.

Either the NAND or NOR basic cell can be used in practical memory circuits. We will use the NAND cell in the following discussion, but similar circuits could be built with the NOR cell.

D-latch

The basic cell is the most rudimentary memory device, and it is useful in certain situations. But by adding only two logic gates to a basic cell, a much more useful memory device called a D-latch can be created. A D-latch uses a basic cell for a memory element, but it only allows the value stored in memory to be changed (or "programmed") when a timing control input is asserted. Thus, a D-latch has two inputs—the timing control input and a data input. The timing control input, commonly called "gate", or "clock", or "latch enable", is used to coordinate when new data can be written·into the memory element, and conversely, when data cannot be written. In the figure on the left below, observe that when the Gate input is not asserted, S and R are driven to "1" and the output Q is determined by the value stored in the basic cell feedback loop (and so Q is showing the stored logic value). In the figure on the right, observe that when the Gate input is asserted, the D (for Data) input drives S and R to opposite levels, forcing a SET or RESET operation on the basic cell. By combining a timing control input and a data input that forces the basic cell to either SET or RESET, an useful memory device is created. The D-latch is widely used in all sorts of modern digital circuits.

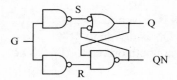 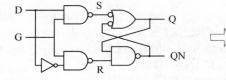

A timing diagram for the D latch is shown below. Note that when the Gate input is asserted, the output Q simply "follows" the input. But when the Gate input is not asserted, the output "remembers" the value present at D at the time the Gate signal was de-asserted.

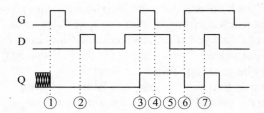

① Q is undefined until G is asserted; Q gets D's value
② D is asserted but G is not; Q unchanged
③ D and G are asserted; Q gets D's value
④ G de-asserted; Q memorizes D's value
⑤ D de-asserted but G also de-asserted; Q unchanged
⑥ G asserted and Q gets D's value
⑦ Q follows D while G asserted

D-flip-flop

All useful memory devices have at least two inputs—one for the Data signal to be memorized, and a timing control signal to define exactly when the data signal should be memorized. As shown in the figure, the current output of a memory device is called the "present state", and the input is called the "next state" because it will define the memory at the next assertion of the timing control input. In a D - latch, the present state and next state are the same as long as the timing control input is asserted. A D-flip-

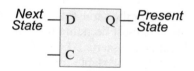

Data input to a memory device is called the *Next State*

Output from a memory device is called the *Present State*

flop modifies the function of a D-latch in a fundamental and important way: the next state (or D-input) can only be written into the memory on the edge (or transition) of the timing signal.

A D-flip-flop (DFF) is one of the most fundamental memory devices. A DFF typically has three inputs: a data input that defines the next state; a timing control input that tells the flip-flop exactly when to "memorize" the data input; and a reset input that can cause the memory to be reset to "0" regardless of the other two inputs. The "D" in DFF arises from the name of the *data* input; thus, the flip-flop may also be called a data flip-flop. The timing control input, called "clock", is used to coordinate when new data can be written into the memory element, and conversely, when data cannot be written. A clock signal is most typically a square wave that regularly repeats at some frequency. A DFF records (or registers) new data whenever an *active* clock edge occurs—the active edge can be either the rising edge or the falling edge. A rising-edge triggered (RET) DFF symbol uses a triangle to show that the flip-flop is edge-triggered; a falling-edge triggered (FET) DFF symbol uses the same triangle, but with a bubble on the outside of the bounding box (just like any other asserted-low input). The timing diagram below illustrates RET DFF behavior. Note that the Q output changes only on the active edge of the clock, and the reset signal forces the output to "0" regardless of the other inputs.

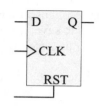

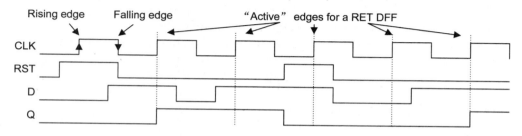

As with the basic cells, a D flip-flop or D-latch can enter a metastable state if the data and control inputs are changed at exactly the same time. In a D-latch, the data must be stable when the control input is de-asserted. In a DFF, the data input must be stable for a time immediately before and immediately after the clock edge. If the data is not stable at the clock edge, a metastable state may be clocked into the memory element. If this happens, the memory

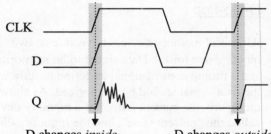

D changes *inside* sampling window, so Q may be metastable

D changes *outside* sampling window, so Q will be stable

element may not be able to immediately resolve to either low voltage or high voltage, and it may oscillate for a time. Thus, when designing circuits using edge-triggered flip-flops, it is important to ensure the data input is stable for adequate time prior to the clock edge (known as the *setup* time), and for a time after the clock edge (known as the *hold* time). Setup and hold times vary between several tens of picoseconds (for designs inside single IC's) to several nanoseconds (for designs using discrete logic chips).

A schematic for a basic D-flip-flop is shown on the right. Several slightly different schematics can be found in various references, but any circuit called a DFF will exhibit the same behavior.

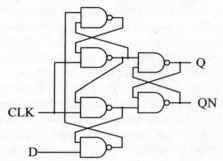

Memory Device Reset Signals

When a memory device is first powered up, it is not possible to predict whether the internal feedback loop will start up storing a "0", "1", or metastable state. Thus, it is typical to add an input signal (or signals) that can force the feedback loop to "1" or "0". Called "reset" or "preset", these signals are independent of the CLK or D inputs, and they override all other inputs to drive the stored value to a "0" or "1" respectively. These signals are most useful when a memory device is first initialized after power-on, but they can be used at any time to force the output low or high regardless of the state of the CLK or D signals.

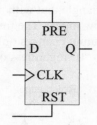

Other Inputs to Memory Devices

In addition to the reset and preset signals, two other signals are often included in memory device circuits. The first, called clock enable (or CE) can be used to render the memory device either responsive or non-responsive to the CLK signal. In many applications, it is convenient to temporarily disable the clock to a memory device. It is tempting to do so by running the clock signal through an AND gate with an enable signal driving one side of the gate. For many reasons, this is a poor design technique that should be avoided, particularly when designing with FPGA's (in fact, many modern CAD tools do not allow logic outputs to drive clock inputs). Although most of the reasons for not "gating the clock" are beyond the scope of this module, one reason is because the output of the clock-gating AND gate can glitch, causing unwanted clock pulses to "leak" through. The CE input has been specially designed to disable the clock while avoiding possible glitches.

Another frequently encountered signal in memory devices is a synchronous reset that drives the memory device output to "0" on the next rising edge of the clock. The synchronous reset signal simply drives one side of an AND gate inside the memory device (with the other side of the AND gate driven by the D input).

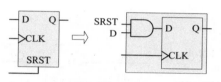

Synchronous reset uses an AND gate on the D input

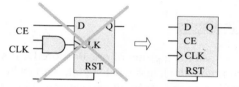

Never gate the clock; use a device with a CE input

Other Flip-flops

The DFF is the simplest and most useful edge-triggered memory device. Its output depends on a data input and the clock input—at the active clock edge, the device output is driven to match the device's data input. The DFF can be used in any application that requires a flip-flop. Over the years, other flip-flops have been designed that behave similar to, but not exactly like a DFF. One common device, called a JK-flip-flop, uses two inputs to direct state changes (the J input sets the output, and the K input resets the output; if both are asserted, the output toggles between "1" and "0"). Another common device, the T-flip-flop, simply toggles between "1" and "0" on each successive clock edge so long as the T input is asserted. These devices were commonly used in older digital systems (especially those built of discrete 7400 logic ICs), but they are rarely encountered in modern designs. Both JKFF and TFF can be easily constructed from DFFs or from first principles using basic cells. In modern digital design, and particularly in designs destined for FPGAs or other complex logic chips, these other flip-flops offer no advantages and they will not be dealt with further here.

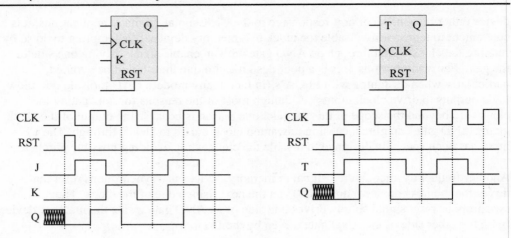

Registers

A register is a group of one or more DFF's that share a common clock and reset signal, with each flip-flop having a separate input and separate output. Registers are used when the contents of an entire bus must be memorized at the same time. Common register sizes include 1-bit (which is just a flip flop), 2-bit, 4-bit, 8-bit, and 16-bit. As with individual flip-flops, registers may have preset, clock enable, or synchronous reset inputs.

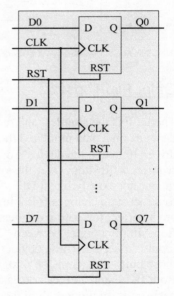

An 8-bit register

Other Memory Circuits

Many other circuit topologies that exhibit memory are used in modern digital circuits. For example, the dynamic memory circuits used in computer memory arrays use a small capacitor to store digital signal levels. Fast SRAM structures (like those used in a computer's cache memory structure) use cross-coupled inverters to form a bistable cell. Cross-coupled inverters present a much smaller RAM cell, but they can only be programmed by "overdriving" the output of the feedback resistor using powerful write buffers. Non-volatile memory devices (such as the FLASH BIOS ROM in PCs) use floating gates to permanently store memory bits. Together, these "other" memory circuits make up the vast majority of memory devices in use today. The basic cell and flip-flop circuits shown here are conceptually simple, but they are not that common in modern digital design. These other memory circuits will be covered in more detail in later exercises.

VHDL Descriptions of Memory Devices

Structural VHDL can be used to describe memory circuits in exactly the same way as conventional "feed-forward" circuits are described. For example, the statements

$$Q <= (S \textbf{ nand } QN) \textbf{ after } 1ns;$$
$$QN <= (R \textbf{ nand } Q) \textbf{ after } 1ns;$$

define a pair of cross-coupled NAND gates that form a basic cell. Similar code can be used to define a D-latch or DFF. Structural VHDL code written in this manner allows more detailed modeling of circuits, because delays can be added to every logic gate.

Behavioral VHDL can also be used to describe flip-flops, latches, and other memory circuits by using a process statement. The process statement is the most fundamental VHDL statement, and it is the "behind the scenes" basis for all signal assignment statements we have seen so far.

Process Statements in VHDL

Assignment statements (like those shown above) can be directly mapped to physical circuit devices, and their simulation requirements are straightforward—whenever a signal on the right-hand side of the assignment operator changes state, the simulator evaluates the logic expression to determine if the output must be driven to a new value. During the time the simulator is evaluating the expression, no physical time passes (here, physical time refers to the time-course of circuit events being modeled by the simulator, as opposed to the computer execution time needed to run the simulation).

A process statement allows more general circuit descriptions than a simple signal assignment statement. It contains a "begin–end" block, wherein multiple VHDL statements can describe more complex behaviors. It also contains a list of signals in a "sensitivity list"; the process is only simulated when one of the listed signals changes state. An assignment statement is simulated whenever one of the signals on the right-hand side of the assignment operator changes state, and therefore it is an "implicit" process. A process statement is explicit, because it lists the signals to which it is sensitive, and provides an area for describing more complex circuits.

All VHDL signal assignment statements are concurrent, meaning they are not executed in any particular sequence, but rather, whenever a signal on the right-hand side of the assignment operator changes state. They are concurrent in the sense that no physical time passes while the assignment statements are being evaluated. Since physical time in a simulator is simply a counter value stored in some variable, any number of assignment statements can be simulated without changing the timer-counter value. This has the effect of allowing any or all assignment statements to be completely evaluated at the same physical time, which defines concurrency (Of course, the computer will require some amount of execution time, but that is not related to the physical time being modeled in the

227

simulator). A process statement is also concurrent, and all statements in the "begin–end" block execute in zero time—that is, without the physical time variable being changed.

Within the "begin–end" block in a process statement, sequence does matter. Statements inside of a process statement are executed in the order written, and events that occur over time can be checked. Because statements inside of a process are subject to sequence and time, if-then-else relationships can be modeled, and this is the key to defining memory behaviorally: if the clock transitions high, then store a new value. If-then-else statements can also be used to describe many other circuit behaviors, but they are only really needed for behavioral descriptions of memory circuits.

In behavioral VHDL, an if-then-else statement must be used inside of a process statement to describe a flip-flop or latch. In fact, when describing circuits for synthesis, there is no need to use a process statement for any other purpose (although many engineers choose to use process statements to make certain code more convenient or more readable). The key to defining memory is to under-specify the if-then-else relationship: "if the clock transitions from low to high, then change the output to match the input". No direction is given on how to drive the output if the clock goes high-to-low, or if the input signal changes. The VHDL analyzer interprets this under-specification, or lack of direction on how to proceed under some input conditions, as an implied request to keep the output at its current level regardless of changes on certain inputs (like the input, or clock going high-to-low), and this defines memory.

The VHDL simulator stores values for all signals in a design during a simulation run, so it can detect which signals are changing at any given physical time. Any time a signal changes, a "signal event" occurs, and that event is stored by the simulator as an attribute of the signal. VHDL code can check signal attributes in an if-then-else statement to determine whether a clock signal has changed state, and that check is

```
process(sig1, sig2)
begin
  if sig1 =' 1' then Y <= ' 0';
    elsif (sig2' event and sig2=' 1')
      then Y <= X;
  end if;
end process;
```

A process statement with attribute check

an essential ingredient in the behavioral description of flip-flops. In the example shown, following the "process" keyword is a list of signals in parenthesis. This is the sensitivity list, and the process will execute whenever sig1 or sig2 changes. The "begin" keyword must follow the sensitivity list, and between the "begin and "end" keywords any valid VHDL statements can be used to describe circuit behaviors. In this example, a nested if-then-else is used, with the second if-statement starting with the keyword "elsif". Using an "elsif" allows the entire compound if-statement to be closed with a single "end if". The same behavior could be described with two independent if-statements (i.e., "else if" instead of "elsif "), but then two "end if " statements would be required. Continuing with the example, if sig1 changes and it is a "1", then the output Y is driven to "0"; if sig2 changes and it is currently a "1", then by definition it must have just become a "1" (i.e., a rising edge occurred), and in that case, the output Y is driven by the input signal X. An if-statement must be closed with "end if", and a process must be closed with "end process", and these are the final two lines in the example.

Several examples of behavioral VHDL defining DFF's are presented to the right and below. In constructing behavioral code for a flip-flop, note that only two signals can cause the output to change—clock and reset. The data signal by itself cannot change the output; rather, the rising edge of the clock changes the output to match the D signal. Thus, only the "clk" and "rst" signals appear in the sensitivity list. The first example shows a flip-flop with a clock enable and an asynchronous reset, where the reset signal drives the output to a "0" regardless of the clock or data input. The second example shows a synchronous reset, where the reset signal drives the output to "0", but only on the rising edge of the clock. The third example shows an 8-bit D-register. Study all the examples, and be sure you understand them, and their differences.

```
entity DFF is
  port (D,clk,rst,ce : in STD_LOGIC;
              Q : out STD_LOGIC);
end DFF;

architecture behavioral of DFF is
begin
  process(clk, rst)
  begin
    if rst ='1' then Q <= '0';
      elsif (CLK'event and CLK='1')
      then if ce = '1' then Q <= D;
      end if;
    end if;
  end process;
end dff_arch;
```

Behavioral D-flip-flop with Clock Enable and Asynchronous Reset

```
entity DFF is
  port (D, clk, rst : in STD_LOGIC;
              Q : out STD_LOGIC);
end DFF;

architecture behavioral of DFF is
begin
  process(clk, rst)
  begin
    if (CLK'event and CLK='1') then
    if rst ='1' then Q <= '0';
    else Q<=D;
  end if;
  end process;
end dff_arch;
```

Behavioral D-flip-flop, Synchronous Reset

229

```
entity DFF is
  port (D : in STD_LOGIC_VECTOR(7 downto 0);
        clk : in STD_LOGIC_VECTOR(7 downto 0);
        rst : in STD_LOGIC_VECTOR(7 downto 0);
        Q : out STD_LOGIC_VECTOR (7 downto 0));
end DFF;

architecture behavioral of DFF is
begin
  process(clk,rst)
  begin
   if rst = '1' then Q <= '0';
     elsif (CLK' event and CLK='1') then Q <= D;
   end if;
  end process;
end dff_arch;
```

Behavioral D-register with Asynchronous Reset

Lab Project 9: Basic Memory Circuits

Print Name   ID Number

Sign Name   Date

Estimated Work Hours

1	2	3	4	5	6	7	8	9	10

1	2	3	4	5	6	7	8	9	10

Overall Weight

Point Scale

4: Exemplary   3: Complete

2: Incomplete   1: Minor effort

0: Not submitted

20% will be deducted from scores for each week late
Score = Points awarded (Pts)× Weight (Wt)

LAB ASSISTANT

#	Demonstration	Wt	Pts	Late	Score	Lab Asst Signature	Date	Total In-Lab Score
5	Source & simulation inspection	3						
6	Source & simulation inspection	3						NA
8	Source & simulation inspection	3						

GRADER

#	Attachments	Wt	Pts	Score	Weeks late	Total Grading Score		Total Score
1	Source and annotated simulation	3						
2	Worksheet	3						
3	Worksheet	3						
4	Source and annotated simulation	4					*Total score is In-lab score plus grading score*	
5	Source, simulation, worksheet	4						
6	Source and simulation	3						
7	Source and simulation	3						
8	Source and simulation	3						
9	Source and simulation	3						

Problem 1. Create a NAND basic cell in the Xilinx tools using structural VHDL methods. Add a 1ns gate delay to both NAND gates (for both rising and falling transitions). Label inputs S and R and the outputs Q and QN as appropriate. Create a VHDL test bench to simulate the circuit, driving the inputs as specified below. Print the waveform output from the simulator, and annotate it with a pen or pencil to indicate the output features in the

list below. Submit the source file and annotated output timing diagram for credit.

De-assert both inputs at the start of the simulation. At 100ns, asset S. At 200 ns, de-assert S. At 300 ns, assert R. At 400 ns, de-assert R. At 500 ns, assert both inputs. At 600 ns, de-assert both inputs. At 700 ns, assert both inputs.

(1) An undefined output
(2) A set operation
(3) A reset operation
(4) A "0" being stored in memory
(5) A "1" being stored in memory
(6) A state where the Q and QN outputs are both driven to the same value
(7) A metastable state

Problem 2. Repeat problem 1, but use a NOR basic cell. Why are the basic cells outputs undefined at the start of the simulation?

Complete the following table by placing the correct letter in the output column. A: set operation; B: reset operation; C: confounded outputs (both outputs at the same voltage); D: storing a value in memory; E: a metastable state.

Set	Reset	NAND Output	NOR Output
$1 \to 0$	$1 \to 1$		
$1 \to 1$	$1 \to 0$		
$1 \to 1$	$1 \to 1$		
$1 \to 0$	$1 \to 0$		
$0 \to 1$	$0 \to 1$		
$0 \to 0$	$0 \to 0$		
$0 \to 0$	$0 \to 1$		
$0 \to 1$	$0 \to 0$		

Problem 3. Modify the test bench for the NAND basic cell by de-asserting S at 600ns and R at 601ns, and resimulate. Comment on any differences in the output, and more importantly, give a reason for any differences seen.

Problem 4.   Starting with the NAND basic cell, create a new source file for a D-latch. Be sure the basic cell NAND gates have a 1 ns gate delay. Create and run a VHDL test bench to simulate this circuit, and be sure to test *all possible* combinations of inputs to fully document the circuit's function. At some point during the simulation, illustrate the property of D-latch transparency (i.e., show the circuit behavior when gate input is high, and the D input changes from L–H–L or H–L–H), and also illustrate a metastable state. Mark on a printout of the simulation waveform the following output behaviors: an undefined output, transparency, storing a "1", storing a "0", and metastability. Submit the source file and annotated timing diagram.

Problem 5.   Create a behavioral source file for a RET DFF. Name the inputs D and CLK, and the output Q. Create a VHDL test bench to simulate the flip-flop, driving CLK and D appropriately. What do you notice about the output Q? Why?

Add an asynchronous reset, and assert the reset signal at the start of the simulation, de-asserting it after a small amount of time. Resimulate, and demonstrate the proper operation of your flip-flop.

Modify the simulation, and try to force a metastable state. Can you force a metastable state? Print and submit your source file, and a single simulation file showing proper flip-flop operation and your attempt to get it into a metastable state. Have the lab assistance inspect your work.

Problem 6.   Create a source file for a FET DFF with clock enable and preset. Simulate the FF, showing all pertinent operating states. Have the lab assistant inspect your work, and print and submit your source file and simulation output.

Problem 7.   Create a source file for an 8-bit D register with both a synchronous reset (named SRST) and an asynchronous reset (named ARST). Simulate the register, showing all pertinent operating states. Submit your source code and simulation outputs.

Problem 8.   Create and simulate a source file for a T-flip-flop. Show all pertinent operating states in the simulation, and have the lab assistant inspect your work. Submit your source and simulation files for credit.

Problem 9.   Create and simulate a source file for a JK-flip-flop. Show all pertinent operating states in the simulation, and submit your source and simulation files for credit.

Chapter 10: Structural Design of Sequential Circuits

1. Overview

This chapter introduces the founding concepts used in the design of sequential circuits. Sequential circuits use memory to store information about past inputs, and they use that information to effect future output changes. Although combinational logic circuits form the backbone of digital circuits, sequential circuits are used in the vast majority of useful devices—there are more than 100 billion in existence.

2. Background

Sequential Circuit Characteristics

Many problems require the detection or generation of a sequence of events. As examples, an electronic combination-lock door controller must detect when a particular sequence of numbered buttons has been pressed, and an elevator controller must create a sequence of signals to shut the doors, move the cabin, and then reopen doors. In such situations, a circuit can only advance to the next action (or next state) if the current action is known. For example, an elevator should not move until the doors are shut, and pressing a "2" at some point on a combination lock may or may not contribute to the unlock sequence. A circuit that operates according to a specific sequence of events is called a "state machine" or "sequential circuit". A state machine requires memory to store information about past actions, and it uses that memory to help determine what action to take next. Outputs from sequential circuits are functions of the current inputs and memorized past inputs—this is in contrast to a combinational circuit, where the outputs are strictly a function of the current inputs.

Most memory-containing circuits provide data storage for computing devices. Examples include RAM arrays for computers, registers and register files for microprocessors, cache memories, accumulators, status indicators, etc. These memory circuits may use flip-flops, latches, or RAM cells (depending on the particular application), and they are only used to store data elements in a processor environment. Memory devices used in sequential circuits do not store data, but rather the operating state of the circuit. The state of a sequential circuit is defined by the collective contents of all of its memory devices. The value stored in each memory device in a state machine is referred to as a state variable. Since a state variable can only take one of two values ("0" or "1"), a circuit with N state variables must be in one of 2^N states, and each state is defined by a unique N-bit binary number. The memory devices in a given state machine are collectively referred to as the state register.

The previous lab presented basic memory devices, including the basic cell, the D-latch, and the DFF. While any of these (or other) memory devices could be used to implement a state register, the sequential machine design process is greatly simplified if memory devices with certain characteristics are used. Those characteristics are: the ability to be driven to a stable operating state ("0" or "1"); a timing signal that generates the smallest possible sampling window to dictate exactly when new data can be written; a single data input that directly programs the memory device; and a single reset signal that can drive the output to "0" regardless of the data or clock input signals. All of these characteristics are contained in a DFF, and DFF's are used in practically all sequential circuits. In fact, DFFs can be used to construct any sequential circuit, and their use will always yield the smallest, simplest sequential circuits.

A sequential circuit follows the general model shown below. The state register is controlled directly by an external clock and reset signal. Data inputs to the state register arise from a "next state" logic block that combines circuit inputs with state register outputs —this feedback of the state variables is the reason a sequential circuit can implement a given sequence of events. Without this feedback, future state register changes could not be based on past events, and so ordered sequences could not be implemented. The output from the state register is called the "present state", and the input to the state register is called the "next state". At each edge of the clock, the next state is written into the state register and so becomes the current state.

Like the next-state logic circuit, the output logic circuit contains only combinational devices. In the figure below, the most general state machine model is shown, with circuit inputs fed forward to the output logic block where they can be combined with state variables to determine overall circuit outputs. This most general model is called the "Mealy" model; in the simpler "Moore" model, only the state variables drive the output logic block, so the feed-forward signal would not be shown (i.e., the red line would be absent). In simpler state machines like counters and other basic sequence generators, the output logic block may not be present at all. In such cases, the state register outputs are used as the overall circuit outputs.

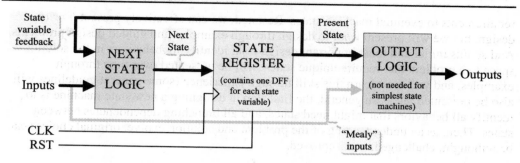

The example timing diagram on the right shows the behavior of a hypothetical state machine (what the state machine does is not important here—just examine the timing diagram). Note that every rising clock edge causes a state transition, where the "next state" is clocked into the state register flip-flops to become the "present state". Each state is uniquely identified by the contents of the state register, called the "state code". This example shows three state variables, so eight distinct states are possible. The state machine progresses from state 0 to states 1, 3, 2, 2, 6, and 4 based on the inputs I0 and I1 and the current state code. Note also that the outputs Y0, Y1, and Y2 change just after the clock—this is generally the case, because the state codes change just after the clock edge, and the state codes are inputs to the output logic block.

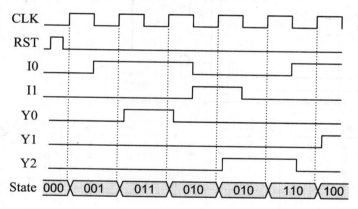

Designing Sequential Circuits

The most difficult task in designing sequential circuits occurs at the very start of the design, in determining what characteristics of a given problem require sequential operations, and more particularly, what behaviors must be represented by a unique state. A poor choice of states coupled with a poor understanding of the problem can make a design lengthy, difficult and error prone. With better understanding and a better choice of states, the same problem might well be trivial. Whereas it is relatively straight-forward to describe sequential circuit structure and define applicable engineering design methods, it is relatively challenging to find analytical methods capable of matching design problem requirements to eventual machine states. Restated, we can effectively present *how* to design, but we will present *what* to design through examples and guided design problems. And so this initial and most important design task, identifying behaviors in the solution-space to a problem that require unique states, will be presented over time through examples, and you must learn this skill through experience (some general guidelines will also be presented later). In general, the first step in designing a new state machine is to identify all behaviors that might need states, and all branching dependencies between states. Then, as an understanding of the problem and solution evolve, original choices can be rethought, challenged, and improved.

One method of capturing the behavioral requirements of a state machine is through the creation of a state table. A state table is nothing more than a truth table that specifies the requirements for the next-state logic, with inputs coming from the state register and from outside the circuit. The state table lists all required states, and all possible next states that might follow a given present state.

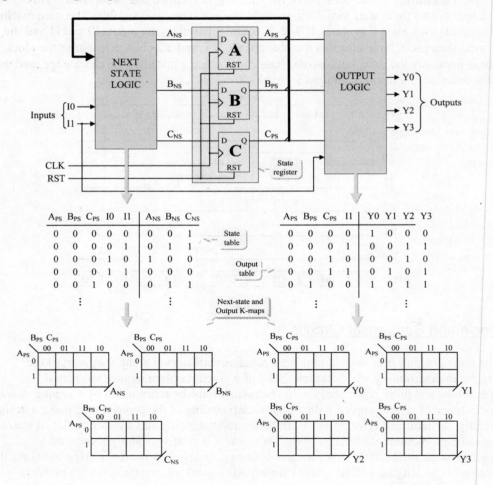

State-to-state transitions can be directed by input signals, so the table must list any input signals required to cause a given transition. The figure above shows an expanded model of a state machine, and illustrates how the state/truth table can be used to find the next-state logic. In the state table, the first four rows all show "000" for the state variables. This is because there are two inputs, and a next state must be specified for all possible combinations of inputs. From the state table, you can deduce that if the machine is in state "000" and the inputs are both "0", then the next state will be "001"; if the machine is in state "000" and the inputs are "0" and "1", then the next state will be "011"; and so on.

The output truth table shows how the state variables and any Mealy inputs are combined to form outputs. In this example, only one of the two inputs (I1) is used by the output logic circuit. The state and output tables can be combined into a single truth table (also called a state table) to specify all combinational logic requirements (i.e., both next-state and output requirements) in a single table.

The next-state truth table requires at maximum N input columns for each of N state variables, and M input columns for each of M circuit inputs. It is not required that all possible states nor all possible combinations of inputs be used; hence, the next-state truth table need not have all $2^{(N+M)}$ rows present. Just which rows are required in the truth table depends on which of the 2^N possible states are used in a given sequential circuit, as well as which inputs are used in each state (again, choosing states and branching conditions is the more difficult engineering challenge, and several examples in this and future lab exercises will help illustrate the process). For each row of the truth table, the next-state output values are assigned according to the desired next state. The use of DFFs in the state register is assumed, so a "1" in an output column will cause the corresponding DFF to transition to a "1" on the next clock edge.

Although truth tables (or state tables) can always be used to specify next-state and output logic, they suffer from a significant drawback: it is difficult to visualize the sequential nature of a circuit's behavior. A more useful method exists for specifying next-state and output logic that has a powerful advantage—it lets us not only specify logic requirements, but also clearly visualize the sequential and/or algorithmic behavior of a circuit.

Designing Sequential Circuits Using State Diagrams

A state diagram represents states with circles, and transitions between states by arrows exiting one circle and arriving at another. A binary number called the "state code" can be written in the state-circle to indicate the value stored in the state register when the state machine is in that state. Directed arrows leaving one state and arriving at another show permissible state transitions. Input variable requirements for transitions are shown immediately next to each transition; the indicated transition will only take place if the input conditions shown are present. Transitions (also called branches) occur at every clock edge; thus, at every edge, the present state is exited, and the next-state entered. Often, it is required that for some input conditions, the machine hold in a given state—this holding condition is shown as a directed arrow leaving and re-entering the same state. In the partial state diagram shown, the state register contains three flip-flops: if the state register is storing "000", then it will remain in that state if A is "0" at the next clock edge; otherwise it will transition out of the state if A is "1". The figure on the right uses VHDL syntax for checking and assigning logic values. Many texts use conventional logic equation symbols instead.

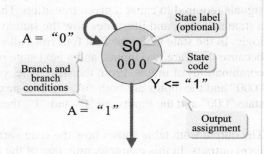

When a state diagram is used as a conceptual tool to help arrive at a given problem solution, it is typically sketched and modified in an iterative fashion. Circles are drawn representing possible states, interconnected according to problem requirements, and redrawn and reconnected as the problem and solution become clearer in the designer's mind. Once a state diagram has been created that captures the design specifications, a fairly automatic procedure can be applied to create a circuit from the diagram.

State-to-state transitions occur when the state register is loaded with new next-state values. Since the state register can only be written on a CLK edge, state-to-state transitions can only occur on the CLK edge. Thus, the presence of the CLK signal is implied in a state machine, and the CLK signal is not shown in the state diagram. Likewise, RST or PRE signals are not shown in a state diagram; rather, an arrow is shown pointing to an initial state that the machine should assume whenever a "reset" signal is asserted. A "0" bit in the reset state requires the RST input of the corresponding state register DFF to be connected to the reset signal, and a "1" in the reset state requires the PRE input to be connected to the reset signal. Thus, RST and PRE signals are not shown in the state diagram—their presence is implied when an initial state is identified. Only signals that are needed by the next-state or output logic circuits are shown in the state diagram.

An example of a simple state diagram is shown below. This machine receives input from three buttons labeled X, Y, and Z, and asserts two signals called "RED" and "GRN": RED if and only if the proper three-button-press sequence X−Z−Y is detected; GRN when a new sequence starts. This "early stage" state diagram does not show state variables or state names. The diagram has evolved by the iterative process mentioned above—states and branching conditions were added and modified as the needs of the problem became clearer, until a complete solution was found.

Note that for each state, the branching conditions take into account all possible input combinations, and no ambiguous branching conditions are present. If some input combinations are not accounted for, or if branching conditions indicate more than one next state, unpredictable operation can occur. The partial state diagrams below illustrate these points—in the diagram on the left, if both A and B are "1", or if C = "0", it is not clear which branch to take. The need to unambiguously show possible next states is important

240

enough that many texts name two rules: the "sum rule" states that all inputs leaving a given state must OR to a logic "1"; and the "mutual exclusion rule" states that any combination of inputs can indicate only one next state.

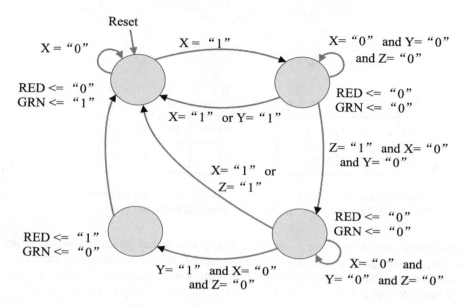

In the figure below, the logic graphs illustrate a simple method for ensuring that both the sum rule and exclusion rule have been obeyed (these graphs resemble, but are not, K-maps). One graph is needed to analyze branching conditions from each state, and the number of input variables determines the graph's size (input variables are used as the axis variables for the logic graph). Each cell in the graph represents the unique combination of inputs indicated by the axis variables, and cell entries show the next state for the branch conditions indicated by the axis variables. Information can be transferred to the logic graph to document the next-states for all branches from a given state. Each cell should have one and only one entry—an empty cell indicates the sum rule has been violated, and more than one entry indicates the exclusion rule has been violated. The state diagram on the left of the figure above shows both sum rule and exclusion rule violations, and so the state diagram must be modified before further design activities are attempted. In the example shown, one possible solution that removes all "unknowns" and redundancies is shown. Note that removing ambiguities changes the branching conditions —it is up to the designer to choose new branches that are consistent with the problem description. In general, after a state diagram has been sketched, and before any further circuit design activities are undertaken, it is good design practice to ensure that neither the sum rule nor the exclusion rule are violated.

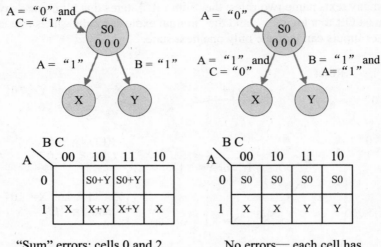

B C				
A	00	10	11	10
0		S0+Y	S0+Y	
1	X	X+Y	X+Y	X

B C				
A	00	10	11	10
0	S0	S0	S0	S0
1	X	X	Y	Y

"Sum" errors: cells 0 and 2
"Exclusion" errors: cells 1,3,5,7

No errors— each cell has
one and only one entry.

Output signal names are shown near every state during which they must be asserted. If an output must to be asserted in consecutive states, the output should be shown on the state diagram in consecutive states. One method of preparing a state diagram is to show output names only near the states in which they are asserted. A better method is to show each output driven to "1" or "0" in every state—this avoids any confusion.

Once the sequential behavior of a problem has been captured with a state diagram, state codes can be assigned to each state. The state codes show the actual contents of the state register when the state machine is in that state. For a state diagram with N states, at least $\log_2 N$ state variables are required so that each state can be assigned a unique number. In the example above, the state diagram has 4 states, so $\log_2 4 = 2$ state variables are required. More than the required number of state variables can be used, but in general, the fewest number of state variables needed are used, since adding more state variables creates a larger and more complex circuit. Any state code can be assigned to any state, but in practice certain rules can be used to guide the assignment of state codes.

In general, state codes are chosen to minimize the required logic in the next state and/or output logic circuits, or to eliminate timing problems in sequential circuit outputs. One rule of thumb is to minimize the number of flip-flops that change state during any state transition. Ideally, only one flip-flop would change state for any transition in the diagram (a state-to-state transition where only one state variable changes is known as "unit-distance coding"). It is usually not possible to create a situation wherein all transitions are unit-distance coded, but it is generally possible to choose state codes that yield the highest

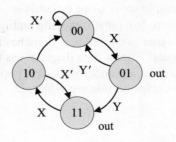

242

number of unit-distant coded states. A second rule of thumb is to match state register bits to output requirements wherever possible. For example, in a four-state machine with an output that must be asserted in two of the states, it may be possible to assign state codes such that the output is asserted only when one of the flip-flops is a "1", thereby eliminating the output logic altogether. The figure on the right above shows both unit-distant coding, and matching an output to state codes (i.e., the output is "1" whenever flip-flip #2 is a "1", meaning no output logic is required).

Structural Design of Sequential Circuits

A state diagram with state codes and complete branching conditions contains all information required for the design of optimal next-state and output logic circuits. In fact, a state diagram contains exactly the same information as the state table (or next-state truth table), with the added benefit of showing sequential flow. By following a few simple rules, the information in a state diagram can be transferred directly to K-maps so that a minimal next state logic circuit can be found.

The process is illustrated in the three figures below using a state diagram similar to the one presented earlier (but in this state diagram, the GRN output is now a Mealy output that combines the X and Y inputs with state codes—see states "01" and "11"). In the first step, all branch conditions are checked to ensure that neither the sum rule nor the exclusion rule is violated (branch condition checking uses the logic graphs as shown). State codes are assigned so that a minimum number of bits change across the set of all state transitions. In this example, it is not possible to use unit-distant coding for all state transitions, nor is it possible to match outputs to state codes. The state codes shown result in the greatest number of transitions having unit-distant codes. The second step is to transfer information from the state diagram to K-maps so that logic circuits can be defined.

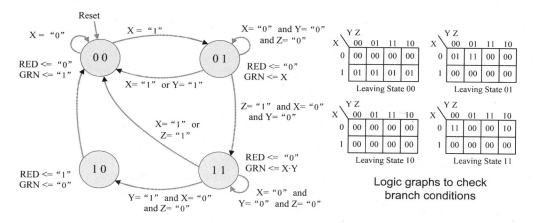

Logic graphs to check branch conditions

In this example, two state variables and two outputs require four K-maps, one for each of the next-state circuit, and one for each output. The next-state circuits will drive the D inputs of the state-variable flip-flops, and the output logic circuits will produce outputs based on the state variables and inputs. The state variables are used as the K-map index variables for all four maps. In the next-state maps, branch condition inputs are shown as entered variables. Thus, loops in the next-state maps will be in terms of the state codes (axis variables) and inputs (entered variables). For output maps, a "1" or "0" is placed in a cell to indicate whether an output is asserted in that state; for Mealy outputs, the input variables that drive the output are placed in the maps as entered variables. The "Rules" below describe to process of populating K-maps in detail.

(1) Sketch one K-map for each state variable and each output. The state variables are the K-map index variables (and so K-map size is determined by the number of state variables). Since state variables are used on the K-map indexes, each cell K-map cell corresponds to a present state.

(2) For next state K-maps, enter branch conditions from each present state into the corresponding K-map cell if and only if the branch leads to a next state where the state DFF being mapped is "1".

(3) For Moore model K-maps, enter a "1" in each K-map cell where the output must be asserted; for Mealy model K-maps, enter a "1" for unconditional outputs, or the variable (or expression) for conditional outputs in each K-map cell where the output must be asserted.

The process is applied to the state diagram above, resulting in the K-maps shown below.

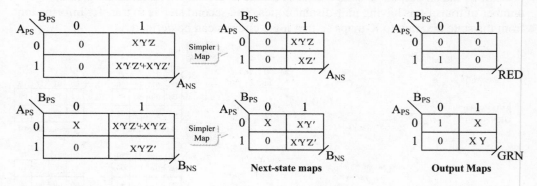

The third and final step is to create a circuit from the equations obtained from looping the K-maps. A block diagram of the circuit is shown below—you should recognize the Mealy model schematic. Following the methods described and with sufficient practice, a wide variety of state machines can be designed.

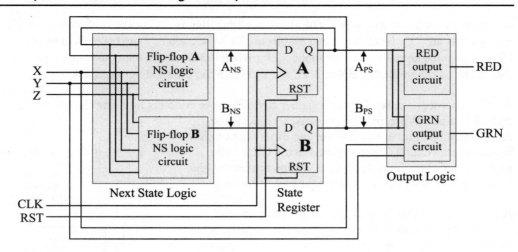

Binary Counters

A binary counter is a simple state machine whose outputs are a repeating sequence of n-bit binary numbers in the range 0 to $2^n - 1$ (see figure below). At each edge of the clock, the output pattern changes from a binary number X to binary number X + 1; at the end of the count range (at binary number $2^n - 1$), the counter rolls over, and the next clock will start the count range over at binary number 0. Practical binary counters come in 4-bit, 8-bit, and 16-bit sizes, with count ranges from 0 to 16, 256, and 64K respectively. Counter output bits toggle at rate equal to $1/2^n$ of the input clock input frequency, where n is the bit position (beginning with "1" for the LSB). Counters find many uses in the design of digital systems. As examples, they are often used to generate sequential addresses into a memory array, to create unique states for use in a state machine, or to implement a specific delay or clock-divide ratio.

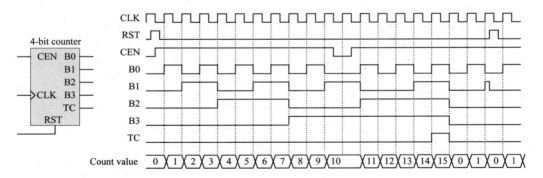

Counters are often designed with a counter enable input (CEN) so that counting can be suspended under certain conditions. When CEN is asserted, the counter will increment with each successive clock edge, and when CEN is not asserted, the counter will simply maintain its current output. Counters are also often designed with a "terminal count" (TC)

245

output that is asserted as the AND of all output bits—that is, TC is asserted only when all counter bits are "1". Note that when all bits are "1", the counter's next state will be all "0"s. Hence the signal name terminal count—when it is asserted, the counter has reached the end of its range. Both CEN and TC are shown in the timing diagram above.

Smaller counters can be chained together to form larger counters by using the TC output and CEN input. When the first, or least significant, or fastest running counter reaches the end of its count range, it will assert TC. If TC is connected to the CEN of the next counter, then the next counter will increment by one each time the first counter reaches the end of its range.

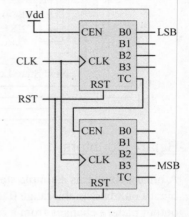

A counter is somewhat unique among state machines in that: the state variables themselves are the circuit outputs; every state code is used; and every next-state state code is simply the present-state state code + 1. A state diagram for a 4-bit binary counter is shown below. The CEN input must be asserted for a state transition to occur. If DFFs with clock enable inputs are used, then the CEN input can connect to all DFFs clock enable inputs. In this case, CEN would not appear in the state diagram since, like the CLK and RST signals, CEN would not be a part of the next state logic (rather, it would connect directly to the flip-flops instead).

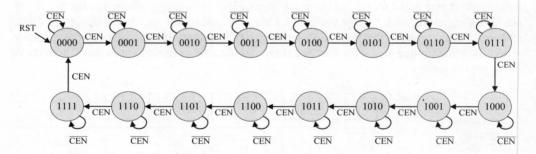

Binary Counters in VHDL

A counter circuit can be implemented using structural or behavioral VHDL. A structural counter design would instantiate the required number of flip-flops as components, and then define next-state logic circuits to drive each flip-flop D input. This design process is rather tedious when compared to a behavioral VHDL design, but in return a much better simulation model could be developed. The structural design of various counters will be covered in depth in a later module.

A behavioral counter can take advantage of the IEEE STD_LOGIC_UNSIGNED library available in any standard VHDL environment. The SLU library allows the use of standard arithmetic operators with STD_LOGIC types (see the fourth line in the example below), making a counter design trivial. Note that the counter output is a vector named B that is defined as an "inout" type so that it can be used on either side of an assignment operator.

```
library IEEE;
use IEEE.STD_LOGIC_1164.all;
use IEEE.STD_LOGIC_ARITH.all;
use IEEE.STD_LOGIC_UNSIGNED.all;

entity counter is
    Port ( clk : in  STD_LOGIC;
           rst : in  STD_LOGIC;
           B : inout  STD_LOGIC_VECTOR (3 downto 0));
end counter;

architecture Behavioral of counter is

begin

process (clk, rst)
  begin
  if rst = '1' then B <= "0000";
    elsif (clk' event and clk='1') then
      B <= B + 1;
    end if;
  end process;
end Behavioral;
```

Behavioral VHDL for a 4-bit binary counter

A "clock divider" is one of the more common applications for counters. In this application, a higher frequency clock signal drives a counter's clock input, and the counter outputs provide lower frequency signals at $1/2^n$ of the input frequency, where n is the counter output bit number (assuming bit #1 is the LSB). Thus, the LSB of the counter provides a frequency of 1/2 the input frequency, bit #2 provides $1/4^{th}$ the input frequency, bit #3 $1/8^{th}$ the frequency, and so on. In most technologies, the output of one flip-flop (such as a counter output bit) can directly drive the clock inputs of other flip-flops.

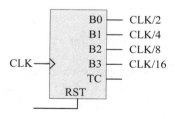

Simple clock divider

A simple divider works well for generating frequencies that are power-of-two divisors of the input frequency. To create divider frequencies that are any integer divisor of the input frequency, an equality comparator can be used to compare the count value to a divisor. If a clock with frequency 1/N is required, then a divisor of N/2 can drive one side of the comparator (with the counter driving the other side). The output of the comparator can be used as a synchronous reset to restart the counter from "0" (at twice the desired frequency), and also as a clock-enable for flip-flop that has its output tied to its input through an inverter (CLKoutA in the figure). The output of this flip-flop will produce the desired frequency with a 50% duty cycle (duty cycle is the fraction of time a signal spends at "1"; a 50% duty cycle means the signal is "1" half the time and "0" half the time) . Note that a simpler circuit can produce a clock frequency of 1/N if a 50% duty cycle is not required (and in most applications, duty cycle is not important). This simpler circuit resets the counter when it reaches N (instead of N/2 as above), and then uses the MSB of the counter as the output clock. This signal will have the desired frequency, but it will not have a 50% duty cycle.

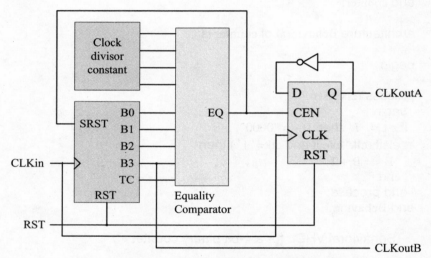

Clock divider for any integer divisor

Behavioral VHDL code for a clock divider that divides a 50MHz clock to a 1Hz clock is shown below. In the example code, note that a constant has been used to define the divider ratio; this constant can be changed to set any desired divider ratio. Note also the MSB of the counter is used as CLKout, resulting in a clock signal with the correct frequency that does not have a 50% duty cycle.

```
library IEEE;
use IEEE.STD_LOGIC_1164.all;
use IEEE.STD_LOGIC_ARITH.all;
use IEEE.STD_LOGIC_UNSIGNED.all;
```

```
entity clkdiv is
   Port ( clk : in  STD_LOGIC;
          rst : in  STD_LOGIC;
          clkout : out  STD_LOGIC);
end clkdiv;

architecture Behavioral of clkdiv is

constant cntendval : STD_LOGIC_VECTOR(25 downto 0) :=
"10111110101111000010000000";
signal cntval : STD_LOGIC_VECTOR (25 downto 0);

begin

process (clk, rst)
  begin
  if rst = '1' then cntval <= "00000000000000000000000000";
    elsif (clk'event and clk='1') then
     if (cntval = cntendval) then cntval <="00000000000000000000000000";
       else cntval <= cntval + 1;
       end if;
    end if;
  end process;

  clkout <= cntval(25);

end Behavioral;
```

249

Exercise 10: Structural Design of Sequential Circuits

STUDENT

I am submitting my own work, and I understand penalties will be assessed if I submit work for credit that is not my own.

Print Name ______________ ID Number ______________

Sign Name ______________ Date ______________

Estimated Work Hours

1	2	3	4	5	6	7	8	9	10

1	2	3	4	5	6	7	8	9	10

Overall Weight

GRADER

#	*Points*	*Score*
1	12	
2	8	
3	20	
4	20	

Total Score

Weeks late

Adjusted Score

Adjusted Score:
Deduct 20% from score for each week late

Problem 1. Assign state codes to the state diagrams below, and discuss the motivation behind your choice of state codes.

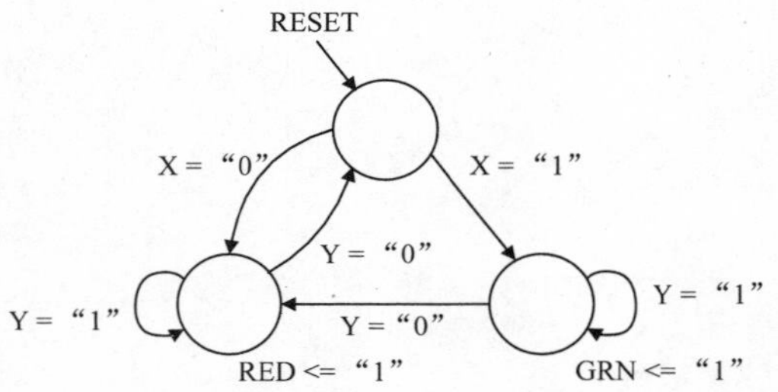

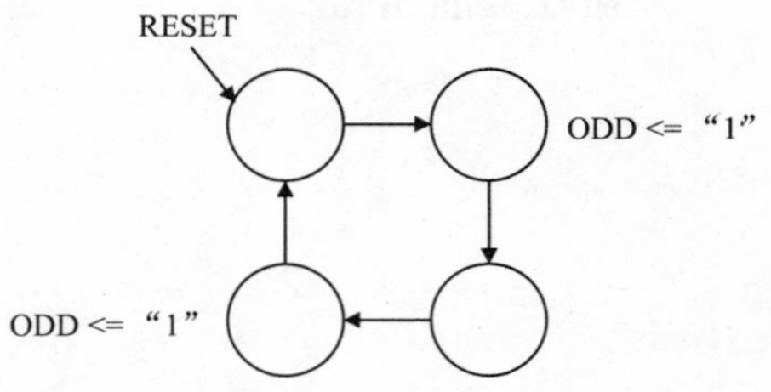

Exercise 10: Structural Design of Sequential Circuits

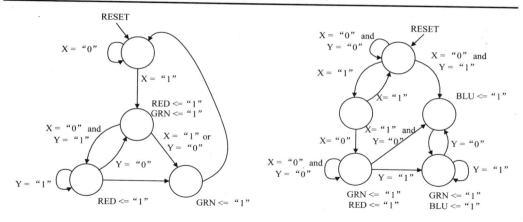

Problem 2. Modify the state diagram branching conditions in the diagrams below as needed to ensure the sum and exclusion rules are obeyed in each case. You can add a holding conditions or change branch codes as desired.

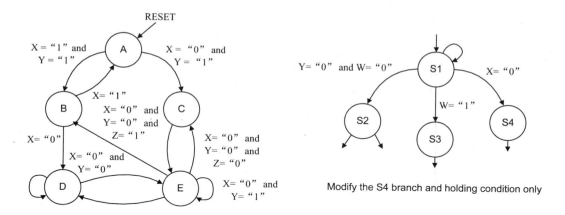

Modify the S4 branch and holding condition only

Problem 3. A vending machine should SELL an item if 30 cents is input. The machine has a coin sensor that can detect nickels, dimes, and quarters, and reject everything else. No change is given (i.e, if two quarters are input, simply assert SELL and keep the fifty cents).

Create a state diagram for a machine that can control a 4-button digital combination lock mechanism, unlocking only if the sequence B0−B3−B1 is detected.

Problem 4. Sketch circuits for the state machines below.

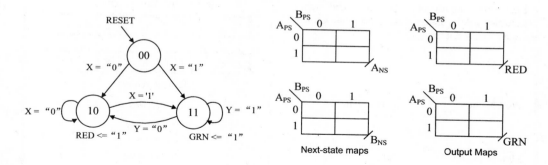

Next-state maps   Output Maps

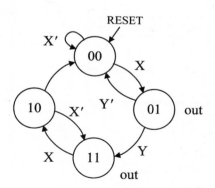

Lab Project 10: Structural Design of Sequential Circuits

STUDENT

I am submitting my own work, and I understand penalties will be assessed if I submit work for credit that is not my own.

_____
Print Name

_____
ID Number

_____
Sign Name

_____
Date

Estimated Work Hours

1	2	3	4	5	6	7	8	9	10

1	2	3	4	5	6	7	8	9	10

Overall Weight

Point Scale

4: Exemplary
3: Complete
2: Incomplete
1: Minor effort
0: Not submitted

20% will be deducted from scores for each week late
Score = Points awarded (Pts) × Weight (Wt)

LAB ASSISTANT

#	Demonstration	Wt	Pts	Late	Score	Lab Asst Signature	Date
3	Circuit demonstration	10					
4	Circuit demonstration	10					

Total In-Lab Score

NA

GRADER

#	Attachments	Wt	Pts	Score
1	Source, simulation, worksheet	6		
2	Source and simulation	3		
3	Worksheets, source and simulation files	10		
4	Source, simulation, and worksheet	10		

Weeks late

Total Grading Score

Total score is In-lab score plus grading score

Total Score

Lab Project 10: Structural Design of Sequential Circuits

Problem 1.   Using the Xilinx CAD tools, create a structural 4-bit counter with CEN and TC functions. You may use schematic methods and the FDCE flip-flop component from the Xilinx library, or structural VHDL methods (in which case you can use the flip-flop you designed in the previous lab). To complete the design, you will need to find next-state logic circuits for the counter. A state diagram and K-maps have been provided below for this purpose (or, nothing is keeping you from "borrowing" a circuit from the Xilinx schematic library, but you must complete the K-maps regardless). When the counter is complete, simulate it using a VHDL a test bench file, and be sure to show all appropriate output states. Print and submit your source and simulation files. (Hint: Extensive XOR patterns are present in the D next-state maps. You will probably want to refer to some circuit schematic source to check your K-map looping.)

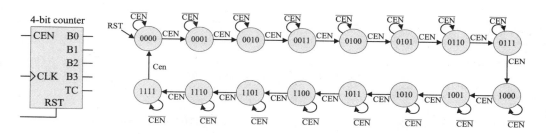

Empty K-maps follow. Note that if you choose to design a counter using DFFs with a CE input, you can ignore the CEN inputs shown in the state diagram above (i.e., the state diagram would only show branches to the next state, without any holding conditions). In this case, the counter's CEN input would directly drive the CE inputs on the DFFs (this makes the K-map loading and looping a fair amount easier – but it is your choice).

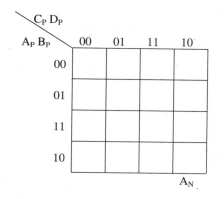

$A_N =$ _____

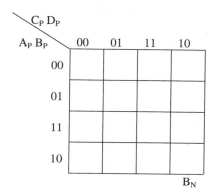

$B_N =$ _____

255

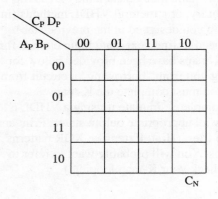

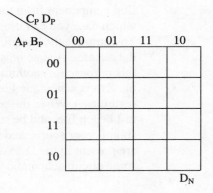

$C_N =$ _____ $D_N =$ _____

Problem 2. Create and simulate a behavioral VHDL 4-bit counter, using a VHDL test bench for the simulation. Print and submit your source and simulation files.

Problem 3. Design a circuit that increments a digit (0–F) shown on the seven-segment display device once each second. The circuit has four pushbutton inputs: one button starts the counter, a second button stops the counter, a third button increments the counter, and the fourth button asynchronously resets all memory devices in the design. The system has the block diagram shown below. You must create the 4-bit counter, a clock divider, a seven-segment display decoder, and a controller circuit. You may use any design tools or methods you wish. You must also create and submit a state diagram for the controller, together with K-maps showing the next-state and output circuits. Have the lab assistant inspect your completed work, and download your design to the Digilent board. Demonstrate your circuit's function to the lab assistant and print and submit your source files for credit.

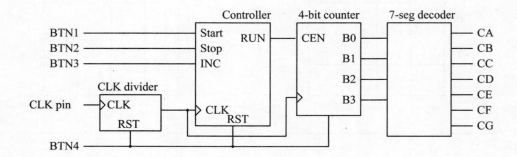

Problem 4.   Modify your circuit so that all four digits on the seven-segment display are driven, and drive the least-significant digit so that it changes at a rate of once per millisecond (and so, the most-significant bit will change at a rate of once per second). This circuit requires a scanning display controller which is discussed in your board's Reference Manual. When complete, demonstrate your circuit to the lab assistant and print and submit your source files for credit. Also create and submit a detailed block diagram of your circuit showing all circuit blocks and signal connections (and make sure to appropriately label all circuit blocks and signals).